PSYCHONIX
MIND OVER MATTER
MIKE BURNETTE

D1713567

PROLOGUE

"Psychokinesis or mind over matter is the motion of the mind, soul, spirit, or breath. I believe we can move objects by supernatural forces, including spirits and ghosts."
~ *Henry Holt, 1914, On The Cosmic Relations*

THOSE INVOLVED IN the *Mind-Body Problem* projects, at Innovations Technology Laboratory, discovered that there was a science to the supernatural. The axiomatic lines separating the fields of study were seemingly erased, once they fortuitously detected a mental substance called PSYCHON radiation and began to develop *psychological bionics*. For the first time this seemed to amplify and enable mind-to-mind communication through what was designated as the *Holt* frequency spectrum. For now, no one could openly discuss the benefits and dangers of this transhuman development.

There have always been programs and weapons that were so classified that public hearings and budgets were deemed inappropriate by the Director of National Intelligence. Those *Black Budgets* were projects that included operating funds for intelligence, CIA, global listening posts of the National Security Agency, the super-secret satellites of the National Reconnaissance Office, and NASA. All these—and only God and the President of the United States knew what else. Sitting on the President's desk now was a top secret folder with the file name:

PSYCHONIX.

The file revealed that there was a sophisticated piece of emerging technology, which could enhance human intellect, physiology, and evidently probe our thoughts and unlock consciousness. If there was indeed a neoteric device that could overcome human limitations, transcend physical reality, and harness *mind over matter*, then they wanted it before the Chinese,

1

or some other economic superpower got their hands on it. It was a matter of the highest national security.

The hard problems of how the mind and body communicated and where consciousness originated had been debated by science and religion for millennia, but not any longer. The ITL staff was now fully testing PSYCHONIX, which was apparently driven by the newly developed *MDSL-1* processor—potentially a modem for the soul. At first the central processing unit would be adapted into virtual reality goggles and used to penetrate the eyes and ears with projected beams of energy, which enhanced the natural PSYCHON radiation recently discovered in our body. That allowed it to be absorbed by the cochlea and retina, and then converted to electrical impulses. It would then be transferred along the auditory and optic nerve, directly to the brain. That was merely in the Alpha phase of the project. It was, however, seriously being considered for a neural implant—and potentially a high-powered, wireless, bionic eye that communicated between the central nervous system and the ITL Control Center.

Theoretically, PSYCHONIX could tap into the areas of the brain that controlled thought, memory, emotion, touch, motor skills, vision, breathing, temperature, hunger, and every process that regulated mind and body. ITL largely understood how the brain worked—but had serious philosophical disagreements about how it was controlled.

One man, Colonel Steven Scott, may become the first person to explore all that the human mind sees, believes, feels, thinks, and loves in this world and the next. He and his stepbrother Dr. Mark Starr were persuaded by the words often attributed to C.S. Lewis: *You do not have a soul. You are a soul. You have a body.*

If Steven can overcome his dysfunctional childhood, PTSD, espionage, and a near death experience in a cryogenic Dewar, called the *Amaranth*, it's then that he may find healing, happiness, and ultimate hope—provided it doesn't kill him first.

CHAPTER ONE

"NASA should start thinking about this planet."
~ *Wally Schirra*

LIFT OFF

THE THEORY WAS sound but complicated. First, the cybernetic team would put Colonel Steven Scott to sleep and then fuse the PSYCHONIX *MDSL-1* processor to his central nervous system. It would become part of the myelin layers and provide better trophic support and neural circuit computation after he died.

Once Steven came to, from having the processor embedded, they would allow him to snugly fit the prosthetic bionic eye with a short metal suction rod. The prosthesis was a serious bonus for a retired Soldier missing his right eye. He was given instructions: *Lift the upper lid with your index finger to create an opening and slide the top edge of the prosthesis under the upper lid.* Done. It popped directly into the socket. Instantly the wireless processor linked to the eye and the Innovations Technology Laboratory network.

"I can hear his thoughts!" Brad Manuszewski said. Even as the primary inventor of the innovative technology, it took his breath away. "Now all we have to do is induce clinical death. In some ways it's simple." He continued to excitedly mumble to himself, not realizing he was on an open mic. "The heart stops beating, blood circulation terminates, and breathing ceases, but let's keep our fingers crossed that we can pull him back."

"Thanks Brad—you know I can still hear you too," Steven said.

Brad grimaced. He had forgotten but wasn't distracted. He double-checked the monitors and cryoprotectants levels. It was tedious, nerve-wracking work for everyone assigned to the project, and a man's life was potentially at stake. Their concentration was paramount.

On the first attempt, Steven would be legally dead for up to one minute. Initially one of the techs asked, "*That's all?*" But that was like asking *that's all*, when talking about Neil Armstrong's first step on the moon. It was certainly a huge day for ITL and Colonel Steven Scott.

They're all as mad as a box of frogs, Dr. Gus Kahn thought, *and we're going to jail for killing this man.*

Fortunately for Steven, Kahn didn't have his headset on, and no one could hear him. As the lights dimmed and the machinery hummed, Steven felt his left eye twitch and his hands tremble slightly from the nervous adrenaline.

"Let's do it! Steven announced through the PSYCHONIX communications system.

"Roger sir, we're ready, in 5-4-3-2..."

The *Amaranth* looked like a rocket waiting on the platform during the final countdown with liquid oxygen and liquid hydrogen clouds of steam escaping from the bleeder valves. There was a risk of the pressure blowing seals or damaging other components, so they had backup systems to their backup system.

Brad placed his left palm on a biometric live-scan and immediately initiated a two-person security protocol with Sabrina Killian, as another technician frenetically punched in launch codes. The rest of the staff adjusted their headsets as they induced sleep and began Steven's lengthy cooling protocol. By the time Brad said *two*, Steven had been fully anesthetized and was out cold. In due time, he wasn't breathing at all. He was gone—flatlined, no breathing, no circulation—nothing worked on its own at this level of deep freeze.

"There are absolutely no electrical activities in the heart or brain that can be detected," the ITL Director, Dr. Mark Starr said. He peered closely at the monitor and screwed up his eyes, trying to make sense of the data. There were only a few tones and beeps and chirps as Steven's PSYCHONIX eye swirled and pulsated red digital patterns throughout the lens. The staff gasped as they saw an illuminated glow shoot from within the *Amaranth* dewar and saw something incredible on their monitors. Over the whir of the machines they heard a retracting soundsnap that descended from a high pitch to low quiet hum. It banged and jarred the room with a gentle shockwave of light.

"His soul jumped!" Sabrina Killian yelled with a startle.

Brad stared unblinking at his monitor. "It was a *luminal boom* that breached the energy dimension," he said. "We broke the speed of light barrier."

Dr. Starr nodded.

As Steven Scott transitioned, the rest of the team saw it too. He was immediately lifted from his body and could see himself lying cradled in the *Amaranth.* Steven heard familiar, distant voices—none that he could quite make out. It was intoxicating, as he turned his head and saw Sabrina break a nail while she pushed buttons and frantically typed more data into the computer. He also heard Brad mention that the Washington Capitals had beaten the Pittsburgh Penguins 1-0 in last night's hockey game.

"What the heck?!" It caught Brad by surprise when he looked in the monitor and saw and heard everything in real-time that Steven Scott was experiencing.

"Just as we thought," Dr. Lui exclaimed, "it's dynamic."

"We've got a Steven's-eye view," Dr. Mark Starr announced over the ITL speakers.

Steven Scott gave him a tip-of-the-hat salute. "Steve-o-vision…it's the latest thing," he said, taking it all in and trying to comprehend his phantasmagoric perspective.

Everyone applauded.

It looks like you're prepared for a NASA lift-off, Steven said.

Everyone either nodded or gave him a thumbs-up. Then they saw him scan the room once again, open his mouth, and start to talk—just as his movements rapidly accelerated. At first, Steven felt a gentle pull, and then his translucent image shot up and soared through the top of the laboratory room. In an instant, he was gone and there wasn't a swish or a pop or thunderous crack. Only profound silence…until there was a staticky pop and they heard Steven breathlessly utter a few descriptions of *Wow* and *Oh Man!*

Fifteen seconds into the transition, they lost the transmission and panicked.

"Get him back," Dr. Starr commanded.

The ITL team hurriedly and expeditiously worked to restore the tenuous connection for their first PSYCHONIX mission. They had trained for it. In moments, they were able to restore audio and could hear him provide play-by-play.

Steven's psychomorphic, peripheral display flashed: **25 SEC.**

"I'm being drawn toward a foggy emerald tunnel through streaming blue and white lights."

And then, just as suddenly, and for no apparent reason—they lost the connection. There was dead silence.

Did we lose him, Dr. Starr thought?

No. However, just prior to the wireless link losing the signal—it happened. It would occur on each of the missions to the other side. In the depths of a nanosecond, Steven Scott's life and more flashed before his eyes.

CHAPTER TWO

"NASA is developing space taxis to shuttle astronauts to the International Space Station.
And just like New York taxis, they're all going to be driven by aliens."
~ *Jimmy Fallon*

FEBRUARY 13, 1989

ELEVEN YEAR OLD Steven Scott pretended that he was living in the 24th century,
whenever he watched the fictional Federation starship *Enterprise,* zipping through the vastness
of the universe. He and his stepbrother Mark Starr could easily survey all of space from the tiny
5.5-inch screen of their portable camping television and AM/FM Radio set. They clung to every
single word, as they camped-out in their spacious backyard:

But Data is Starfleet property, not a sentient being, Riker said.

The boys were superglued to the tiny screen, as they watched their favorite series, Star Trek:
The Next Generation. It showed on channel 21 UHF in Walla Walla, Washington, one of the
four channels they had—and their silver TV antenna could pick up. It was a program that they
rarely, if ever, missed. This episode was *The Measure of a Man* with a courtroom scene
featuring an android and the question of his humanity or the lack thereof.

Their imaginations ran wild with the possibilities of alien interaction. They pretended that
they were zooming around the outer edges of unknown space, from planet to planet, speaking
with radically diverse groups of intelligent and sometimes aggressive life forms. They fantasized
about not needing a vehicle but being able to efficiently and cleanly teleport their bodies from

9

location to location, like they had seen on their TV show. In their childhood make-believe, they could easily establish communication with beings from other worlds and escape ephemeral dangers with their ultra-advanced, jury-rigged technologies.

He can't choose to resign. He can't choose anything!

Understood, the captain said, presiding over the space court of appeals. *…but, can you please show me a means of measuring consciousness for anyone?*

They couldn't. No one could, and it seemed as though a fatal blow to the argument had been dealt. Even in the future, consciousness was thought of as a personal and qualitative thing, but how could a robot have it? There was nothing to put under a microscope and say, *yes there it is—that's consciousness.* They couldn't put their finger on it, but instinctively knew it was there—and that it was invisible. Even 11 year old Steven and his 8 year old stepbrother Mark knew that.

In light of the evidence, I rule that Mr. Data has self-determination—the right to choose for himself.

Mark, at this time, with nothing but food on his mind, dashed toward the backdoor of their white aluminum-sided house, to make a quick snack pit-stop, and get their little dog Buddy. He didn't hear the ruling come down on the TV show, but Steven did. He stayed transfixed to the creative television images and at the incredible, if not implausible, thought of an android robot having any kind of inherent human rights.

His mouth was agape as he tried to understand their nuanced procedures concerning: *The right to life, liberty, and freedom from slavery and torture. Freedom of opinion and expression, the right to work, and education*—or even how it was possible for a complex machine to be afforded genuine *hope* or be delivered from a finite material existence?

Steven unclipped his walkie-talkie from his well-worn, brown leather belt, raised the retractable silver antennae about two feet and pressed the key to deliver his important message. His little brother, Mark, waited impatiently by their back porch with his own walkie-talkie in hand and their dog by his side. Steven could see him from the opened flap of their make-shift Army tent, lit ever-so faintly by the small glass-encased, amber backdoor light. He thought the glow made Buddy look like a tiny, yellow cyclops.

Their mother had promised to restock their camping supply of goodies: comics, cookies, popcorn, and a mostly full Tupperware container of Kool-Aid with a round, clear, Snap-On top for easy pouring. They would use it to pour into their olive drab plastic Army canteens—helping them stay hydrated while they camped in their backyard jungle and ran around the neighborhood wreaking havoc.

"Data has SELF-DETERMINATION!" Steven repeated loudly and empathetically, after hearing the court ruling announced on TV.

Mark responded quickly on his walkie-talkie. "That sounds pretty cool, what is it?"

"Self-determination means that you get to decide what you want to do, all by yourself."

"Right on, I'm for that!"

It would be years to come before they ever heard of John Searle's *Chinese room* argument, which held that a digital computer that executed a program couldn't be shown to have a mind, understanding, or consciousness, regardless of how intelligent or human-like the program may make the computer behave. But who cared?

"Copy!" That was a cool term that he had recently overheard from *Miami Vice*, a crime drama that his parents watched each week. The program focused on two GQ, Metro-Dade Police Department detectives, working undercover in Miami. So, he knew that "Copy" meant that he had fully received the information and understood it. There were a lot of other unfavorable words that they had also learned from that show and their parents—which usually got them into a lot of trouble.

Both brothers had creative, wandering minds, and often imagined themselves being in full command of a crucial, deep-space outpost. So, that was what their make-shift tent became—a futuristic outpost to the vast universe. In their imaginations, the TV show that they were listening to was a live message from worlds unknown—and an advance warning of hostile aliens that required extremely close monitoring. Next to the TV, they had positioned a red *Dr. Cool Lunar Telescope* to explore the stars, the Moon, and its craters. It was a gift from two Christmases ago—that they mostly used for identifying local aliens and spying on the neighbors.

Steven keyed his walkie-talkie again with further instructions, "Steven for Mark! Since robots have now earned the right to *choose*, we must protect earth, more than ever." He looked up at the stars, then glanced through the futuristic telescope, with his right eye, as he spoke. He couldn't possibly have known that as an adult he would be missing that eye, and that because of 21st Century technology he would be able to see and hear far beyond anything he could fathom.

"If not earth, then let's at least defend the neighborhood!" Mark said

"Copy," Steven said, as he noticed something in his *Marx Toys Sooper Snooper, 4-way Periscope*, and sounded the intrusion alarm. "Small alien-girls approaching! Headed towards the DiBuono's house with adult-like creatures in tow! Must take immediate action! Engage with combat water-balloons," Steven added. He already had five in reserve, waiting to be launched.

In actuality, the oblivious adults were taking their children to a sleepover with Marlina DiBuono and six of her closest little girlfriends. The boys would have, no doubt, been in a lot more hot water if they had been discovered pelting the 10 year old girls and their parents with a barrage of balloons, as they arrived, but they did it anyway—and ran like crazy. They zigzagged wildly through the adjoining neighborhood yards, and into the woods, to recover their well-hidden, 3-speed, *Raleigh Chopper* getaway bikes.

To their childish minds there was a marked thrill of excitement at being chased like this. So much so that they had fondly named these cunning get-a-ways: *The Chase.* That night, they executed their planned chase and escaped perfectly. They instinctively communicated—practically able to understand what the other brother was thinking.

Each had to take different routes as they fled on their bikes, but Steven somehow sensed that his kid brother was hurt and circled back. When they met up, he asked Mark, "Are you okay?" Back then it seemed a rather benign question and neither of them followed up with why or how he had sensed his brother's dilemma—but he did.

"Yeah, I ran my bike right through a freak'n rose bush and kissed that tree," he said, pointing to his arm and the way his chopper handlebars were bent back at an angle and to the side. His main concern, for the time being, was straightening the crooked handles and washing off the minor traces of blood, so he wouldn't have to go home and explain it to his inquisitive mother.

Neither of the boys understood why, but they shared a special connection beyond that of ordinary siblings. It was similar to, but stronger than, the unique bond of twins, who seemed to be endowed with extraordinary and seemingly empathic or telepathic qualities. Steven was usually the first to recognize that something was happening or have a greater sensation that something was wrong. But clearly, Mark was on the same wavelength, whenever he was near Steven.

An hour or so later, they meandered around the block, rode the sidewalks and popped wheelies, as they headed back to their house and abandoned tent outpost. On the way, they both guiltlessly waved at a police cruiser, which slowly made its regular neighborhood rounds. The cops waved back. They both did a superb job acting as though nothing had happened. To their young minds, *nothing worth admitting* had happened. Steven even rendered a Cub Scout salute, to the cops, he had seen a kid at school do. They eventually parked their bikes and replenished their aqua arsenal.

"Make more water balloons!" Steven barked.

"10-4, on it!" Mark said, as he finished filling the last of the flexible water grenades from their outside water spigot and tied them off.

"Bringing in backup supplies too, right after Buddy goes potty!" Buddy was their nine-pound Maltese, whose dutiful bark provided an alarm of imminent alien intrusions.

"Copy!"

Just then Mrs. Scott poked her head out the backdoor, and handed Mark a large brown grocery bag full of their favorite goodies and a *Captain America* backpack stuffed with comics, gizmos, and gadgets—all necessary to defend planet earth overnight. Though not typically a warm and affectionate woman, Mrs. Scott felt rather mellow from copious glasses of Pinot Grigio. Mark smelled it lingering on her breath but didn't see her lean in—and catch him off-guard with a stolen peck on the cheek.

"*Mo-om!*" He acted as though his mother had turned into one of those more aggressive aliens that his stepbrother had warned him about. He promptly and fiercely wiped the obviously *poison* smudge of red lipstick off with the back of his baggy shirtsleeve. "*Sheesh!* People can see!"

14

With her mission accomplished, Mrs. Scott meandered back into the house, wearing a buzzed smirk on her face, as she so often did. Mark did an abrupt, military, *about-face* and made his way back to the tent, posthaste. He carried the survival bag of supplies in one hand and the retractable dog-leash in the other.

"The universe must be saved, Mark! Do you read me? Over!" Steven transmitted and cradled the receiver snuggly to his mouth, to ensure that his brother could clearly hear him. Mark's hands were too full to answer his brother immediately, so he began jogging double-time toward their camp site. He was doing his best to listen to Steven, but heard an unintelligible, garbled interference on the line too. It was like there were other people trying to talk.

Could it be aliens?

Steven barked the distress signal again, just as Mark popped his head in the tent and said, "I read you—I read you, already! Grab the bag!" He plopped to his knees, at the entrance, and released Buddy to run freely in the grass.

"Who are those other voices on the line?" Mark asked.

"Voices?"

"Yeah, I picked up something on the walkie-talkie while I was waiting—and whenever I turned up the volume, it disappeared."

Steven stared at him. "Creepy!" he said, as his eyes darted side-to-side. He pretended that whoever it was, might still be close at hand—or behind them in the shadows. "Maybe it was an alien!" Steven sharply blurted out, which startled Mark and made him jump. Simultaneously, Steven shined a flashlight under his face, which also made him look quite eerie. Because of the elongated shadows, his teeth seemed more prominent, and he spoke with a Transylvanian accent: "*Maybe* they'll come back for a quick *bite*. Bwa-ha-ha-haaa!"

Mark nervously begged Steven not to do that. "That's not funny—those shadows look real!" It was a normal 8-year-old's reaction. He was easily frightened and could spontaneously conjure up his own imaginative versions of the boogeyman—without any help. Just three years younger than his brother, but still young enough to believe in spooky things and potentially suffer traumatic nightmares from thinking about them. For the rest of the night, his Army angle-head flashlight was fastened tightly to his belt, or close at hand, even as they carried out their late-evening water-balloon expedition.

The boys kept their mobile television-set strategically balanced atop a blue plastic milk crate full of old used cables and wires that their dad had thrown away. It made it look more like a real spaceship. When not in use, their walkie-talkies were also conveniently strapped on their hips, opposite their Army canteens. It would be an enjoyable nighttime adventure. They were well prepared in their jury-rigged, backyard command post, assembled from a few worn-out woolen Army blankets, tautly strung over the clothesline, and loosely fastened with clothespins. It resembled a real tent, in nature. As best they could, they nailed and weighed-down the fringe edges of the blankets with rocks and sticks, or whatever could be gathered from a nearby field.

The boys were now safe and secure from outside threats. They were also well-stocked, but as an added insurance policy a reconnaissance was conducted earlier that evening—liberating even more supplies from their mother's well-furnished pantry. It would be a day, or maybe two, before she would discover anything missing, but that was of little consequence to them. For now—they were *roughing* it—clearly able to survive, until called into the house for breakfast, which usually consisted of two toasted Kellogg Pop-Tarts and a glass of Tang. *If it was good enough for John Glenn to drink on his 1962 Mercury flight, then it's good enough for me,* Steven thought.

16

For now, they would make do, from their backyard bivouac, welcoming friendly new life forms, and keeping the galaxy safe from unfriendly aliens and girls—neither variety of species was welcome.

They eventually found out that the walkie-talkie interference that they heard was frequency bleed over, coming from the little girl's sleepover next door. *Hmmm.* They, too, had some toy walkie-talkies, but with a much shorter range. To the boys it was a welcome—and diabolically useful discovery! They thought it would be quite entertaining to *eavesdrop* on the girls. The closer they got to the house, the clearer the reception became, but the more boring it got for the boys. They rapidly grew tired of hearing the girls replay *New Kids On The Block* music, and practice cheers, or talk about their latest Barbies, Cabbage Patch Kids, or just how cute Uncle Jesse from *Full House* was on TV. It took them less than an hour before they grew tired of it and developed yet another cunning plan: *Operation Scare Girls.*

Not a well-thought-out battle plan, but sufficiently decent for two smart little boys camping out in their backyard. It was mostly a simple assessment of where the *enemy girls* were located and how to best upset them. What else did you need to know? There were a lot of delicious options.

"They're in the *front living room*," Mark said. He had spotted them, as he scanned the yard again with their telescope.

"Copy! Collect all the loose acorns you can and when I give the word…throw them, as hard as you can at the windowpanes and yell into your walkie-talkie…like a *MONSTER!*"

The look on Steven's face, when he said monster, spoke volumes. He was enjoying this.

It worked. The terrified girls made high-pitched coyote-like howls. You could hear them all, as they scurried back-and-forth, bumped into each other, and shrieked in terror. One little girl had passed out, and another cried out sadly: *I wanna to go home!* Eight-year-old Marlina DiBuono sat on the floor and comforted her with a hug. She wasn't at all happy. It was her party and some nasty boys had ruined it.

All-in-all, it was a successful late evening for two ornery boys camped out to defend the universe. That was until a highly perturbed and overly exhausted Mr. DiBuono bolted from his backdoor and into the yard, barefooted, wearing Bermuda shorts and a white muscle shirt. He cupped his hands around his mouth and shouted into the darkness of the nearby woods, "I call da carabinieri on you boyz!" He corrected himself. "Da police!"

He wasn't quite fluent in English, so in the excitement he used the first Italian words that came to mind. "Basta!" meant that he had enough!

Who could blame him for his irritation? He had worked a long day and had half-a-dozen little girls squealing and frantically scurrying inside his house. Girls that would no doubt inform their parents that they had been attacked by monsters at the sleepover. Just then Mrs. DiBuono stepped outside, onto the porch, and calmly motioned for her husband to come back inside. She smiled and said, "*Che vuoi, sono maschi!*" Boys will be boys.

"Come Papa, I have extra cannoli for you. V*a bene*," meant that they would be all right.

He shook his head and smiled. "*Bene! Bene!*"

There was a lot of excitement that night, but it was hardly the crime of the century. If nothing else, it certainly caused quite a stir up in the DiBuono household—and that was the goal. Mrs. DiBuono recognized that kids teasing other kids wasn't exactly something new in the world. Not in Italy nor in America. She also knew that the behavior had to be stopped—before it got out of hand. At this point in their juvenile history, she had more than a few good reasons to suspect the two young boys next door, so she tried to give the Scotts an informative phone call. Mrs.

DiBuono let the phone ring half-a-dozen times while she waited for them to pick up—but to no avail. It seems that Steven and Mark had some foresight and anticipated the trouble that might follow their evening raid. They had already unplugged their home phone at the wall. Mrs. DiBuono shook her head and gave up. The Scotts would hear about this soon enough.

Later that evening, after the exhilaration of a water-balloon victory, scaring the girls half to death, and the relief of not being caught, Steven brought Mark up to speed on the details of their favorite TV space show. They also watched the rest of another program while they ate popcorn, and talked about all the important issues that night—and throughout the rest of the *ginormous galaxy*:

"I don't think they should kill Data," Mark said, with a somber pout.

"You can't kill a machine," Steven asserted. "They're just disassembling him—because he's not conscious."

"What?"

"We don't kill the TV when we're done with it, do we?" he said, reaching over and turning it off. It caused a pop with a staticky, high-pitched blip, as the screen faded into a small white dot.

Mark quickly turned it back on and asked, "How do you know?" It was the beginning of deeper psychological and philosophical, life related questions that he would ask much later in his chosen profession.

It was a serious question, well above the pay grade of an eleven-year-old big brother, but Steven didn't want to look stupid. So, as they both snuggled into their nylon, mummy-style sleeping bags with their flashlights, snacks, heads poked out the end of the tent, and stared up at the night sky, Steven said, "I just do—that's all! The TV didn't happen by accident. It came from the store, right? So, a person had to make it and put it there."

"So!"

"So…*Mr. Knucklebrain*, things don't just appear…and things don't pop into existence, all by themselves."

"But, didn't someone make us too?" Mark asked, innocently. "And the stars?"

"Yeah, but TVs and stars can't think or believe in Santa Claus, or know what it's like to be a person," Steven said, as he fumbled around in his backpack, and pulled out two large zip-lock baggies of mom's homemade toothsome cookies and candy—an even variety of cookies and fudge. All their favorites: peanut-butter, snickerdoodles, chocolate chip, and brown sugar fudge. "Or know what these cookies taste like—or what it feels like not to get one," he said, with a taunting laugh. He dangled them toward Mark's face and just as quickly pulled them back, as he strained to reach for them.

Mark clumsily pawed at the goodie-bags, missed, and desperately lunged toward them and his brother. He fussed and painfully grunted, as they collided and desperately wrestled back-and-forth for possession of the sugary treats. They heartily laughed and rolled out of the tent flaps, all arms and legs tangled, breathlessly coming to an abrupt rest in the coolness of the grass. There they laid side-by-side, on their backs, and looked up at the wide-open night sky.

"Wow, I wonder where the end of space is?" Mark asked, still breathless, as he chomped down on a huge bite out of his well-earned peanut butter cookie.

With their bare eyes, and no moon, clouds, or haze to block their vision, the boys could see half of the stars visible to the eye alone, from the Earth's summer night sky. Somewhere around *5,000,* he learned in school. Steven's 6th grade teacher had taped up a large poster, including twelve of the constellations, and he loved looking at it: *Aries, Taurus, Gemini, Cancer, Leo, Virgo, Libra, Scorpius, Sagittarius, Capricorn, Aquarius and Pisces.*

He couldn't remember them all, but the fact that Sagittarius was a centaur with a man's head and torso on a horse's body, got his attention. *It's pretty cool that he had a bow and arrow!* He thought.

That was the best constellation when you were 11 and 8 years old, respectively. They often pretended that was what they were—*Centaurs*, shooting arrows—as they popped successive wheelies, and trampled new paths in the woods on their *Raleigh Choppers*.

As they settled into their tent outpost, Steven said, "My science teacher says space is growing, out of nothing."

That didn't compute in his naïve young mind. *It's growing—out of nothing?*

"That's dumb!" Mark said, rolling his eyes. "You can't make something out of nothing—even I know that much!"

"Yeah, me too! Teachers can say some pretty dumb stuff, huh?!"

They both agreed and stretched out on top of their sleeping bags. They pondered the thought and enjoyed the view of the well-lit night sky—as they scrunched up their little faces to intently consider where the universe actually came from.

"Something or someone had to be pretty smart and powerful to make all that stuff," Steven said.

"Yep," Mark sighed, "but I don't know anybody with that kind of power—not even *Superman*."

Steven nodded. "Do you think we'll live forever?"

"I don't know. How long is that?"

"A long, long time. It means you never ever die."

"Ever?"

"Nope."

"I don't want to be stuck in the fourth grade forever," Mark said, wearing a hangdog look, as though he had been sentenced to a life in the county prison.

"Well, we'll keep getting older—so you'd be done with school by then." It was a good, big-brother answer that satisfied him.

"Okay, good—so, I guess that would be pretty cool then, especially if we didn't have to follow dumb-old-rules.

Steven's eyes lit up with a new thought. "If it was only us, then we could make up our own rules."

"First rule: no baths!"

"—and NO bedtimes."

"—and cookies every morning for breakfast."

"—and ice cream any time. And...since I'm your big brother I'll be in charge—so, you can make all the cookies."

Mark stood up in defiance. "No way—that's not fair! Why do you get to be in charge?"

"Because, I'm the oldest!" He stood up, too, and looked intimidatingly down at his little brother, who was easily seven inches shorter than him.

"You can't be in charge JUST BECAUSE you were born FIRST. That's not fair!"

"Can too! If I live forever, then I get to decide what's fair—and the first rule is that I'm the President."

Mark shook his head. "No, the FIRST rule is no baths, remember?"

"Okay, then the second rule."

"You can't just make stuff up."

"Yes, I can. I'm the President."

"Well, then I'm the King."

"Okay, I'll be the Emperor!"

"Then I'm whatever is higher than an Emperor—whatever that is!" Mark said, with satisfaction.

"That would be God," Steven said, reflectively, pausing and looking up at the sky. "But you can't be God."

"Why not?" he said, with a huge encumbered mouthful of cookies. Not making any attempt at showing manners or concealing his chocolate covered teeth and crumb-covered lips, he mumbled the words—sounding more like: *rye-lot?*

"Because, whoever made us probably has that job—and the only thing you're good at is eating cookies," he said, snatching the zip-lock bag away from Mark. Immediately he was tackled around the knees by his kid brother, as he attempted to flee with the treats. Both boys stopped cold when they heard a loud crash, sharp words, and an unpleasant commotion coming directly from their house. Sounds that they had heard many times before, toward the end of some serious, *hellraising,* weekend parties. They didn't mind because they usually got to do whatever they wanted to do.

They were still frozen and listening. They heard a muddled cacophony of slamming and hollering and swearing, punctuated by the sound of random things breaking and the screech of tires, as their dad roared away from their home. They knew what had happened, but barely cared. Yesterday, Mark overheard an elderly neighbor lady say to another nosey neighbor:

Their daddy has a short fuse and their mommy has the matches. Poor boys.

Their best bet was to stand clear of the ground-zero explosion. They glanced at each other and nodded with sad eyes and pursed lips, as though the calamity was unfortunate but expected. The disrespect and hate-filled words that their parents spewed had become an inevitable part of their life. The peaceful night of camping in the backyard suddenly shattered, as another drunken poker party touched down, and jealous accusations flew.

They didn't like it but were used to it by now. Their only option—*block it out.*

Steven reached over to turn up the volume on their TV.

"You think we'll ever get out of here?" Mark asked.

"I hope so!

CHAPTER THREE

"The Earth is the cradle of humanity, but mankind cannot stay in the cradle forever."
~ Konstantin Tsiolkovsky

GOING BACK

IT HAD ALL HAPPENED in a wink. Steven Scott's earliest childhood memories flooded his mind. Each moment had chronologically flashed before his eyes, as he laid staring up from the *Amaranth* dewar.

"It was incredible," Steven Scott said. "I could remember every detail of my childhood."

On the second trip, Steven would flatline for one-point-five minutes, no more and no less. It was vigilantly calculated to ensure his safety. They would slowly increase and regulate the limits to better understand the capabilities and uniformly regulate the cryoprotectant fluids. A chemical fixative called glutaraldehyde was injected to instantly stop decay, allowing them to add fluids more slowly and to prevent dehydration. They were in totally new territory.

The PSYCHONIX systems new power supply was exponentially increased, which allowed Steven to make it through the foggy emerald tunnel of lights that he had previously described in detail. Evidently, not everything on his journey to the other side could be seen by the ITL team, so Steven's vivid descriptions were enlightening.

"It was an opening into another dimension—sort of like Heaven, I guess. And it wasn't a bunch of fluffy clouds with angels playing harps and lyres. No, it seemed very real and beautiful—and I was met by a spirit guide."

"And you knew this how?" Dr. Gus Kahn asked.

"I —I felt it," Steven said. He couldn't exactly explain it. "Nothing was said with words, but I knew that he was there to welcome me."

"Did he have a name?" Dr. Feinberg asked.

"I don't know. It all happened so quickly. I saw him and then I was pulled back."

Dr. Kahn nodded as though he was speaking to a crazy person. "Hmm, I see. Perhaps you're remembering your dreams as an engram."

"Sure, okay," Steven said. He had no idea what Kahn meant. "There were important moments of my life that flashed and were vividly replayed in my mind. I know. I experienced them as I was drawn through the brilliant flashes of multi-colored lights. It seemed to be a lot more than just memories or dreams."

The subsequent split-second trips were just as incredible and became more and more fascinating—especially when he could start to decipher the memories from the dreams and nightmares.

CHAPTER FOUR

"Of all the things I've lost, I miss my mind the most."
~ *Mark Twain*

GRANDMA'S HOUSE

"MY MOTHER-IN-LAW is 85 years old," Mrs. Brenda Scott remarked with a high sense of urgency in her voice. She was on the phone to a local Walla Walla nursing home, dourly inquiring about the services and cost of elderly nursing care.

"Oh, dear—that much," she said. "Do you have anything cheaper?"

There were numerous physical and fiduciary questions that needed to be answered about meals, physical therapy, hospice care, and special units for patients with mental illness—if that's what Grandma Scott had. *Sure, seems like it*, she thought.

The bleak but necessary plans had to be made in case they needed to admit Grandma soon. Brenda's boorish disposition was on full display and Mr. Scott soon gave in to her determined wishes. If they sent his mother to a senior living facility, he insisted that they find a place nearby, so they could visit. She agreed and couched her intractable position as the best way to provide for grandma's health and welfare when, in reality, she just didn't want to assume responsibility for the person, she called the *old lady*. She argued that the house wasn't big enough or suited for grandma's needs.

"She'll be close enough," Brenda churlishly chided her husband.

Sometimes in her typical impatience, selfishness, and aggravation, she would lash out at her unresponsive husband. "She's your mother—and you'd think that you'd care more about this!" It was just one more stressful reason for them to argue and it usually resulted in Mr. Scott sulking at the corner bar.

Even though *Mom* hadn't manifested any other obvious signs, they both suspected a serious condition had emerged. Mr. Scott had dolefully contemplated this time of life and figured that they would eventually have to provide more care for his mother. He knew that there were always medical issues to deal with, as one advanced in age, and it was his responsibility to be the caring son. So, together, they kept a closer eye on her.

"Grandma seems sharp enough for now and she hasn't lost her memory—yet." That was how Mrs. Scott explained it to the lady from the nursing home. "But she's definitely shown signs of impaired judgment—and last night's little episode was the last straw."

From the dispassionate tone in her voice, the lady at the nursing home realized something needed to be done. They agreed to meet and scheduled a convenient time to sit-down and discuss the possibilities for grandma's long-term health care: medications and therapies and the best end of life care. It was explained to them that this was, likely, the best path forward and that those were the steps that would best accommodate their aging mother. The nurse on the other end of the line remained calm and sympathetic, as she provided the Scotts with a glimmer of *hope*. She even asked if she could pray. It felt awkward and weird, but they indulged her.

"Grandma would want it," Mr. Scott said. He bowed his head.

On one call to the house, Steven and Mark perked up when they overheard the gist of the conversation. They scooted closer and keenly listened from the living room. That was where they liked to hang-out and watched *The Jetsons* cartoons, as they ate their after-school snacks and waded through boring homework assignments. They were both bright kids, and took normal classes without ever seeing any real connection to their everyday lives, like most kids.

It wasn't something that you could always communicate to your children—not until there was a need for it. There was plainly no *real-life* experience for them to compare it to in their young minds. Perhaps that was why, as much as possible, they avoided doing their homework. At least until report cards and teachers' conferences and the threat of restriction was looming over them.

The teachers reported: *They can obviously do the work. They just don't.*

The boys listened as Mrs. Scott continued to explain her mother-in-law's condition to the nurse. "She is moderately active, despite walking with a cane. And she's still driving—some— even goes to church and attends water aerobics three times a week at the Walla Walla YMCA."

The nurse asked more about her mother-in-law's marital status. "Well, she lost her husband about three years ago," Mrs. Scott replied, "but appears to manage quite well on her own. Of course, we take her shopping, to dinner—you know, the regular stuff like that." She said the right words, but her glaring, passionless tone spoke volumes about her ostensible concerns.

Her husband, Grandpa Scott, retired at Walla Walla Air Force Base nearly twenty-five years ago, as a Fuels Supply Sergeant with the Air Defense Command, 325th Fighter Wing out of McChord Air Force Base. The base had since shutdown because of base realignment and consolidation programs. Since his passing, Grandma still got a small Chief's pension from the United States Air Force. It was a good check but hadn't kept up with the cost of living and was not nearly enough to meet all her growing medical, housing, and transportation needs. It did, however, provide her a modicum of independence and kept her sufficiently above water.

Brenda Scott volunteered. "We have to help her pay her bills." She responded to a series of other questions on the line. "I don't know—but recently she just seems unusually frightened about things. She has a lot of trouble sleeping—and getting the right words out."

Brenda paused and listened to the lady from the nursing home. "Uh-huh, right—lately—I would definitely say that she's been showing signs of paranoia. At first, we were completely dumbfounded—couldn't really believe it, but she told us—my husband and me—that she heard the voices of her grandchildren in her bedroom the other night." She paused to hear the nurses response. "No, she doesn't even live here—in the same house."

The lady said she thought that was indeed *an interesting development,* and asked Brenda what medications her mother-in-law was taking, and whether or not she had any sort of hallucinations before.

"No—but she phoned me and my husband, pretty close to mid-night—completely hysterical. He fetched her, as fast as he could, and brought her back to our house. But, she's still quite rattled. Upset. Trembling hands and lips. We've never seen her so terribly shaken and panicked before."

The nurse questioned her current mental state and whether she had settled down at all.

"Yes, but it took her awhile to calm down. The first night she took a sleeping pill, but she's been able to go to sleep since."

Steven and Mark laughed so wildly and inappropriately out of control that they found it difficult to breathe. In a near state of asphyxia, they snorted their *Capri Sun* drinks through their noses and eventually caught a breath, as they rolled-off the living room sofa and tumbled to the soft carpeted floor below. Now they were nearly choked from uncontrolled laughter, as they tactlessly mimicked the phone conversation, between gasps for air.

"Did you hear that?" Steven asked, as he smiled guiltily at Mark. "Grandma—seems to be hearing voices!"

Mark uproariously asked, "I wonder if—they sounded anything like us?"

"How could they?" Steven deadpanned with a mischievous smirk beaming from his face.

"We never left the house."

Both boys simultaneously pulled out their two-way walkie-talkies, from behind the couch, and keyed the mic as they marched around the living room. "Grandma, come in—can you hear us?!"

From the kitchen door, Mrs. Scott noticed, but hadn't quite caught on to their silly antics yet. But she would—*oh, would she ever.*

Steven continued his silliness, "Outer-space to grandma, *oo-OOO-oo!*" like he was a ghost from a scary, distant planet trying to make contact with geriatric life forms.

"We have come for you, *bleep-bleep!*" Mark said, acting out the rigid mechanical movements of an alien robot, as he marched around the room. "*Bleep-bleep!*"

Grandma's house was approximately two miles away from theirs, an easy twelve-minute bike ride through the neighborhood, to her driveway, if you didn't stop. It only took a few more minutes than that to find the spare backdoor key, wedged under a stone in the garden shed, and to circumspectly set foot in her house. Everything went smoothly, as planned.

The concealed walkie-talkie that they placed under her *Edyth* four poster bed, the night before, had a terrifically strong three mile range—and it worked better than advertised. It had enough of a coverage range to accomplish their semi-diabolical mission: *Scare Grandma!*

Mission accomplished—they had scared her witless.

Consequently, there was an even wider range of unfavorable emotions being dealt with by the adults, at the Scott household, that evening—annoyance, anger, exasperation, and trace shadows of black humor, veiled primarily in dad's pursed lips and grinning eyes. He fleetingly referred to it as a *rather amusing moment but* was shot down by the steely glares of his wife and mother. He had to profess solidarity, because they were still absolutely livid. Although it was quite stressful during these tortuous, long-drawn-out moments, for the rest of Steven's and Mark's natural lives it would be an often-repeated tale—that never died. It practically became a holiday tradition.

However—tonight, "It wasn't a bit funny!" according to their highly-agitated mother and completely flustered grandma.

"Hey, look on the bright side," Steven pled, "Grandma Scott isn't losing her mind."

From the facial expressions, it was to no avail, nor was it of consolation to anyone involved.

Mark nodded and added with a modicum of practiced sincerity, "And the good news is that she won't have to be committed to a nursing home either." He genuinely loved his grandma, but that practiced argument also fell on unsympathetic ears. They couldn't run from this problem.

It was true that grandma wouldn't be committed to a home today, but truly—it would also be quite a while before either of the boys ventured outside of their own home.

CHAPTER FIVE

"Failure is not an option." ~ *Gene Kranz*

SCRUBBED

THE COLD BARE concrete floor shook, began to crack, and splintered out like the electrical bloom of lighting in an angry night sky. Fog suspiciously hugged the malfunctioning equipment and probingly crept along the low-lying surfaces of the laboratory. A single, bare lightbulb dangled and hypnotically swung back and forth above Steven Scott's face. It transfixed him as he laid immobile staring up from the *Amaranth.*

He could see the exposed wooden beams in the ceiling shift. Circuit boards, microchips, and wires balanced around him began to smoke and combust. A burly arc welder, in gray overalls, stood at the foot of the dewar, pulled down his auto-darkening mask and fired up his torch.

"Don't worry, we'll have ya outta there in a jiff."

In the corner was an old RCA TV/Radio console, balanced on two wooden planks, between two metal drums full of jumbled computer parts. The nightly news was on, but the only sound heard was classical music, which lofted from the radio and was piped throughout the building. Behind it there was a large mirror. Staring through the glass sides of the *Amaranth,* Steven could see his reflection and the bulky piece of technology that held him. He thought that he looked like a baby swaddled in an assortment of metal items, reclaimed from electronic junk. He could see gleaming swaths of stainless steel being spot welded by the man with the torch.

Standing behind seven foot high steel cylinders of chemicals were two geeks in white laboratory jump-suits and black framed glasses. In the reddish glare of the *Amaranth* they madly flipped through an instruction manual on *Lines, Tubes, and Drains: What to know about Acute Treatment.* One of them shook his head wildly, slid back a sleek, floor to ceiling cabinet, and took out a sternal saw.

"Open wide," he said.

CHAPTER SIX

"Two things that you will never have to chase: true friends and true love."
~ *Mandy Hale*

BLOOD BROTHERS

THE AMARANTH FLASHED and Steven was once again swept through a cascade of brilliant lights to a time of his youth...

The young gentle eyes and tender ears of Steven and Mark didn't miss a thing at their house. Even as they matured into teens and young adults, they were exposed to unwarranted verbal abuse—more often than not, caught in the crossfire of their immature parents.

They couldn't help but absorb the sights, sounds, and attitudes that were on full display and handed down. Sadly, the good, bad, and ugly behaviors, instilled in them, would become their family inheritance.

Steven joked, "Our parents' final wills will probably say *we didn't leave you anything—get over it.*"

"No, it'll be more like, *there's bourbon and pills in the cabinet, and cigarettes in the armoire,*" Mark said. "*Help yourself.*"

They had a good laugh about it.

The stepbrothers had regrettably devolved into the pitiable teenage reflections of their parent's deficient moral nurturing, guidance, and distorted temperaments. They weren't bad kids, just angry.

Like discolored sponges, molding in the dark, they had soaked in an assortment of abusive sights and sounds that psychologically damaged and misshaped their most formative years. They didn't know who they could trust, and it triggered irritation, frustration, anger, and a macabre sense of humor.

For now, their raw memories were budding emotional seeds, but the boys knew that things were clearly wrong with their family's crummy disposition, and that the apples hadn't fallen far from the tree.

"Who knows—we probably caused our folks to argue and drink," Mark said.

"—but who cares," Steve added quickly. Although not true, he acted as though he was okay with taking the blame.

"My thoughts exactly."

"Deal with it," Steven flippantly said. From his tone, it was quite apparent that he hadn't yet developed an understanding of how to *deal with it.*

"Yeah, what's wrong with you boy?" Mark said with a wink, and other well-rehearsed words from his father's catalog of hurtful words. Some thoughts, so traumatic that they were hidden deep in the shadowed crevasses of their brains—never consciously accessed. They didn't understand how or know why, but it shaped them and the way they thought about things. It had caused them to act differently, to withdraw, and sometimes react inappropriately.

They initially blamed themselves for all the addictive problems with alcohol and incessant quarreling within their family—but there was nothing that they could have done to change or stop it. The dysfunctional merry-go-round spun and spiraled out of control. It was sadly ironic that they were headed down the exact same, disruptive path as their parents. That was the hardest part to swallow. At heart, they were good kids and usually in a lot more trouble than they had deserved. Their saving grace was that they were, almost always, clever enough to stay one step ahead of their problems, with an uncanny ability to sense trouble, before it happened.

Sadly, they had been born in the wrong place, at the wrong time, and to childish, undisciplined parents, who weren't entirely equipped to cope with their youthful exuberance. So instead of being *raised* well in Walla Walla—they were *ignored* and, for the most part, left to their own devices.

In many ways, it seemed as though emotional providence had spitefully dealt the boys a losing hand. For better or worse, they had survived in an unsupportive and unstable family. That had precipitated a protective detachment from close relationships—leaving them, as teenagers, to trust no one but each other. That was something that they were about to seal with an ancient ritual.

"I saw this on TV," Steven said, pulling out a blue bandana and his Swiss Army pocketknife.

Mark stepped back; eyes wide. "What's that for?"

"It's for our *Blood Brother Pact*."

"You're crazy!"

"No, I'm serious. Warriors used to have a ceremony and swear a loyalty oath to each other, where each person makes a small cut, and the two cuts are pressed together and bound."

"You've gotta stop watching so much TV."

"No, I want us to do this, seriously.

Mark listened—apprehensively.

"First we prick our hands, mingle the blood, and then wrap them together to make us one."

He turned to walk away. "Well, I don't know about all that—let's just say we did."

Steven stopped him. "It's okay, we'll only make a small cut—and you can do yours first."

Steven foisted the pocket-knife on Mark before he could leave.

"Me, why me?"

"Because I've got to tie us together with the bandana."

"How about—I tie us, and you go first?"

"Don't be such a scaredy-cat." Steven goaded him with his big brother, *I dare you*, look.

Mark crossed his arms and shook his head *No!* with pursed lips, but then reluctantly said,
"Oh, alright, let me have it."

He took the knife and grimaced as he lightly scored his palm with the thin metal blade.

"Harder!" Steven commanded. "It didn't cut the skin."

"Harder?! You do it!"

"Okay!" He impatiently snatched the knife back and gently slit his palm, until a few tiny droplets of blood erupted and trickled across his hand. "See—it's just a nick. There's nothing to it." He handed the knife back to Mark. "Your turn."

Mark furrowed his forehead and trepidly took the knife back. He then screwed-up his face, to anticipate the pain, and firmly ran the blade across a one inch part of his palm. It immediately brought tears to his eyes.

"Good job! Now hold my hand, like we're arm-wrestling, and let's mingle the blood."

"What for?"

"It makes us become part of each other."

Mark nodded, and they smooshed their hands and blood together, like they were scrubbing it with a thick red soap.

"That should be enough," Steven said, as he draped the bandana around their hands, and tied it off with the help of his other hand and teeth.

"Do we have to say any special words?" Mark asked.

"No, it's just sort of an unspoken, magical agreement."

Mark was okay with that because, if nothing else, they now had each other—as loyal blood brothers. Steven even started calling him *Blood* after that.

They had always struggled with new relationships and vulnerable conversations, but now they knew they had each other, come thick or thin. They fought for each other and against the world. One day—when and if the brothers ever connected and unloaded their burdens to an actual counselor—one would have to cue an orchestra of violins to start playing. Theirs was a long, sad story. But there would be no crying violins today. Today, their only *hope* appeared to be in their imminent survival—and they were pretty darn good at doing that.

Isolation seemed to be the key. It was the only mutually agreeable solution for their transitory situation. They knew that neither one of them would be at home forever, so until then they needed a plan to coexist, or at least until their circumstances vastly improved. It occupied their minds a lot. It was their belief that they could coexist best by not existing in the same time or space as their parents—or any other authority figures. It was basically *Newton's Third Law of Motion* about collisions between two objects:

In a collision between two objects, both objects experience forces that are equal in magnitude and opposite in direction. Such forces often cause one object to speed up and the other object to slow down.

They had no intentions of slowing down and wouldn't have to, if they only avoided their parents. So, whenever possible they went in the opposite direction. At home they barricaded themselves in their rooms or left the house, circumventing their incurious parents whenever possible. Away from home, they invariably ran toward trouble and away from the law.

In their earliest teenage years, they chose to stonewall people they didn't trust. Their strategy: *Radio Silence!* It gave them what they thought was a cool persona.

They withdrew from serious engagements and communication, and often got fueled up on cheap booze and cigarettes to help them cope with their situations. It was unwittingly and unsuccessfully used to self-medicate and escape their depressed, anxiety riddled childhood.

As an adult, Mark would later admit, "And it worked for a while. I didn't have to deal with my childhood feelings of neglect, confusion, and distrust. So, nothing was damaged—other than my sleep, health, energy, creativity, clarity, and relationships." If nothing else, over the years, he had mastered being facetious.

He admitted that a taciturn manner probably wasn't the best communications weapon for two boys entirely dependent on their parents for food, clothing, and housing. But it didn't discernibly matter to them back then. They would never think of asking their parents for anything—even if it meant a *five-finger discount* every now and then. The only other option was leaving home for good, but they were still too young for that.

Steven and Mark were understandably miserable and intended to leave home as soon as they possibly could. Both had mentally withered in what seemed like a never-ending cycle of affliction.

How did we get so lucky? Each of them thought at one time or another. Somehow stupidity, desperation, and/or sex had brought together Steven's quick-tempered, alcoholic father and manipulative stepmother. The only up-side to this disastrous marriage was his simpatico stepbrother, who he now had as a blood brother. They shared everything, including an ornery sense of humor.

"Steven, you're JUST GREAT, you only hear what you want to hear," Mrs. Scott said, constantly nagging him about his personal choices.

He nodded, "I am great, aren't I?"

It was his typical teenage, passive-aggressive way of responding.

"You know what I like about you Mother Dear?"

"No?"

"Me neither!" It was irritatingly smug enough to get under her skin and just about right for helping him cope with her *annoying crap.*

Mark loved his mother but acknowledged, without apology, that she was doltish and certainly no candidate for sainthood. After the ill-planned, blended marriage, he kept his mother's previous married name, *Starr.* Given the complicated paperwork and cost, it was just easier for them to keep it that way. Steven kept his father's last name, *Scott.* From the beginning the stepbrothers had a great pact relationship, which helped them to adjust and survive the surrounding conflicts. Fear of separation and random visits from *Child Protective Service* counselors could do that to young children.

On the plus side, it helped them form a protective bond that remains unbroken to this day. Their biggest challenge for now would be to avoid their toxic parents—and *hope* for an eventual escape.

Lights danced and there was another metallic luminance boom that echoed and swept the laboratory.

Steven Scott was returned to his body in the *Amaranth* and they began to reanimate him. On subsequent trips or nights, the memories or dreams or nightmares were too interspersed for his mind to parse.

CHAPTER SEVEN

"Good to the last drop." ~ *Teddy Roosevelt*

PERCOLATE

STEVEN SHOT HIS good eye toward the foot of the *Amaranth*.

"We'll have you outta there in a jiff," The welder laughed to himself as he repeated part of it again. "...in a jiff!" The second part echoed in the hollowness of the eerie laboratory. Steven noticed a digital read out scroll across the auto-darkening portion of the welder's vision screen: **OUT OF ORDER.**

How strange, Steven thought.

Steven shifted his eye back to the left. There was a mass spectrometer, centrifuge, and a particle accelerator attached to the top and sides of three large, high tech, *Imperial* 40 cup percolator coffee makers with an assortment of tubes running from each to dispense multi-colored cryoprotectants.

I don't want that crap in me, he thought, but his thoughts keep registering inaccurately on the old RCA TV/Radio console straddled between the two metal drums in the corner.

It read: **YOU WILL DIE.**

Then, Steven looked across at the welder's mask and it too had another message scroll across the vision screen: **YOU WILL DIE.**

"That's not what I said!" he screamed. The white coated technicians looked at him curiously and turned to punch more buttons and type codes—and then the TV blinked off with a small white dot disappearing into the dark screen.

"That TV didn't deserve to live," the first technician laughed.

The other technician walked over. "Sir, you're missed-thoughts *are* closed-caption, captures, captioned*, missing—error*," she slurred the mis-jumbled words as though she had wound down and run out of power. Now, she was frozen in place with her head cocked to the side and her index finger pointed up, toward the bed-bound patient mirror hanging above Steven's head.

He looked straight up and caught his reflection in the mirror. Everything below the collarbone had been discarded, with only tubal connections left protruding from the double-walled flask. It was as though he had been housed and assimilated by the *Amaranth* with thousands of minds trying to control him. He jerked and spasmed as he fought off the mental invasion. His Native American Army battle-buddy, *Red Feather,* walked in, took out an arrow, and broke it in two. He shook his head sadly and left.

Steven was somehow alive, but unable to speak, frozen between life and death.

Another technician came to assess Steven and spoke with a mechanical patter. "We are unable to upgrade your outdated applications."

She's an android, he thought.

"You are inferior, so we have determined—your termination."

Robot after robot entered the lab and repeated parts of the sentence: *We have...Determined...Your termination.*

Steven reeled from sheer terror and couldn't believe what he saw. Everyone at ITL was an android.

CHAPTER EIGHT

"I listen to the Trumpet of Jesus, while the world hears a different sound.
I march to the drumbeat of God Almighty, while the others just wander around..."
~ *The Imperials*

BEST PLACE TO MEET GIRLS

IT WAS DIFFICULT, if not impossible, to know. Yes, the *Amaranth* was undoubtedly a catalyst for penetrating dimensions, but since its *MDSL-1* processor had broken the speed of light barrier—had it also become an ingress that enabled time travel? Or was Steven Scott simply remembering the past? As he laid frozen in the dewar, the light explosion from the luminance boom bullwhipped the laboratory with the subtle and otherworldly sound of multiple sonic lasers passing overhead—and he returned to the early 1990's...

Flash.

For the foreseeable future the brothers were distracted by academics and girls—but, mostly girls. Somehow the little girls in the neighborhood had sprouted-up and evolved from the threatening aliens that they had been, into heartbreakers. The boys were, strangely, no longer plotting to chase them away with acorns and water balloons.

It became obvious, early-on, that some of the prettiest girls, on their block and from school, attended a local church youth group. So, it was of no great wonder that was where you would find Steven and Mark every Friday night, *religiously*.

As Mrs. DiBuono said, when they were a bit younger, *Boys will be boys!*

In the beginning, they attended the youth group primarily for the serendipitous opportunities to pick up girls and catch a fly rock band called *CFM* playing. It didn't hurt that the band was made up of three pretty girls—K.C, Harper, and Lulu.

Their group was entertaining, the music full of attitude—and just loud enough to fill the empty spaces, so that you didn't have to talk too much. The guys were really into it. Of course, neither Steven nor Mark bought the whole church thing, but they weren't raised to hate it either, since their grandma was what they called *religious*. *C'est la vie* they thought. They didn't have a strong opinion about it one way or the other. If pressed—they certainly sometimes wondered; *why would God allow so much pain and suffering in our family?* But the thought didn't linger. There were too many more interesting things happening and they were having a lot more fun meeting girls—than finding existential answers.

Tonight, they were having a blast hanging out and hearing music—even if it meant hanging with a few *Poindexters* and some cute, notable exceptions.

Marlina stared at Steven while he talked to friends—and he caught her. He shyly grinned and she quickly looked down and then back up. Steven still had his gaze set on her and they both smiled from across the room. It was their first teenage introduction, since scaring her sleepover friends, half to death, nearly six years ago. He made his way through the crowd, to say hello.

"Hey."

"Hey."

"I'm Steven!" He said over the loud music.

"I know."

"You do?"

"Uh-huh. My daddy said your names, often, after you and your brother threw acorns at our windows."

"Yeah—ah…about that…" Steven turned nervously, finger-combed his hair and his knees involuntarily gyrated a little like Elvis Presley had possessed him.

Marlina smiled. She thought it was cute that he got nervous like that.

Not knowing what else to say, Steven asked, "Would you like to dance?"

"Sure."

It wasn't what you'd call a quiet, romantic dance, but it was a special moment that they would remember forever. Marlina's parents didn't allow her to date, until she turned sixteen, but it didn't matter at the moment. They danced and talked, and he felt an immediate connection. He would wait and do whatever he needed to do, to be able see her again—and she didn't discourage it.

Later in life, Steven recalled that the church band rocked out—but they were the exception back then. In some cases, during the 1980's and early 1990's, you were considered on a *slippery slope,* if you dared to sing one of Bill Gaither's songs, like *Because He Lives.* In a few conservative denominations, your salvation was in question if your church had a drum-set or guitars, and you were certainly being deceived by the devil, if you ventured to listen to any music from the Jesus Movement rock bands of that era. Anything else—and you were unquestionably going to hell! That kind of self-righteous, judgmental attitude still made him nauseous.

He could remember banned artists from a list that was handed to him by a church lady with ancient horn-rimmed spectacles, a list that seemed mild by today's standards: *Keith Green, Larry*

Norman, Barry McGuire, Love Song, The Imperials, 2nd Chapter of Acts, Don Francisco and Phil Keaggy.

"One local church even posted lists of groups that parents should be aware of," Mark said. "But, back then, we didn't trouble ourselves with their *holier-than-thou* rules. I watched what I wanted to watch and listened to what I wanted to listen to—Aerosmith, Led Zeppelin, Tom Petty, and Will To Power. Man, I loved their medley of Baby I Love Your Way and Freebird." Years later, he would still have *SiriusXM 80's* music programmed in his Tesla.

None of the conservative regulations were of much consequence to the brothers, since they lived by their own set of rules. But they played it cool, just so they could attend for a couple hours a week. Why not? The food was free, the music was upbeat and fun, and the girls were different in a nice way. Especially that Italian American girl who lived in his neighborhood. After living around the block for years, he was finally getting a chance to really know her and certainly no longer regarded her as an *alien.*

While they were waiting outside for their rides, Steve said, "I hope I'll see you again."

"Well, maybe the next time you'll throw rocks at my window," she teased.

"What? Oh, well, I wouldn't do th—."

Marlina grinned.

"You know, like Romeo did, throwing pebbles gently against Juliet's window."

Her friends called her away. "Our ride's here!" She gave him a peck on the cheek.

Steven saw Mark having a good time talking to one of the girls, as they left, and walked over to ask him a question. "Who's this Romeo guy?"

Mark shrugged.

The brothers still had great memories about hanging out there and how they were treated. "We always felt welcome at that youth group," Mark said. "And no one tried to push a bunch of religious *mumbo-jumbo* down our throats."

"Honestly, I felt like we were really missed when we didn't show up," Steven replied.

The adults knew their names and they were trusted and treated with respect—something they rarely, if ever, got at home.

CHAPTER NINE

"You see things; and you say, 'Why?'
But I dream things that never were; and I say, 'Why not?'" ~ *George Bernard Shaw*

FIX IT

SOFT CLASSICAL music was still being piped throughout the lab and the heavy scent of day-old coffee overlaid the slight smell of disinfectant. Steven Scott could smell it but was still entrapped by the *Amaranth*. He couldn't move or express himself.

The three cryoprotectant coffee machines hummed and spewed as they pumped out fluids through the long tubes attached to Steven's arms, legs, head, and neck. He squirmed to free himself as a raging deluge of the cryosolution erupted under his skin, like tiny volcanoes finding their way to the surface.

The earth began to swirl around him, and he became immersed in *much of muchness* as he passed under rainbows, doorways, and bridges. His first kiss. His proposal and marriage to Marlina. The birth of their children and a wonderful life together. Horrific times on the battlefields, his friends dying, and every important mistake he had ever made.

Then there were rings around the Earth that gyrated, and Steven felt as though he was rocketing toward Jupiter. His life seemed out of balance and his whole future was on the line, if he didn't confront it now.

I'll fix it. I'll fix it! He called out as he struggled to toss and turn and tumbled from his bed in a tangle of sweaty sheets. The impact of hitting the floor had shaken him awake from another bad dream.

CHAPTER TEN

"It is the very nature of truth that presents us with this reality. Truth by definition is exclusive. Everything cannot be true. If everything is true, then nothing is false. And if nothing is false, then it would also be true to say everything is false." ~ *Ravi Zacharias,* The Logic of God

PRAYER GROUP

Steven Scott tested the theory of superluminal time travel and attempted to change the past. In the fiery sparks of flatlining synapses, and he remembered...

THE YOUTH PASTOR never pressured them about religious matters, how they dressed, or what music they listened to—although in Steven and Mark's own words: *there was always a dull message stuck somewhere in-between all the fun.*

No buzzkill. That's how they thought about it, even though it was strange to their way of thinking. Some of their new friends at the youth group called it a *real drag,* but they didn't see it as all that bad. It was certainly no worse or weirder than some of their non-religious friends.

The group was made up of mostly kids that didn't normally attend or were required to attend church by their zealous families.

At first it wasn't a glaring inconsistency, but in their mind, it became an obvious and strange disconnect. The biggest troublemakers in the group were often the preacher's and deacon's kids, who were nearly as clever as the stepbrothers. They watched them categorically disavow their involvement with the *pagan* kids, but who cared? They made their own fun and started their own late-night party called the *Prayer Group.* It was a great cover, because the kids could always say that they were late, because they were in a prayer group.

"Where were you tonight son?"

"Oh, ah...prayer group went long."

"Oh, that's nice dear!"

Prayer Group was usually held in the church parking lot, long after all the other kids were picked up and the adults had gone home. It usually entailed sharing cigarettes, six-packs of beer, and exploring the joys and terrors of weed with the rest of the uninformed and *born-again hypocrites*. Mark and Steven weren't alarmed—they half-expected it and gladly joined in their mock atheist communions.

Hey, who are we to judge? Pass me a joint!

Most of the time they enjoyed the relaxed, friendly scene, and tolerated the *Jesus Stuff.* To them the *holier-than-thou* folks were way too preachy and could moralize and drone on to no end, but as far as they could see, it didn't hurt anybody. And, it was certainly nothing that they hadn't already ignored from their grandma. Each time they visited her, they were tenderly manipulated into learning bits and pieces about God. It usually happened when their parents separated. That's when they would invariably be packed in the car and shuffled over to Grandma Scott's house. *At least she's a good cook*, they thought.

Grandma had a big family Bible on her Colonial American coffee table, crammed full of photos, pressed flowers, and obituary bookmarks with verses on them. No one dared touch it, but sometimes she would open it and read to herself. At dinner one night she read a verse and asked Steven to pray.

He speedily uttered, "Dear God, my grandma tells me that you have a reason for everything on Earth, I guess broccoli is one of your mysteries. Amen."

Mark grinned and exuberantly exclaimed, "Amen!" and quickly dipped half a fishstick in ketchup and crammed it in his mouth. Grandma Scott was patient. She smiled and shook her head. The most important thing to her was that they were safe and loved—*what else mattered?*

"It's a precious memory, even though we probably tormented the poor soul to death," Mark said. He fondly remembered her affirming bedtime words: *Jesus loves you—and I do too!* That was what they heard after she gently kissed them goodnight and acted out short stories from her ten-volume set of Arthur S. Maxwell, *The Bible Story* books—at least until they were old enough to decline.

"She always said she was praying for us," Steven recalled, "I remember when we were really little that she would rock us and sing: *Jesus Loves the little children—all the children of the world...*"

Maybe it was due to their conditioning or their grandma's touching words *I'm praying for you,* but they soon found that the youth leader's messages were getting through their hard heads. It helped them make a little more sense of life—and it gave them exactly what they needed: *Answers.* They were captivated—and encouraged by her stories of meaning and purpose, and the never-ending life thing really captured their attention.

They thought, *Who wouldn't want that?*

Steven and Mark began to attend the youth group regularly and surprised themselves by signing up for a youth camp. They had never heard of such a thing, until they were handed a flier and a permission slip. It was offered, conveniently, during a time when their parents were separated. The boys were staying with Grandma Scott again, at least until the marital issues could be resolved. She signed the permission slip and they were going.

Why not? More, food, fun, and girls! They thought. It was set and they were going.

When they arrived at the youth camp all the leaders introduced themselves and the first speaker was from their group.

"Hey, thanks for coming—I'm Bobby Smith. I work for a *global enterprise* that has outlets in nearly every country in the world. We've got hospitals, homeless shelters, hostels, hospices, orphanages, food banks, and feeding programs. We also do marriage, mental health, and justice work. Basically, I'd say that we look after people from birth to death and we deal with the area of behavioral alterations." He paused.

That got their attention. *Behavioral alterations*—cool.

"It's called the Church. Have you heard of it?"

Some of the kids laughed and some moaned.

Whenever Pastor Bobby spoke it was entertaining and personal and powerful.

"He even died for you and came back to life to prove that He was in charge of everything," Bobby creatively added.

"It seemed like he was talking straight to me!" Steven remembered. "He spoke about this real God with skin, who had already sent us messages of hope from another dimension and visited our earth to protect all the people."

Bobby continued. "Here's some more good news. Over the course of the week the *Jovian Players*, from Jupiter Florida, are performing *The Lion, the Witch, and the Wardrobe* for us, adapted from the C.S. Lewis book. But here's the twist. By paying close attention to subtle clues in the story, your team will have the chance to decipher a code and unlock this large wardrobe full of sweetness," Bobby said, pointing to an unevenly stained, standing cabinet in the corner. One could only imagine what candied delights might be secured behind those mysterious, plain paneled doors.

"The clues may be hidden to the uninitiated but are actually right before your eyes. So—to help things along, I'll give the clever sleuths among you a few hints. Take the lamppost in the story, for instance, it's like a compass in *Narnia* that leads the children back into the real world. Also, it's always winter and there's no Christmas or goodness until Aslan, the talking lion, returns. And the final hint—he gives his life to save one of the children and later rises from the dead, vanquishes the White Witch, and crowns the children Kings and Queens of Narnia. That's all you get—and my goodness—that's a lot."

Steven and Mark were quite intrigued. They loved a good puzzle and worked hard at not just solving it but winning. Some of grandma's old bible stories popped in their head and they wasted no time piecing things together.

Just like at their own local youth group, there was plenty of great food, games, a rocking band, and plenty of tolerable speakers. Except, at this event, there were a lot more kids, food, activities, music, and longer messages. But it only took one speaker to connect and deliver a much-needed message of *hope.* It was the last night and things had started to wind down. The food was nearly gone, and the band had sung all their songs multiple times. Most of the kids had even packed, prepared to get out of Dodge as fast as possible when it was over, *but God spoke.* Not audibly, but in their soul.

At the end of one of Bobby's shorter, heartfelt messages, the band played the only slow song that they knew: *Open the Eyes of My Heart.* He then invited everyone to bow their heads and pray—and asked if they wanted to have a personal relationship with the God of the universe.

"I had never heard it put like that," Mark said, "I was into mythology—and loved astrology as a kid, but this was way different. It was about a real person, places, and things that happened in history—nothing ever rang so true to me."

As he remembered it, both he and Steven stood up at the same time and echoed the pastor's prayer with *Amen!* Both boys were dumbfounded that the God of the entire universe cared so much about them.

It was a powerful, memorable event, but also resisted and mocked by a few oblivious agitators who found the entire notion, synonymous with being *narrow-minded, fanatical, judgmental, puritanical, medieval, homophobic, and Neanderthal*—at least that was how one of the older boys described them at *Prayer Group*. It sounded like he had memorized the line. Others were there strictly for the fun. They talked, passed notes, snickered, and waited impatiently to hear things conclude, so they could exit as quickly as possible. It was a rude but presumed behavior for teens at a large youth camp.

Neither Steven nor Mark were sure what it all meant, but they had searched for some type of religious identity that made logical sense. This was it. They had tried everything from the moral relativism of Wicca—to becoming a left-wing, politically active Buddhist vegan and closet atheist. This Jesus thing seemed entirely different and reasonable. It gave them some of the stuff that the other religions and myths didn't. At the time, they couldn't articulate the answers it provided for objective morality, meaning, destiny, or the origins of the universe—*but it sure seemed right.*

It was like a big weight had been taken off their shoulders and they couldn't be happier about their decision. *Radiant* was how Bobby described them. But this was only the beginning of their spiritual journey. He told them that there would be ups and downs, but an indescribable joy and strength would carry them through the harder times.

One thing was for sure, they had a lot of complicated questions waiting on the shelf and didn't wake up the next morning with angel wings, ready to perfectly serve God.

Marlina was beyond ecstatic and showed it. She was a generally expressive person, and quite animated and vocally enthusiastic about Steven's spiritual decision. She could barely contain her happiness. She skipped and ran as she approached—her expressive Italian hand's waved in the air. Steven could see her coming, all the way, from the back of the auditorium. From gestures, to food, art, and of course a romantic language, the Italians were known for being passionate in everything they did. Marlina was no exception, as she hugged him up tight.

Marlina DiBuono had hoped for this moment but hadn't pushed it. It had to be genuine—and Steven's personal decision. She was neither the kind of girl who led a guy on, nor the type that dated with hopes of converting someone to her faith—and she, technically, didn't consider going to youth group a date. His decision, however, was a delightful surprise and welcomed relief to the strongly religious Mama and Papa DiBuono.

Throughout their high school years, Pastor Bobby invested in the boys both spiritually and in personal matters of life. He knew firsthand that teenagers often acted impulsively on matters that didn't stick. And he didn't want their young impressionable minds making purely emotional decisions. He knew that in this type of energized religious atmosphere that they were particularly vulnerable. That wasn't necessarily a bad thing, but it was a great responsibility that needed to be handled with wisdom. He also knew that many kids left church because of unanswered or poorly answered questions, so he was there for them.

He also knew just how responsive they were to positive reinforcement and reasoning—especially Mark. He drank it in like water. Bobby did his best to wisely guide both brothers, hoping to instill a strong moral code, knowledge, principles, and wisdom, all aimed at serving and living their lives with meaning and purpose. He also encouraged them to study and challenge their beliefs.

"If you can't challenge your beliefs, then it's not worth believing—and it's the only way to grow," he told them. "Don't blindly accept everything you hear from me, or anyone else."

Both boys were staying exceptionally busy. They attended church, volunteered, and worked community-faith projects. In an effort to make things right, they tried to reconcile with their parents—but neither bought into their *goody-goody* act.

"It's one of those religious phases," their dad said. "Give them some time—and it'll pass."

They tried to make amends and in their minds that was good enough. For now, their new life kept them busy, out of trouble, and away from their parents—so all-in-all it had worked in their favor. They liked making a difference, feeding the homeless, assisting at the crisis pregnancy center, and holding workdays at the homes of the elderly and disabled. They took to heart the message about *faith without works being dead* and couldn't imagine not being active in their small-town community of Walla Walla, Washington.

During one of their lessons, Pastor Bobby introduced them to the term *apologetics*, which they totally misunderstood.

"Well, I don't think it's right to apologize for something you believe in," Mark said. "If you believe something is true, then you shouldn't have to apologize for it, right?"

"Right," Bobby said. "The reason you believe something is because you think it's true. That's the basic definition of a belief. But A*pologetics* isn't about apologizing. It's a branch of theology that helps us discover the reasons why we believe something is true and how to defend it."

"Like you would in a court of law—," Steven said.

"—with evidence," Mark finished his sentence.

"Yes."

Steven scrunched up his face and tried to follow what he felt was an overly complicated way of believing something. A deeper conversation than he personally cared for. "Look—I just believe it, okay?"

The Pastor explained to him that it was okay, but that apologetics was about providing solid arguments about what you believe. It strengthens your beliefs and helps you defend those ideas to others."

Steven continued, "It all seems pretty basic to me—like why wouldn't you believe it, right? And who needs an argument? I don't like arguing anyways!" He grew up with a lot of fighting and it had nothing but a negative connotation to him. "I'll pass."

"You misunderstood this definition of *argument,* Steven. In the apologetics sense, it means a reasoned out forensic debate, not a quarrel," Bobby instructed. "As you said—it's more like something a lawyer would do, as he defends a case."

"Okay—sure, but I'm not a lawyer either. So, I don't need a bunch of complicated *fancy-schmancy* arguments to believe it—I just do."

Bobby didn't *argue or make an argument* with him about it. He believed that personal belief and experience were some of the strongest basic arguments for the existence of God. The other supportive stuff would come along in time and with maturity. He wanted to tell Steven that apologetics would help communicate his faith better and provide *hope* and strength in times of pain and suffering—but he left it there. He understood from his own journey that each person had to process and practice their faith, at their own pace.

Mark on the other hand, dove in headfirst. He asked questions and read everything he could get his hands on from: Alvin Plantinga, William Lane Craig, J.P. Moreland, John Lennox, Gary Habermas, and others. He had a much deeper thirst for spiritual knowledge. An academic need to know about why things are the way they are.

Where did we come from?

Where are we going?

What is our purpose?

How can we know?

What makes Christianity true?

Mark also had a desire to seek out and consume scientific information and resolve those great mysteries—some that even the greatest minds had struggled to understand. He took great pleasure in doing so and pondered whether he would ever be able to reconcile that with his faith. It seemed like a conflict—but it challenged him to think, all the more. Thoughts that he had as a young boy staring up at the night sky still echoed in his mind.

Something or someone had to be pretty smart and powerful to make all that stuff.

Bobby didn't go into the science vs. Christianity warfare mentality in a heavy fashion, but simply shared a quote from C.S. Lewis: "Men became scientific because they expected Law in Nature, and they expected Law in Nature because they believed in a *Legislator*."

CHAPTER ELEVEN

"You never know how strong you are until being strong is the only choice you have."
~ *Bob Marley*

ARMY

ITL now knows that Multidimensional Spatial Travel cascades via the gateways of memory and the mind. That was the reason for the dreams; however, no perceptible time travel or ability to change events has been discovered.

ON THE NEXT journey in the *Amaranth*, Steven Scott's life once again flashed to a later part of his life. A time right before he joined the Army and parted ways with Mark. Most of the memories were good, but you could see his strained face peering from the *Amaranth*, whenever he recalled the more difficult moments of training and challenges in his life. A time when he pursued the one thing that he thought he could count on—the U.S. Army.

It happened in a vapor, just before he flatlined and the *Amaranth* sounded *Beep, beep, beee*—.

There's an adage that says, *change is the one thing that you can always count on.* It was inevitable—and true. Whether it was within your organization or in your personal life, change was going to happen. Steven Scott was reeled back to a time when, whether he knew it or not, big changes were on the horizon. Things were beginning to happen that required a lot of blood, sweat, and tears.

Right after graduating from high school, he was unceremoniously dropped off at the Seattle Military Entrance Processing Station or MEPS by his father.

"You just head through those doors—take care," his dad said. No hug. No instructions.

With everything he owned in a gray-blue leather suitcase and backpack he made a beeline toward the door and never looked back.

MEPS was responsible for determining an applicant's qualifications: aptitude, physical fitness, and background screening. Not all military jobs were created equal. Some were dangerous and some highly technical, but most fell somewhere in between. He would take the ASVAB or *The Armed Services Vocational Aptitude Battery* to figure out where he landed within those categories.

Steven Scott met all the cursory medical standards and blew the test out of the water with a General Technical score of 138 and a Combat Operations score of 98. He had no idea of what that meant, but apparently it was one of the best scores that they had ever seen. Each of the MEPS counselors took notice—and offered him special career advice. Because of his aptitude scores, his career options were wide-open—everything from a slick-sleeved grunt to eventually becoming a commissioned Officer. But there was one military occupational specialty or MOS that appealed to him the most: **SPECIAL FORCES.**

I qualify for Special Forces! That was what he wanted—and the mere thought of it, simultaneously made him feel both nervous and cocky.

Special Forces candidates attended *Infantry One Station Unit Training*, which combined Army Basic Combat Training and Advanced Individual Training into a 14 week course. Once completed, he would then attend Airborne Training, followed by a 4 week Special Operations Preparation Course and the Special Forces Assessment and Selection program, where his physical, emotional and *mental stamina* would be put to the test. They would only accept the best of the best. *That's me*, he thought.

Steven Scott qualified for the Special Forces option, but first had to board a Greyhound bus to get to his training post and then make it through a rigorous boot-camp. So, with one well-worn travel suitcase, and a canvas backpack full of snacks, he headed out on his next adventure. It kind of reminded him, a little, of his childhood camping excursions in the backyard with Mark— except this time he would be living in real tents and preparing to fight real adversaries.

When he finally got off the bus at Fort Benning, Georgia, changes happened faster than he had anticipated. *It's a day that I'll never forget*, he wrote to his brother Mark. *When I got off the bus with the other recruits, we were immediately ambushed by a herd of Drill Sergeants in their olive drab campaign hats. They looked like Smokey Bear hats, but not as friendly. It was quite a chaotic day as they welcomed us to the REAL Army.*"

The Drill Sergeants introduced the recruits to the tougher physical, mental, and emotional elements of military service—and that seemed to require a little more dramatic shock and awe.

"In basic they immediately began the intense process of turning civilians into soldiers, taught us to march, shoot, an array of survival skills, and prepared us for life in the *real Army*. Here, we have regular Basic, but also have to earn the right to be a Green Beret. It's a lot tougher. We sleep in the mud—if we get to sleep at all, get buried in dark holes, eat bugs, and shoot all kinds of weapons!" Steven relayed on a short call home.

Mark was envious. "Get out! What about grenades?"

"Yep—and I'm getting pretty good at it too! I guess all those years of throwing water-balloons and dirt-clods finally paid-off, huh?"

"You always had a good arm."

"Oh, and I'm getting used to this short haircut," Steven said, as he rubbed the palm of his hand, back-and-forth, over the surface of his prickly, fresh cut, hair fuzz. "It's sort of a rite of passage during military basic training. And—it makes me look pretty darn tough—if I say so myself," he said, as he caught a glimpse of his reflection in the phone-booth glass. At the same time, a Drill Sergeant stared back, through the glass, at the strange recruit and pointed to his watch.

"Yeah, I'm not sure how you get used to all the bad food—and being told what to do—and being yelled at, every day," Mark said.

"Just like home!"

"Ha, yeah!"

"Except, I know what to expect."

"Wish I could say the same—things are still a little—well, you know the deal."

Steven sighed "Yeah," as he changed the subject. "Anyone special in your life these days?"

Mark, always the joker said, "Well, you know the old high school cafeteria lady with the big hairy mole?"

"Yeah?"

"Well—we're eloping!"

"Oh brother!" Steven exclaimed, as he palmed his forehead.

"It's like that old 60's song says," he sang, "*if you wanna be happy for the rest of your life, never make a pretty woman your wife!*

"Ha—you can have her—ladies' man!" Steven cracked up. It felt good to shoot the breeze with someone from back home. "Besides, you'll never guess—."

"What?"

"Marlina and I are engaged! But I'm marrying a pretty wife."

"Wow—I guess I knew that was coming. Congratulations!"

"Yep, she came down on my weekend pass, I popped the question, and she said she'd have me!"

"That's great Steven—I'm happy for you!"

"Thanks! Hey—I'm out of *Stalag Benning* in another few weeks—and then we'll get married. Then, I've got a one-week break before heading to the *Military Intelligence Electronic Warfare College* at Fort Sill, Oklahoma, and on to Afghanistan."

"Wow, where?"

"Can't really talk about it—but I can say that I'll be in *Military Intelligence*—in Afghanistan. Green Beret!"

"No kidding, Green Beret?! That's really cool—but, Military Intelligence—why'd they pick you for that?" he teased.

"I guess they're scraping the barrel," he paused to adjust to a more serious tone. "Look, I won't have a lot of time, but I was hoping you'd be my best man."

"It'll be my honor, man," Mark said.

"Yeah?"

"Yeah—I look forward to it."

"Well, *gotta* go little bro—my times up. The Sergeant is breathing down my neck to wrap it up! And other guys are lined-up to use the phone—later!

"Love you Steven!"

Steven looked around to see if he was being noticed. "Yeah, right back at you blood!" His *I love you too* tone came through, even though he had difficulty saying the specific words within earshot of his Drill Sergeant.

CHAPTER TWELVE

"I imagine headaches as tiny neurons repairing the insides of my head with miniature hammers."
~ YQ Baba

HEADACHE

THE TRIPS WERE becoming more vivid, but the details confused and conflated. Life past, present, and who knows. "Was it all a dream or a PTSD flashback?" Steven Scott didn't know anymore—but he had seen something present and real. More than anything he was conflicted about his desire to live in this world and the opportunity to discover another dimension. *How could life ever return to normal?* He thought, after crossing over. Now that he knew there was more, he wanted to find out as much as he could about it.

"Did you see the spirit guide or guardian angel this time?" Dr. Kahn asked suspiciously.

"Yes, I did. I saw a lot, but it happened so quickly. The being looked like a Roman soldier. Then I saw flashes of Mama and Papa Millie rocking on a wooden porch, a beautiful field of flowers, and Marlina staring into a waterfall."

"What do you think it meant?" Dr. Feinberg asked.

"I don't know. Maybe nothing."

"Probably just the people, in your memory, that you miss," Dr. Kahn added.

"I don't know," Dr. Starr said. "You're obviously going somewhere."

"And I've got to go back—but first I could sure use some Tylenol," Steven said, rubbing his head. "Dying causes the worst headache."

CHAPTER THIRTEEN

"Bootcamp is really easy, it's just like riding a bike. Except the bike is on fire. So are you. And everything around you is on fire. Because you're in hell." ~ *Unknown*

BACK FROM BOOTCAMP

AFTER 18 GRUELING weeks of bad Army haircuts, humiliation, and organized havoc, Steven Scott, the disorganized civilian, returned home as PFC Steven Scott wearing a Green Beret and a canvas duffle bag full of funny stories, from his time in training.

Shortly after his arrival, he and his brother Mark were doing what most guys did, as one's wedding date quickly approached—bought a ring, rented a tux, and waited for it to happen. After all, Marlina was the one doing the heavy lifting: dress fittings, food, band, flowers, venues, sent out invitations—hair, nails, and on-and-on. They had planned their one-week honeymoon at *The Edgewater* in Seattle with brunch overlooking Elliot Bay and the majestic Olympic Mountains. Then it was off to his first assignment. *Alone.* Marlina never got used to it but being alone became an expected part of their Special Forces military life.

For now, the brothers bided their time, and sat on a rusted-out picnic table, at their favorite local hang-out. They ate fries and foot-long chili dogs with mustard and onions. Both agreed that it was their favorite combination and went down best with a fresh, thick strawberry milkshake. A combination that always reminded them of their childhood—the good parts.

Prominently displayed on a billboard behind them was a sunbaked, dilapidated sign that read: *Olympia Dairy Bar, the Best Custard and Burgers since 1956.* It was the *Best*, especially after weeks on end of eating nothing but scrumptious Army chow and field rations.

"Congratulations, you made it through," Mark said, as he clinked his paper milkshake cup against Steven's, as though it were a crystal wine glass. "How was training?"

"Not bad, once you endured being stuck with a full assortment of vaccinations and remembered to follow rule number one—."

"Which is—no baths?" He remembered their childhood conversations about rules and who was in charge.

He chuckled and said firmly, "No, never volunteer—for anything!"

"Ha! *Yeah*," Mark grinned.

"And rule number two," Steven said, "don't say *yeah* when the Drill Sergeant asks you a question."

"Why is that?" Mark asked.

"You never ask why in the Army—you just do it! One guy in our squadron learned that the hard way."

"How?"

"It's a funny story really. There was this guy from New York City—David Ammon, who answered the Drill Sergeant's question with *yeah*. Boy—did he ever pay for that," Steven said, as he shook his head. "He had to stand at attention in front of a barracks toilet—for about fifteen-minutes—and flush all the *yeahs* out of his system.

"Are —you kidding?!"

"Nope! For 15 minutes straight that's all the kid did—salute, scream *yeah,* flush, and repeat."

"That's insane!"

"Nope, that's just how the Army builds character!"

"Weird."

"Yeah—I suppose it is, but persevering and overcoming adversity in the form of humiliation can teach you a few things—like learning attention to detail and how to maintain your military bearing under pressure."

"Military bearing?" Mark asked.

"It means you stay calm or don't get rattled too fast, when things go south. You learn to roll with the punches—and not sweat the small stuff."

"Okay, I could see that. I always thought we were pretty good at it."

He nodded. "Right, they know that in battle we'll get hit with a lot, so they want us to focus on training, teamwork, and the mission at hand."

"Wow, and all along I thought that the Army was just about fighting wars and stuff like that."

"It is—but a lot more. It's about service before self, God, and country and—you know, patriotic things like that! The leaders are mostly about mentorship now-a-days, but every-now-and-then we're threatened with *wall-to-wall counselling,*" he said with a raised eyebrow that divulged sinister intent.

Mark shrugged.

"It means that you're going to get your butt kicked, to put it nicely, for being such a screw-up."

"Are they supposed to treat people that way?" Mark asked.

"No, it's not—supposed to happen that way," Steven replied, "but there are a lot of things in life that aren't supposed to go down like that, right?" Steven gave Mark a worldly-wise wink.

"However, Army Boot Camp is where recruits are transformed into Soldiers, and prepared for the real Army and combat zone, where things can get crazy. They're trying to shape us—so we can fight and win America's wars."

He paused while he took another big bite of his tasty chili dog and a long pull on his red-striped milkshake straw. "They've got to know that you can take a lot more than a simple beating—and that they can count on you, when the going gets tough. It's then that the *tough—tough, get going*," he sang out the Billy Ocean song that they used to work out to.

"I don't think I could ever make it in the Army. But, mostly—I'm just hoping to make it out of high school," Mark said. He was still eighteen months from graduation, maybe sooner if he squeezed in AP classes and went to summer school.

"Sure, you could, but remember it's not just about you—it's about something much bigger," Steven said. It's a *sifting process*—like getting along with people at church or preparing for Heaven. It shapes and refines us as we learn to serve, trust, and have confidence in each other. We also learn how to communicate and work together as part of a team." Steven slurped the last sip of his milkshake and threw it in the trash with his hotdog wrapper. Still a perspicacious young man, he had easily picked up on how Mark felt without him having to say too much.

"Don't worry about it buddy—you're going to college anyways."

"I *hope* so."

"*Hope's not a plan!*" Steven quipped, echoing an aggressive Army mindset that effectively made hope sound like a dirty word.

"Wow, lighten up MacArthur!"

As Mark said the name *MacArthur*, Steven Scott found himself waking up, remembering where he was, and knew that he had once again dreamed about his life upon reentry—and was

71

now being reanimated. He was at ITL, lying in the *Amaranth* and his skin tingled. He couldn't move, but consciously noticed a pain in his left shoulder. Most likely from lying still for so long. He also felt thirsty and called out, "Hello, anybody there? I'm thirsty and ready to get out of here."

CHAPTER FOURTEEN

"It's a war within yourself that never goes away" ~ *Sgt. Brandon Ketchum*

PTSD

THE TRANSITIONS WERE smooth, but the dreams were becoming more vivid and PTSD dreams kept getting worse, so Marlina asked Steven to see a doctor. He knew that he should, because he hadn't been sleeping well and felt irritable. He typically woke up at three or four a.m. and couldn't return to sleep. Sometimes he tossed and turned for hours, unable to fall asleep at all. He had anxious thoughts and worries that would flood his mind and expel the sandman.

His threatening nightmares left him overcharged and thrashing around in his bed or waking up in a blind panic, soaked in sweat and ready to fight. Last night was the final straw. He saw the worried look on Marlina's face.

"I'm gonna call Mark," Steven said.

"I think that's a good idea."

"Maybe he's got some good ideas about how to deal with this."

CHAPTER FIFTEEN

"Family is like fudge; mostly sweet with a few nuts!"
~ *Unknown*

MAY 3, 2023

REGRETTABLY—IT OFTEN takes a family funeral, birth, marriage, or mental illness to bring families back together again and such was the case now. Steven Scott and Mark Starr had drifted apart. They weren't estranged, just busy. It inevitably happened, even in close, loving families. At first you missed birthdays and anniversary celebrations and then you couldn't make the family reunion or won't be home for Christmas this year. You hoped that your schedules would clear up and you could make it home soon, but things almost always got in the way—namely life.

It had been a while now since they had spoken, but Steven Scott picked up the phone and told Mark all of his complicated troubles. They were deep and Mark knew it would require a professional counselor.

"Can you recommend anyone?" Steven asked.

"I can. Dr. Peggy Feinberg. I trust her judgment." Mark made the arrangements at her office in Baltimore and mentioned something to Steven about becoming a volunteer for their *Mind-Body Problem* study.

"It just means we won't use your name," Mark said. "Only select data that Peggy gathers during the counseling. And best of all, my company, Innovations Technology Laboratory would cover your cost."

"Why?"

"We're funded for it, as part of a research program."

"Works for me," Steven said. "I appreciate your help and the price is right."

Steven Scott's troubles started long before he picked up the phone to call Mark. Ever since he left home, for the Army, life had gotten in his way. He took on more and bigger responsibilities, went to war, returned damaged, and was mentally exhausted. He had unconsciously gone into a survival mode. It was instinctive. He woke up each morning—and hung on for dear life.

For Mark, it wasn't nearly as bad. It took a while but eventually things got going. At first, he struggled through his prerequisite college courses, but in the end got the hang of things. So well, in fact, that he graduated *summa cum laude*, got into a great medical school, and then specialized in psychiatry and brain surgery. It seemed like he spent his life savings and life in school.

Steven Scott was immensely proud of his little brother and joked that he himself eventually graduated, *Oh Lawdy*. It was an old family joke that they never tired of. School was important to Steven, but the Army came first. It had to be that way. However, he was disheartened when he learned that he couldn't make Mark's first college graduation ceremony, but it was unavoidable. He was otherwise detained by the current world conflict. This time deployed with KFOR, a NATO-led international peacekeeping force that secured Kosovo.

"My first night, I slept in a sleeping bag under the stars," he said, recalling his childhood campouts. "This next time, I slept in a substandard bunk—somewhere in a building, in the city." He wrote home, but that was all he could tell anyone, except for the nebulous mission statement: *We're deterring hostility and threats against Kosovo by Yugoslav and Serb forces!* It was standard military-speak for; *we're doing a lot of stuff that we can't talk about.* Or he would just cavalierly write: *Someone's gotta do it, right?!*

The brothers were living their dreams, each successful in his own right. They were happy for each other and stayed in contact, as much as possible. Regrettably, their careers drove their hectic schedules in opposite directions, on different sides of the planet. They rarely met up, except for a family reunion, or conference that landed them near each other in a city along the way. Then they would stop and have a leisurely cup of coffee or breakfast, before going their own way again. Scattered to the wind. They both spoke of how nice it would be if, sometime soon they could share Christmas together—*maybe next year.* They would plan on it. Unluckily, their plans didn't work out as well as they did when they were kids. It was much harder when being *chased* by life's demands.

As children they loved Christmas and living in a small Washington town with neighbors that knew each other. I suppose most children do, if it's part of their tradition. But they really loved it because of their grandma and the way she celebrated it. Those were the good memories. The ones they held on too. It had captivated them as little boys and it was a special shared memory for them now, too.

They remembered wearing their blue fur-lined parkas, riding their new bikes—and touring the vast neighborhood Christmas light displays, which offered residents a winter wonderland, complete with thousands of illuminated bulbs and decorations. They still talked about it in letters, then later with email, and on social media. It delighted them and turned them into little kids all over again. Perhaps, one day, they would try to get back home and recapture the good things that they remembered about *small-town Christmases*.

When they were growing up, everyone in Walla Walla started putting up Christmas lights months in advance. If you pulled up in front of any local home, you could see the lights as they twinkled and flashed to upbeat Christmas music. During one of Steven's Afghanistan and Iraq deployments, he found a *YouTube* video of his hometown Christmas lights and showed it to his troops. It brought him a touch of home that he needed in a faraway land. Whenever he called home, he would joke with Marlina about being able to see those lights flash in the night sky.

"I can see it all over Southwest and South-Central Asia," he said. He pictured the houses there being like the Clark Griswold scene, from *National Lampoon's Christmas Vacation*, and laughed whenever he thought about Chevy Chase playing the looney dad.

Steven took college classes whenever time allowed and eventually accepted a regular commission as a 2nd Lieutenant in the Army. Fellow service members referred to that rank as a *Butter Bar,* because the insignia was a small gold bar, about the shape of a small stick of butter. As a junior officer, he was now earning more money than ever before, but took on a whole lot more responsibility. In the long run, it provided a better quality of life for himself, Marlina, and their two children, Vito and Donna. His son, Vito, was a traveling nurse who worked in Bluefield, Virginia, and his daughter Donna had followed in daddy's footsteps and joined the United States Air Force, as a Public Affairs Officer. She was now a *Butter Bar* too.

While on active duty, Steven Scott was what they called a *burner.* He climbed the ladder faster than most of his peers and pinned-on *Full Bird Colonel* in twenty-two years. It was nicknamed that because the rank-insignia is an eagle and because Lieutenant Colonels are also referred to as *Colonel.*

He had earned a chest-full of ribbons, *or fruit salad*, proudly displayed for his brave accomplishments. They included the Purple Heart and Silver Star awarded for being wounded and gallantry in action against an enemy of the United States.

He was happy and their marriage couldn't have been going better—aside from some bad dreams that got worse. But even with Marlina's faithful support as an Army spouse, the long hours at work, deployments, and his injuries took their toll on his physical and mental health. He lost his right eye in the chaotic fury of a fierce battle in Afghanistan. The bullet pierced his face in the right temple and zipped out the right eye socket. It blinded him and he was forced to endure more than twenty surgeries, which included a reconstruction of his face. They had done a good reconstruction surgery, but that was on the outside. He also fought feelings of anxiety and remorse, and slowly learned to accept it and regain his confidence, but that was the least of his current problems.

He had shielded Marlina and their unwitting friends for as long as he could. PTSD slowly crept up and reared its ugly head. The residual effects became more and more evident in the expression of his frequent bad moods and short temper. There were also other personal issues that he hadn't quite come to terms with yet. For the sake of their marriage and his own health, it became necessary to put in for retirement and seek mental health counseling. That was the first time he called Mark to ask for help.

We often feel paralyzed by the choices of life. Still, we've got to make a choice to accept our circumstances or change them. It's the unknown that scares us and the uncertainty of the ripple effect—the little day-to-day things that often direct our path—because one never knows where that will lead them and as to whether it's random or providence. Either way Steven Scott knew what he had to do.

CHAPTER SIXTEEN

"If it's free, it's advice; if you pay for it, it's counseling; if you can use either one, it's a miracle."
~ Jack Adams

SHRINK

"I'M NOT THRILLED about being seen by a shrink—no offense—much less being videoed by a complete stranger," Steven Scott said. He folded his arms against his chest, a classic gesture of defensiveness, born from his uneasiness in unfamiliar environments. Even though he had volunteered, he still hadn't fully come to terms with the idea of opening up to a complete stranger in a private counseling session—even in the name of research. He had done this once before with an Army doctor but wasn't satisfied. In his mind the doctor was a *kid* and didn't take PTSD as seriously as he should have. This time the therapy would be a bit more involved.

"None taken," Dr. Peggy Feinberg said, in response to being called a *shrink*. She operated her own private practice but had recently been contracted to the Innovations Technology Laboratory (ITL) to assist with the *Mind-Body Problem* project—something, for the time being, she would have to keep discreet. Even though the counseling sessions would provide project data for Dr. Mark Starr, she now focused on how she could best help Steven Scott's situation. She had read his intake interview notes and seen his Army medical records. Her plan was to relax Steven, be an active listener, and compose her thoughts. That allowed him to take their conversation in whatever direction he liked.

Steven uncrossed his arms and sat up straighter in his chair.

"Let's chat for a moment while the team gets the recording equipment set up." Dr. Feinberg motioned toward a beverage cart on the wall. "Help yourself to some coffee, or whatever you'd prefer."

"Thanks."

She liked to use the studio set up time to ease into a pre-interview. It made the client more comfortable and it helped her get to know people, build a rapport, and focus the conversation. The recordings were also useful for training and helped the client to not be distracted by excessive note taking.

He nodded. "This is my first big, well—you know—," he paused and started to fidget with his gold wedding band. As he spun it slowly and nervously, he thought about where he was now—*a nicely decorated counseling room with a large rectangular mirror on the wall.*

"It's my first time being seen by one of you guys," he said, trying to neither overthink his situation, or who he was talking to right now.

"I'm glad," Feinberg said reassuringly. "…glad you made the choice to come in and talk. Tell me a little bit about yourself."

Steven continued his introduction and talked about his mental health concerns with PTSD—at least what he had recently experienced and been told about it at the Landstuhl Regional Medical Center in Germany. To him, that active duty screening seemed more like a bureaucratic stopgap, since the staff was overwhelmed by triaging and treating the ones with visible wounds.

"I'm grateful that you could fit me in. My family has been worried about me," he said. "And my brother Mark too, but I guess you already know that."

She knew exactly who he was referring to. It was his younger stepbrother, the Director of ITL, Dr. Mark Starr. He had referred Steven and arranged for the private counseling sessions. She knew that it had to be done discreetly, because of her recent contract with ITL. Because of the new development in her employment situation and his direct tie with an ITL family member, she and Dr. Mark Starr agreed that they were treading in a gray area of dual relationships. Dr. Starr told her that proper logistics would be paramount. He wanted to help his brother, but also avoid any perceived ethical issues regarding ITL's objectivity and confidentiality. There was a lot of research dollars on the line, not to mention their personal ethics.

"Yes, Dr. Starr is the one that referred you."

"Right, because some odd things have been happening—and well, he thinks that I could benefit from this—whatever *this* is."

Dr. Feinberg nodded.

Steven Scott paused for a silent, reflective moment—maybe five or ten seconds to diffuse his gradually accumulated anxiety with a slow, controlled exhale. "I guess I do, too," he said. "You know—think that I could benefit from this—crazy, right?

"No, not at all," Feinberg stated. "It's actually a good thing that you've recognized the need for counseling—and that you took the first steps."

He held his chin in his right hand and restlessly drummed his fingers on the right arm of the chair, as he mulled over her words and other issues that he had seen on the *health history questionnaire* she had provided him in advance. Things that he had never thought about before his wartime injuries; *stressful, frightening experiences or distressing events* that could trigger various levels of PTSD symptoms in any of us. Add to that, Steven's earliest developmental years had been riddled with humiliation, embarrassment, constant put-downs, hypercriticism, and withdrawal of affection from his parents. The latter had hit its target the hardest and it reeled him back to his childhood, an emotionally difficult place that he continued to run from in his mind. You could see the painful shadows of anguish reflected on his face.

"It seems like life is made up of a lot of firsts, huh?" he queried, examining his shoes.

Dr. Feinberg nodded.

It was uncomfortable for him to open up like that at first. It wasn't exactly a conversation that a seasoned Army vet, or perhaps anyone, relished. So, Dr. Feinberg did her best to put him at ease. "You're having trouble putting words to it, but I see that it disturbs you."

He furrowed his brow and pursed his lips. "Yes, it does."

She did her best to assuage his fears. "I can see how that could make you feel uneasy. So, as we begin, let's talk about some of the things that you're more comfortable with mentioning, okay?"

His inner John Wayne would have been more comfortable not talking about it at all. Or, he would have been more open to talking about other firsts in his life, like when he lost his first tooth or rode a bike without training wheels—or even sex for that matter. That would have been easier for him to talk about than his emotions and apparent struggles with PTSD. Dr. Feinberg realized that most of us lived in the wake of our experiences. Whether they were good or bad, the surface tensions usually made a significant impact on us and were often the result of an underlying turbulence.

"You sort of assume that there aren't too many other firsts going on in your life," he said, fretfully looking around the room with his good left eye. He lowered his voice, so as not to be heard by anyone else who might happen by, "until you start hearing—and seeing—things."

She nodded with a reassuring expression. "I am happy to address those issues with you, Mr. Scott. It's not as uncommon as you might think for someone with PTSD to see something—or hear voices."

That seemed to relax him. "Please—call me Steven."

"Alright, Steven." It was important for her personal etiquette to address clients as they wished, Mr., Mrs., Ms., or by their given name. She would never presume to address them by first name without their permission. It also helped her relax and him to loosen up. He sat there and *hoped* that he had made the right decision. Steven sought the help—even though he wasn't sure what that meant or entailed. *But, hey, what could it hurt?* He thought.

The office where she saw Steven Scott was located within walking distance of the historical Johns Hopkins Hospital, but in a newer, brick, medical facility. As a self-employed private therapist, she had established multiple offices, in different locations, to meet the needs of hospitals, substance abuse rehabilitation facilities, and a few colleges. She stayed busy seeing clients and teaching. But now, due to her contractual relationship with ITL, she had freed her schedule a bit, to be more accessible to the new research being conducted. It wasn't a relationship that she was free to discuss with anyone yet.

Due to the newly developed *top secret* nature of ITL's mission they had commandeered all three floors of the Johns Hopkins Hospital wing, which included the *Octagon* unit. It was where, in the past, physicians who visited patients were said to be doing their *rounds*, a clear reference to making their way around the octagon. That was long ago, but now there were no signs or indicators of anything significant going on in the old Victorian-style building—other than select staff members entering and exiting with special access badges and an ocular-based recognition, iris-scan.

This would be the ideal place to clandestinely pursue their *Black Budget* government funded project—surrounded by other normal doctors going about their duties. There was also a huge video archive of mental health cases accessible for their research. That, along with other institutionalized mental health patients being treated and studied, would prove invaluable data for the *Mind-Body Problem* project. It afforded them up-close opportunities to study the individual actions, reactions, progress, and setbacks that patients experienced. They would make their rounds later with interns.

A studio producer fastidiously prepared for today's session, typed in font information for the TV, focused cameras, and adjusted lights. When the recording began, they would intermittently superimpose a few tidbits over the lower-left corner of the video to identify with whom they were speaking:

> Client: *Steven F. Scott, Colonel, U.S. Army, (Retired)*
> Age: *46* Born: *Walla Walla, WA*
> Marital Status: *Married*
> Condition: *PTSD*

"This session is only the first phase of your evaluation, counseling, and potential future treatment," Dr. Feinberg said. "And it will assist us in arriving at a proper diagnosis and plan, as we advance in our sessions."

One of the studio technicians poked his head in the room and updated Dr. Feinberg. "Ma'am we're having some last-minute issues with the equipment—and have to replace all the *Intel Quad-Core Celeron* processors that one of the doctors requested."

That could take a while and they may as well have been speaking Chinese to her.

"The what?"

"It's a special Motherboard/CPU Combo that was ordered to be installed on all the computers." In truth it was a sophisticated piece of *malware* that Dr. Lui had specifically requested and it was now being installed on essential pieces of equipment. No one took notice or was suspicious, because the request and requirement was ostensibly meant for greater speed and capacity on all ITL computers. But in truth—it doubled as an encrypted satellite phone-home apparatus. It hid as a surreptitious system file and then called the owner of the system, the moment he was on the network, streaming confidential communication via a *GMR-2 cipher algorithm*. It could be accessed remotely and manipulated, if no one was on the computer. It also reported network location, username, and allowed someone to take over the mic, cameras, and relay computer files at will.

It still made no sense to Dr. Feinberg. "How long will it take?"

"Maybe another twenty-minutes—tops."

She glanced at her watch and nodded. "Let's take a short break, Steven, and meet back here in thirty minutes." She wondered, *why are they requesting last minute equipment changes?*

CHAPTER SEVENTEEN

"The real voyage of discovery consists not in seeking new landscapes, but in having new eyes."
~ *Marcel Proust*

CLEARED

THE DIRECTOR OF National Intelligence, Donald McCullagh, walked into the oval office and laid the President's Daily Brief (PDB) on the *Resolute Desk*. He was trailed by a slender special agent in black heels who carried a Secret Service messenger briefcase by her side.

"Thanks," he said. The President picked it up and slowly leaned back in his chair. After he adjusted his reading glasses on his nose, he slowly and methodically thumbed through the highly classified intelligence. It was a *top secret* document that fused intelligence from the CIA, the Defense Intelligence Agency, the National Security Agency, the FBI, and other members of the U.S. Intelligence Community.

"What's the BLUFF Don?" It meant that he wanted to know the bottom-line-up-front.

"Same threats, nothing significant to report sir," Director McCullagh said. "But there's one other matter." He nodded toward the special agent and she produced another *top secret* folder with the word **PSYCHONIX** written in a small rectangular box, as the file name. She handed it directly to the President.

The project had captured the National Security team's attention and they were closely watching it on the Senate Intel Committee; however, no one mentioned it in meetings, and it would *never* be included in the regular PDB. It was imperative that the technology not be compromised or fall into the wrong hands. The Secretary of Defense had advised that it could have significant national security ramifications and it would best be funded under a *Black Budget*—funds used for super-secret operations that only God and the President's National Security team were cognizant of.

To ensure that it remained secure, Innovations Technology Laboratory leadership coordinated, collaborated, and communicated with a small group of select agents in the Intelligence Community. They would ensure that it was hidden and fit nicely into the already established *Mind-Body Problem* projects.

The President handed the file directly back to the agent and she immediately secured it in the messenger bag. She was an attractive and ambitious 33 year-old Secret Service agent, acknowledged only by her rolling cryptonym: *NOUS-1*. One of three agents that would liaison around the clock with ITL during the PSYCHONIX project. The agents blended in with the other physicians with white coats, except that they had every government clearance imaginable—and then some. These high-level clearances were compulsory for special assignments, like the White House Medical Office, and were required in this case due to ITL's recent cognitive discoveries.

As luck and a National Security Intelligence (NSI) policy letter would have it, Dr. Starr had just received the government's greenlight for the project. That cleared the path for more, close-hold, internal information sharing. He would have his first briefing about it soon, but first the staff members who handled the highly classified *telepath communication technology*, including Dr. Peggy Feinberg, were dragged through a labyrinth of background checks. They had to make sure that the new discovery was properly safeguarded. Everyone on the small team held an important piece to the puzzle, but only now were they learning the full context of this new piece of equipment. Now everyone working the *Mind-Body Problem* research knew the full context that they played in the development. It came as a bigger surprise to some than others. The new technology was apparently *capable of transmitting and reading a person's thoughts.*

Dr. Mark Starr convened the first staff briefing, which they referred to as an *in-progress review* or IPR. It was their opportunity to go over the mission requirements and recent findings. Until now the groups had been segregated and their assignments parsed into subprojects, tasks, and milestones—but now they were all together, about to connect the dots.

Before attending the meeting, everyone had to re-read and sign the Invention Secrecy Act of 1951. It warned them about the *disclosure of new inventions and technologies that present a possible threat to the national security, national defense, or economic stability of the United States.*

"I have some exciting news to share with you today," Dr. Starr spoke privately to his most trusted inner circle. After all the vetting and veiled planning, they were more than ready to hear the *exciting news.* All six members of the science-technologies team gathered into the main lab in the Octagon unit. Some of them stood along the walls, others swiveled their black computer chairs in the direction of Dr. Mark Starr.

"First, I'd like to introduce some of you to Dr. Lui Wei or as it's spoken in China, Dr. Lui. A couple of you already know him from our research and development team."

ITL had expanded its commitment to scientific research and it showed in their aggressive recruitment. "Two years ago, we recruited Dr. Lui from Lumni Gongsi or *Lumni Corporation* in China's tech hub of Nanjing, near Shanghai—and just six months ago, I'm happy to report, he decided to become a U.S. Citizen." The doctor stood up, gave a slight bow of respect, and sat back down as everyone congratulated and warmly welcomed him with applause.

"He is well versed on the new technologies and will be the team lead on our new PSYCHONIX project."

"What new project?" Dr. Gus Kahn asked.

"I'm getting there, Gus." Dr. Starr ambled around the large central conference table, to the front of the room, before he continued the announcement. "It's a huge breakthrough and I wouldn't have believed it, if I hadn't witnessed it for myself. While pursuing bionics research and cognitive development projects, our senior engineer, Brad Manuszewski, stumbled on a mind-blowing communications capability."

Everyone applauded. Brad stood up, regally waved, and said, "Thank you. Thank you," in his genuine surfer drawl. He was from Southern California and recruited straight out of U.C. Berkley seven years ago.

Dr. Lui, as the team lead, was one of the first vetted and thoroughly read into the broad scope of the project. He added in his good, but still occasionally broken, English, "I have fully read research and examined findings. In the past, it seems, we have focused more on brain imaging technology, but there is—for all intents and purposes—a new technology for controlling and amplifying the mind or brain states."

Dr. Starr expanded, "It's a form of telepathic communication."

"Impossible," Dr. Kahn said.

"Unbelievable," Dr. Feinberg added.

"I'll say," Dr. Starr said. They mostly agreed that it was unbelievable—but was it true? Starr continued, "It seems to provide us evidence that we're all mentally connected in some unique way."

"Sure, wireless EEG electrodes are capable of connecting and measuring changes of electrical activity in the brain—faster than ever before," Dr. Kahn said. "The data we see on current scans is what we detect from the thin-aluminum disc—which can be placed anywhere on your scalp like a *zucchetto* or *kippah*." He placed his hand on the crown of his head, as though it were a skullcap that Roman Catholic clergy or Rabbis wore.

"Right, but this is completely different, Gus—it's not an EEG or a recorded image in any form or function. We're not merely talking about the dynamic imaging of persistent brain imaging—we're talking about transmitting and receiving human thoughts."

"In what way?" Dr. Feinberg asked.

"From one person's mind to another person's mind."

Dr. Kahn was a short, balding man with a gray tuft of hair that stuck up in the middle of his forehead, which he continuously pushed over and matted down with his hand. He also had a thin strip of hair that grew in the shape of a horseshoe around the edges of his ears and neck. He had ruddy-cheeks and a bumpy, red, swollen nose—mostly from the Kentucky bourbon he had indulged in too often.

Even though Dr. Kahn was quite brilliant, he was a cartoonish figure who resembled W.C. Fields, but not nearly as charming or funny. He chafed in utter disbelief and massaged his temples, trying to sooth his encroaching headache and make sense of it.

"That's ridiculous to more ridiculous," Dr Kahn said. He dismissed it out-of-hand and seemed to have no desire to find out whether this telepathic phenomenon was real or not.

Dr. Starr, unaffected by his *apriori* dismissal, continued to brief the PSYCHONIX project. "As far as we can tell, it's a telepathic technology, which allows us to communicate through auditory and optic neural signals."

"What if you're blind and deaf?" Dr. Kahn asked skeptically.

"Good question—since it's channeled through the brain's central nerve centers, it doesn't seem to *matter*."

"It can bypass the eyes and ears?!" Dr. Feinberg asked.

"It appears so," Dr. Starr said. "Although in our alpha testing, the highly adapted goggles use the person as the conduit with access to our servers, as well as souped-up virtual, augmented, and mixed reality technologies.

"That's amazing," she said.

"Yes—quite. A sophisticated processor in the goggles amplifies cognitive signals and penetrates the ears and retina through electromagnetic and mechanical waves of energy. At that point, they are absorbed by the cochlea and retina, and converted to electrical impulses before being transferred along the auditory and optic nerve, and to the brain.

"All through these new super-goggles?" Dr. Kahn asked, holding them up for inspection.

"Yes, while wearing them a person merely thinks about what they want to say, and the equipment amplifies and transmits it to the recipient—another person wearing goggles."

"It sounds like ESP," Feinberg said. "But, seems like it would be impossible to control transmissions like that—in a purely mechanical way."

"Yes, I think that's right, but it's not technically ESP or mechanical. Our engineers call it PSYCHONIX—short for *Psychological Bionics*. And as far as control—I'll cover that later in great detail. The most interesting point of fact, with this newly discovered technology, is that we've learned how to amplify certain elements or frequencies, or something like a frequency, which radiates from our own body. Brad and Dr. Lui theorize that it's found in all human beings to one degree or another."

"I can't hear anything," Dr. Kahn muttered sarcastically. He squinted his eyes and pretended to listen very hard to Peggy's thoughts. "Are you thinking anything now?"

She rolled her eyes. *If you only knew what I was thinking!*

Dr. Starr shook his head. "No, you can't hear anything that way—at least no one we're aware of can. But we now have reasons to believe that our mind is sending and receiving signals, and that they can be amplified and heard by others—if they have the right equipment.

They all nodded with great interest.

"It's similar, for example, to radio waves being amplified and picked up by an antenna. If you're on the right frequency, then you can pick up the signal. However, in this case, you're the transmitter and antenna."

"People?" Dr. Kahn asked.

"Yes, it appears that humans radiate signals that we're calling PSYCHONS," Brad said. In the earliest versions of our alpha testing, I discovered how to amplify the signals that our body produces with an *MDSL-1* processor. I built it into a pair of simple pair of virtual reality goggles—and that's what picks up and amplifies the PSYCHONS."

Prior to his discovery, Brad had consumed, and was inspired by the voluminous works of Gottfried Leibniz on dynamism or motion. Leibniz's ingenious theories provided a metaphysical groundwork for a complete and unified science of dynamics. His theory of a pre-established harmony suggested that there was an essential, indestructible force at work, where both mind and bodies causally interact with each other in the universe, because they have been programmed by

God in advance to harmonize with each other. Leibniz called the substances *windowless monads*, which didn't occupy space. The force sounded much like a soul, but this was a scientific laboratory—Brad called them PSYCHONS.

"This is just the first phase," Dr. Lui added. "It doesn't yet contain all features that we envision for the implanted version."

"No kidding," Sabrina Killian exclaimed—one of the younger members of the engineering staff, out of MIT. "An implant!"

"The *MDSL-1* is really just a tiny central processing unit or CPU that communicates with the mother of all motherboards—the brain," Todd Lopez said, another young *Stanford University* brainiac that assisted in Brad's portion of the research and discovery.

"Passing through the central nerve centers of the eyes and ears?" Dr. Feinberg silently repeated to herself. "*Wow!*"

"An *MDSL-1* processor?" Dr. Kahn repeated questioningly. "I've never heard of such a thing."

"No—because it didn't exist. *M-D-S-L*," Dr. Starr repeated slowly. "It's short for *Multi-Dimensional Spatial Lattice*. Up until now that was primarily in Brad Manuszewski's wheelhouse—but we now have the greenlight from the U.S. Government to pursue advanced testing. Although, as you know, it's completely *top secret*. As he just told you, Brad believes it can be fused directly to an optic and auditory nerve somewhere behind the eyes.

"Of course, we don't have a volunteer for that yet." Brad raised his arm and added with a humorous tone, "Do I see any hands?"

"So, it reaches other dimensions?" Dr. Feinberg asked, focused on the name. "Multidimensional?" She shared some of Kahn's skepticism, but wasn't entirely dismissive about the idea.

"I don't know—theoretically yes," Brad answered. "I suppose it could be used to communicate within other dimensions," he shrugged and looked toward Dr. Lui for some support, "If there were someone to communicate with." Dr. Lui didn't notice, as he scribbled extensive notes in cursive Chinese calligraphy—that no one else could read.

Brad continued, "It's a cool thought, but for now we're more concerned with this dimension, and the ethics and ramifications of potentially intruding on another person's thoughts."

At this point, even Dr. Starr wasn't quite sure where things were headed for the new project. *Were there bio-technical limitations or could mankind become a single consciousness?* It was an interesting thought and it remained to be seen—or heard.

"Yes, I was wondering about that." Dr Feinberg said.

"So far, Brad has only interacted with the alpha-version of PSYCHONIX to interface with complex computer games and single-player logic puzzles," Dr. Lui said. "However, the team is eager to work out the bugs—and begin more multi-player and person-to-person communication testing as soon as possible."

"You mean like you do with a *walkie-talkie*," Dr. Kahn asked.

"Yes, Gus, but it's a much more sophisticated version," Dr. Starr said. "Instead of a walkie-talkie, think of it as an exponentially accelerated, two-way police radio scanner for the mind or brain."

While briefing, analogies seemed like the best way to communicate the idea of PSYCHONIX. It was more effective than the confusing, complicated, technical explanations. "We all know that the air around us is bursting with radio waves, right?"

"Sure, it's an ocean of electromagnetic and mechanical signals," Dr. Feinberg replied.

"Well, the communication ocean of signals or PSYCHON radiation that our own bodies generate is a much larger source than you might imagine," Brad said. "And I'm not sure yet, exactly how to categorize those signals."

"We've barely scratched the surface," Dr. Lui added.

"In our early testing of PSYCHONIX," Brad said, "we have successfully transmitted and received frequencies from far below 7 Hertz and well above 300 kHz. That is lower than what the *Blue Whale* can hear and higher than what the *Greater wax moth* can hear."

"I highly doubt that," Dr. Kahn said. He was primarily interested in the results of EEG testing and scans and was still highly involved with examining the brains of institutionalized patients. To him, the whole telepathy thing seemed highly implausible.

"*Oh, contraire mon ami!*" Dr. Starr said. "It's more than just possible. It's tested and true. I've witnessed it and soon you will too. But—I really must say that it's a whole lot more than just a communication technology—the U.S Government thinks so too. I suppose the bigger discovery has been of PSYCHONS or *PSYCHON radiation* and how our team has been able to harness this entirely new spectrum of electromagnetic fields called the *Holt.*"

"The *Holt?*" Feinberg and Kahn echoed.

"Yes, the Holt," Brad repeated for the third time. "You can think of it as being similar to the Hertz, but it's actually a completely new operating system in a completely different frequency range—if you can even call it that."

"How—?" Dr. Kahn asked.

"That's all he can say about it today, but we'll learn more—in due time."

"What do the bionics look like?" Dr. Feinberg asked. "The *psychological bionics*?"

"PSYCHONIX—for short. It's a mechanism about the size of a grain of rice. Small enough to implant—and potentially powerful enough to transmit neural signals directly into the primary visual and auditory cortexes."

"So, the eyes truly are the window to the *soul*!" Dr. Feinberg exclaimed. "I can't wait to see where this takes us."

"Indeed." Dr. Starr said.

Our team discovered a revolutionary technology that appears to read and amplify signals from the mind. Honestly, I'm still having trouble believing it myself. It's probably how Alexander Graham Bell felt in 1876, when he invented the telephone. Or how excited Reginald Fessenden was in 1906, when he gave us the first wireless radio broadcast for entertainment and music. Each of the technologies was a complete departure from the transmission of dots and dashes, widely used for Morse Code.

How far we've come—and we still have no idea exactly where we're going.

CHAPTER EIGHTEEN

"Look at an interview as an organic part of building a relationship"
~ *Caroline Ghosn*

PRE-INTERVIEW

THE MALWARE POSING as a central processing unit had been replaced in the ITL recording studio and in Dr. Peggy Feinberg's office. It was an unscheduled delay, but she and Steven Scott were back in their seats and ready to continue the counseling session. Peggy wasn't concerned or distressed about the delay, because her schedule had been freed up specifically for these sessions with Steven Scott. To her it was an ideal time to become more acquainted with her client and she wanted to be as transparent as possible, before starting the counseling.

"Today we'll address your primary reason for being here—and build upon that as we go—and throughout any future sessions," she informed him. "Secondly, you agreed that we may use the lessons learned here as part of the ITL *Mind-Body Problem* project and any future tests found to be necessary. Are you still okay with that?" He was and she checked off the box.

That was all he needed to know about the project at this stage. The flow was meant to keep him informed and give him time to adjust and relax, but he merely gave an indifferent shoulder shrug. "Sure, whatever." It was an expected response. What layman could begin to fathom what the idea of a *Mind-Body Problem* meant?

"It's an academic portion of our studies and means that we're trying to figure out how a conscious mind emerges from the gray matter between our ears."

"Oh—is that all." He had a tough-guy persona and teasing sense of humor, which Peggy quickly picked up on. "You guys couldn't figure it out—so you needed my rapier-like mind?"

"Yes, well no—." She regrouped, folded her hands, and smiled. "That's not all. ITL has a team studying physical brain functions as well—and they have a reasonably complete understanding of how that works with MRIs and EEGs. One of the biggest issues they're trying to figure out—is how does a physical, material brain, which is basically a biological machine, become sentient?"

"Self-aware?" He remembered that word and the idea from all the *Star Trek* TV reruns he watched as a kid.

But Data is Starfleet property, not a sentient being!

"Yes, aware of one's own existence: feelings, sensations, thoughts, beliefs—and self-determination and awareness," she said. "That's a bit trickier to explain."

The conversation triggered moments from his childhood. As a young boy he shouted the words *self-determination* into his walkie-talkie to update his brother about their TV show. "Well, I can't speak for you," he said with a self-satisfied grin, "but I know I'm here. I volunteered."

She nodded. "Indeed." Dr. Feinberg continued to let him know what he could expect throughout the course of the sessions. "We'll do these video interviews, psychological exams, and adjust medications, if necessary. I've already reviewed your medical records."

"Sounds good to me."

Even though it wasn't the primary reason for the visit, he was naturally curious and found the idea of the *Mind-Body Problem* fascinating. He was eager to know more. "Why is it a problem?" he asked.

She explained to him that the *Mind–Body Problem* was an unsolved problem concerning the relationship between thought and consciousness in the human mind and the brain, as part of the physical body—and how it communicates.

"It's an age-old debate in which science, philosophy, and religion operate—discussed for millennia."

"That long?"

"Yes," she said smiling, "that long."

Steven nodded.

"I was recently recruited as a mental health contractor and project aid and will provide research data gleaned from these sessions—and hopefully provide better data about what makes our *mind* and *body* collaborate so well—or what makes consciousness *tick*."

She's got her job cut out for her trying to find out what makes me tick.

"After all, if you don't know yourself and your thoughts and feelings—who does, right?" She asked rhetorically.

"I'm just an android, Dr. Feinberg—nothing but an *advanced calculator* from a distant planet," he said robotically with a sly smirk. "No thoughts or feelings to share with you."

She looked at him curiously, not especially getting the android references.

"Sorry, I'm a *Star Trek* fan—disregard." That was his Army way of stopping a train of thought and moving on—*disregard*.

Then, just as though someone hit a light switch, he immediately felt anxious and sat up rigidly straight. It came on fast and he struggled to find his words. "But, lately—I'm having trouble—making sense of things."

"What do you mean?"

"There are times that—I can't seem to keep my head on straight. I mean, even simple decisions—aren't simple. It's difficult to concentrate—like now. I get confused and an overwhelmed feeling comes over me."

"*Uh-huh*, I see," she said, noticing his alert posture and changes in speech. "Thanks for sharing that with me Steven."

It was his first breakthrough. The first real moment of opening up in a session and it distressed him. "That's why I'm here for you." Dr. Feinberg wanted the initial tone of her voice and first words to be confidence-boosting. She knew that his problems with concentration were likely influenced by his PTSD and the levels of dopamine in his body, but she would have some blood work done. The right balance was vital for both physical and mental well-being.

He looked up and made direct eye contact. "Good."

"We're going to sort this out together, Steven—and discover what's going on," Dr. Feinberg assured him. Steven nodded as she continued to answer his question about the project. "You know, the fact that we can even think about ourselves has raised some key issues in our *Mind-Body Problem* project. If you're really curious about it, then you should know that your brother Mark will be hosting a three-part, *Mind Over Matter*, video series about it."

"About what?"

"About our *consciousness* or *self-awareness* and where it comes from. I think you'd find it fascinating."

"Great, I can't wait to miss that," he joked impatiently under his breath.

"What was that?" she asked.

"Nothing." He had learned that, even when joking, some thoughts were best not repeated. Little did he know that the guest, on the three-part series, would be an old friend from Walla Walla, Washington.

"There was an Army chaplain that I knew in Europe," he added, "who told me that everything we think...is an illusion. He told me that you could change your reality, just by thinking about it—and even change yourself."

"That's certainly an opinion that some people have—is that what you believe?" she asked, not wanting to contradict him or be too controversial with the interview.

"Mm—no, I thought he was pretty weird—but it's partially true I suppose."

"Right, on its face, it sure seems true that we can influence our thoughts and the thoughts of others—and even change our own mind, but—the truth is that we can't fundamentally change what it is that we *believe,* at least not without accepting a new set of facts."

Steven nodded. Dr. Feinberg was stating the philosophic obvious, but her explanation sounded overly complicated to him. He never liked that. He had always preferred plain living room English, instead of the semantic gymnastics of academics.

"Say again?" It was military slang for *repeat,* because you never used the word *repeat* in a war zone. It could be confused with the word *retreat.*

"Look at it this way—you can't decide to change a belief like you do a pair of socks. You can merely influence your beliefs with information that you've learned. Now, you could certainly lie about it—even lie to yourself! But you can't just decide to not believe something that you believe to be true—like the fact that you were in the Army."

"Roger." He playfully rendered a salute.

"It also seems plainly true that we can make choices, which change us mentally and physically and morally. Choices about self-educating, relaxing, losing weight or deciding where we want to live and work."

"And it's your choice?" he asked. He was still showing subtle signs of impatience through his persistent fidgeting.

"There are some people who would say *no*. They think that we're biologically hard-wired, and that everything we do and think is pre-determined for survival. "But to answer your question...yes...I think it's ultimately our choice, because we can force ourselves to do things that we wouldn't normally do, like put ourselves in jeopardy—because of hope and love. We can also choose to protect others and follow our moral code or deep-seated belief in times of personal danger."

He nodded as she spoke.

"There are those who say that you don't really have a *free will* or *choice* about anything, but that we're merely evolved, bio-chemical combinations of natural selection and random variations—which adapt and promote survival. But I don't subscribe to that way of thinking— rationality seems like something else."

"Sure. Whatever," He said with a nonplussed expression. He didn't mean to sound rude, but neither did he pretend like he knew what she was talking about.

Dr. Feinberg faintly smiled and put her hands up in a mock surrender. "Sorry, Steven, I'll try to break it down better."

He said, "Yes, ma'am." He sat up straighter. It had been ingrained in him, by the Army, to respond that way. He waited for her to clear up what he regarded as a *gobbledygook explanation*.

"You see, if we're just a brain—an evolved bio-chemical machine or computational circuitry—."

"Or calculator."

"Yes, as you say—if we're just a calculator," she said, "then how does that account for our personal, conscious mind? It's the million-dollar question, right?"

It was a thought that the ITL staff had ruminated on for some time now. Calculators, computers, and brains all required some type of programming—but brains adapted and seemed to rewrite their own dynamic programming.

But who programs the programmer? he thought. That was a metaphysical question and he remembered telling Mark many years ago that TVs and stars didn't just pop into existence. *Something or someone had to be pretty smart and powerful to make all that stuff…*

They weren't questions that he had thought about much since those days when he had camped under a blanket of stars. But he definitely accepted that calculators, TVs, and androids couldn't think on their own—at least not in a conscious way.

"I guess you just keep trying to trace it backwards," Steven said, "and figure out where a brain and a mind could come from and who made or created them, right?"

"Yes, and that's what we're trying to do at ITL—trace it back to its origins and gain a better understanding of its controlling form and function—and where it came from. The team is focused on the emergence of consciousness and asking: *Is it an epiphenomenal emergence of brain activity or is there a mind that unifies our thoughts but is controlled by the brain?* We are also heavily focused on finding out what it is that unifies the 100 billion neurons in our brain—and causes us to refer to ourselves in the singular."

He politely said, "Makes some sense I guess." *This is going on forever—are we ready to record yet?*

"It does—and if the mind is different from the brain, then we want to know that too. It would be a real breakthrough. And it leads us to many other theories and existential questions that we're also open to investigating."

"But—the only thing I know of—that can think and produce another person is—."

She finished his sentence, "—another person!

"Right!"

"And from a philosophical perspective—it seems right that only an ultimate mind or necessary, uncaused, transcendent, spaceless, timeless, immensely powerful, personal being would have to exist in order to create other minds or persons."

There she goes again, he thought. Steven tilted his head back and said, "Wow, that's a mouthful."

"Yes, I learned that from your brother, Mark."

"Oh, no wonder," he nodded. "That's what eleven years of advanced schooling will do for you—trust me, he fully paid for his *mind* and *brain*." Peggy thought that was funny and covered her mouth to stifle a laugh.

Steven chuckled, too. "Sometimes he goes off and I have no idea what he's talking about. You just have to ask him to speak plain English." He was proud of his brother but would rather hear it in layman's terms.

"The necessary, uncaused line of thinking is apparently a part of *first cause* arguments dating all the way back to Aristotle, Aquinas, and early Christianity. I read that it's really the only way to avoid the impossibility of an *infinite regress*."

He nodded and motioned with his hands, as if to say *okay whatever you say*. She elaborated that an *infinite regress* was about a sequence of reasoning or justification, which could never come to an end. "You can't just continue to go backwards with explanations—it makes no sense."

Steven scrunched up his face and nodded, trying to follow.

"Ultimately it seems like there has to be a metaphysically necessary being, in order to explain why something exists rather than nothing."

Why can't she just say God? "So how does a mind do all that, according to those big guys— Aristotle and Aquin—?"

"Aquinas! He was a *13th* Century Italian philosopher who argued for the existence of God based on reason and our ordinary experiences in nature." She glanced down and out of habit, checked the condition of her nail polish, as she considered his question.

Steven noticed. "You missed your appointment, didn't you?" he asked.

How did he know that? She looked at him and continued her thought. "A better question might be: why is it that humans can choose to sacrifice their life, liberty, and happiness for others? What is it, in us, that allows for that aspect of *consciousness*—and how does it gel with the theory of natural selection?"

"You mean why would we choose to forfeit our lives for the sake of others?"

"Right—why is it that we aren't all selfish and obsessed with our own survival? You would certainly think that natural selection would have killed off all the unselfish people by now, right?"

Steven nodded. He never thought of that. "You know—I thought a lot about personal freedom and choices, when I was in the Army. So, I'd say it comes from our *service-before-self values.*"

"But Steven—values aren't scientific—they're moral beliefs."

"What?"

"Morals are in an entirely different category from science. For instance, how could you scientifically demonstrate that your values are superior to mine?"

"I guess you couldn't," he said, "when you put it like that."

"You see, it's not the job of science to measure human values. The objective of science is to organize knowledge in the form of testable explanations and predictions about the universe."

"I'll buy that. So—to make a short-story long...," he said, humorously, hinting that it was a lot to absorb.

She pursed her lips, smiled, and nodded again. There was a simple conclusion that she wanted to draw. "If we're not more than our brains, then we're entirely made up of *adaptive neural processes* struggling to survive in an unguided, mindless universe—not freely choosing anything. No *self-determination*—only being nudged along by the blind forces of nature."

Steven thought about her words, as he filtered through a variety of inquisitive facial expressions, until he said the first thing that came to his mind.

"I believe in God and that we all have souls."

"A soul? Yes—I believe that way too Steven. I suppose you could say that our *Mind-Body Problem* project is partially concerned with the possibility and location of a *soul*—or whatever it is that has enabled and drives our conscious mind. However, as scientists—we must always manage our biases—and remember that truth is truth, regardless of the consequences."

"Right, that is—if there's a person, who can choose to manage it all," he said whimsically. "If not, then we can't ignore it anyways, right?"

"Touché. You're a fast learner." She smiled and nodded as a small, unobtrusive red recording studio light came on over Steven's left shoulder. Her cue to begin the more official portions of the interview.

CHAPTER NINETEEN

"A world without radio is a deaf world. A world without television is a blind world. A world without telephone is a dumb world. A world without communication is indeed a crippled world"
~ *Ernest Agyemang Yeboah*

MULTIDIMENSIONAL

AT 5:30 A.M. Dr. Mark Starr braved the early morning commuter traffic of Highway 97, from his Annapolis condo to get a head start on the newly developing PSYCHONIX project. It gave him plenty of time to say good morning to everyone, drink a cup of coffee, and quietly read his email before the normal workday began. While driving to work from his Annapolis condo, he redeemed the time by listening to the news on WTOP—a station that broadcast in the Metro Washington, D.C. area or 95.1 Shine FM. Today was different.

Today, quite by accident, his radio scanner stopped on WAVA, FM 105.1—a religious talk-formatted radio station. He only caught the final few minutes of the broadcast, but what he heard fascinated him—it clearly related to the wireless communications aspect of his *Mind-Body Problem* project.

"If you think about it—Jesus has multidimensional capabilities," Pastor Kenny Barrett said. "Meaning he can materialize and dematerialize in different realities—while remaining *locally active and consciously aware* of what's going on in all our lives. You know the verses in John and Psalms—God is greater than our heart and knows all things—and His understanding is infinite."

He's locally active and consciously aware. I never thought about it like that before, Mark thought.

This was a new insight from ancient verses that Mark could totally relate to his *Mind-Body Problem* project: *the problem of how the mind and body communicate at a conscious level.* As a person of Faith, Mark had reasons to believe that the body was simply the home for our consciousness and that consciousness wasn't limited to being contained within a physical body. In his own mind, it was simply a gateway that connected us all with our *Maker* and could make us aware of things that were beyond our body's ability to sense.

"In this way—He's everywhere," the radio pastor continued. "He is sustaining command and control from a parallel reality—we call Heaven. In the Bible *"heavenly places"* is code for certain kinds of dimensions."

Sounds like something from Star Trek!

"If you've ever watched *Star Trek*, then you know that the *Starship Enterprise* had a policy about engaging other beings, parallel worlds, and dimensions."

He's reading my mind.

"It's called the Prime Directive, Starfleet General Order One, prohibiting the protagonist from interfering with the internal development of alien civilizations. I think you would agree that since the beginning of time there have been outside interferences, but the *Creator* of our world gave us a communication directive as well. One that has been relayed to us through ancient Hebrew, Greek, and Aramaic documents."

Hmm, that's a thought—perhaps we should establish some type of communication policy prior to launching PSYCHONIX. I'll talk it over with the staff. I wonder if spiritual communication could be considered a form of a PSYCHON transmission.

Pastor Barrett continued, "And the fact is that we are influenced and communicated to by beings in other dimensions—every day. And we communicate to them through our thought life, actions, and prayers."

Somehow PSYCHONIX is bridging all of our thoughts, but I never really thought of it in light of a prayer—but why not? He thought that it could certainly be the case. There was without a doubt some sort of cognitive tie that they had tapped into. *Maybe it's the same spiritual channel that God communicates on—sheesh, now I'm really reaching.* As he drove, he shook his head and rolled his eyes at the thought and continued listening to the message.

"You probably thought that the first human space travel happened with *Vostok 1* and Russian Lt. Yuri Gagarin orbiting Earth on April 12, 1961, but—you would be wrong! Jesus did it, and more than two-thousand-years ago the Apostle John left Earth—and gave us a play-by-play:

I was in the spirit and behold! A throne was standing in heaven and there was someone sitting on the throne. The one sitting on the throne was like jasper and sardius in appearance. An emerald-colored rainbow was around the throne. Around the throne I saw twenty-four thrones. On those twenty-four thrones were elders wearing white clothes and golden crowns on their heads. Coming from the throne was lightning, noise, and thunder...

"It was one of the first *Heaven is Real* accounts of *I died and went to heaven and came back and this is what I experienced.* John, no doubt had a vision and perhaps what many would call a near death experience. He was apparently taken into a heavenly dimension—and did you notice that he saw someone—and could see lightning and hear noise and thunder? He was in the spirit but could still hear and see everything that was going on around him. *Evidence,* I think, that our *mind* or *soul* can go places that our current body can't!

Evidence—I wonder how Gus Kahn would feel about that—ha!

111

It drizzled rain all morning but had now evolved into a downpour as Mark passed the Severn Run Natural Environment Area. He steadily crept his F250 up the highway—deep in thought as the hypnotic *swish-swish-swish* of his windshield wipers orchestrated a lentando tempo for the early morning traffic.

I wish I could pray this traffic jam away.

Mark exited off I 97 to the right and sluggishly rounded I 895 before he transited the E-ZPass toll lane. He lost the radio signal as he dropped into the 1.4 mile-long Baltimore Harbor Tunnel.

CHAPTER TWENTY

"The present chasm between the generations has been brought about almost entirely by a change in the concept of truth." ~ *Francis Schaeffer*

GETTING STARTED

"SO, WHAT BRINGS you here?" Dr. Peggy Feinberg asked. It was a non-threatening, open-ended question, which she used at the beginning of every counseling session. This one was being recorded, so she reintroduced and set the stage. She had read his intake interview and medical records, and knew why he was there, but this greeting was intended to open the gate. It was broad enough of a question to get him started, but not delve into every detail of his life. It was Peggy's style.

It set the tone for a confident clinical interaction and acknowledgment of his rights and whatever he believed was the most pertinent thing to talk about—even if it was just a little social banter and levity at first. *It would promote his own sense of self-determination*," Peggy thought.

She glanced up and frowned when she noticed the camera shot of herself in the wall-mounted TV. Like the *On-Air* light, it was mounted on an angle, behind the interviewee, out of the client's view and used to monitor the signal. Unconsciously, she crossed and recrossed her legs, adjusted her skirt, and used her hands to brush back her auburn hair. Her professional credentials also flashed up on the lower third of the monitor each time she engaged Steven Scott.

Dr. Peggy Feinberg, MD
Assistant Professor of Neurology, Innovations Technology Laboratory
Director, Neuromodulation and Advanced Therapies Clinic

"I don't know—I suppose it was a pushy family that got me to come here," he said, trying to appear casually calm and relaxed. He nervously grinned, as he tested the counseling waters.

"Interesting, that's the same way I got through med school," she smiled back.

It was instinctive. She understood that a friendly exchange could relax and open up a client and it taught you more than endless hours of lectures or reading textbooks. It was a good start to their session. She paused and listened as Steven Scott moved the conversation along at his own comfortable pace.

"I'm not sure where to start," he said. "The Army told me I've got PTSD." He paused to consider how to best explain it. "Early on I was told by Army doctors that some of my issues stemmed from the anxieties of war and sleep deprivation, but there was no way around it—that's the normal rhythm of battle in the military."

"What issues?" Dr. Feinberg asked.

"More than once, back then, I thought that I was hearing things and the medic told me that I just needed to get some rest—and he seemed to be right. It went away. I didn't think twice about it…I mean it happened to guys all the time in Special Ops training."

"Interesting."

"Once, right after I was wounded, I had mild hallucinations from a morphine high. That was wild—in a Jimi Hendricks, psychedelic kind of way," Steven said with a broad, goofy smile. "But since I retired, it's gotten worse."

Dr. Feinberg nodded. He didn't have to say it. She was well aware of the residual psychotic symptoms that could be triggered by PTSD, including intrusive thoughts, disturbed sleep patterns, aggression, and flashbacks. She knew that people with PTSD processed threats differently, in part because the balance of chemicals in their brain were out of whack. They also had an easily triggered "*fight or flight*" response, which made them jumpy and on edge. Trying to constantly shut that down, often made them feel emotionally cold and removed.

"They tried a few things, but eventually balanced me out with a light cocktail of Zoloft and Seroquel."

"Do you still take them?"

"Yeah, low doses."

She looked at his chart, wrote something down, and nodded. "I'm going to recommend we slightly increase your dose."

"Great," he deadpanned.

Steven wasn't keen on taking medicine or talking about himself, so he began to ask her a variety of his own distracting questions. "One of your walls is purple—is that your favorite color?" As a veteran of wars, he had mastered misdirection, deception, and the ability to *pop smoke*, military slang for leaving a place undercover when necessary. It was useful for distracting and confusing the enemy, but an ineffective tactic to employ on a professional mental health counselor, in the middle of her own psychological operation. It had worked on teachers when he was in school, but however doggedly he tried he couldn't derail Peggy. *I respect that!* He thought.

"Yes, I like lavender. It goes with my flower pictures." She noticed how Steven feigned interest with a head nod but played along and hoped for more insight about him. "They're petunias."

He crossed his arms and partially covered his mouth and chin, stroking it with his finger and thumb—teasing her as though he were a psychiatrist. "So how long have you had this fascination with *petunias*?"

Ironically, the petunia is a striking flower, which symbolized resentment and anger. Someone else doing a Freudian psychoanalysis might have said that she really knew what it meant and that it revealed her subconscious feelings—but in fact, it was simply a picture that she enjoyed.

"Oh, I see—now you're the counselor analyzing me," she teased back, stating the obvious, and still not rushing headlong into the conversation. Even this side of him was teaching her vital things about his inner self. His humor and need for control, as well as having an analytical mind.

"I like to feel comfortable at work, that's all. It's an important quality of life thing for me."

In her years of psychotherapy, she had worked in several counseling environments, youth centers, training facilities, and now private practice. The counseling rooms provided ranged from ugly and depressing to comfortable and friendly. This was one of her best situations and she had spared no expense in making it look nice. Dr. Feinberg believed that the atmosphere contributed to productivity, efficiency, and in addition boosted her morale. She didn't mind talking about it. "And I want you to be as comfortable as possible too," she said with another polite smile.

If the environment nourished her and was welcoming, then she believed it would most likely be nourishing to her clients as well. Dr. Feinberg had a lot of experience and designed her office accordingly. She screened off any potentially offending equipment and included personal objects of value. That included her genteel 3-way *Adelaide* table lamp with a cast-iron base and scalloped glass shade, accented with hand-painted, dark-red floral patterns.

"My grandmother had a lamp just like that," Steven said. "My brother Mark has it now at his house. We both have fond memories of visiting Grandma and seeing that cozy living room lamp warmly lit in her bay window."

"You had a good relationship with your grandmother?"

He nodded. "Yes, let's just say—Grandma Scott was very kind and forgiving. Sometimes we had to stay with her while the folks worked things out."

"What kinds of things?"

"Arguments. Fights. Separations—you know. The normal family stuff."

Dr. Feinberg didn't nod or acknowledge that it was *normal* in any sense. She just listened.

"The times we spent at her house were some of the best times of our life. I remember a number of special Christmases there. She would move the lamp to the side of the window, during the holidays, to make room for a *kitschy*, silver-aluminum Christmas tree with a color-wheel."

"I don't think I've ever seen one of those."

"If you were lucky," he said with a sarcastic lilt, "enough to have one growing up, then you would absolutely remember it." He and Mark never cared for the Charlie Brown reject of a tree, but it was their earliest memory of Christmas.

"Those 1965 tinsel beauties added a lot of space age sparkle to your holiday décor, so Grandma never saw a need to change it—ever."

"But it's a good memory," she stated.

"Yeah, I guess it is—it smelled nice, too, with the fake evergreen spray that she used," he said, sniffing the air, "but not as nice as the smell of your office."

Steven had trouble staying focused. It was part of his condition. He patted both arms of the chair with the palms of his hands—and scouted the room with his good eye. He wore a black eyepatch over the other to cover his battle wound. He never liked it—but it had grown on him.

Steven looked about the room and grabbed at another opportunity to talk about anything, other than the issues at hand. He sniffed the air again— "Hmm, I like that smell. What is it?" Peggy liked to introduce pleasant fragrances to counter any potentially sterile medical smells: Lavender, jasmine, rosemary, sometimes lemon. Mostly lemon, because it promoted *concentration*. It also had a calming and clarifying effect when clients were feeling angry, anxious, or run-down.

"I'm glad you like it—it's lemon," she said, pausing to take in a deep breath of air.

Steven dodged and distracted like a pro. He was a regular *Rubik's Cube* of difficult behaviors, but it was a useless endeavor. Dr. Feinberg dealt with an array of potential problems and personalities. She knew how to deal with the manipulators, resisters, monopolizers, sarcasm, and silence. It was her job to promote a positive interchange and facilitate the conversation, and she did it well.

"So, what's going on Steven?" she asked again in a different way. She did this in an attempt to pull him back into their primary reason for being there. They had limited time together and, within reason, she would have to keep him on track.

"I'm tired," Steven said. "I don't sleep well, and my emotions are up and down like a roller coaster. Sometimes I feel incredibly excited and happy. Other times, I feel sad, anxious or downright miserable," he said with a slight cringe of his lips and subtle hint of sadness in his voice. "I *hope* you can help."

Feinberg nodded again. "Me too, Steven. Can I ask you a few more questions?" She leaned back, crossed her legs in the opposite direction, and reclined to one side of the chair with her hands folded. It was one of two white leather chairs placed at right angles to each other—so Steven could look past her without turning his head. It positioned them in view of the video camera, yet was hidden from the *On-Air* light and monitor, or anything that revealed that the counseling session was all still being recorded.

"Sure, ask away." He leaned in, took a sip of coffee and sat his paper cup on the corner of a small decorative table between them. He then took another slow, deliberate look around the room.

"You have a nice office," he said, still inspecting the décor.

"Thank you. I like it."

"I can see why," he said as he stood up. "Do you mind?"

"No, go ahead."

He stretched his arms and rubbed his hands together. It was chilly in the room with the temperature set low to protect the video equipment. This routine went on for a good minute. He even ran one of his fingers along the upper-side of the antique, burnished white wall unit, and showed her that it was dusty—an old military inspection habit. She shrugged with a slightly embarrassed smile.

He noticed the personal things. Items Peggy had chosen to display from home and her career. Those things that brought comfort and led to a feeling of relaxation. It was intentional. Being relaxed led to opening up. Opening up would help Dr. Feinberg understand Steven Scott's mental health issues and advance their study of the *Mind-Body Problem* and human consciousness. It was a win-win.

"It's quite cozy in here." He felt comfortable and liked her and sensed that she was a good and honest person.

"Yes, the room is comfortable in a—cozy cottage sort of way I suppose," she agreed and moved the conversation along. "Does it remind you of anything?"

"Well, while deployed, I mostly lived in the OD Green and Desert Tan modular Army tents and B-Hut housing that we had in Iraq and Afghanistan." B-huts were simply built rows of wooden cabins, constructed to house Soldiers on deployment. Steven knew them all too well from his many years living far from his home in Washington State. "You could say they were some of my first real homes away from home."

"Where's home?" she asked.

Guys in the service were always hard-pressed to answer that question: *Where's home?* "Do you mean where I was born, where I'm from, where I'm going, or where I live now?"

"Perhaps you could give me an overview?" she asked curiously.

It was never a simple answer, but home had become the next name on his Army PCS Orders. Permanent Change of Station. "Even though it was a far cry from my childhood home—I always felt at home whenever I found a clean bunk, hot chow, and American Forces Radio." She keyed in on the words: *it's a far cry from my childhood home.*

She probed. "So, how do you feel about your childhood home?" It was a slow pitch down the middle. No reason not to swing.

"To be honest—I didn't like it. I didn't care for my home, parents, or my life in general growing up. That's why I got on a Greyhound bus and scooted out of town, as soon as I could— and joined the Army. That was my home. I had to get out of Walla Walla—and knew that there was something better out there—and there was."

His stepbrother Mark had to endure their home life a couple years longer. Alone. But then he was off to college and never looked back. They had both, ostensibly, broken the surly bonds of their childhood—and gotten out of Dodge as fast as possible, but he didn't go into all of that.

"You know—none of the foreign places I lived ever had anything close to your counseling office," he said, skirting her questions again. It had almost become humorous to Peggy, but she also thought that it might be a subconscious diversion for coping with his PTSD.

It was a nice office; faux wooden floors, mostly lilac colored walls and tasteful accents, and knick knacks placed on the ledge of an eclectic and artsy double-window behind them. He slowly walked around the room again—and admired the other pictures of flowers along the side walls. A field of lavender flowers. *He called them purple* and it was her favorite color. He wanted to question her more about it. It was part of Steve Scott's nature as a former military intelligence officer. He knew that there had to be a story there. But she was on her game and he wasn't going to get another chance to play counselor today.

There was, however, an interesting but unrelated story about the flowers. They reminded Peggy of her late mother and a special bucket-list trip that they had taken to Keukenhof, Holland to see the springtime tulips. She had never seen so many beautiful flowers and colors. It was a place of refreshing that she hoped to visit again someday. That's how she recharged. She also advised her clients to find those special self-reflective sanctuaries or havens.

Steven noticed the galvanized watering can with red Sycamore leaf branches artfully displayed, *Rodin's Thinker* bookend set with two non-descript books, and a vintage wall clock leaned slightly back in the middle of the wall unit—not keeping time.

That seems so impractical! he thought.

Then he focused again on the large mirrored window on the front wall. From the time he sat down he knew that something wasn't quite right—just like when he was a kid. He felt it. Something had immediately triggered his Spidey senses. It was a trait that he had honed in the military—he noticed everything!

On deployments his life depended on keeping his head on a swivel—and knowing what was going on around him.

"So, let's get back into this thing," Steven said, as he sat down, eager to continue. "Go ahead and work your *headshrinker* voodoo on me!"

CHAPTER TWENTY-ONE

"What is a soul? It's like electricity—we don't really know what it is, but it's a force that can light a room." ~ *Ray Charles*

HOLT CONCERTO

"THE INCREDIBLE TECHNOLOGY that powers psychological bionics is the *MDSL-1* processor," Brad Manuszewski said. It was the central processing unit that synchronized and orchestrated transmissions within the *Holt* frequency spectrum if you could call it that. It wasn't a frequency nor a relatable spectrum—in any empirical sense. "For simplification we just call it PSYCHONIX," he explained again to Doctors Starr and Kahn. Dr. Feinberg was still in a counseling session and would be briefed.

"Psychological Bionics," Sabrina Killian repeated it aloud, completely enamored by the idea.

"Yes—and the microprocessor weaves a series of less than hair-thin *Quantope-Crystals,* 40 x 50 x 10 micrometers, into a crisscrossed lattice. Once it's used in a highly adapted pair of goggles or embedded into an auditory and optic nerve, the lattice then scans for each person's PSYCHON Radiation.

"That's truly amazing," Dr. Feinberg remarked.

"Didn't you say that the processor encodes, decodes, and amplifies signals like radio and television frequencies?" Dr. Starr asked,

"Yes, in a way it does—but not in the same way," Brad said.

"Then, it's just more vivid metabolic imagery that we're capturing?" Dr. Kahn asked, still not able to get past the idea of something that was superior to MRI or EEG imaging.

"No—it's quite dynamic—live signals that penetrate the retina and cochlea," Dr. Lui answered. As the new team lead, he was fully immersed in the project and could articulate its use quite well. "As you know, an MRI uses radio waves to generate *images* of various organs in the body. An EEG monitors brain waves, but it only falls into the range of 1–20 Hertz. This is a far more powerful technology that we've discovered. It somehow communicates directly with the central and peripheral nervous systems—Brad discovered it." He said, as he glanced toward Dr. Kahn and nodded.

"Interestingly enough—prior to our discovery of the *Holt Scale*, any activity below or above the 1-20 Hertz range was considered to be false readings," Brad said. "We were always suspicious of those *false* readings—and that's what put me on the trail of testing and eventually discovering the PSYCHON radiation."

Dr. Starr smiled broadly, as he thought about the ability to receive new kinds of radio signals and having other channels interfere. He couldn't help but share one of his over-imaginative childhood quests. "When I was a kid, my brother and I used our walkie-talkies to communicate with galaxies, billions of light years away—to protect Earth, or at least the neighborhood, from aliens."

"That's amusing make-believe stuff," Dr. Kahn said, cutting him short, "but this is the real world Mark."

"I know—but that's quite often where innovations start," Dr. Starr said. "The idea of communicating telepathically isn't the same as a walkie-talkie, but the basic principles are similar."

Dr. Kahn nodded impatiently, after his attempt to rudely shut Brad down didn't work.

"I'm more concerned with finding a volunteer for the PSYCHONIX implant," Brad said, changing the subject. "That's something we need to start addressing, because it will be a much more invasive part of the project."

"Imagine how this *new frequency spectrum* could be used for national defense," Sabrina speculated. "We could mentally communicate with commands, soldiers, or even connect to SETI technology in our search for extraterrestrial intelligence."

Something in Dr. Kahn's countenance shifted when Sabrina spoke of national defense and space operations. It was in his expression, something indicative of an inner, moral struggle. No one noticed, when he nodded back toward Dr. Lui.

CHAPTER TWENTY-TWO

"Psychology: the science that tells you what you already know, using words you cannot understand. ~ *Unknown*

HEADSHRINKER

Go ahead and work your headshrinker voodoo on me! Dr. Peggy Feinberg shook her head and smiled at Steven Scott's indelicate statement. Some psychotherapists might have been put-off, pulled back and become defensive when they heard the term: *Headshrinker!* But it was a label that she had grown accustomed to hearing over the years. *Headshrinker, indeed,* she thought.

Thomas Pynchon had coined the term in his 1966 book *The Crying of Lot 49*. And people still humorously compared the process of psychotherapy to primitive tribal practices of shrinking the heads of enemies. No one completely agreed on why that was, but the ill-suited moniker stuck.

"I think I'd rather expand your mind—than shrink it," she parried with a clever riposte. "Let's concentrate on you. What was it like for you growing up?"

Steven fidgeted with his hands and spun his wedding band again but settled in and told his unhappy story. "It was a sad, horrible time—other than the moments Mark and I spent together. Those were great and we survived it together. To this day it bothers me whenever I see children being mistreated or a teen ignored or dismissed. We had too much of that—and it's just not right," he said with an adamant flicker of historic anger foaming up in his crackling voice and watering eyes.

"I considered it my seven years of tribulation—like in the Bible. So, if there's a hell—I already did my time—thank you."

"Feeling down or sad sometimes is normal," Dr. Feinberg said. "But if you've been struggling with it, then I think we should talk about it."

She didn't recount the differences between normal human emotions to him, but she knew that every single person would, at some point, experience that kind of a low. She herself could appreciate a good cry. It was a much-needed release. Depression, on the other hand, was a hollowed out feeling, which often had overpowering effects on a person's life. It included feelings of sadness, discouragement, loss of interest in activities, and *hopelessness*. She would focus on the latter.

"It's okay, Steven, our sad emotions connect us to our body and our body connects us with our emotions and with joy and beauty." It sounded like a bunch of psychobabble, but he nodded acknowledgement. Dr. Feinberg didn't elaborate, because he still showed some outward signs of distress. She looked at his chart again, erased the number she had written beside a recommended medication—and increased it by 100 mg.

Steven Scott had been to war, but he faced a different sort of enemy this time. The emotions and floodgates of past hurts had been tapped into—childhood abuse, neglect, and feelings of abandonment japed and hooked from all sides. All our emotions flowed through the same channel and this was now a clear channel for him, skipping across every part of his brain. He had been given permission to express himself and opened up like never before.

Dr. Feinberg drilled down past the superficial questions and responses. She looked for causes and symptoms, confused thinking, excessive fear, worries, guilt, extreme mood changes, anger, and/or a detachment from reality. She didn't want to rewatch the entire video session, so she glanced down and jotted a note or two on the chart.

"What are you writing?" he asked.

"Just what you said about your life and how you feel—being tired and sad."

"Don't forget, miserable."

"Right, miserable," she repeated.

He wasn't exactly miserable, but it was obvious from the escalating volume of his words, tone, and body language, that he was having trouble communicating what was actually on his mind and was becoming a little annoyed with the counseling process. Dr. Feinberg thought that perhaps his impatience was a symptom of PTSD. He showed all the signs.

"I know you're struggling, but—are you thinking about hurting or killing yourself?" she asked, slipping it in naturally without worrying about the directness or offensiveness of the words. She did her best to be clear and non-judgmental. Trying to understand.

That's how it's done, she thought. It doesn't have to be hard. Just cut to the chase and say it. She watched his left eye, read his body language, and listened closely to each of his words.

"Sure, I've thought about it. But that's it! Only thoughts!" he said brusquely. He stretched out each syllable of the word for special emphasis. "Who wouldn't? My parents were whack-jobs. Not to mention I've got PTSD, I'm missing my right eye from a disgusting combat wound, and I'm—well, life sucks all over, right?"

"It can, but what were you going to say—you're what?"

"I'm just tired of it all, Doc—whatever it is," he said. "It's even starting to affect my sex life." He folded his arms across his chest again and sighed.

"Okay—I know that's important, but let's drill down a bit."

He nodded and seemed to be okay with that.

Steven paused, looked up, and started spinning his wedding band again. It was his "tell" and she had already noticed it, from the corner of her eye, as she scribbled one more note. She suspected that his fidgeting with his wedding band was related to whatever it was that worried him. He had other things to say but couldn't get them out. That much was obvious. You didn't have to be a counselor to see it. Something else weighed heavily on his mind. And his whole temperament shifted—for the worse.

"Look, I manage it," he said curtly, as though that was all there was to say about the matter. "Case closed."

"No plans?"

Now he was getting really irritated. He felt that she had leaned on him too much—it was too personal and intrusive, even though she was obligated to ask. "I've got this—believe me! *Bee-leeve mee*. If I wanted to kill myself, it would've happened a long time ago, Doc! I'm well acquainted with the nasty, rotten smell of war. This time—I'm not going to be collateral damage." He was strong-willed, but also protective, and had a strong desire to live.

"I'm sure war's not a pretty thing. I know it hurts—."

He cut her off. "You don't know anything!"

Had she slipped up? *No.* She had merely empathized with his feelings and suffering—but he was overly sensitive about it because of his PTSD. Peggy remained calm and let Steven Scott talk it out—and vent as much as necessary.

Steven Scott's hands started to shake ever so slightly and tears welled up in his good eye. "War is ugly. It hurts," he said. He lifted his black eyepatch so she could see his hideous wound.

It caused her to flinch inside, but she remained composed.

"And it kills—it kills your best friends!" he said. It was a poetic moment of breakthrough. It was the darkest part of the pain he felt—being injured and having watched his friends die in battle.

They sat silently while Steven Scott continued to study his feet and the floor. He tried to regroup his thoughts, nervously rubbed the palms of his hands, and then interlaced his fingers like he was praying. He had done this many times before, but now it was used to collect his dwindling sanity.

They stopped talking and the one minute that passed seemed like an eternity. In his state of mind, it seemed as though time had crawled to a stop. He sat there wide-eyed and replayed a loop of horrific memories; death and destruction on the battlefield—visions of body parts that hung like macabre ornaments from a Christmas tree. He went silent—and Dr. Feinberg was okay with that: *Silence is golden—sometimes.* It could prod a person into speaking through the discomfort, but you had to read the situation and prevent them from retreating into themselves.

It was a time to reflect on what you heard, learned, and wanted to say next. A time to filter through your client's words, body language, and emotions. You may occasionally have an *Ah-Ha!* moment and time to reset a thought or change directions in your plan. At the very least, a moment to remove yourself from all the inane small talk and chaos of work, traffic, and surface relationships. It was certainly one of the benefits of seeing a counselor—the intentional, uninterrupted silence.   It was a psychotherapeutic strategy that Peggy was comfortable with using.

Typically, therapy was an energized conversation between the client and therapist to assist in understanding what's going on and why.   She knew just how to *ride those waves of communication to the shores of meaning.*   She had actually been brave enough to put that on a slide at a psychiatric conference, which had received amused groans.

"I'd like to follow-up on what you've told me Steven."   It was a back-and-forth exchange. Connecting the dots.   He raised questions, concerns, and observations about himself while she clarified, summarized, and tried to make connections between past and present or thoughts and behaviors.

"So, what else can you tell me?"   That's all she needed to say, because it was rare that a lack of words was the problem in a counseling session.   She needed to engage and know things and he needed to talk.   He had never realized it before, but he did.   It was long overdue.   He had too many buried feelings and needed to talk about what had happened in his life and what was happening now.

"I've lost a lot of good friends in battle and I've been close to death myself.   It comes with the territory," he said.   He paused again and raised his left hand, rubbed and pressed down on the corners of his mouth with his thumb and forefinger, before he covered it completely with the palm of his hand.   It was as though he had stopped himself from speaking.

There was a doleful blank look in his good left eye.   It was frozen in a painful, prolonged thought.   He peered at Peggy with a wan smile.   "I really don't want to talk about it."

"You don't have to, Steven.   I'm sure you've gone through some unimaginable things."

"Yeah—like I said, you had to be there."

"Okay—that may be true—but it still might do you some good to talk about it," she suggested. So, he did. He spoke nearly non-stop. Floods of memories and experiences flowed for a solid hour and twenty-minutes—a full session.

Later, after Steven had warmed-up to the counseling, he told her more about a seriously traumatic time in his life. A time when he was shot and had nearly died on the battlefield with his buddies. He wasn't the kind of man to be visibly shaken or scared, but subconsciously—he was still terrified. She could tell.

"I was *concerned*," he would often say. He didn't use words like scared and afraid. He was an Army Warrior—bold and brave. "I was an experienced soldier and I'm trying to enjoy retirement now, so I'd like to get this stuff resolved." He approached it like he did all his plans, but there was still a wake of fear involved that he couldn't plan for or outrun. Mentally, at times, he was still stuck in the middle of a tumultuous Iraq and Afghanistan. He remembered seeing his comrades die and always felt suspicious of any unattended items or packages left behind or patches of discolored dirt—where a pipe bomb might have been planted. He knew you could only take the wrong step once, so it often paralyzed his thinking. Dr. Feinberg plainly saw the strain on his already tensed face and sensed it in the tone of his exasperated words.

Steven's life experiences spilled over and busted through a dam of pent-up emotions. He liked to talk when he had something that he wanted to say, and he had plenty. He was also a take-charge leader, but Peggy knew she needed to guide him. She knew that a torrent of unfocused thoughts could get in the way of their progress and perhaps even set him back. She thought that his endless stream of thoughts could even be a defense mechanism that prevented him from engaging with his deepest feelings. Because even though he was jabbering away, he was repeating himself. Steven was a *type-A* personality—so it wasn't always easy for him to let go and make himself vulnerable in this way. Dr. Feinberg slowed him down, and he fell silent again.

In his Army world, you weren't always encouraged to vocalize negative thoughts. In a war zone it could be interpreted as fear or cowardice. For a man that led men into battle, it was a foreign concept to express those kinds of emotions. He was used to leading the way, so he broke the silence first.

"The worst part—is the stuff I can't get out of my head," he pointed to the top of his forehead with his big, long, callused right index finger. "In my old noggin—and I think it's getting worse. I'm not sure how to describe it other than there have been these—persistent, overlapping voices and images that I can't get out of my head. The voices are soft and calm at first, and then sometimes considerably louder." He stopped talking—and heaved a deep, slow, but heavy sigh.

"Okay," she said, just to acknowledge that she was still present.

"I did my best to ignore it. Like I am right now."

"What are you experiencing now?"

"I'm hearing *Chinese* sounding words and someone muttering about *trust*. I don't know—I just don't know—it's not clear!" he said as a stressed look spread across his face.

"Do you see things as well or is it just auditory?" Dr. Feinberg asked. It was a good question; it was the next obvious question.

"Both," he said. "But what I saw wasn't clear. It came to me in a couple quick flashes."

"Flashes of what?"

"Shadows at first and then of two people. It sounds nuts, but one of the guys was bald. I couldn't clearly make out the other one—it sounded foreign."

"Believe it or not," she said, "according to the *World Health Organization,* about 1 in 20 people have experienced at least one hallucination in their lifetime, which wasn't connected to drugs, alcohol, or PTSD. So, there's no need for immediate concern. Based on what you've told me, I can say that what you're experiencing is likely a symptom of psychosis—maybe a hallucination like you had when you were treated with morphine."

"Oh, so I'm crazy!" he said, shaking his head back and forth.

"No, of course not—it doesn't mean that you're crazy, Steven. If you were, then I probably couldn't help you. It could just be temporary or at the very least treatable," Dr. Feinberg said. "Many people live happy, prosperous lives with various forms of psychosis." She paused. "Now—tell me about this latest episode."

"At first it was just a weird sound, more like someone was blowing through a warbled, out of tune, whistle. Then I started hearing a mumble of voices," he glanced up and around the room, as though he might be hearing them again at that moment. He was.

"Does it happen often?"

He nodded and gently bit down on his lower lip as he thought about it. "After I got out of the Army—I started hearing voices louder and more clearly. Sometimes it felt like someone, or at times a group was talking to me. A few times I saw something moving on the edge of my peripheral vision."

"Just shadows?"

"No—the same as a few moments ago. I saw shadows followed by clearer flashes of people and places.

"Do these people say anything or tell you to do things?" Dr. Feinberg asked.

"No, it's usually a jumble of sounds, but it sounded like one of them said—*You Can't Trust Marlina.*"

"Your wife?"

"Yeah."

CHAPTER TWENTY-THREE

"The most important thing in communication is hearing what isn't said."
~ *Peter F. Drucker*

READ MY LIPS

"WHY IS TODD mouthing Sabrina's words while listening to her speak?" Dr. Starr asked, as the Innovations Technology Lab engineers demonstrated the PSYCHONIX goggles for the whole staff.

"It's just a residual psychological condition called echolalia," Dr. Lui added. He seemed to enjoy the relationship with his new team and made fast friends with Dr. Kahn. They were even meeting after work for tennis and golf dates. Even though he was the PSYCHONIX project team lead, not much was really known about him personally, other than he was a sharp dresser, emigrated from China, and was a relatively new American citizen.

It was also common knowledge that Dr. Lui had worked at *Lumni Gongsi* in the Chinese tech hub of Nanjing, 186 miles up the Yangtze River from Shanghai. Gongsi was just their word for company. ITL considered him a good catch. He was vetted like the rest, but unbeknownst to ITL and the U.S. Government, the city of Nanjing had developed a similar research park to foster China's next generation of technology giants. If Dr. Lui hadn't been vetted as an American citizen, then it would have been a flashing red light and glaring conflict of interest. Gongsi was still a hot place to generate, attract and retain science and technology and talent that aligned with the goals of the Chinese State research laboratories and universities.

"We noted the mouth movements when Brad brought us up-to-speed on the PSYCHONIX goggles. He said it has had absolutely no bearing on the test results," Sabrina Killian said matter-of-factly.

Sabrina and Todd eagerly filled the team in on some of the more tangential issues. Brad, who leaned coolly to the introverted side, was observant and talkative one-on-one, but only weighed in when the other two didn't know the answer or reached an impasse.

"People who move their lips like that are usually very smart and sometimes introverted," Todd said, as Sabrina leapfrogged his explanation and said, "—and they have a sensory need to reform the words that they hear with their own mouths, in order to fully process their meaning."

"Could be," Dr. Starr agreed. "But not all of us move our mouth this way."

"My father-in-law does the same thing, only *after* speaking rather than while listening," Todd added, giving Sabrina a rueful look as she once again continued the thought. "Their mouths silently re-form the words after they speak them," she said.

"It's not uncommon at all," Todd said, holding up the palm of his hand toward Sabrina, as a stop sign—so he could explain. "It even happens as we read to ourselves, when we silently say words in our head. It's a way we acknowledge the word we're hearing or reading in our brain, for memory purposes."

"Right, and our memory is basically nothing more than the record left behind by learning," Dr. Kahn stated. "It's a process that helps us store and retrieve information for future use."

"I heard, once," Sabrina said, as she caught an opening, "that they subconsciously want to make sure that what they said was really what they meant to say. Sort of a mental double-check, I guess—however that works."

"That really has no bearing on the test," Brad admonished them both. He didn't like the one-upmanship and rapid fire back-and-forth going on between Todd and Sabrina.

Dr. Lui crossed his arms to gesture *time out*. "Okay!" he said, in an effort to refocus the briefing. "We are talking to Dr. Starr's section—about the effectiveness of the PSYCHONIX goggles." He paused for a short moment to get their mutual agreement and continued.

"Brad, fill us in again on the details of the *MDSL-1* internal processor," Dr. Starr requested.

"Yes sir, it's truly innovative—in the strictest sense. Unlike Steven Hawking's speech processor of the past—this machinery doesn't require any sort of physical interaction, like eye movement or facial cues, to help us communicate with the PSYCHONIX technology."

"How's that possible?" Dr. Kahn asked.

"Sir, the equipment sends and receives PSYCHON radiation emanating from each person's mind or brain—depending on how you want to think about it."

"Brad discovered that we all have this unusual radiation in varied amounts," Dr. Lui said, "and that every person's is uniquely coded, like a fingerprint."

"And," Brad continued Dr. Lui's thought, "to read that mental fingerprint the equipment must be fine-tuned to the person's individual *Holt frequency!*"

"It's like we all have our own internal, narrow bandwidth channel to communicate on," Dr. Starr said excitedly."

"Exactly!" Brad said.

CHAPTER TWENTY-FOUR

"If you would be a real seeker after truth, it is necessary that at least once in your life you doubt, as far as possible, all things. ~ *Rene Descartes*

COGITO, ERGO SUM!

DR. MARK STARR had pondered physical and metaphysical concepts since he was a child in Washington State. He and his stepbrother, Steven Scott, laid under the stars and looked up at Aquila, Cygnus, Hercules, Lyra, Ophiuchus, Scorpius, and Sagittarius, the centaur with a man's head and torso on a horse's body. The one who held a bow and arrow. It was the one that he and his brother Steven pretended to be while they rode their bikes and shot suction cup arrows at each other in the neighborhood. Even as he relaxed with a friend in the ITL break room, the idea of traveling to the stars still took his breath away and captured his imagination. He had always believed that we were more than the sum of our parts and it had influenced the way he approached the science of the PSYCHONIX project.

"I heard a TED Talk once where the speaker said *reality is just a hallucination we all agree upon,*" Peggy said. "What do you think about that?" It was another one of their mind-expanding, casual talks over coffee, before they made rounds with a group of local interns who shadowed them for the week. Mark and Peggy met for coffee often and caught precious few minutes alone, whenever possible. They weren't dating, but there was a definite spark.

"No, I don't think it makes a lot of sense that a group of people could witness the same hallucination or delusion—since it is, by definition, a personal *firmly fixed false belief*," Mark answered.

"But—I suppose—if you could share someone else's subjective perceptions it would be one of three things," Peggy said. "You're privy to their delusion, you're being tricked, or you misremembered."

"Or it's true," Mark said. "You could both be witnessing what is actually happening."

"Interesting, I never considered that," she said with a flirty touch to the top of his hand. He smiled, looked around, and placed his hand on top of hers.

Peggy had a PSYCHONIX related question. "Given that it's true, here's a hypothetical— what if PSYCHON radiation unified all our minds at once—wouldn't that change reality?"

It was a fun question. They both relished the brainstorming and spit-balling of new ideas.

"Hmm, I really hadn't thought about that aspect of it. What do you think?"

"Well—it doesn't seem to me like it would change reality. Because, if it were possible to communicate like that, then I think that it would just change how we experience reality—at most."

"Good point," Mark said. "Unless there's an underlying psychosis."

"But it seems to me like a hallucination could still be recognizable as an unwarranted delusion, even if we're all connected with one mind."

"You mean, identify the truth in the same way we do personally?"

"Yes, we would most likely still be able to identify that the other person, who we are connected to, had experienced mental problems—because it could be tested through our reasoning."

"I think that makes sense. It would, in essence, be the same—whether it's here and now or experienced through a PSYCHONIX connection."

"Right," Peggy said, "but that may not *matter* since we don't believe that we can experience someone else's thoughts without their *willing assent*.

"True but take it another step. If it was an actual group communication, then I'd classify that as a vision, not a delusion or someone playing a trick on us."

"A vision—from a higher mind?"

"Yes, like from God—who it's reported, knows everyone's mind simultaneously. I've even heard of large Muslim communities having a mass vision of Jesus."

"In the sense that it's a wide-spread mental communication?"

"Yes."

"Interesting, but what do you mean, *someone playing a trick*?"

"I mean that each of us can easily be *fooled*. For instance, we can witness the same magical illusion—but it's only a *trick* that has been played on our senses. There's a reasonable explanation for it. There's an actual rabbit in the hat and a magician manipulating us. But when it comes to a delusion—it's *your* senses that are playing a trick on you—about something that never actually happened."

"Okay," Peggy said. "And—so, then a vision would also require a reasonable explanation?"

"Yes, but that's for another time. Suffice it to say that in each case *you* are the common denominator. If you weren't *tricked*, then something really happened that requires an explanation."

"Or—you're delusional."

"Hey, don't call me names." They smiled and clinked coffee cups.

It was shades of Descartes. *Cogito, ergo sum!* Latin for: *I think, therefore I am.* While other *knowledge* could be a figment of imagination, deception, or a mistake, French Philosopher René Descartes said that *the very act of doubting one's own existence served, at minimum, as proof of the reality of one's own mind.*

They sat there for a few more minutes talking, subtly flirting, smiling, and laughing—a bit more than normal. Mark complimented Peggy's hair.

"Oh, you probably say that to all the doctors," she said with a wink.

She thanked him and subconsciously combed her curly auburn hair back with her fingers. Mark thought this might be a great opportunity, so he cleared his throat and awkwardly floated the question.

"Speaking of things that really happen or maybe—need to happen—how'd you like to go out for dinner sometime?"

"No *tricks*?" she joked, referencing their magician versus delusions and visions conversation.

"None—you have my word as a fully paid member of the *Psi Chi, Chi Sigma Iota* honor society, and the Boy Scouts—well I was never in the Boy Scouts, but I'm always prepared," he humorously added. He held up the three fingers of the Boy Scout salute.

Peggy gazed around to ensure that they were still alone and quieted him with a gentle touch of her finger to his lips. "Yes Mark—I'll go out with you," she replied sweetly. "Just let me know when."

He lingered with a chirpy grin, as she took another sip of her coffee and smiled back with her eyes.

Descartes argued that *there is no passion that some particular expression of the **eyes** does not reveal.* That passion was now the likely cause of his dumbstruck grin.

CHAPTER TWENTY-FIVE

"Courage, sacrifice, determination, commitment, toughness, heart, talent, guts. That's what little girls are made of." ~ *Bethany Hamilton*

PRINCESS

CHELSEA PUT HER face in her hands for a few seconds before she squealed with excitement. She was on vacation with her family and about to receive an early birthday gift. Her mouth dropped open, her eyeballs popped wide, and she danced with uninhibited joy when she saw her *Royal Highness Princess* costume peeking out of the gift bag. Her mom picked it up for $19.99 at Party City and held it up for her to see as she entered the bedroom. Chelsea started breathing faster. It was her seventh birthday and she got to *choose* what she wanted to be.

"Calm down," her mother said. "You'll get to put it on for our special trip today."

Chelsea flailed her hands and bubbled-over with a surge of childish glee. She looked up at her mom with skyrocketing energy, as she jumped around and bounced on her bed and yelled again. "Oh, oh, oh! I get to be a princess!"

Today she was *Princess Chelsea Marie Croxon* and would exhibit all the refinement and royal manners of a seven-year-old.

"There are important rules," her daddy pronounced in a faux British accent. "The princess must curtsy, sit politely, cross her legs at the ankles, and hold her princess teacup with an extended royal pinky." He demonstrated and she giggled. "And she must always, always stick safely close to her mummy and daddy." In this case, her daddy was the Honorable John Croxon,

144

U.S. Senator from the Commonwealth of Virginia. He worked in D.C., but his home was near Richlands, Virginia.

The senator was simply reinforcing the important rules of safety, before he escorted his daughter to the old Reynolds Tavern for a traditional English afternoon tea. It was an elegant atmosphere with an offering fit for a Princess—a pot of tea, savory finger sandwiches, tarts, and homemade scones with whipped cream and strawberry preserves. She was in *heaven*.

John went all out for Chelsea's seventh birthday and was dressed in his top hat and a 3-piece tailcoat suit. He courteously opened the car door for her.

"We've arrived, *m'lady*," he said as he bowed his head to honor her presence.

"Thank you, pa-pa,!" she replied with a giggle.

"You're welcome *m'lady*."

It was family fun for an innocent, wide-eyed little girl, caught up in the wonder of imagination, dreams, and fantasy. Her family planned a dinner party for a little later, to be held on-board the ship, Pirate Adventures Chesapeake. There she could *escape the world* and pretend that she was being saved by Peter Pan, before Captain Hook made her walk the plank. All the fun plans and birthday adventures danced in her head, as they strolled through Colonial Annapolis.

The walking-man pedestrian symbol turned white in front of *Chick & Ruth's Delly,* and Chelsea held her mommy's hand as she skipped merrily through the crosswalk to the other side of Conduit and Main Street. As she walked, she ruled her kingdom and blessed her subjects with a wave of her pink feathered princess wand. Not a bad deal for $4.95. Passersby smiled, charmed by her delightful innocence.

CHAPTER TWENTY-SIX

"Always trust your gut, it knows what your head hasn't yet figured out." ~ *Unknown*

TRUST

AS THEY BEGAN another counseling session, you could tell by Steven Scott's body language, that he had strong feelings of revulsion after, believing, he heard something as outlandish as *You Can't Trust Marlina!*

That's absurd, he thought. *I must've misheard it.* The conspicuous, emotional strain was plastered evenly across his already combat-haggard face as they continued the session.

"Would you like to pick up where we left-off last time?" Dr. Feinberg asked.

Steven nodded.

"Tell me about your wife and how you met."

The last session was uncomfortable and pushed him outside his comfort zone. It had invaded his personal sense of privacy, so he started by making something clear. "Since we started dating as teenagers, I've wholeheartedly and unreservedly trusted her—and still do. She was always so classy that I sometimes referred to her as *The Lovely Marlina*," Steven said with a smile. "She thought it was cute."

It was his unique way of expressing his love for her. He used *The Lovely* as though it were a royal cognomen or noble sobriquet, like William *the Conqueror* or *Bloody* Mary I of England.

"I've—loved everything about her from the beginning. Her smile and approachable hazel eyes. Her wit and her long chestnut-brown hair. She's a stunning Italian-American lady with an appreciation for living life and laughing—she brings out the best in me," Steven said.

"Marlina DiBuono Scott taught me how to love and has been the love of my life for twenty-six years now. What else is there to say? We raised two wonderful, beautiful, gifted children, Vito and Donna."

"What do they do?"

"Well, as children, they worked at their grandparents' restaurant in the summers and on breaks. Now, they're on their own. Vito was accepted into nursing school and is working as a traveling nurse at the Bluefield Regional Medical Center in West Virginia."

"What about your daughter?"

"Donna, my oldest, joined the Air Force as a public affairs officer."

"You must be very proud."

"Yes, I am. She's deployed now, working with ISAF and USFOR-A in Kabul," he said with a mixed sense of pride and sadness. "She's been working for the Commander of the International Security Assistance Force and U.S. Forces–Afghanistan for six long months now."

"How do you feel about that?" Dr. Feinberg asked.

"It's a tough world, but she's a patriot and knows the risk," he said, as he took another sip of coffee and pondered the risks, which he knew all too well. "But I'm glad she's doing it and I still believe that America is an indispensable force for good. She believes it too."

Dr. Feinberg nodded. "Do you and your wife get to speak with her often?"

"Yeah— but it's a different war nowadays, Doc, in a different time. We get to *FaceTime* once a week, so she can talk to the Momma Bear. Italians are tight like that."

Marlina's maiden name was DiBuono. She was a proud first-generation Italian American with old country roots in Riccia, Italy.

"Marlina's parents found their way to New York City," he said, "and eventually to Washington State in 1959, as lovesick newlyweds. It was a scary journey for them, but they landed on their feet, as they say, in the New World."

It was a new life, in a new country, full of *hopes*, dreams, and opportunities.

"They worked really hard for everything that they got," Steven said. "For three years, they worked their fingers to the bone in local restaurants. They washed dishes, mopped floors, waited tables—barely scraping by, as they tried to learn English."

Even though times were lean, the DiBuonos were strong and believed that with enough hard work that they could make it on their own and be successful.

"Her momma used to always say: *A chi vuole, non mancano modi.* Roughly translated, it means, *Where there is a will, there is a way.* It was a quote proudly displayed on a rustic plaque that hung over the antique restaurant bar that they owned."

They had the *will* and now everyone who liked great Italian food made their way to the new family business in Walla Walla. A little mom and pop place they called *DiBuono's Steak & Submarine Shop* in College Place. "With lots of fabulous food for the dollar," is how Papa sold it to the customers.

"Marlina and I sort of knew each other from around the neighborhood, growing up, but we weren't an *item* until about midway through high school. Ha! I remember that exact wonderful day, when things really started to click between the two of us. I was walking home and ducked into their family restaurant to avoid a random Washington downpour. I darted in for shelter, completely drenched—and just wanted to wait by the door. That was really my only choice, since I didn't have any money to spend on food. But Mrs. DiBuono wouldn't hear of it. She sat me down at the counter, close to a window booth where Marlina was doing homework. I didn't know what to expect—but she brought me out a plate of *Mama Millie's Meatballs,* always a special on their menu. There was so much sauce that I had to ask for extra napkins.

Mama said, *"You-ah-big boy, so you get-ah extra sauce, extra cheese, extra bread, and extra napkins too."*

"Saying the word *extra* became a long-running joke or replacement word between me and the DiBuono family," Steven said. "They used it in the place of *molto*, so that instead of something being *molto bene*, it was *extra good*. And instead of telling Marlina she was molto bella; I would translate it to *you're extra beautiful*!"

"That's sweet," Dr. Feinberg said. "They sound like a wonderful family."

"That's the way they were. Mama Millie would say in her sweetest Italian American accent, *for-ah big Steven, there is-ah-no extra charge* and she would hug me so tightly and laugh a healthy Italian family laugh. I could hear her say, *Ha, I love, love, love dis ah-boy* as she walked to the kitchen, *you hear me, no extra charge-ah!* And usually there was no charge whatsoever, once I seriously began dating their daughter."

"You have some warm, vivid memories with Marlina?" Dr. Feinberg asked.

"Yeah, we were first reacquainted at a dance, but then the restaurant meeting happened and many other special moments. Our relationship has always been strong: *Un sacco d'amore!* is what Mama Millie used to call it. *A lot of love.* So you see—I fully trust my wife. The voices that I heard—are unwarranted."

149

"So, what do you think about the voices that you're hearing?" Dr. Feinberg asked again. More of a "let's pick up and move on from here" reiteration of what they had talked about, instead of a follow-up question.

Steven found the notion entirely strange. Not just about hearing voices but the surreal conversation about it, like they were discussing the NFL draft. "I don't believe it. I may be going crazy or my meds may be off, but I'm not stupid."

"Of course, you're not—I'm just trying to…"

Steven cut her off in mid-sentence. He wasn't offended but had a forthright military attitude that wanted to set things straight and get right to the point. "You know—it's odd and disturbs me just how real the voices, images, and shadows have been, and what was said about *trust*." He paused and took a slow deep breath, as he collected himself. "It doesn't jive with reality."

"That's good Steven—I mean I'm glad that you can filter that and that you don't believe what you're hearing. You seem to have a strong ability to navigate these episodes."

"Episodes?"

"It sounds like you're having mild hallucinations. They're of course usually associated with those kinds of false beliefs."

"Why me?'

"Who knows exactly how they arise? Maybe it's a result of stress—perhaps your combat injuries, or not getting enough rest and food."

He nodded.

"It could even be from drinking too much alcohol."

He interrupted her again. "I rarely drink and I'm not tired." *It feels like she's minimizing this*, he thought. Once again, he began to have intense feelings of distress as tragic, anxiety-riddled moments replayed in his mind. "It seems very real—maybe it is."

Dr. Feinberg made a mental note: *He thinks that what he saw and heard could be real.* It was a question that would soon be answered.

"What happens when you ignore it?" she asked.

"I don't know, really. It hasn't been happening all that long," he said. "At least not in a prolonged way. The last few days they mumble more than talk and I haven't had any of those images flash in my thoughts—until late last night."

"What happened?" she asked.

"My bedroom wall art suddenly changed into a string of nasty obscenities. There's a romantic picture that hangs above our bed, which reads: *Love of My Life & My Best Friend Forever.* The words were somehow exchanged for a cluster of vile, tasteless graffiti," Steven said with an unamused scowl. "Then, suddenly it changed it back."

"My goodness," she said. "Who was it—and why do you think that it happened?"

"I don't know!" he said, visibly agitated. "You tell me!"

"Do you think it could have just been a nightmare?" she asked.

"Maybe, I don't know." That seemed to calm him some.

It could have likely been a nightmare, but it was also another *ah-hah* moment for Dr. Feinberg. She had just adjusted his meds. And even though the medications were similar, people could react differently to them. Steven had only been on them for a few days and his fidgety body language revealed that he was becoming more agitated, on edge.

Steven noticeably bounced his knees and wrung his hands. His eye…wide open. His face transfixed on the *8' x 10'* glass mirror, which took up most of the front center of the counseling room wall.

I hope it's just the meds, she thought.

CHAPTER TWENTY-SEVEN

"A hallucination is a strictly sensational form of consciousness, as good and true a sensation as if there were a real object there. The object happens to be not there, that is all."
~*William James*

INTERVIEWS

"WHEREAS HALLUCINATIONS ARE incorrect perceptions of objects or events involving the senses, a delusion is defined as a *fixed false belief* not commensurate with the person's educational and cultural background," Dr. Mark Starr lectured a synapse of intern neurologists, who shadowed the mental health interviews on *Mental Health Unit-B*. "And although delusions can be idiosyncratic beliefs or impressions that are firmly maintained, despite being contradicted by reality or rational argument—it is typically a symptom of mental disorder."

He would use this time as an on-hands teaching opportunity; however, only he, Dr. Feinberg, and Dr. Kahn knew that these were the more severe, institutionalized cases that had been selected for the *Mind-Body Problem* research.

Doctors Starr, Kahn, and Feinberg were all slated to conduct a series of their own interviews this week. After it concluded, Dr. Kahn's major part would be to analyze their EEG and MRI scans to see how their brains reacted to various stimuli.

"Hallucinations are sometimes categorized as secondary delusions," Dr. Starr continue, "if they involve having a false belief in the voice that they are hearing, or other sensations they are experiencing—but a delusion is almost universally associated with schizophrenia and other psychotic disorders."

The group continued to make their rounds as he expanded on lessons that they had learned during a class. "But if we apply the notion that a fixed false belief is delusional, then several other psychiatric disorders would qualify as well. Consider the following."

He showed them a chart on the wall-monitor.

Personality Disorder   Major Depressive Disorder   Obsessive-Compulsive   PTSD

Anxiety   Hypochondriasis   Anorexia Nervosa   Body Dysmorphic Disorder

"As we make our rounds today, I want to challenge your presumptions and what you may take for granted in the *Diagnostic and Statistical Manual of Mental Disorders*. In the DSM, psychotic disorders are set aside as just one section of seventeen types of disorders. I hope to convince you that a thread of psychotic thinking can be identified across many of the other sixteen supposedly *nonpsychotic* groupings," Mark said. "Even OCD has been suggested as an early and overlapping symptom in schizophrenia, where hallucinations may occur. So, let's keep that in mind as you listen to our patient interviews this week."

He knew that the patient interview was the gateway to the health of the patient, because it was both a science and an art. A science that drove research, methodology, diagnoses, and an art fed by imaginative ideas, creativity—and given to some Freudian styled interpretations.

He advised them. "The contact has to be done directly, person-to-person, not by machines. And you were asked to follow me today, because only another *person* could absorb and adjust to the full range of another person's emotions," Dr. Starr stated. He continued the short lecture on the importance of face-to-face visits, as they shuffled down the hallway together.

"You may have heard that robots are coming for our jobs, or maybe that super-intelligent programs could cause an apocalypse, but when you look closely, humans still have many advantages over artificial intelligence. Even in the realm of cognitive deficits or just plain *ignorance*, the human mind still remains the master of using common-sense reasoning to solve and adapt to new problems, feeling emotions and understanding the emotions of others, and creativity."

They each took their own notes and nodded their understanding.

"For example, I heard Elon Musk once say that an example of something a human can do that a computer struggles with is putting two loose tubes together. You see, a human can spontaneously grab the tubes and put them together while a computer may miss the tubes all together, and not even realize it. We can use common-sense reasoning on the fly to make the necessary adjustments, whereas a computer will never know or feel anything in a conscious way—unless we tell it to in our programming."

Some of the interns stood there and wondered why the heck this guy was talking about putting tubes together. But to Mark it wasn't a non sequitur. The idea of comparing robots with humans had fascinated him since childhood.

"We visit our patients because that's where we engage genuine feelings, empathy, and find it easier to understand the nuances of emotions. We have something that even the most sophisticated AI can't express—true empathy. There's no algorithm for that. Empathy is one of the most human traits and it allows us medical folks to better care for others."

He went on to say, "We can even build social companion robot programs, which are pleasant for humans to interact with and be around, but they will never understand what it's like to be a human—to love and to feel creative. You see, we can dream and write books that touch the heart of readers and paint gasp-worthy works of art from scratch—that resonate with people. You can't resonate with a robot."

AI was the product of very strict rules and explicit instructions, the exact opposite of creativity.

"Humans alone can generate or recognize ideas, alternatives, or possibilities that might be useful in solving problems. We communicate and entertain ourselves and others—robots can't do that spontaneously!" Dr. Starr said to bobbing heads. "It's certainly possible to design an algorithm that can churn out an endless sequence of paintings, but it is difficult to teach an algorithm the difference between the *emotionally powerful* and *rubbish*. So—you can rest assured that no robot, as we know them, will ever come to take the arts or medical caretaking profession away from us," he said. He looked at the group of interns and nodded as he wound his way farther down the hallway.

Dr. Starr engaged his patients, mostly from the *art* angle—if one wanted to call it that. He knew and used many humorous ice-breakers—sometimes to pursed-lipped-smiles, raised eyebrows, and audible groans. Sometimes to radio silence. But everyone knew he cared about them.

This was his favorite: "Did you hear the one about the three *Freudians* that go into a bar? The bartender asks them for some *id*." He paused to the sound of crickets chirping, "You'll laugh about that one later...or you've obviously had an odd relationship with your mother."

Mark had a small stable of benign jokes that he would trot out and circulate with each new group. In this way, he and Dr. Kahn were very much alike. They were noted for enjoying their own sense of humor with a self-congratulatory chuckle. To some, that was the sole indication that something funny had been said.

As the interns took copious notes, he added, "First I try to lighten the mood, but one must read the room correctly. Psychiatric patients may feel too troubled to care much about ball games, traffic jams, the weather, or even jokes—and if you don't know what they're suffering from—at a minimum, show genuine interest and ask.

All the rounds were being recorded today, just as they were with Steven Scott and Dr. Feinberg. Except these patients were a bit less cooperative and under stricter observation. Each member of the core team—Starr, Feinberg, and Kahn—were assigned three clients each to interview. The intern neurologists were merely there to observe:

Patient 1

"Being bipolar plagues me every single day. My emotions have been like the stock market or a bottom-feeding Tug-Of-War between extreme mania and crippling depression."

"Yes, Mm-hmm," said Dr. Gus Kahn. "I hear you." He excelled at analyzing data, but not at empathy.

Patient 2

"My first psychotic break happened while I was away at college. It was my first day of school and the first time I ever saw demons. Have you ever seen demons? It screwed me up so bad that I couldn't focus on anything else—family, friends, or class. To top it off, I had the most violent urges—and I'm still hearing voices."

"Please explain to me what you mean by *violent urges*," Dr. Mark Starr requested. The process of counseling and diagnosing were important, but *so was one's safety*.

"It's an overwhelming urge to hit, stab, or strangle someone," he said, as Mark cautiously distanced himself from the bed. This particular patient had attempted to hurt himself and was now threatening to hurt others.

Patient 3

"I can't trust myself and I don't trust you either. I don't know you!" This patient randomly flashed looks to the left and right—and never looked at who he was speaking with. "Do I?! People abandon you—you know?! But it doesn't really matter, does it?! I don't like being around people anyways. And I can tell that they don't like me either—when it starts."

"Starts?"

"Some of my worst nightmares. It's hard to describe, but things—things have been happening to me while I'm asleep and while I'm awake."

It carries over. Interesting.

"And, I don't even know who I am anymore. I hear what I'm saying—the words coming out of my mouth and I wonder where did that come from? Sure, it's me talking—but then it's just another version of me—and then it's not me at all—I swear—it's not me! When it's happening, I feel like a statue possessed by something or someone else!"

"So, do you feel like a statue possessed by something, someone else right now?" Dr. Feinberg noticed that her client was frozen in an awkward, statuesque posture with his left arm raised.

Patient 4

"I've been diagnosed with major depression—not just your regular hometown variety, mind you," he said, as he slowly raised his head to speak to Dr. Kahn. "No—I get the extreme version—thanks," he said in an impassive manner. His expression and feelings were flat and hollowed out and he had been unable to get out of bed for months. "You don't want to know about the vivid dreams that torment my sleep. I'll dream that I'm roasting in hell and wake up drenched in sweat—still feeling like I'm on fire, gasping for breath and thinking about the most damnable things."

"Earlier on, you said that you thought a lot about death. Why do you think that is?" Dr. Kahn asked.

Kahn would never say it, but he believed that people like this had been indoctrinated about God, from youth, and conditioned to fear hell. They were afraid of the consequences—if they didn't accept the cultic-teachings. To him it was just enough psychological trauma to trigger guilt and fear in those he felt were weak-minded or genetically predisposed.

Patient 5

"Who are you and why am I here!?"

"You were in an accident." Dr. Starr glanced down at the foot of the hospital bed and noticed the word *Dissociative* checked-off on the medical placard. He knew that times of stress and trauma could cause some to keep difficult memories at bay or develop multiple personalities— that didn't seem to be the case here.

"An accident?!"

"Yes, it was—more or less a disaster, which you survived. Apparently, a tornado touched down in your trailer park and knocked you around pretty good. You've been here for three months now. You can't remember telling us about that?

"*Whoa!* You're kidding—man, that's wild." This fellow had the entire dissociative bundle: breakdowns of memory, consciousness, awareness, identity and perception. Worst of all, he didn't cooperate when a nurse gave him his medicine and a paper cup of water to take it with. "No, I'm NOT taking any more pills—I have my rights." He looked nervously around the room for confirmation or help of any kind but got none. "Look, no matter how many pills you say I have to take—or get forced down my throat—or *electroshocks* you give me. No matter what you say—it WON'T help! You try living like this… man—it's a brutal neighborhood."

"Do you drink?" Dr. Starr asked. When they brought him in, his blood alcohol concentration was at 0.43 percent. Death occurred in most people at 0.45, but there was always the exception. One man in Poland was recorded at 1.480 percent. Doctors say he survived his brush with death, but later died of injuries sustained in the car crash.

"Nah, I never touch the stuff."

Patient 6

He was restrained to his bed and quite agitated as the team entered his room.

"I'll cut you! You don't think I will, but you're wrong—I will!" he yelled. "I'm a soldier—I've seen people die and I know exactly how to do it."

Earlier this client screamed profanities and threw himself against the wall multiple times. He had to be restrained for his own welfare.

"Let's take a break," Feinberg said to the interns. "It's probably best if this patient is allowed to calm down and rest.

Patient 7

"I'd never wish this on anybody. Imagine yourself being strapped to a bed and tortured by insane jabbering. Hallucinations attempting to steal your personality! I have *eleven* alternate personalities besides me and it's pure hell. One of them is a *liar* and another *cuts* me."

He was shifting personalities faster than he or the staff could keep up with it. One of them was extremely violent, so they had to keep him restrained when he presented that personality.

"Who am I talking to now?" Dr. Kahn asked. It would have been funny, if it wasn't so sad.

Patient 8

"You know that feeling you have when you lose your balance and struggle to gain control—trying to get your feet back under you? It's like you're on a tightrope over the Grand Canyon, always about to fall, but you don't. That's what it's like to have a *panic attack*, but it goes on and on and on. It's literally driving me crazy."

"What do you feel like you can control?" Dr. Starr asked to help her focus more positively.

"Reading, watching TV—anything but being alone in my thoughts."

Patient 9

Client number nine was uncooperative and aggressive. She threw a food tray against the door and refused her meds with two raised middle-fingers and a few well-seasoned words. Words that would've made George Carlin blush, but didn't faze the experienced psychiatric staff. They were faced with multiple forms of hostility, aggression, and assault on a daily basis.

"We'll circle back and check on her later," Dr. Starr said. Her aggressive condition would also be discussed later in the classroom. He would allow everyone to go over the other cases as well. They would share notes and practice making diagnoses.

"Some illnesses start at birth, but others take years to discover or unravel or diagnose," Dr. Mark Starr said. At the end of the week he brought the team together for a tag-team *hotwash* with the interns—a time for feedback and advice.

"Throughout your career you'll encounter everything from anxiety disorders, mood disorders, and schizophrenia to psychotic disorders, dementia, and eating disorders," Dr. Feinberg said. "But there seems to be no rhyme or reason as to who, why, and when they get it."

"There was a rare case reported of a woman in India with the onset of schizophrenia—who was 100 years old," Kahn said. "It's rare, but it happens."

"It's difficult to even imagine anyone having a mental illness," Feinberg said. "It can be a mixed bag of anxiety, psychosis, depression, obsessions, mixed mental states, mania and hypomania, which can lead to delirium."

"For homework, I want you to read through the cases, and rack and stack your recommendations in categories of diagnosis." Dr. Starr said, then wrapped it up. "Most of the disorders are treatable to some extent. But let's be honest—for the majority, it's basically incurable.

I do my best to provide health, healing, and hope to my patients. I have learned a lot about the power of hope and hopelessness in people. People who have hit a brick wall and become suicidal.

Sometimes our hopes can be demolished by shattered dreams, unemployment, death, and mental illness. They can all feel like degrees of death. Those are the feelings that often lead to depression and incalculable misery. The hardest part is seeing those who feel their hope is entirely lost. I know that feeling—I felt it as a child.

'My whole world is collapsing all around me!' That's the message that I heard from clients today. They've been mentally defeated in the worst ways possible and it's painful to hear their cries. Some have support, others don't. I wish that I could tell them that there's something more. But most of them couldn't hear it through their brick wall of pain and misery.

CHAPTER TWENTY-EIGHT

"Research is what I'm doing when I don't know what I'm doing." ~Wernher von Braun

PSYCHONS

INNOVATIONS TECHNOLOGY LABORATORY paid a lot of attention to finding the source of consciousness. Including the hush-hush *Black Budget* government funding, they became the first institution to breach the $2 billion research barrier. Yet, no one had an answer as to how consciousness emerges in the brain or where it came from.

The ITL teams slowly started to gather in the Octagon for the next In-Progress Review.

"This PSYCHONIX project is bringing in beaucoup research dollars," Dr. Gus Kahn said enthusiastically. The thought of making a lot of cash was more important to him now than it normally would have been—but if you considered his recent divorce and gambling debts—not strange at all. No one at ITL knew it at the time, but he was completely strapped for cash and privately Dr. Lui had loaned him $3,000 to make last month's rent. A friendly yet subtle move, however, Dr. Lui had personal reasons.

"Big research questions usually bring in research dollars," Dr. Starr said, "and we're asking some of the biggest, most expensive questions on the planet. Luckily, our research project is supported well."

"Right, it doesn't get much bigger than *how does consciousness emerge from a three-pound gelatinous ball of gray wrinkled tissue and unify our thoughts*," Dr. Feinberg stated. "Much less, transfer from one mind to another."

"Yeah, that should earn us a tidy sum to retire somewhere in the Florida Keys," Dr. Kahn added, nearly inaudibly. He pondered and calculated the financial ramifications, rather than the worthiness of their research. "Or wherever or whatever you want to spend it on, right?" he added with dubious clarification.

Everyone trickled into the lab and gathered around the conference table for their third IPR. Dr. Feinberg led off. "What do these *PSYCHONS* look like?"

"We can't see them with our available technology ma'am," Sabrina Killian said. "Even the normal electromagnetic spectrum is only nanometers across.

"But PSYCHONS aren't visible at all," Todd quickly added.

"And, so you know they exist, how?" Dr. Kahn asked skeptically.

"In the same way that we know that the wind exists—you can feel it and see its effects," Todd said. "On a sailboat, you can feel the wind blowing and see it inflate the sail, right?"

"And—you can also hear it," Brad added, "When it whistles outside your window!"

"Yes—so, it's the same concept—except now," Dr. Lui assured Dr. Kahn, "we can detect a mental substance called PSYCHONS by its effects.

"Why do you call it a mental substance?" Dr. Kahn asked.

"Because it's not made of a physical substance that we know of," Sabrina said. "It's only detectable in conscious beings."

"With the *MDSL-1* processor?" Dr. Feinberg asked.

"Yes, the processor picks up what is radiated from the voids within the gray matter," Brad said. "Incredibly—that's what is triggered by sub-vocalized thoughts."

"Huh?" Dr. Kahn said. Everyone in the room had that puzzled look on their faces too. "You mean like a throat mic that cops use?"

"No, not exactly. In other words, there is no need for words or vibrations," Brad said. "At least not in the way that we process sounds in the eardrum or convert them to motor-neuron impulses that feed your spinal cord or muscles."

"How could that be?" Dr. Kahn asked.

"Because, evidently, we all transmit and receive PSYCHONS organically," Brad said. "Each of us, to various degrees and ranges, emit them. As we discussed before, the PSYCHONIX goggles or implants merely capture and amplify what is already there—nearly before thought happens."

"Why before?" Dr. Feinberg asked. "How could it know what you're saying, prior to saying it?"

"PSYCHON radiation has a cascading effect, much like dominoes—but it can predict the neuron path prior to activation," Sabrina said. "I suppose it's just the way we're built."

"I call it an *ephemeral subconscious experience*," Brad said.

"Why ephemeral?" Dr. Feinberg asked.

"Because the thoughts reside subliminally—in subconscious nano-moments that disappear and that we aren't even aware of summoning."

"Like our brain instructing our lungs to breathe and our hearts to beat," Sabrina added.

"Yes," Brad continued, "Think of it like this—as we talk, we're continuously anticipating new words, thoughts, and memories. You're perpetually loading subconscious thoughts into your brain—anticipating what to think and say next. Some thoughts, which may or may not be conscious, relevant—or even appropriate, but they're all there—ready to go."

"But I wouldn't want everyone hearing my thoughts," Dr. Feinberg said, being the more reticent member of the group—especially when it concerned her personal affairs. "Not that I'm thinking anything terrible—of course, but it's the principle."

"They couldn't hear you, if they wanted to," Sabrina said reassuringly. "It's not like all your thoughts are just hanging out there for all the world to hear when they want to. We don't know why—but there appears to be something in the *radiation coding* that's only triggered by *mental assent*. Once you're willing to share it—it's available."

"Only the things you want to be heard?" Dr. Feinberg followed-up.

"Yes, it's not like your mind is an old-fashioned party-line or that someone could randomly choose to read your thoughts, as you walked by," Todd said smiling. "At least we haven't found that *gifted* person yet."

"Is this technology mind-reading?" Dr. Kahn asked.

"No—not in the strictest sense. It's a thought amplifier," Brad said, "But that was partially the impetus for my discovery. People have been claiming telepathic abilities for centuries, but we've just learned that they were apparently on to something very real."

"You're saying the charlatans with so-called *psychic abilities* are real?" Dr. Kahn asked with his usual tone of doubt.

"No, No—I'm not saying that at all, but whether those people knew it or not, they were on to something. I just ran with the theory and tested certain aspects, which I thought might have validity. In this case—it did! I discovered the reason for what people call telepathic abilities—PSYCHONS!"

Dr. Lui nodded. "In China, PSYCHONS have long been theorized as hypothetical particles of consciousness, which drive our evolution and behavior. We call it: *kàn bu jiàn Yìshí* or unseen awareness. It's an element of our: *jīng shén*, essence or mind. "It's thought of as the thing that's holding everything together."

Dr. Starr nodded. "I'm speechless." He didn't share his current thought with the group, but a familiar verse came to mind: *And He is before all things, and in him all things hold together.*

"And of course, speechless is the best environment for PSYCHONS," Brad said jokingly.

"Since Brad's initial discovery we've also learned that everyone's PSYCHONS transmit their own unique frequency," Todd said. "It's a specific code, which is fundamentally—more like a harmony."

"Wow—the sounds are so amazingly beautiful. They look like modern art in our psychographs," Sabrina said. The creative, right side of her brain kicked in as she expressed it. "It's like *our souls are dancing together."* She motioned with her pen like a baton in a figure-eight and hummed a few lines from Beethoven's *Fur Elise.* Todd joined in as they very briefly choreographed a comical minuet and bowed. Dr. Lui found the entire scene much too childish for his liking and shooed them when they tried to take his hand for part of the dance.

"Yeah—thanks for that lovely performance," Brad said with a shake of his head and wry look of bemusement.

"Todd, why did you say it's a harmony?" Dr. Starr asked.

"Because, it's like a series of piano chords played in combination."

"Or really—interdependent tones that roll in different combination sets," Sabrina said, "to produce an individual's *unique frequency code* or private UFC."

"What do you mean—roll?" Dr. Starr asked.

"Let me explain it this way," Brad said, trying to simplify their explanations. "Your UFC is a dynamic code that no one else has access to—it's sort of a mental security lock."

"It's a personal code that operates using an ever-changing mental authenticator," Todd said, "your mind."

"And it's basically dynamic time-based verification," Sabrina added, "like security programs that implement two-step verification services using a one-time password algorithm."

"But in this case, it's much more than two steps and it's unlocked by *willing assent*," Todd stressed. It's a perfect syzygy of *mind and body*."

Brad nodded and continued his explanation. "Try imagining the greatest pianist's fingers dancing and weaving across all 88 black and white ivories. The musician able to write within seven octaves, plus a minor third, from A0 to C8—able to produce all the polyphonic tones in the universe—that's what we have in the PSYCHON radiation code."

"Right, but in this case," Dr. Starr restated, "what you're saying is that we can each control and share our own unique harmony at will."

"Yes, exactly, however, it's apparently stronger in some than in others," Brad said. "But PSYCHONIX equalized that for us. We've harnessed and amplified the mind, so that it doesn't *matter*.

CHAPTER TWENTY-NINE

"I was amazed as people must be who are seized and kidnapped, and who realize that in the strange world of their captors they have a value absolutely unconnected with anything they know about themselves." ~ *Alice Munro*

RIDE HOME

SEVEN-YEAR-OLD Chelsea Marie Croxon was on a fun-filled family vacation to celebrate her birthday and busy reigning over her imaginary kingdom, as three other happy-go-lucky elementary school children were just getting out of class in Annapolis, Maryland. If Chelsea was a princess, then the woman who picked up those other children was a wicked witch, who had cast an evil spell over their lives—forever.

The woman's name was Ashlynn Peterson. She was married and childless and would never be able to have children. It troubled her greatly and she couldn't wrap her mind around the fact. She dreamt of being a mom since she was a little girl playing with dolls. Now she desperately wanted her own children and wanted all the children she met to call her *Mommy*. It had become a strange obsession—impelled by drugs, alcohol, and her first, second, and third psychotic episodes. She was supposed to take medicine, but didn't. That induced irrational thoughts and delusional fantasies—usually unnoticed by her inattentive husband.

There are a lot of impolite words to describe Ashlynn: *nutso, squirrelly, wacko, buggy, daft,* and *touched* to name a few, but neurotic, psychotic, and deranged were more precise and accurate. She was unstable enough to kidnap little children, but just stable enough to convince and coerce them, winning their trust and friendship. They were young enough to be easy, vulnerable, and convenient targets.

Ashlynn spotted one of the children—with a name pinned on her jacket. It made the job of kidnapping that much easier. Eight-year-old Elizabeth Simmons was enticed into Ashlynn's air-conditioned van at 3:00 p.m. with the promise of an *ice cream cone* and *a little doll that needs a friend*.

"Hi Elizabeth, your parents had to go to the hospital for a boo-boo and asked me to watch you for a little while."

"Are they okay?" she asked.

"Oh yes, of course—but they'll be a little late getting home. So, I'm thinking we could get some ice cream—and look here," she said as she pulled out a doll. "Let me introduce you to my old friend, *Mrs. Beasley*." Ashlynn sold it in a soft, gentle, sweet voice that one might hear a second grade teacher use with her class.

Mrs. Beasley was Ashlynn's 50th anniversary replica doll from the five year TV hit show, *Family Affair*. The little girl, Buffy, from the show, carried her around wherever she went and spoke to her and confided in her, like she was a real person. This didn't seem strange at all for a child. The doll was outfitted in a blue dress with white polka-dots and rectangular wire-rim glasses, like many people wore in the late 1960's and early 1970's. She didn't have any frills or special abilities. She couldn't pee, or cry, or say momma like dolls do nowadays. In that era, one's imagination and pretend-playing were expected behaviors.

"Can you give her a hug?" Ashlynn asked. "She really needs a friend today." It was a loving gesture, easy distraction, tempting lure, and a sweet reward for a guileless, naïve little girl. "I'm her mommy."

171

Elizabeth held Mrs. Beasley tightly in her arms, and then asked *Miss Ashlynn* to buckle her into the car seat too. "That's what my mommy and daddy do." She was innocently unsuspecting and saw no reason for not taking a pretty doll from a nice lady who knew her name.

What could be wrong with that?

Ashlynn proved to be very adept, as well as disarming in her artful deception. She was merely passing along instructions from Elizabeith's parents to get them ice cream while they waited. The friendly tone made it clear that there was no reason for alarm.

The 12 and 10 year old boys came out and looked around for their little sister and the school bus that they normally rode home. Then they saw Elizabeth sitting contentedly in a gray Chrysler Pacifica van, playing with a weird looking doll with glasses. Boys being boys, they were oblivious to the imminent danger and got directly into the van with a convincing story, a smile, and a similar offer of ice cream, *any flavor, your choice.*

Each year, about ten abductions were committed by women who desired children of their own, usually babies. Sometimes it was done to preserve a relationship with a man. In cases like that, they would try to convince him that the baby she suddenly had was really his. It's a little tougher to pull off when you're kidnapping three children—8, 10, and 12 years old. She wouldn't try to fool her husband. As far as he was concerned she was babysitting again.

The children got into the van. They were much too young to notice her blank, distant stare, facial twitches, and flickering eyes when she said, "I'm sad today and it would make me *very, very* happy if you would call me *Mommy*."

The oldest, 12 year old Gary, soon realized that they had made a huge mistake getting into the van. He didn't want to *alarm the lady*, so he relented to Ashlynn's odd requests and played along. He also coached the others, as soon as it dawned on him that she was acting *really, really weird.* Until he could figure out how to get away, Gary made a game out of it for the others—and comforted Tommy and Elizabeth with a smile and a wink. Later, he would be the first to mount an escape.

Ashlynn was extremely convincing, but it was a *ruse,* an *easy lie* that was often perfected by experienced addicts and drunks to exploit naiveté or compassion and protect their own miserable self-absorbed, perverted, delusional lives. They lied to everyone. But on the first trip down the rabbit hole they lied to themselves the most. It's not a stretch when you're already *losing your mind.* Ashlynn wasn't perverted or naive, but she was confused, ill, and quite broken in spirit.

The children had been lured away from their elementary school under false pretenses—and driven away in a family van. They got their ice cream, but the only taste that they had in their mouths now was from the polyethylene coating of Duct tape that had been wrapped around their mouth, wrists, and ankles. She flashed her pistol and forced them to the ground, so she could wind the tape tight. Ashlynn wanted children and now she had them. They were bound and quietly seated on her couch.

His ballgame was on, so her half-deaf and distracted husband retreated and listened to his blaring television from their den. It would have taken an atomic bomb to interrupt him.

Some child abductions began as less complicated crimes. Usually the victims were lured into cars or alleys, for such short times that they were never really considered missing at all. In some cases, things went terribly wrong. Someone interrupted the crime and perhaps the pedophile panicked. Child abduction wasn't a growing menace, but it was a heinous one, particularly when violence ensued. Perhaps it was unintentional violence, from a large, panicked person trying to subdue a frightened, screaming child. Maybe the ploy didn't work the way that they had planned and made them feel like there were no other options. They might even see themselves as the victim or the one who was dealt a bad hand. They rationalized:

I told you to listen. It's not my fault you got hurt! Only it was entirely their fault. *If the children don't behave, then they'll get what they deserve.* It's certainly a startling and tragic event for the child and the 115 families involved each year in abuse.

What kind of person did that? The answer was that they were usually the seedier, socially bereft outcasts, with few friends. Sociopaths. Losers. Pedophiles. Perhaps people who themselves were abused as children. Mostly *non-violent* until they became desperate and convinced that it was *needed*. Mentally deranged individuals, intent on abducting and keeping the children for pornography, sexual abuse, social companionship, or parenthood.

The children were terrified—and they had a right to be.

CHAPTER THIRTY

"You don't have to control your thoughts. You just have to stop letting them control you."
~ Dan Millman

CONSENT

PRIOR TO HIS counseling sessions, and the subsequent *Mind-Body Problem* issues being studied, Steven Scott was given a battery of tests and an informed consent letter to sign. It informed him of his legal rights and how the information that they gleaned might be used at ITL—if he chose to participate. He did, and gladly signed it. He understood that the nature of the research was confidential and wouldn't be shared with anyone—including the clients. He trusted his brother's advice and willingly accepted the gratis counseling with the full understanding that all residual clinical studies and projects solely belonged to Innovations Technology Laboratory.

Prior to ITL's unforeseen association with a super-secret project and being assigned a team of Secret Service agents, they had budgeted for staff, equipment, lectures, lessons, and the recording of counseling sessions in their new media center. It was state-of-the-art. It was business as usual. But now there were immediate staffing adjustments that had to be made. Studying the *Mind-Body Problem* brought significant amounts of attention from the government. Since they began to officially work on psychological bionics—there was a seemly endless flow of resources. It was all happening so fast.

Dr. Starr had recommended his brother for counseling prior to the U.S. Government entering into the PSYCHONIX project. Now he wasn't so sure that it was a good idea. But with things snowballing so quickly, he didn't see a need for changing plans in mid-stream. Steven still had needs and ITL could benefit from studying his case. It might even raise unnecessary red flags, if he changed course now. He had never been a part of a big government operation. He liked it. However, this was a major deal and he was nervous about messing something up.

So, for now—it was business as usual. Steven Scott proceeded with his planned counseling. Though before sitting down in the comfortable doctor's office, he first had to take an *unusual series* of psychological tests, all the while seated in an undersized tablet arm school desk.

"I felt like I was still in school," he later told his brother, "when a lackadaisical attendant trudged over, handed me a stack of medical forms and instructed me to write down any pending criminal charges and/or illegal drug use."

His brother Mark laughed and explained. "It's an important discriminating factor that helps us weed out unqualified volunteers—and to find volunteers most suited to our *Mind-Body Problem* research. For your portion, we're looking for people with typical concerns—like your PTSD."

"Folks that you think you could help."

"Yes, that's right. You take low doses of meds, but otherwise lead a normal life."

"Yeah—*mostly*," he nodded. "But Dr. Feinberg just put me on *something new.*"

"We've collected great data about how the brain actually works but need to increase our qualitative assessments about the mind. That's where you fit in."

"Concerning?"

"It's quite technical but think of it like this—your brain is part of the visible, tangible world of your body. Your mind, on the other hand, is part of the invisible, transcendent world of thought, feeling, attitude, belief and imagination."

"The qualities that you can't measure as easily?"

"Right, especially since I don't believe that the mind is confined to the brain."

"Meaning you're thinking of it as a soul?"

"Meaning, yes. But for our research we have to keep an *open mind*."

"Noted." Steven appreciated the pun.

"We need *normal* folks like you," Mark said with a raised eyebrow, "—that are more receptive and responsive to counseling and can provide us a different source of data for our *Mind-Body Problem* study." In the back of his mind, Mark was also thinking about a new direction the research was going now. Incorporating and expanding on the PSYCHONIX project would be an interesting, innovative challenge—and one that he couldn't reveal to his brother, yet.

"Did you just call me *normal*?" Steven asked with another grin.

"Don't let it go to your head. You all done with psych-testing?"

"Yep."

Steven took the written psychological test and exited as soon as he and Mark were done talking. The following week, he received an acceptance letter.

Thank you for your interest in the Innovations Technology Laboratory Volunteer Program. You've been accepted as a volunteer into the Mind-Body Problem project. You are eligible for this study if you are receiving counseling. Please read, sign, and follow the reporting instructions on the back. It was good news, but at this point it was more or less a formality, because the sessions with Dr. Feinberg had already started.

Steven Scott would later recall to friends and family, "There were a bunch of asinine multiple-choice questions on the test." Even to the staff there were, admittedly, many bizarre ones in the one hundred questions listed:

Would you rather be a ballerina, than a firefighter? Why?

Some, like that one, were semantic and paradoxical traps that forced honest, if not confused, answers and potentially delusional responses. Who would believe that three Yale University professors had come up with it—most likely over a few drinks?

How often do you torture small animals?

How long have you known you were Jesus?

Other questions included:

1) *True/False: If people had not had it in for me, then I would have been much more successful.*

2) *True/False: At times I feel like smashing things.*

3) *True/False: I have had peculiar and strange visitors, not from Earth.*

4) *True/False: I have not lived the right kind of life.*

5) *True/False: I'd rather sit and daydream, than do anything else.*

6) *True/False: Once in a while, I think of things too bad to talk about.*

7) *True/False: A person should be guided by their dreams?*

8) *True/False: Everything is turning out, just like the prophets in the Bible said it would.*

9) *True/False: I do not always tell the truth.*

10) *True/False: I have better solutions to problems than others.*

The questions became more thought provoking, invasive, and paradoxical.

11) *True/False: I intend to answer some of the questions falsely.* "Well, yes, no, maybe—huh?" It could be a troublesome paradox for the person struggling with mental health issues. He could truthfully answer *no* and that would make some of his answers a lie or answer *yes* with no intention of telling the truth—another lie. A truly sane person would just find it all quite humorous.

"The goal is to discover the person's mental health and potential biases. It may prove helpful in how we place them in the study," Dr. Kahn explained to Steven. "This is just a psychological snapshot." It was a good fit for Dr. Kahn's data driven personality.

He nodded.

Dr. Kahn assessed the questionnaires and sent them to Dr. Starr for further review. As the director, he would be the one making recommendations.

CHAPTER THIRTY-ONE

"Sometimes in life you just need a hug. No words, no advice. Just a hug to make you feel better."
~ Author Unknown

BORN TO BE WILD

AS AN OFF-DUTY police sergeant exited ITL, he recognized a person in a car doing donuts in the parking lot. It was Brian McGhee. He also wanted gratis counseling and to participate in the *Mind-Body Problem* research. Brian was supposed to arrive by 2 o'clock for his psychological evaluation, and that's exactly when he showed up. According to his earlier intake interview, he didn't do drugs, but that was quite misleading. To everyone's displeasure, he had consumed a lot of beer, and was drinking one while spinning his blue 1967 Chevy Malibu in a circle. He also blared his CD player with *You Never Even Called Me By My Name* and sang it at the top of his lungs. It was an off-key clarion, country-steeped vocal, somewhere between David Allen Coe and Kurt Cobain.

But you don't have to call me darlin', darlin'…You never even called me by my name…

The off-duty officer immediately called it in as a 10-96, a *mental subject*. Inside the building, the word spread quickly among the staff members: *there's a Cranial Rectosis in the main entrance parking lot!* It was a grandiloquent, yet unflattering way to refer to the physical location of one's head—presumably at the point when a patient has his head completely up his butt. Unfortunately, the person of interest was actively removing himself from the *Mind-Body*

180

Problem project. Security responded first and the cops arrived shortly thereafter. It wasn't the kind of spectacle that one necessarily wanted in the vicinity of the PSYCHONIX project, but on the other hand—it was in front of a mental health hospital.

Mental health, behavioral health, and psychiatric hospitals all came with their own unique set of risks and safety requirements. Later, an investigation discovered that Brian McGhee had mixed drugs and alcohol—specifically psychotropic mood stabilizers. It had revved-up his erratic behavior and put the staff in an undesirable position as well. The emergency room updated Dr. Starr's team as it happened. For now, he could only read the reports as he watched from his office window.

Brian consumed too much alcohol, mixed drugs, and denies that he has a problem. Now, he has refused to take his regular medication for anxiety. He says that he was misdiagnosed and that he doesn't need them anymore.

Dr. Starr briefed the ITL staff, "He's too erratic, plus if he's unwilling to comply, then we can't use him in the PSYCHONIX project. Best we found out now."

A nurse on *Mental Health Unit-B* reported, "Brian has been irascible and continues to argue and demonstrate extremely poor judgement."

"His blatant recklessness poses an unacceptable risk to the program," Dr. Kahn stated firmly.

"And—more importantly, to himself and the safety of everyone around him," Dr. Feinberg added compassionately.

"You're right, we can't have this," Dr. Starr replied.

It took security the better part of the morning to apprehend Brian McGhee. Until his car had stalled, and he calmly got out. The report from security said, *he wasn't violent—quite the opposite. He started wandering around the parking lot, asking everyone he saw for a hug—until we approached him. As soon as he spotted us, he was uncooperative and surprisingly nimble in evading everyone—taunting us, staying just out of our grasp.*

He did, however, stroll through the hospital doors when a smart nurse reminded him that his *2 o'clock session* was about to start. That was when two muscular orderlies efficiently secured him, one on each side, and escorted him to a room of his own. He was checked-in as a 5150, *Detention of Mentally Disordered Persons for Evaluation and Treatment.*

Brian McGhee had become a danger to himself and others, and was firmly invited to *Unit-B* for the next 72 hours to be evaluated and treated as necessary. Everything was above board and legally approved by the State Department of Health Care Services. Dr. Feinberg took immediate charge of the admission—and temporarily secluded Brian for his own safety, and to be evaluated. He wasn't violent, so the decision was made not to restrain him. They didn't want to trigger fears or cause unnecessary psychosocial trauma.

Dr. Feinberg reported to Dr. Starr, "There was no way we could release him in his current state. He's relatively peaceful now but having a variety of psychotic episodes—more specifically presenting an array of hallucinatory sensory experiences."

CHAPTER THIRTY-TWO

"Timeo Danaos et dona ferentes." ~ *Virgil*

FOLLOW THE STARR

ELEGANTLY TUCKED INTO the fourth-story gables of the old Johns Hopkins Hospital, directly above the *Octagon* unit, was Dr. Mark Starr's executive office. It was from there that he usually answered messages and occasionally received clients. As you entered, the first thing that drew your eyes was an antique mahogany desk pointed toward tastefully draped French doors, and a wood-framed balcony that overlooked the courtyard and mature gardens below. He worked there a lot and the pleasant scenery refreshed him. It energized and allowed him to think more clearly about the matters of the day.

He sat there and casually reviewed a half-dozen pages or so, which had just been entered into Brian McGhee's medical file. They assessed his condition, progress, and the next best steps for him and the *Mind-Body Problem* project—now minus another candidate. Brian remained in seclusion and was being treated. Since he had to be dropped from the program, that would leave them with only one candidate now—his brother Steven. They had hoped for more. It wasn't ideal, but they had to do what was in Brian's best interest.

It was a tough situation and a setback, but certainly not a deal breaker. However, Mark had to rethink his plans. He had a lot on his mind but did his best hard thinking in the early morning. It was then that he wrestled with the most difficult issues, while he gazed out at the fall foliage, and sipped a frothy hot cappuccino from his *Bunn* espresso machine. His desk phone buzzed.

Sheila, his administrative assistant, reported over the intercom, "Sir, you have a visitor—your brother Steven Scott is here—to—." She had barely uttered the first words, when Steven heedlessly waltzed past her and strode through Mark's office door. "Sir—you can't...," she stood up and tried to block him, but she couldn't move fast enough. However, she hurriedly followed close behind.

Before Sheila could utter another protest, he was already standing in front of Mark's desk. "Great," Mark said with an acquiescent tone of sarcasm. "Send him right in." He was genuinely happy to see his brother.

Steven looked at them both and threw up his arms in a '*hey what did I do*' gesture.

Sheila shrugged *sorry*, as Mark calmly waved her off. He was used to his brother's antics. Steven grinned, intentionally oblivious to their office protocol.

"I have followed the *Starr* and come bearing gifts from afar," he jovially proclaimed and waved a decorative tin of peanut butter cookies under Mark's nose, and then pulled it back as he reached for them. It was the way that he had teased his brother since childhood.

"You'll get these—when I get some answers, little brother." He laid the tin on the front corner of Mark's desk. They would, of course, be shared and eaten by day's end. They would also go quite well with a cappuccino for Mark and strong, black coffee for Steven. He never quite embraced the idea of defiling the drink with milk and sugar or overcharging for a cup of *frou-frou* coffee.

"Answers—for what?" They embraced in a strong bear hug. Steven strolled around to admire and case the joint. The military had ingrained it in him to assess his environment and that was what he did. He looked at the countless prestigious awards that lined the walls of his brother's pristine office.

"Oh…I think you know very well…" It was a speculative guilt trip ploy that they had used as kids to solicit potential answers from strangers, but he couldn't keep a straight face—and they broke into laughter.

"I thought for a moment—that maybe your sessions weren't going so well." He was also subtly fishing for how his brother felt.

"Yeah, it's fine. I'm fine. Everything's fine," he said off-handedly.

"Well…that certainly sounds…*fine,*" he mimicked.

In truth, Steven Scott's morning session with Dr. Peggy Feinberg had once again kicked off a cascade of anxiety-riddled effects—that sent his pulse racing. It also made his palms sweaty and hands a little shaky. His brewing feelings of anxiety had tweaked his nervous system more than a little. His body was prepared to react to the imminent threat that he was seeing and hearing from the mirror, whatever it was. For the time-being, he was *fine* with well-hidden shadows of not so fine that bubbled beneath the surface. Hopefully the new meds Dr. Feinberg prescribed for him would settle the physical, neurological, and emotional duress of his PTSD attacks.

"Yeah—I thought I'd come up—and bug you before my head gets completely shrunk," he said, instinctively continuing his survey of the office. He admired Mark's *I Love Me* wall and walked back-and-forth from one decorated end to the other. "Wow, check out just how big *your britches* are."

Regardless of how much he teased, he was nevertheless extremely proud and impressed by his brother's successes. He hadn't realized exactly how accomplished Mark was in the medical community. "I only have a few minutes before my next session starts, but—this *Mark Museum* could take all day."

Mark smiled again at his brother's droll humor and disarming frankness. He motioned for him to sit down on a tufted black leather sofa next to the window. As if on cue, he pulled out his best cups from an antique coffee station and started to make drinks. Steven pointed and commented on one of the larger framed awards in the middle of the wall. He could read the large diploma font from where he was seated across the room.

"What the heck is a *PFISTER*?!" Steven asked, "Is that like *hemorrhoids?*"

Mark laughed. "Not hardly!" The awards on his wall represented a lifetime of achievements and Mark was most proud of the *PFISTER AWARD.* "I got that for outstanding contributions in the fields of Psychiatry and Religion—something that I'm still researching as part of our *Mind-Body Problem* project." He went on to say that recipients got to deliver a lecture at an *American Psychological Association* conference during the year he got the award. That was when he ran into their mutual friend from Walla Walla.

"Remember Pastor Bobby?" Mark asked.

"Yeah, I always liked him."

"Well—we met up while attending a cordial, after conference, dinner party at the *PFISTER AWARD* ceremony last year."

"No kidding. That's great—but why was Bobby there?"

"Well, he's Dr. Robert W. Smith now and teaches at Houston Baptist University."

"Pastor Bobby, a professor—it doesn't surprise me," Steven said. "What does he teach?"

"He's an analytical philosopher and apologetics professor. You know the heady stuff he always liked to talk to us about when we were kids."

"Right, ten-dollar seminary words for Jesus, God, and love," he remembered Mark's love of esoteric jargon, but hadn't had much use for it. To him it was pretentious.

"Well, we've spoken a lot since our *PFISTER* reunion—even tossed around the idea of writing a book together."

"Wow, that sounds great! Are you going to do it?"

"Yeah, I like the thought of working with him—especially in the areas of psychology and religion."

"How would that work?

"For now, we're still tossing it around, but we've discussed writing something related to the spiritual and physical connections between our *mind and body*—focusing on consciousness. It's an overlapping area of interest for me at ITL."

"Right, Peggy mentioned that to me. She said I might have an opportunity to participate in a new project—whatever that means."

"We're still figuring that out," Mark said. He was in deep thought as he examined his brother's face closely. He contemplated the black eyepatch over his missing right eye and the possibilities of an *MDSL-1* implant with a bionic eye. It wasn't an entirely new thought. They already had considered the fact that someone with a missing eye would make it much easier to access for the implant. Steven would be perfect for this, but it was too much to ask for. It wasn't like he was asking his brother for a kidney. This was more complicated with so many unknowns.

"The one thing I can divulge is that it's a *top secret* project, so I can't go into any details. But what I can say, brother-to-brother, is that we've developed a communications device—and we're investigating the possibility of a cerebral implant—maybe something bionic."

"No kidding." The Six-Million Dollar Man immediately popped in his mind. "You know, it wouldn't be too hard to install something behind my eye," he said, lifting his patch. "Because I ain't got one," he softly chuckled. He wasn't shy talking about his injury. It had been years since his injuries, and he had learned to live with it.

Mark nodded. "The thought had crossed my mind."

"Sometimes I wear a glass eye."

That's all that they discussed about the new projects, but it triggered ideas.

CHAPTER THIRTY-THREE

"I am just a child who has never grown up. I still keep asking these 'how' and 'why' questions. Occasionally, I find an answer." ~*Stephen Hawking*

500 TRILLION SYNAPSES

THE INNOVATIONS TECHNOLOGY Laboratory team was the crème de la crème. They taught, researched, and orchestrated psychological operations related to many new technologies. They were a trusted, flexible, and responsive team, and now even closer knit as they pursued the PSYCHONIX project. They effectively engaged each other in problem-solving, shared decision-making, and oversight of the project. Each watched, inspired, and motivated the others to excellence. It was truly the innovations part of their program.

They exhaustively combed through all of the data: video interviews, ITL files, and peer-reviewed research. That was how theories were formed, and how discoveries were made. However, this morning's IPR bordered on the philosophic.

"*What* questions are important for figuring out *how* things operate in a mechanical sense, but the *Why* questions take us a lot deeper, down the philosophical paths of meaning and purpose." Dr. Mark Starr reiterated to the team. "Those are paths that we would like to identify in our project, whether they're traveled or not."

Dr. Mark Starr worked in scientific research around some of the brightest minds that he had ever met, not like the weird eccentrics or dogmatic know-it-alls you might conjure up in your mind. At least they were no stranger than the general population. Most people in his psychiatric medical community were people with a lot of heart, passion, and compassion. He personally believed that one of the most striking things about what they shared was compassion.

"It's an important qualitative approach for us physicians to remember as we move forward in our nascent projects—to remember that we suffer with them," Dr. Starr said.

He explained that being relational affected one's level of compassion—and that compassion literally meant: *to suffer with*. "It's an emotion that springs from the recognition that the human experience is imperfect and that we're fallible. Why else would we say *it's only human* when we comfort someone who made a mistake?" He himself was willing to take risks and make mistakes in his own research. *That's how one learns,* he thought.

When you study something intensely enough, for long enough, you realize just how little you know and how little you can ever know.

It's very humbling.

Dr. Starr was fond of reminding his staff that the only people who think they know everything are those who don't realize how much there is to know. Mark never felt like he had arrived, nor was he egotistical, but he instinctively trusted his common sense and entertained some ideas that appeared radical to others in the scientific community.

"Wouldn't it be amazing if we could communicate with beings from other dimensions?" Dr. Starr asked rhetorically, even though he knew that wasn't their primary objective. It was still interesting, and he knew that radical ideas sent a man to the moon.

Naysayers never dissuaded him. He had the *sacred fire* or *feu sacré,* as the French called it. It was what he thought about all the time. Like the others on his team, he too had a lot of heart, passion, and compassion for his clients and patients. He believed in what he was doing and believed it was his duty to question convention, reinvent, and teach others—and that was what he did. One of his biggest personal concerns was about exposing his brother to the PSYCHONIX project and the problems that might come about as a result. For now, at least, his brother was being helped with his PTSD issues. So, Mark concentrated on the tasks at hand.

"*Why* should we trust chemically induced thoughts, produced by nearly *500 trillion synapses*?" he continued. It wasn't a popular neurological pursuit, maybe more philosophical or neurotheological. "Why should we trust *neurotransmitters* handing off crucial biological computations that underlie our perceptions and thoughts? What is it that we're *trusting*—biology?"

"I'm trusting the science," Dr. Kahn said glibly.

"I'm trusting the evidence, wherever it leads us," Dr. Peggy Feinberg added. "I think we need to be open-minded—and open to the possibilities."

"Yeah, but let's get real," Kahn interrupted. "This is nonsense."

"Let's recognize and admit that science can't explain everything—and move forward from there."

"Yes, it can." Dr. Kahn asserted.

Dr. Starr shook his head and Dr. Feinberg heaved a slow sigh. To Mark, she was a breath of fresh air and a conflict resolution facilitator at the same time. She often took the steam out of an argument before it even got started. Peggy knew that, in some cases, it was probably better to drop the conversation.

She's a smart lady, Dr. Starr thought *and quite beautiful.* "I agree with Peggy."

"I don't agree," Dr. Kahn said. His tetchy demeanor was not exactly breaking news for anyone on the ITL team.

Dr. Feinberg brought a unique perspective to the scientific conversations and ITL was lucky to have her onboard, especially since most organizations were having a hard time retaining women at the highest levels of STEM *or Science, Technology, Engineering, and Math.* Unable to contain herself, Dr. Feinberg reentered the tête-à-tête. "Well, there are a number of things that can't be scientifically proven that we are still rational to believe."

"Like?"

Dr. Starr tagged up. "Like whether or not there are other minds, other than our own,"

"…and whether or not the past wasn't created five minutes ago with the appearance of age," Peggy continued with a wink. "I just read that—in the book you loaned me."

She's smart, principled, and beautiful, Starr thought again. Peggy systematically destroyed Gus' arguments and connected the dots, as well as any scientific mind could.

"I also read that logic, math, and even science—can't strictly be proven by science," she said. "Because that would be circular reasoning."

That caused Dr. Kahn an imperceptible twitch. He filtered through a medley of facial contortions: alarm, shock, and surprise—but offered no response.

Starr looked at Kahn and punctuated their back-and-forth with, "But you'll have to read the book." He knew that their worldviews were at odds and that no amount of evidence would persuade him.

Dr. Starr maintained that a cumulative approach was the best plan—not just one argument. His philosophic education started in junior high and that had opened his mental aperture and entirely changed his way of thinking.

Now he asked intriguing questions and wrestled with the biggest philosophical questions associated with science, but he recalled, "My curiosity started in the backyard at the age of eight as I looked up at the expansive night sky, wondering: *Didn't someone make us too, and the stars?"*

His questions and curiosity continued into adulthood:

Why are we here?

Why is there something, rather than nothing?

How do we know anything?

They were deeply philosophical questions that had informed his worldview.

"I sure hope we can trust our brain," Dr. Starr said in a goading tone, targeted at Dr. Kahn. "If not, then we're all completely screwed."

CHAPTER THIRTY-FOUR

"Electric communication will never be a substitute for the face of someone who with their soul encourages another person to be brave and true." ~ *Charles Dickens*

HELLO—IS ANYBODY IN THERE?

THE PSYCHONIX SYSTEMS were in place—but no one really knew the full extent of its capabilities. Theoretically they knew quite a lot, but not much had actually been done with it. Many of the computer models had been run and forecasted nearly every imaginable outcome.

"Can you strengthen the PSYCHONIX signal?" Dr. Feinberg asked.

"Yes, we believe tweaking amplification up is a relatively simple process," Dr. Lui assured her. "We're operating it now, at its lowest level."

"What about hearing the signals more clearly—and in real time?" Dr. Starr asked.

"It's nearly in real time," Sabrina chimed. "As you know sir—in the past, it took our normal NASA signals more than 19 hours to reach Voyager, which is approximately 13 billion miles from Earth. However, the finely-tuned PSYCHONIX *MDSL-1 or Multi-Dimensional Spatial Lattice* fibers have exponentially cut that speed—to within minutes."

"*Ahem!* I'm happy to announce that it's in *real time* now," Dr. Lui added as he quickly walked into the room and settled into his workstation. Brad followed close behind, because they were now in possession of new information, discovered within the last couple hours.

The state of incredulity in the room was palpable. No one could fathom minutes, much less immediate communication with a spacecraft—that far away. Dr. Lui nodded toward Brad, who pressed a digital playback button on the console to start a pre-recorded audio transmission. It was a responsive reading. Dr. Lui spoke the first seven words from Luke 2:14 and Brad delivered the final eight words: *Glory to God in the highest and—on earth peace to men of good will.*

"As of 10 o'clock this morning there have been *dramatic developments*," Brad said. "We spoke those words from separate locations and were able to hear and respond to the verse in real time."

"No delay?" Dr. Kahn asked.

"Imperceptible," Dr. Lui interjected. "The transmission was sent to Voyager 1, bounced to Voyager 2 , and was immediately recorded here in our lab."

"What kind of distance did that cover?" Dr. Feinberg asked.

"The space-probes are 13.7 billion and 10.5 billion miles from earth, respectively," Brad said, "and we communicated to each other like we were talking on a cellphone with full bars."

"Yeah—I'd call that a *dramatic development*," Dr. Starr said excitedly.

"What we're doing now makes our current communication with the Deep *Space Network* parabolic dish, high-gain antenna, look like the *Pony Express*," Todd Lopez said in his embellished nerdy way.

"Something that *was* in the realm of impossible," Sabrina said.

"Yes, it was considered utterly impossible in the same way that we used to think about heavier-than-air flight, the sound barrier being broken, manned space flight, landing on Mars, and harnessing nuclear energy." Brad got a room full of expressive head nods.

His point was well taken by everyone but Dr. Kahn, who had already tuned out. He was fully distracted by something he had to do in the next room and stopped listening when they quoted the Bible verse. Already with his back turned, he slipped into the adjacent office, as clandestinely as possible to retrieve his cellphone. He returned within seconds and furtively glanced around the room—before he secretively handed Dr. Lui his phone as well.

"We've done it," Dr. Starr said. "Thanks to the smart ITL work—daily seeking, discovering, and exploiting the impossible."

"It was a happy accident," Brad said. "I initially stumbled upon this, late one evening, as Todd and I began to explore the possibilities of superluminal, faster-than-light communication."

"Nonsense," Dr. Starr replied to startled looks. But Brad smiled broadly when he continued the thought. "Your so-called happy accident was an elemental part of your innovative genius young man. You're like a hiker who stumbled upon a jewel, as he journeyed up a mountain. I'm proud of the smart work you've pursued."

"We never dreamed, in a million years that our experimentations with *quantope-chrystal* effects would lead us to discover PSYCHON radiation," Todd said. "Oh, and—for the record— we were using the lowest settings. So, if there's something out there worth listening to—we'll hear it."

CHAPTER THIRTY-FIVE

"The shadows are as important as the light." ~ *Charlotte Bronte*

SHADOW PEOPLE

IT MENTALLY TAXED Steven Scott from the onset, but he stayed with it. Going to counseling was stressful for everyone, but Dr. Peggy Feinberg guided him and made it as easy as possible. His twisted expression was reflected in the large rectangular mirror, set into the front wall. He noticed and unmindfully brushed his fingers through his graying black hair. Unconsciously, he massaged his hairline and temples, as he thought about the most recent events and relayed the story of his ostensible PTSD induced hallucinations. He was taking the new med that Dr. Feinberg prescribed, but hadn't seen any benefits—quite the opposite.

"I'm hearing and seeing something!" he declared with a renewed sense of surprise. Saying it out loud didn't make him feel any better. He shook his head. *It seems so real!*

In her mind, Dr. Feinberg had loosely categorized Steven's latest hallucination about Marlina and the profane wall-hanging as a secondary delusion.

Maybe his meds need to be adjusted. Perhaps it's too low, she thought.

He was certainly stable enough to question and debate the reality of what he was experiencing, but the last time that they were together he told her about the so-called *invasion* at his home—by what he called *shadow people* and *flashes of images.* Whoever or whatever, it was had apparently exchanged a framed inspirational quote hanging above his bed for a string of vile, tasteless graffiti and then changed it back. It upset him and greatly alarmed Marlina, when he finally told her about it. Steven had already been diagnosed with PTSD, so it wasn't a stretch to think that he might hallucinate in that way. Still it was so vivid in his mind. *It was there, but it just as suddenly disappeared. I swear!*

He steadfastly panned the room with his good left eye and sighed a deep, slow breath. He felt an increased, unanticipated anxiety overtake him. There was a shortness of breath that, in the end, left him terrifically nervous—to the point that he couldn't breathe in deeply enough.

"I think they're here," he said again.

"Who's here?" Dr. Feinberg asked,

Steven Scott scanned the room—fixated on the mirror. "I don't know—I hear them—the shadow people I guess."

Dr. Feinberg acknowledged his beliefs without being patronizing.

"Yes, of course—we'll talk more about that Steven, but first let's relax," she recommended. "And take things a bit slower." She wanted to reassure and comfort him but, of course, she had no idea how Steven's psychotic episodes would present themselves.

She thought to herself: *PTSD can cause this.* "I want you to take your time and try to relax your breathing." She handed him a bottle of water and they sat quietly for a few moments. That seemed to settle him down—at least enough to resume their talk. She knew from having treated these types of symptoms that it could be brought on by something as simple as anxiety or dehydration.

"It sounds crazy—I know, but sometimes I scream at the images—to go away!" he said.

"I see."

"But it hasn't helped."

To Steven it was like he was being taunted and poked, but there was nothing to fight back against.

"Can you control it at all, Steven?" she asked.

"Control?" he deadpanned like it was the most vacuous question that he had ever heard.

"Yes, perhaps by singing happy birthday or merely counting to ten. You see—we've found that if you can control *the haunting voices* by doing that, then it would show that you have some control over when you hear them. And since it's your mind—maybe you could simply force them to leave."

"I'll try anything," he said. "It's all so—mind-blowing." He paused. "But come to think of it, when I read, talk, exercise, or even when I'm listening to music it goes away for a while—for weeks." He paused to consider it. "But, other than that—I guess there's not a lot I can do about it," he said. He expressed distress and annoyance at his apparent lack of control. "It can be overwhelming."

Dr. Feinberg nodded. "I could offer you some insight or perhaps a brief explanation of what we know about psychosis or the things you're experiencing, if you don't mind."

"Okay."

"The *neurology* behind the voices is what we call it." She explained to him that there were some successful treatments, if it didn't subside on its own. "We also have a variety of other antipsychotic medications we could try at some point."

Just then a rash of fear spread across Steven's face and his eye shot to the right. "Did you see that?" he said softly, interrupting Dr. Feinberg's scientific explanation. He slowly panned the room with his good left eye rapidly blinking.

His eye then cut sharply to the left and darted back-and-forth, as though he had spotted something moving, something that was invisible to everyone else in the room.

"It's there." He pointed and whispered confidentially to Feinberg. "Why am I—seeing this crap?" He started to slightly hyperventilate.

Dr. Feinberg knew that it was critical for her to help him navigate through his thoughts and feelings.

"Try to focus on me and what we're talking about," she said supportively. Dr. Feinberg believed that if she continued to talk and used the cognitive approach of explaining and teaching, it might help him cope. But it didn't seem to work. Steven covered his ears and started singing *Happy Birthday*. He raised the volume of his voice to cover the sounds he was hearing.

"*Happy birthday to you. Happy Birthday to you. Happy*—." But it didn't stop. His singing was out of tune and it made the song seem a bit eerie sung this way.

Dr. Feinberg cut-in and spoke as he sang and hummed. "You may be having what we call: *overlapping voice-thoughts*," she said. "Granted, some dysfunctional voice-thoughts, but never-the-less internal communication generated from your brain. We all have them, but we don't all hear them like you do."

"Right," he said staring straight ahead. He didn't attempt to make eye contact with Dr. Feinberg—still fixated on the mirror.

"Did singing help?" Dr. Feinberg asked.

"No."

"Steven—we all have thoughts that aren't true. Things that we know and assess as being right, wrong, good or bad. They're part of a vast number of things that we process every day. We do it in the act of *assessing possibilities* and deciding what to do or what to believe. The various possibilities that we filter through in our mind are called *counterfactuals*. All the things that could or would happen, depending on the choices made. It helps us in our decision making."

He was doing his best to focus. "For example?"

"For instance, if I don't stop my car at the red light, then perhaps I would hit that baby stroller in the crosswalk and injure the baby. If I do stop, then it would be safe. I process and know both thoughts, almost simultaneously, as I decide on what to do. Those thoughts signal to us what our choices are and what the consequences *could be* or *might be*—not what they *will* be. Those *could be* and *might be* voices and images are always in your head too. That's what you're hearing, but you can still make a choice."

He nodded. "Well—this may sound strange, but I see two shadows and could swear that I just heard something in *Ch*-Chinese." He stuttered the last word and began singing again.

"Yes, but first remember what I said—Steven." She interrupted and repeated his name often to redirect and hold his attention. Steven—remember that *you're in control*." She accidentally startled him with a compassionate touch on the forearm and caused him to reflexively wrench his hand away, with a light yank. She apologized.

Steven stared straight ahead and felt like his choices were limited. In a state of despair, he glanced over and wearily shook his head. "You don't understand doc—it's like there's a war going on in my brain—and I'm not sure how to choose sides."

He was reacting to the emotional and physical tension and began to reel from the mental demands being placed on him. His anxiety mounted. Dr. Feinberg recognized it and knew that short bursts of stress were useful in helping one avoid danger, but this wasn't normal. It dragged on way too long, even for her own comfort level.

She made every attempt to calm and parse Steven's vivid stream of jumbled thoughts. "Most of us have an internal switch that allows us to consider our possibilities and the consequences of our actions," she said. "It's what helps us to make good, rational decisions." She stopped talking and measured her words more cautiously. "The point is, if we do have improper thoughts, we can gauge them against what we know to be true—like everything Marlina has done to demonstrate her love to you. You know that's true."

He slowly turned his head back toward Peggy when she said that and nodded. It was another breakthrough moment. "Yes, I know Marlina loves me."

"Many of the things you're hearing—the *voices*—are likely pieces of information buried deep inside your memory—so, that when your brain's speech, hearing, and memory centers hold an unscheduled meeting, you get to hear it all," she explained. It was an oversimplified explanation of hallucinations but got the message across.

Steven Scott was fully and deeply engrossed in his disorganized thoughts with incertitude at the core of his current situation. He hadn't heard a word that Peggy said.

"Are you with me Steven?" she prodded.

"What?"

"Did you understand my explanation?" she asked to his glassy-eyed, unwinking stare.

"Uh-huh, what?" he said again, in a disinterested, unmoving trance. His right cheek flinched apprehensively. He was visibly upset and barely able to utter, "Something moved—in the mirror!"

Dr. Feinberg stood up and looked closer. It was evident. Something had indeed moved.

CHAPTER THIRTY-SIX

"Knowing is speculation distilled into certainty."
~ *Callum Bradbury*

MORE THAN MEETS THE EYE

TONIGHT, PSYCHONIX BETA-TESTING was underway. It allowed the engineering staff to more fully test-drive the virtual reality goggles needed for the inscrutable task of mind-to-mind communication. It was a noble scientific pursuit. Though not much was said, they were excited about the potential for metaphysical observations. If nothing else, there was plenty of talk about it as the technicians challenged each through competitive and cooperative video games, using their wireless headsets.

"If they don't find someone for the implant, then I'll volunteer. How bad could it be? The processor is no thicker than a grain of rice," Todd Lopez said. He slipped the stretchy black strap up and snugly over his head and then positioned the darkened mask across his eyes. "What have I got to lose?"

"Sure, it's all fun and games until someone pokes an eye out," Sabrina teased since she was the first one to suggest using a blind person or someone with a missing eye, and going through the eye socket to insert the *MDSL-1*.

"I'm not kidding—I'd like to volunteer for it," Todd said.

Sabrina Killian didn't care who did it. She slipped her visor down over her eyes too. "Ready to begin, sir! You know—I've always believed," she said with dramatic flair, "that our eyes are the window to the soul!" She adjusted the goggle straps and settled in for the first real person-to-person test. "Let's find out."

"Right." Kahn exclaimed with his typical eye-roll.

Brad Manuszewski sat down, turned toward the master control board and keyed in the commands. "Your PSYCHON radiation code was received and calibrated to the *MDSL-1* processor—*Holt* readings are strong," he said. "You're linked and cleared to interface with the computer or other available users."

There were only two users in the room, but it sounded impressive to say it that way. The computer whirred a low hum with a digital display of computer lights that danced to the laboratory processors. Brad adjusted the monitor's on-screen displays. It illuminated the nearly endless variety of patterns exhibited.

"Hey, maybe it's picking up our souls," Sabrina said as she peered hopefully at the kaleidoscopic bursts of PSYCHON radiation patterns, all displayed in a holographic frame in the top left corner of her visor. "Wouldn't that just be the coolest?"

At 24, she was the youngest and most exuberant member of the team. Although, even the most serious-minded members of the staff enjoyed her vibrant, if not childlike, enthusiasm.

"All systems go," Brad said with a strong thumbs-up. They were ready to begin the process of communicating their thoughts to each other telepathically. And that's exactly what they did for more than three-hours. The technicians coordinated their moves and were also able to interface with the computer controls using the highly adapted goggles.

Todd Lopez was a slightly chubby, narcissistic, and extroverted intellectual. You usually knew what he was thinking, because it flowed, unfiltered from his mouth. A bit of an unusual personality type—in the scientific community, but not a stretch. Sabrina was a Mensa-smart gal and quite attractive—but she didn't know it. It was disguised by her studious black-rimmed glasses, baggy clothes, and hair pulled back in a tight classic bun. However, she liked Todd—and it had become more and more obvious in her flirtatious words and mannerisms. Tonight, however, no words were needed. No words had even been spoken—when Todd's face turned a bright red—and even redder when she called him out for staring at her legs. The whole team heard it as it was piped into the monitors. At some subconscious level he must have wanted her to know what he was thinking and granted assent.

"Now, now, eyes up here young man!" she said telepathically via the PSYCHONIX processor. Embarrassed, he pushed the goggles off and apologized. Sabrina smiled and waved him off with a *don't worry about it* gesture. It was an interesting aspect of the study, because no one knew where the psychological boundaries were for mental assent.

"This is going to take us some time," Dr. Lui said to Starr, Kahn, and Feinberg. "So, if there are no further questions—we'll get tonight's testing underway." He sat down with the other engineers and began monitoring the alpha-test, ensuring that systems functioned correctly.

"Dr. Kahn, if you would be so kind as to hand me my cell phone from the table, I would be grateful," Dr. Lui said.

"No problem," Dr. Kahn said. He handed him his phone and then plugged his own into the table charger. It was a subtle covert dance. "I'll leave mine here to charge tonight, if you don't mind."

Dr. Lui nodded. He would be in the lab for a while to monitor the tests and file the nightly briefing. The next day he would update Dr. Starr and the rest of the ITL team during their morning staff meeting. It was the best forum to address the newest discoveries, innovations, and problems.

The overnight testing was rigorous, but it seemed more like a fun-sleepover than a test to the young scientists who conducted it. Two of them took a go at using the PSYCHONIX goggles, while the other ran the board and then they switched up.

"Is the popcorn ready?" Sabrina asked later that evening, during a short bathroom break.

"Nearly," Lopez said. He stood by the monitors, steps from the microwave.

Brad returned to the lab and tossed a handful of candy bars at them and pronounced, "In the name of science, I'm going to test these goggles with the new VR programming we modified for *Elder Scrolls Online*." *ESO* was a Massively Multiplayer Online Role-playing Game (MMORPG). For it to work, ITL would immediately need the gaming rights to their PSYCHONIX modifications, but they didn't have that much power or money or influence. In the interest of time it would require the full backing of the U.S. Government to secure all the necessary legal rights through Bethesda Softworks, Bethesda Game Studios, and Zenimax.

He and Sabrina met up online and spent nearly two more hours using their minds to navigate quests, random events, and freely explore the continent of *Tamriel*; two millennia before the events of *Elder Scrolls V*. They were amazed with the system's ability to manipulate the game and track each other's thoughts.

Success.

"We did all that with our minds!" Brad said to the prerecorded applause that he played after having reached *Level Five*. He and Sabrina held up their arms and high-fived their accomplishment. Not just for winning the game but having mentally coordinated movements so well.

They reeled from the experience and the unexpected awe of a well-regulated, telepathic communication. "It was as though our minds intermingled within the game," Sabrina exclaimed.

Brad nodded his agreement.

"Right," Brad said, "our collaborative response time was way accelerated."

"Imagine what that could do for our military."

He nodded, knowing that was likely the reason for the Department of Defense's interest in the project.

Time passed quickly while they tested and played. No one had eaten or had anything to drink for a long while. Todd, who was a diabetic, let it slip up on him and completely forgot to take his insulin. When his hands started to shake again, he called for a break. He had already ignored the early signs of feeling tired, weak, and shaky for far too long.

CHAPTER THIRTY-SEVEN

"I'm not upset that you lied to me, I'm upset that from now on I can't believe you."
~ *Friedrich Nietzsche*

COMMITTED

IT TURNS OUT that most of us are adept at lying, when we feel that we must, or when we're put on the spot. Most of us choose not to—or do it so innocently that it doesn't morally faze us. However, society was strewn with crafty, pathological liars that practiced deceiving. It was easy for them. A little turn of phrase, bending of the truth, and spinning of the facts—sometimes influenced and guided by pride, shame, stress, bias, misunderstanding, misremembering, greed, drugs, or perhaps a delusion, or interwoven combination.

Ashlynn had committed to her lie, but for her it didn't require a tremendous effort. In her mind it was the truth, so she believed it—unfortunately, it was really a delusion.

I'm sad today and it would make me very, very happy if you would call me mommy! She told the three children that she had kidnapped them.

Her delusions were predictably triggered by her addictions, genetics, and an overwhelming desire to be a mother. Her grandmother had severe mental health issues that no one ever spoke of, except to say that she was an *odd bird*. The family talked about her, but no one did an intervention or sought treatment for her. Ashlynn fit the bill; she was an *odd bird*. Not only was she depressed and her life a complete mess, but now her muddled mind had unraveled nearly beyond control.

The Annapolis Police Department dealt with lies and liars and crazy people every day. They didn't have the time or money to parse out truths, lies, and delusions. If you broke the law, then they had to intervene and there were usually consequences. It was as simple as that—mental health counseling, public service, fines, and sometimes jail.

Their days encompassed facts, behaviors, and safety issues. In the case of a domestic disturbance, they were more concerned with whether or not anyone had been or was about to be threatened or harmed.

When there was a potential for harm, it was called to the attention of the police. It could become a crisis situation and the police were trained for it. They used their *L.I.E.E.* model: Locate, Isolate, Evacuate, and Eliminate. This was ironically a *noble lie* that helped them enforce social harmony, when necessary. It was ingrained in them from day one, since quite often they only had a split second to make the right decision. You didn't want someone on the force to freeze up, when an immediate response was required. So, they quickly assessed the offender, medical problems, conditions, and possibilities. They thought: *what are the next best steps if the conflict escalates or violence continues?*

First impressions and cooperation were a big deal to law enforcement officers. Everyone's safety was at stake, and they were committed to keeping everyone safe, including themselves. The officers usually started with a peaceful, preliminary chat. They looked for unusual signs. They noticed, telling, body language. Was the person nervous, sweating, scared, bragging, confident, and half-way intelligent, or were there other behavioral clues of concern?

They asked common-sense questions like: *what seems to be the problem?* They let the person speak, as they listened for facts and inconsistencies. *Details matter.*

An abundance of details and using words like *honestly* and *frankly* and *to tell you the truth* too much, often belied the truth. It showed that the person had time to make up a story. One of the strategies the first responder used was to remain quiet and allow for guilty paranoia to set in. Maybe by having another officer whisper in your ear or by making the suspect wait, unnecessarily. It caused guilt to set in and mouths to open.

They asked firm, direct, detailed questions about where a subject may have been, possible involvement with drugs or alcohol, and hidden weapons. They were alert and on-guard, never knowing what could happen from one moment to the next.

Officers knew that a firm commanding presence kept everything on an even keel but were also well aware that things could escalate fast, and that they should react with a *proportional use of force*. This afternoon they would use the minimum necessary force to get the job done.

At 4:15 p.m. two patrol officers from the Annapolis Maryland Police Department arrived at 147th Main Street, after they were alerted to a *'lively' domestic squabble.* Sergeant Jose Ibarra and Corporal Joe Lacdon arrived with a high sense of urgency, parked on the street, and cautiously exited their Ford cruiser. They looked up and down the colonial street and toward the address numbers posted on two adjacent, black mailboxes to the left of the front door.

They moved in tandem. Sergeant Ibarra rang the street-level doorbell once and Corporal Lacdon simultaneously rapped three times on the outer edge of the blue wood-framed glass door. It was a clear glass door, so you could see up a narrow stairway that led to two small apartments, one above the other. They were over *Kokopelli's,* a travel boutique that sold clothing, jewelry, and accessories.

On the facade of the building there were eight colonial style, double-hung, multi-pane windows, and white shutters that faced Main Street. The vinyl roller shades were pulled halfway up. There were four windows on the second floor and four on the third floor of the old, remodeled structure. The windows provided effective ventilation, when it was built in the 1780's and still allowed in a cool harbor breeze in 2023, when left ajar.

A thirty-five year old white male heard the officers knock from the street. He unlocked and raised the right center window, leaned halfway out, and shouted loudly down to the street level below, "*Whatchuwant?!*"

"We want to talk to you," Sergeant Ibarra said firmly. Not in a mean or aggressive way, but in a commanding voice that meant business. His resolute presence was rarely ignored, and he wasn't intimidated by someone too uncouth, scared, or inebriated to speak with him face-to-face. He dealt with the rough-hewn part of humanity every day. The one-percenters. But he never allowed his confidence to outrun his competence.

His motto: *remain humble and compassionate and have a plan to subdue or kill everyone you meet.* "Come on down," he commanded, channeling his inner Danny Reagan from the television show Blue Bloods. Through the glass door the two police officers watched a pale and portly man—dressed in a dirty, sweat-stained t-shirt and corduroy pants, make his way down the steps. He held a green bottle of *Chesapeake Brewing BEAT ARMY Golden Lager* in one hand and a half-burned cigarette in the other. It was a local brew, being enjoyed in a Navy town. *No foul.*

The man was relaxed at his home in his stocking feet like a lot of guys do after work. You could see his misshapen, drooping pants, as he turned the bulk of his husky body side-ways, gripped both black iron handrails tightly and slowly descended the uneven steps. Every one of the squeaky wooden planks was a different height from the last in the old house, making it difficult to properly judge how high to lift his stocking feet. At times he stumbled forward where he expected it to stop or misjudged and kicked the lip of the next step. It took him longer than most to navigate the steep, wooden stairway, to the Main Street entrance below, but he arrived on *his* schedule.

"Do you mind putting the cigarette out, sir?" Corporal Lacdon asked.

He flicked it to the street and stared straight ahead with a past-tipsy, self-satisfied look on his face. You could smell the alcohol on him, strong. He was hammered, but since there was a disturbance reported, you still had to ask.

"Have you been drinking, sir?" Sgt. Ibarra asked rhetorically.

There was no doubt that he had been drinking. It would have been obvious to tourists that cruised the *Annapolis Bay Bridge*, six miles from the city dock. The displeasing crotch and underarm sweat and stink that oozed from his booze-ridden pores, totally gave him away.

He staggered slightly backward and swayed as he paced the narrow entrance of the landing. And then he leaned and steadied himself against the right side of the door frame. "Yeah—I've been drinking—it's Friday!" he exclaimed with a few saltier words sprinkled in. Like that meant something big and important in his universe.

Sergeant Ibarra looked at Corporal Lacdon with a raised eyebrow, to say *yep, this is gonna be fun.*

"Lemmegetchaboyzone!" slurred out as one word. He was still legally on his property with the beer, but too drunk to realize what a *clown-bone* he was acting like, and why his neighbors had reported him. It had been building up, over time.

Enough is enough—his neighbors thought. No one wanted to hear his television playing at full volume and the poetic obscenities, randomly screamed at his friends and family when he didn't get what he wanted, or it wasn't fast enough, or if he simply felt disagreeable.

It was a routine Friday night for Ibarra and Lacdon. The knuckleheads were out again in full-force, along with the other nasty dregs of society they would have to encounter that evening—ignore, tolerate or threaten to lock up. Taking someone into custody wasn't their first choice, but they had a job to do.

"On the weekend I always do a *brewski,*" he spat, *"*or two or ten." His tone was playful and intentionally irreverent, and he made it known that he was annoyed by their visit.

"What's your name sir?" Corporal Lacdon asked.

"Ty."

"Ty what?"

"Tyrone Peterson." But again, it was a drunken mumbled word that came out as *Tyrn Pizzan.*

Again, no foul. No one faulted a man for unwinding at home with a beer. After duty, Sergeant Ibara and Corporal Lacdon occasionally threw one back at *Heroes Pub*, a local firehouse-themed pub that featured draft beers, burgers & live music every night. The problem was that this drunken fool wasn't aware of a kidnapping that had taken place, right under his nose.

CHAPTER THIRTY-EIGHT

"Fear is your growth agent in disguise, only if you choose fight over flight.
It compels you to up your game to survive." ~ *Drishti Bablani*

FIGHT OR FLIGHT

SOMETHING HAD INDEED moved from behind the mirror. There could be no serious arguments about that. Dr. Feinberg hadn't seen it at first, but it was there. Something…or someone had in fact been speaking and stood up beside another shadowy figure in the mirror. That triggered Steven Scott's anxiety and a PTSD chain-reaction that completely immobilized him. He froze in place, like a statue, but in a hypervigilant state of mind. It was an oh-so-sudden and steep descent into a condition that precipitously turned for the worst.

"I suppose you're going to tell me this is a nightmare," Steven said, "and it's all in my head."

Dr. Feinberg began to wonder if she had prescribed the right medicine or even dose for him. He appeared distressed and presented in markedly unusual ways, with a waxy silent stare, broken by a random wince or two.

"No, but we'll get to the bottom of it," she answered.

She could tell that his extreme preoccupation with whatever happened in the mirror had paralyzed him. From the get-go, the second interview session had been riddled with stressful moments, and unfortunately it had just escalated. Peggy knew that it was mostly likely a chemical reason, related to his dopamine levels, but she hadn't seen any blood work yet. It would be a necessary piece of the puzzle. If information wasn't being transmitted correctly from one brain cell to another, it caused disruptions to important brain functions.

"You saw it too, didn't you?" he asked.

She nodded.

It had taken Dr. Feinberg a few moments to zero-in and finally figure out exactly what had happened—then she saw it too. It could likely explain his elevated PTSD symptoms of psychosis. There was a well-founded explanation for the movements in the mirror. The reason why his emotions surged and caused him to grow tenser and more fearful by the second. There were indeed two shadows faintly detectable behind the mirror, and one of them was retreating from view. She acknowledged it to herself with a slight nod. *He's not seeing things after all.*

"It's just a mirror," Dr. Feinberg explained. "A two-way mirror. There's another room behind that mirror, where we keep our video equipment—and where other counselors can sit—so, you don't have to see them. I know you don't like crowds," she improvised. But the fact that he had also *heard* something too, was a bit harder to explain. *Maybe he has great hearing.*

What she didn't know was that since his childhood, Steven had always had a mostly untapped sixth sense. It wasn't a strong sense and it didn't manifest itself often. In fact, the episodes were so few and far between that he actually never recognized it as an ability—and wrote it off as being intuitive. He certainly never thought of it as possessing a skill that others didn't have. Steven Scott was simply born with the gift and wrote it off as normal.

Her impromptu explanations were made in an effort to comfort Steven Scott and to be as transparent as possible. "One of our team members, Dr. Gus Kahn, is in the other room taking notes right now—he's assisting me. That's the way we do it at ITL, working in pairs." She held up a sheet of paper with a bio, including the other physician's photo and credentials:

Dr. Gus Kahn, M.A., M.D., Ph.D.
Associate Professor of Neurosurgery, Innovations Technology Laboratory
Associate Professor of Biomedical Engineering

Dr. Feinberg's explanation of events made sense, but it had already pulled the trigger on his anxiety. If she wasn't careful—that, combined with his new regimen of meds, was about to thrust him into a full relapse.

A message came in through her IFB earpiece. "—and, apparently Dr. Lui came in to talk to him a few moments ago. He is Chinese and had to walk into the hallway to take a personal call."

"Isn't that room soundproof?" Steven asked.

Dr. Feinberg nodded. It was a great point and she didn't have a good answer.

Due to his PTSD issues, Steven had undoubtedly hallucinated or had a nightmare about something at home, but it was undeniable that he heard men talking behind the mirror.

How? She thought.

No one knew how, but in future weeks and months, he would continue to experience increased sounds and sustained flashes of images. For now, though, Dr. Feinberg concluded that *Steven's PTSD triggered a cascade of psychological issues that he struggled to parse from reality.* In other words, he had thoughts that triggered a chain reaction or breakdown that nearly put him and the PSYCHONIX project in jeopardy.

The two-way mirror worked well if you sat still and observed from a certain distance. However, it was noticeably transparent if you got too close. When the people who were behind the glass moved around, it was detectable to Steven, a retired military intelligence Soldier who noticed everything.

For many, the two-way mirror was a familiar scene from every police show that they had ever seen. In those shows there was always a brightly lit room with a *perp* being questioned, and in an adjacent dark room there were two unshaven officers who watched with a cup of day-old coffee. It was just like that, except it wasn't. This was a well-lit psychological therapy session with another physician taking notes and being supercharged on a *Mean Bean Java Monster* energy drink. The hours were long, and it was needed.

"I don't like it!" Steven said. He glanced up and then quickly back down at the floor. "That's what they use!"

"What do you mean?" Dr. Feinberg asked. "*They* use the mirrors for what?"

"The shadows and flashes enter that way. They're the ones who changed the picture letters at my house, aren't they?" It was an anxiety-riddled moment of paranoia, so far *out of left field* that there was no making sense of it. She just listened with serious concern.

Pfff! Steven made that sound as he exhaled and struggled with the residual effects of severe anxiety—beginning to ride the early waves of psychosis. He hadn't experienced anything like this since his sleep deprived and morphine-induced hallucinations on the battlefield. And now it appeared that he was having conflated flashbacks of science-fiction television shows and being under attack. Singing *Happy Birthday* wouldn't make it go away.

"The intruders—are coming through the mirror to screw with me again. I know I can!" he shouted toward the mirror.

"You know you can—what Steven?"

"*Trust*—Marlina!" His head sharply turned and his eye darted toward Peggy. She couldn't afford to take any more chances and motioned quickly for Dr. Kahn to come to the room. In most other sessions she may have stopped, but this was being recorded for research.

"This is Dr. Kahn," She said calmly, "the person that I told you about. He and Dr. Lui were on the other side of the mirror."

Dr. Kahn nodded hello and took a seat against the wall.

Steven nodded and exhaled with another *Pfff,* like he was blowing pesky gnats away from his face. By all accounts his imagination, PTSD, and a new medicine had mingled his thoughts and caused him to mishear things. He exhaled again in short anxious breaths, while trying to communicate one-word-at-a-time, and then he suddenly whisked his left index finger up to his lips. A quiet sign for Dr. Feinberg to stop and listen. A short minute passed as he listened and abruptly stood up and paced and looked closely into the mirror.

He's mentally unraveling, she thought. *Not good.* His psychosis had been conjured-up and provoked by a load of stressors. His condition was further exacerbated by the belief that other beings had entered the room, through the mirror. Maybe he got the mirror idea from pieces of scenes in Alfred Hitchcock, Twilight Zone, or Star Trek programs. A flashback from childhood about mirrors and beings from other dimensions.

Aliens approaching...must take immediate action...do you read me? Over!

Dr. Feinberg never verbalized things like *it's just in your mind.* Of course, it was in your mind. Everything was in your mind. She understood that perceptions were usually a part of a person's reality—true or not. The mind had amazing imaginative and unifying powers.

Steven Scott's blue, panic-stricken eye was dilated with agonizing dread, as he slowly drifted deeper into his thoughts. He stared, mute, and immobile with his distraught mind precariously negotiating the thin line separating him from reality. *It was real to him.*

He thrust both of his white-knuckled hands, deep-down, between the arms of the chair and the cushion—and clutched the sides of the white leather seat cushion for dear life. Elbows locked.

Steven's pupil grew ever wider, which provided him the best possible vision for self-protection. It was nature's way of helping us identify the cause of our fear. It was that specific effect, his keen vision, and a *Leupold VX-5HD* rifle scope that contributed to his survival in Southwest Asia many years ago. Now he was simply trying to survive another therapy session.

Steven's eye worked rapidly again. He scanned the room, as his head twitched back-and-forth in a *seizure-like staccato.* To the right. To the center, left, and back. Back-and-forth. He had sudden strong emotions, on the outskirts of overwhelming, and he systematically gauged his situation. It was a skill he had learned well in the Army: *Define the battlefield environment, describe the battlefield's effects, evaluate the threat, and determine your courses of action.*

Dr. Feinberg pulled out all the stops. She tried to get Steven to open up, but he showed more and more signs of agitation. Instinctively she knew that they had taken this far enough. It was time to wind up their session. She meticulously sifted through the range of possibilities but wasn't ready for a diagnostic label beyond PTSD. Labels stuck and could stigmatize people with a stereotypical mark of disgrace. It could be a brand that affected one's relationships, interactions, and attitudes.

Dr. Feinberg looked for the obvious—the horses instead of the zebras. Not the exotic diagnosis, when a more commonplace explanation was likely. She reformed and re-asked questions and tried to identify the nature of his issues.

"So, Steven—," she said.

"Huh?" he responded in a flat, mechanical tone, as he stressfully rubbed his face with the palms of his hands. He then leaned forward and tightly gripped the arms of the chair.

"Before we wrap up are there any other problems that you can tell me about?" she asked, sensing that Steven had totally lost focus.

"No," he answered curtly. His fear and anxiety were steadily converging.

Why is she asking me all these personal questions? Even though he had requested the sessions, his unsubstantiated mistrust made him feel like she had burrowed too far into his mind. Steven Scott furtively glanced between Dr. Peggy Feinberg and the mirror. He scooted closer to the edge of his seat, and without warning—ran for it!

CHAPTER THIRTY-NINE

"Machines have limited, programmed creativity, programmed by a person.
Limited subjective judgement, programmed by a person, and craftsmanship limited to the
parameters, set by, you guessed it. A person." ~ *John Lennox*

PSYCHOMETRICS

"FIVE-BUCKS IS all you're worth—at least that's the value of your basic human elements," Dr. Kahn said as he led off the morning portion of ITL's local lecture series. The training was conducted by each member of the staff and was a vital part of their education, research, and recruitment program—as they searched for the best and the brightest.

The courses rotated around to various satellite campuses throughout the East Coast— including the NCR or National Capital Region, but today he was talking to interns at the Johns Hopkins Kennedy Krieger Institute in Baltimore. It was an institution dedicated to improving the lives of children and young adults with pediatric developmental disabilities and disorders of the brain, spinal cord and musculoskeletal system.

"99.9999999 percent of your body is empty space," Dr. Kahn said. "Sure, some days I know that you may feel like you're a pretty substantial person, but the reality is that you could be shrunk down and molded into the size of a sugar cube." Kahn's lecture involved slide after slide of what some would consider boring neuroimaging. So, he did his best to make his talks entertaining. "But consider this before you do it. Prior to being dehydrated and shrink-wrapped you could potentially fetch upwards of 45 million dollars in body parts—if you were sold separately at Walmart."

Since it was his primary area of expertise, Dr. Kahn's lecture addressed a wide variety of techniques to either directly or indirectly image the structure and functions of the brain. That's what made sense to him. He could see it. He could measure it. It was something material.

"Imaging the brain this way is a relatively new discipline within medicine and neuroscience-psychology," Dr. Kahn said. "This type of *functional imaging* allows us to see the workings of the brain being visualized directly by our computers. There are some people who will tell you that there's more to you than just brain functions—they're wrong—that's who you are!" he proclaimed and pointed with his red laser. He circled the colorful blobs on the screen with his pointer. These images were institutionalized cases that he had recorded from patients in *Unit-B*.

"See this area of the brain scan that's lit up—that is a *metabolism increase*. It will also light up as you're dying. When you're—no doubt—dreaming or having some type of near-death hallucination of immortality," he said matter-of-factly.

He had a substantial belief in the power of scientific knowledge and techniques, and also wasn't shy about sharing his *scientism*.

"The mythical idea of a soul is—unscientific. End of discussion. So, I really don't want to hear all the religious drivel—don't mention them in your papers," Dr. Kahn said. "At bottom, there is no ultimate meaning and purpose. As Dawkins says, 'DNA neither cares nor knows. DNA just is. And we dance to its music.' You make your own happiness in the time that you have—so enjoy yourself now. Science can or will eventually provide us an explanation for everything. We know that the universe rolled out of nothing, even though we don't know how, just yet. But give us time and we'll emerge from another cave of ignorance."

Nearly all of his lectures were humorous and devolved into forthright rants—today was no exception. "When someone talks to you about a god, an after-life, or living forever," he said, "you should rightly be skeptical. Personally, I think that Richard Dawkins got it right—they're delusional."

Dr. Mark Starr stood outside of Dr. Kahn's class, shaking his head. He always welcomed diverse opinions but couldn't help thinking—*the exact same could be said of Kahn's firm, fixed denial of God.*

CHAPTER FORTY

"Occasionally, amazing claims turn out to be true." ~ *Unknown*

A BARGAIN

"EVEN FOR A good con-artist, the going rate for immortality might be a bit difficult to negotiate," Dr. Gus Kahn said, as he continued the afternoon portion of his entertaining, if not biased, lecture series.

"Homer Simpson sold his soul to *Devil Flanders* for a one-dollar *Dunkin Donut,"* he said. "Jesus Christ, while on Earth, was offered all the kingdoms of the world. But he didn't sell—even though he was being offered nearly 80 trillion dollars, given the world's current GDP market value."

Dr. Kahn walked purposefully to his metal lectern and flipped on a second screen projector and continued to speak. Two cartoonish brain scans showed up on the large auditorium screen. "If we imaged Homer Simpson's brains and mine, then the same areas of the brain would light up, of course—but as you can see here," he pointed again with his laser pointer. "In Homer's brain there's an image of a toy monkey with a stupid grin, chattering, jumping up and down, and banging two cymbals together—that's what they call the rhythm of life." A few laughed to themselves and waited for the testable material to drop.

"We know relatively little about our *neuron-dense* brains, so in that sense it's safe to say that we're all a little *dense*," he chuckled to himself. "But we use every single bit of our tiny brains to discover what is scientifically verifiable. In the end, that's all that *matters*."

Privately, one of the interns muttered to another, "I doubt Kahn's sense of humor is scientifically verifiable," which caused an uncontrollable laugh that had them detained after class.

Dr. Kahn was a venerated physician and member of the ITL team. He sought the truth, even though his version of it would never allow for metaphysical ideas.

To him, *there is no ultimate meaning and purpose. You make your own happiness in the time you have.*

He was, as he would say, *a mostly moral man.* Also, a benevolent, if not feisty, mentor to all the resident interns. He made himself available to his students, morning, noon, and night. He advised, guided, consulted, counseled, and unfortunately recycled his torturous jokes. For him, a good joke never lost its savor. Every year during one of his initial lectures, he told a story about his cousin Sherman in Columbus, Ohio. Someone asked him how big his car engine was—wanting to know the horsepower—of course. He laughed and said, "*Pretty big, I guess…it takes up the whole area.*"

Each year he paused, almost always to imperceptible laughter and a smattering of painful groans. This particular time, two male residents in the back row started to slowly but steadily clap out of sync. It was meant to be a sarcastic way of telling him he wasn't all that funny. However, he just bowed and grinned, all the more, at his captive audience.

"*Ahem*, okay—so, that's what it's like with our brain," he continued, oblivious to ridicule, jeering, or mockery. "We don't know a lot about it, but it takes up the whole brain compartment in your skull, if you will. The truth is that we've barely scratched the surface in psychology—maybe 10 percent." At the very least, he made memorable points in his lectures.

"My final point is that we can capture what's happening in the brain with psychometrics. It is a field of its own, which uses samples of behavior in order to assess cognitive and emotional functioning. It measures your brain activity." He flipped off the projector and in his poetically grumpy style said, "That's all we have. That's all there is—class dismissed."

CHAPTER FORTY-ONE

"…you cannot outrun insanity, anymore that you can outrun your own shadow." *~Alyssa Reyans*

RUN

STEVEN SCOTT LAUNCHED from his comfortable white leather counseling chair, like a rocket from Cape Canaveral. He egressed up and out, running and colliding with the therapy room door as briskly as his size-fourteen brown steel-toe *Duluth* work boots could carry him. He made it out of the room before Dr. Feinberg and Dr. Kahn registered what had happened. It was unexpected because he was there voluntarily. He wasn't considered a *flight risk,* or in danger of running—but he did. He ran as fast as his feet could carry him.

Steven Scott streaked thirty yards toward the hospital entrance in no more than five seconds flat. Not accelerating with the super-speed of Barry Allen or challenging Mickey Mantle's 1952, home-to-first, blistering 3.1 seconds record, but at a good clip nonetheless. Especially if you considered that he had just hurled himself through the counseling room door, two swinging metal doors at the end of the hallway, shoulder-blocked an intern, and successfully frightened a room full of mental health patients waiting in the lobby.

He ran with one hand out in front of him, his elbow stiff, and his head down like a football player trying to gain extra yardage. He threaded himself down the hallway with a fixed, vacant, yet resolute stare in his eye and stiff-arming the hospital's side door exit with a thud.

He escaped, unhinging everything and everyone in his path. Escaping, although technically never a captive. Trivial details for one being chased by PTSD memories.

As he raced out the door, he bounded over and down eleven perilous concrete steps. He missed every step on his flight to the bottom and landed with a harrowing painful groan. If he had any delusions about his ability to fly, it was immediately and stubbornly resolved by gravity and the impending pursuit of the security and mental health staff.

Steven Scott fumbled for his balance and tumbled into and over the evergreen *Japanese Boxwood* hedge that lined the ornate walkway and led from the road to the side entrance. As he struggled to remain upright and steady, he shuffled, limped, and strained against his one good leg, unable to maneuver as quickly as before.

The sudden impact at the bottom of the stairs had slowed his terror-stricken attempt to flee and given one heroic security guard a negligible opportunity for a diving tackle.

Textbook: stay low, lift as you hit, break momentum, and wrap up the knees. Oof!

Steven Scott resisted with fierce determination. He flailed anxiously as the security guard grappled and maneuvered his tight grip around his knees, up his legs, and tightly against his torso. Legs spread wide in a V, which helped him maintain balance. He shielded his arms with the broadside of his body. It was no small matter—given Steven's strength and military training.

He was joined by a second security guard who leveraged a *Judo* chokehold, meant to cause *syncope* or temporary loss of consciousness. It was non-lethal in under a minute. He firmly pulled one side of Steven's black t-shirt collar across his throat and constricted the air flow. Just enough to slow him and distract him while a nurse injected him with a lorazepam and haloperidol combo with *no fries*. The first-line treatment for this type of acute agitation.

He was immediately restrained and hauled off and put in isolation. Sharp objects were taken, along with his shoelaces and belt. The only thing that wasn't removed was a glowing ember of dignity that remained and would eventually guide him back to sanity. His first night stay at a psychiatric hospital was nothing like he had expected. If he had ever expected anything—it wouldn't have been like this.

Face-down, immobile, and alone.

Face-down to keep him from swallowing his tongue, or throwing-up and drowning on his own vomit if he got sick. But he didn't throw-up and the meds immediately took effect. He felt much better and calmer now and his thoughts were clearing up, at least enough to rationally consider his situation.

Am I really crazy?

He wasn't crazy, but—right now it felt like he was stuck in a hellish *8' x 12'* prison. He would later see the place as a sanctuary for the broken, the bruised, and for those mending.

The unsettling events of the night seemed to drag on forever in the mental health unit. Steven was afraid that he would never get out, and Marlina was fearful of what she might find when she finally saw him. She had unfortunately witnessed his apprehension from the front lobby, where she had been waiting and reading a slightly tattered *People* magazine. Like anyone in love, she was terribly shaken. But instinctively—almost in a trance-like state—she trailed behind the medical response team. There were plenty of seats, but she couldn't sit down. Marlina restlessly paced the *14 x 20* waiting room of the ward, until Mark returned to update her.

Her brother-in-law gave her a firm, compassionate hug and held both of her hands as he spoke. "He'll be fine. We just want to watch him a while," he said. Of course, he didn't know for sure that he would be alright. It would depend on a host of things. "You would do well to grab a bite to eat and go get some rest." She nodded, but there was little chance of that happening. They were kind, instructive words meant to console, but she wasn't going anywhere until she saw Steven with her own eyes and knew that he was doing okay.

The rest of the family wouldn't learn about tonight's dispiriting events. Not yet—not tomorrow—maybe never. It was too early now, and she needed to process it all, as best as humanly possible. This type of thing had never happened in their family before—and it was on the far side of frightening and disturbing. Her immediate concern—she insisted—was seeing Steven. So, Mark led her past a broad-chested security guard, through a keypad access door, and down another narrow hallway with six small isolated rooms. He pointed toward a seclusion room and a vertical window slit.

"He's in there—but you're not going to like what you see."

Steven was secluded in an observation room and being monitored to protect everyone's physical safety. Securing psychiatric patients could be challenging but ITL didn't throw people into windowless rooms or rooms with jail-like bars on the windows. They tried to create a safe, caring, home-like atmosphere with durable psychiatric windows that provided natural light and unrestricted views through the doors and to the outside—but, still able to withstand high impacts and frustrate escape attempts. Currently, there were other things besides the room that were closing in on Steven.

His shoulders, waist, arms and legs were bound securely with the wide cloth belts of a *Pinel* restraint.

Marlina covered her mouth and cried.

CHAPTER FORTY-TWO

"Placebos are like the lollipop of optimism, but we can do much better by dealing directly with the mind...and it works!" ~*Matthieu Ricard*

PLACEBO

TO SOME EXTENT your brain is easy to control, if you aren't under the influence of clever marketing, or persuasion tricks, drugs, hypnosis or an outright lie. However, lying happens all the time in the name of science. But it goes by a much friendlier name—the *Placebo Effect.* Basically, someone is given a harmless pill, medicine, or procedure prescribed more for the psychological benefit to the patient, than for any physiological affect—or how it would affect the body.

The ITL test being conducted tonight entailed monitoring the effects of consciousness and/or the brain. It was critical, because they were still scientifically undecided as to whether the mind was a function of the brain or a soul limited by the brain. They were hopeful that tonight's testing would provide another piece to the *Mind-Body Problem* puzzle. Sabrina Killian and Brad Manuszewski shared briefing duties as the evening's experiment began.

"The experimental assessments are being conducted with two separate volunteer groups," Sabrina said. "A and B."

"They will all have EEG caps placed on their heads," Brad said, "that will use electrodes to analyze their brainwaves while they sleep—but here's the catch."

Sabrina interrupted him to finish her explanation. "*Control Group A* will be told that they got a full eight hours of rest. *The secondary Group B* will be told they only got four-hours of rest."

"When in reality—each of the groups got approximately eight hours of sleep," Brad punctuated, as an important detail in his explanation.

"Won't the ranges of sleep time and REM differ with each person?" Dr. Feinberg asked.

"Yes, but that's why we have *five* people in each group. We will also use other smoothing factors to control fluctuating input. It's complicated, but we've accounted for as many variations as possible," Brad said.

"We've ensured that they are all of similar age and health—and are asked to follow a specific, week-long regiment of diet and exercise," Sabrina informed them.

Dr. Starr nodded that he was impressed, "Ah, okay, that makes sense."

Most of the testing data needed would be collected by the ITL engineers monitoring overnight, and would be shared with Starr, Feinberg, and Kahn, the next morning. The crew had everything under control, so with that they thanked the volunteers and headed home.

Each of the two test groups were then fully briefed on the importance of adequate rest and that they would each be tested the next morning. They acknowledged the instructions and understood that everyone needed to have at least a couple hours of REM sleep, *Rapid Eye Movement,* to successfully complete their sleep test. Then they were all led down an adjacent corridor—to specially assigned, windowless rooms. That was an important factor. Neither group had access to any visual time references: no clocks, no watches, and no communication with each other. Their only contact was an attendant who would hook them up, wake them up, and tell them exactly how much rest they had received.

After each group slept approximately eight hours, a technician returned to awaken them and remove their sensors:

Control Group A, you got eight hours of sleep.

Secondary Group B, you got four hours of sleep.

Immediately, each person was escorted to separate classrooms, seated, and administered virtually identical cognitive tests—written, visual, and responsive. It tested their ability to make choices and the time it took for them to decide an issue.

Control Group A, as expected, performed notably better. They rightly believed that they had a complete *eight hours* of rest. *Group B* was told that they only got *four-hours* of sleep, when they actually got a full *eight hours.* The same as the control group. There was a negligible difference in the amount of rest each group received.

Notably, however, *Group B* was sluggish and apathetic. They strained to keep their eyes open and missed twenty percent more of the questions asked on the test. They had the same amount of rest, but performed poorer on the exam, ostensibly because they hadn't been given sufficient time to rest.

In the final analysis, the *Placebo Effect* test had provided valuable information concerning the power of the mind over the brain. It was as suspected but would only be part of their cognitive tests. Later they would perform a compelling hypnosis evaluation. That was of particular interest to Dr. Mark Starr.

For now, it seemed patently clear to Dr. Starr. "It's *mind over matter*," he concluded. He recalled a comical *placebo effect* from his own childhood. One that he had told before, but he loved to tell stories to new staff and interns.

"I remember back when our family lived in Walla Walla, Washington," he said. "My brother and I were so overheated and exhausted from racing our bikes around the neighborhood all day and building Army forts in the backyard—that we hadn't had enough to drink. Well—that day in particular our mom packed lunches—to help us rough it in the great outdoors of suburbia.

We ventured out with two small brown paper bags with our first names boldly scribbled on the outside in black marker. Each bag was packed with a thick peanut butter and jelly sandwich, potato chips, a *Snickers Bar*, and a can of *A & W Root Beer*—wrapped in a thin sheet of aluminum foil, scrunched at the ends to help keep it cold. Unfortunately for us, it was an extremely hot August day and by the time we ate, the sodas were no longer cold. In fact, they were quite hot and just barely drinkable," he said. He stuck out his tongue to mimic the disgust of drinking a hot can of soda-pop on a summer day.

"As the youngest—I was gullible and susceptible to older brother shenanigans. Mind you, I was barely eight-years old then," Mark said. He dramatically set the stage for his story. "Not exactly the worldly-wise eleven-year-old that my brother was, so of course I trusted him. And— long story short, it didn't take much convincing—for me to believe that a warm can of *A&W Root Beer* could make you drunk."

Everyone roared with laughter. They could see just how that may have played out in his young mind. As a child, Mark Starr had seen his mom, stepfather, and their friends get loaded at parties and remembered exactly how silly and mean people got after they drank too much alcohol.

"So—the more *A&W Root Beer* I drank—the sillier I got," Mark said with a mildly-inebriated expression on his face, "and the drunker I behaved. *Ha!* I had convinced myself that I was getting drunk, so my little tongue felt darted around and my speech began to slur. I felt totally wasted on warm root beer," he said, doing his best *Foster Brooks* impersonation.

"What did your mother do?" Sabrina asked.

"Oh, she didn't find out for many years—and Steven quickly swore me to secrecy," he said. "He also bribed me with comic books and cookies and candy—all well-known antidotes for juvenile hangovers."

The story never lost its humorous punch and he liked remembering Steven the way he was.

CHAPTER FORTY-THREE

"…but be transformed by the renewal of your mind, that by testing you may discern what is the will of God, what is good and acceptable and perfect." ~ Romans 12:2

MAKING SENSE OF IT ALL

MARK STARR FINISHED a short conversation and hung up his cellphone. "Dr. Kahn can't make it. He and Dr. Lui are taking a little longer than expected in their psych assessments—said he'll try to join us later."

Dr. Starr reviewed the various *Mind-Body Problem* tests with Dr. Feinberg and discussed the phenomenon of memory and conscious thought. It amazed him that we, as humans, could call up a memory from long ago and apply it to something that we were doing now. Peggy also caught Mark up on his brother's situation. It hadn't been easy on either of them.

The persistent counseling wasn't always easy for Dr. Feinberg, but she was experienced and knew that sometimes things went a little sideways. It was still mentally tough on her and she had to occasionally decompress and distance herself by taking a run. It helped void compassion burnout out or excessive stress. She too had to strike a balance of emotional care that didn't cause her to over-empathize. To further combat stressors, she also had a counselor. It had helped her to control her own emotional life, as well as that of other people. She took a long run today, but couldn't shake the last stressful session with Steven.

"There's nothing we can do right now Peggy. He's asleep, but we'll check on him soon."

236

She nodded and Mark changed the subject.

"I overheard Gus talking about Dr. Wilder Penfield's brain-mapping and experiments in one of his lectures," he said.

"Yeah?"

"But he left something out."

"What?"

"Dr. Wilder Penfield began his career as a materialist, convinced that the mind was wholly a product of the brain. But he finished his career as an emphatic dualist—and believed that there must be a scientific theory to account for the soul. That was the basis for his centrencephalic system, *the switchboard* in the brain. There, if anywhere, he believed spirit met flesh and the two were joined—and it was a lot more than the wishful thinking that some wish to attribute."

"Interesting," Peggy said. "Didn't he also do the *déjà vu* and memory recall experiments?"

"Yep—and he literally opened up the heads of living patients to pinpoint the source of a seizure and remove it."

"And in the process mapped how areas relate to sensations in the body."

"Right, and after hearing Gus speak it made me think about memory recall," Mark said. "And the incredible fact that I can recall something from thirty years ago—and my brain will find it."

"Hmm. It is quite miraculous."

"It caused me to consider our *Mind-Body Problem* research a lot more and made me wonder— where do we keep our memories? And how do we link and unify thoughts in our brain?"

"And then—what did you do after lunch?" Peggy teased.

He modestly shrugged.

In one of the ITL tests, Dr. Starr revisited an experiment by Dr. Wilder Penfield, one where he had attached an *electrode to the motor-cortex*. Just as in the Penfield experiment, he could amazingly trigger a person to do several things involuntarily.

"When it comes to brain function, I can cause someone to raise their arms, make sounds, and recall memories," he said to Peggy. "But you know what I can't do?" he asked rhetorically. She nodded with interest.

"I can't hypnotize and cause you to commit the *perfect murder* or involuntarily do something that you don't want to do. I know it's distasteful, but…I couldn't force you to fill a bathtub full of green paint, strip naked, submerge yourself in the tub and choke yourself to death, by swallowing your tongue." Mark noticed Peggy's stunned and unamused look of shock. It was priceless.

"That's disgusting."

He quickly apologized and continued. "It worked brilliantly in the Lee Child novel, but it's not that easy."

The *Penfield* experiments reconfirmed decades of old studies and revealed that the *mind is probably not in the brain chemistry* and couldn't be explained by it. Thus, the mind, as Wilder Penfield understood it, could be influenced by *matter* but wasn't generated by *matter.* However, he did believe that the mind and brain were somehow entangled—but how? That was the million-dollar-question for ITL.

What does it mean to entangle thoughts and memories in the brain?

What causes consciousness: electrons, neurons, chemicals, or something invisible, like a soul?

How does one measure a conscious thought, a belief, a desire or that thing you call—you?

There were no pat answers. As Dr. Starr reviewed slides from the study he spoke aloud—more to himself than to Dr. Feinberg. "The systems of our brain have been thoroughly mapped, so there is apparently no physical place in our brain that is responsible for *consciousness* or for unifying our perceptions of reality."

"You can't say here's where a thought resides," she added. "Much less a central place of unification."

"Right, a place that is responsible for weaving or entangling everything together that we experience—into a seamless thought or stream of reality—so that we can make sense of it all." He flashed up another slide on the lab screen that read: *The Visual Binding Problem.*

It seemed like that was an aspect of what ITL had tapped in to with PSYCHONIX. The thing that bound our thoughts together. PYCHONS or *the soul.* The largest part of the *problem* was that there was no known place in the brain where it combined the electrical impulses of information into one *unified perception* of reality.

"If there's no known place that exists, then how do we explain it?" she asked.

"I think it does exist—in our *mind*!" Dr. Starr declared. "I think that our mind is synonymous with what we call our soul and that it can manipulate a healthy brain through free will."

"Okay, that makes sense."

"Okay, think of it like this—we each make our own choices—choices apparently not predetermined or directed by our biochemistry, right? "

"Right."

"So, even though we are highly influenced by our memories and environment, we can still choose what we want to think about—unless of course our brain is defective. In that case it's just like driving a damaged car—so to speak."

"That's an apropos analogy," Dr. Feinberg said.

"Yes, I think it is. Consider this—if your body was a car, then your mind or soul would be the driver. So, no matter what your mind desired to do, it would be facilitated or impeded by the condition of the car."

"You're part of the same cognitive operation. So, if your brain misfires, would it *matter* what your soul desires?"

"Yes, of course."

"Then, you're saying that would lead us to believe the manipulation or influence over our brain comes from our soul."

"Yes, I think so. It's a truly cooperative and miraculous process," Dr. Starr replied. "In essence we're sculpting *our mind* through mental exercises. Of course, at times hampered or limited by drugs, aging, and/or disease."

"So, then—perhaps we're not exactly slaves to our genetics or brain chemistry," Dr. Feinberg deduced.

"That's a great point! It's common knowledge that our mind can influence healing and influence our behaviors—making us happy or sad or optimistic," Dr. Starr said. "Sometimes causing us to worry, which also triggers anxiety, causes ulcers, and raises or lowers our heart rate or blood pressure. The thing that intrigues me most—the thing I believe—is that it's not the brain that causes these events—because a machine can't worry. *It's the mind that matters*."

CHAPTER FORTY-FOUR

"Blindness separates us from things but deafness separates us from people." *~Helen Keller*

WHAT?

TYRONE PETERSON OR *Trip* as he was known by his friends, family, and workmates, was an obnoxious, mean drunk with a lot of glaring faults. It didn't help that he was also hard of hearing. His wife Ashlynn had absolutely no patience for it, and inevitably screamed at him at the top of her lungs.

In part, she screamed because she lost patience, but also because he was deaf in his left ear. It was due to the sharp end of a pencil that had penetrated and completely ruptured his eardrum as a child. It kept him from his early dream to serve in the U.S. Air Force when he turned eighteen. He still held in a lot of anger over missing out on that. He was still furious and bitter about not being accepted into the service, 17 years later.

You had to speak to him directly, clearly, and more loudly than you normally would when talking to a friend. And, for him to enjoy his television programs, the volume had to be maxed-out. Ashlynn often wore earplugs or made him wear headphones. Today, in his stubborn drunkenness, he arbitrarily decided that headphones wouldn't do. So, he turned up the TV volume—all the way.

Compound that with the fact that he could never quite regulate exactly how loud he was speaking, and it was the perfect storm. The sounds of a loud television and him trying to talk over it was maddening. Even friends said that they could hear him from a mile away. Since he couldn't hear you or himself—he was prone to rudely interrupt mid-sentence.

At first, that didn't set well with officers Ibarra and Lacdon.

First impressions.

He was loud, irreverent, dirty, drunk, and they were initially unaware of his hearing disability. However, Sergeant Ibarra stayed cool and mentally rehearsed his personal mantra:

Remain humble and compassionate and have a plan to kill everyone you meet. As an experienced cop, he wasn't sweating it.

Seasonal and sporadic work in Trip's economically depressed hometown of Hazard, Kentucky and a live-in girlfriend, had pressured him to move to Anne Arundel County, Maryland in 1995. He eventually married the girl, and soon found out that they couldn't have children. He didn't care and it wasn't the end of the world. He enjoyed his beer and his privacy.

So, when he came home, it agitated him that there were three children in his house. "Ashlynn! Why are these kids here?!" She told him a brief story about babysitting. He grunted, rushed off to the den, and never noticed that their mouths were taped shut. He settled into his recliner for the game and she brought him a TV dinner that she had just popped out of the microwave.

Ashlynn plopped it on his lap tray. "Here—you like meatloaf and there's some cinnamon apples for dessert!"

"What?!"

She didn't respond, as she headed back to the kitchen, opened her silverware drawer—and took out her fully loaded pistol.

CHAPTER FORTY-FIVE

"Those weeks before diagnosis can be among the most torturous times. There is a reason you're called a patient once the plastic bracelet goes on." ~ *David Rakoff*

SECURE

ONCE STEVEN SCOTT was admitted to an isolation room, in the ITL mental health unit, Marlina was provided with an array of information about the medical and legal processes. She felt completely overwhelmed, but it was good to know that he was in safe hands. Steven was being closely monitored and assessed for adequate levels of comprehension and the need for any further treatments and/or medications or adjustments that might be required, to stabilize his condition and minimize harm to himself.

Marlina visited Steven every day in the unit and placed a couple of his old Army awards around his room. It encouraged and reminded him of better times and obstacles that he had overcome. He was a hero but apparently fighting a different sort of war with PTSD—and no one got a medal for that.

He was undergoing a high-level medical review—and purely on an educated whim, Dr. Feinberg scheduled him for a PSYCHON radiation test with Brad. Earlier she noted his unusual awareness, and that he knew that she had missed an appointment. He couldn't have known that. She and Dr. Starr found it even more curious that he had overheard pieces of information, spoken in a soundproof room, behind a two-way mirror.

An investigation would eventually reveal all the facts, but it took a while to all come out. Notably, the fact that Dr. Kahn was going through a nasty divorce and privately told Dr. Lui *you can't trust the diva*. The stressful scenario of seeing and hearing things had certainly triggered Steven Scott's hypervigilant condition and caused him to run. But was spurred on by real events. They also learned that he had conflated *you can't trust the diva* with *you can't trust Marlina* and the mirrors that he imagined were merely parts of his dreams and flashbacks.

Prior to the volunteer project, Steven had signed-off on a long series of legal and medical documents. Like everyone else, he was considered a candidate with rights and choices, but that was before he showed signs of psychosis and made a run for it. Because of that, for the time being, Marlina would have to represent him and see to his personal needs. Although, for the next 96 hours, or four days, Steven had no visible choices. He had been strictly confined, during the same amount of time that it would take to make a coast-to-coast drive across America. That was if you took the southern route: started at the southern tip of Florida and headed toward the bottom corner of California, while busting through bayou country, on a Miami-to-San Diego trip.

Toward the end of his first day in isolation he was removed from the *Pinel* restraints and stood peering out his window—into the ITL courtyard. He was still a bit foggy headed from the valium that he had been given. If he had been on a trip across the country, then he would have been well on his way by now. But woefully—he wasn't going anywhere.

The mental health staff supervised and structured his day from breakfast, to therapy, to bedtime. They regularly saw these types of cases, conditions, and symptoms—which sometimes improved and sometimes escalated out of control. They saw it primarily through a clinical lens, although it could take its toll on them as well. Although they were professionals and knew how to cope.

The distraught Marlina—had aged about ten years in the last two days—and was completely terrified, when they body-tackled Steven in the courtyard and wheeled him through the front doors. She couldn't help but replay it over and over again in her mind. Watching her husband get strapped down and rolled away on a gurney isn't an everyday event, in her world.

Even though it was a standard procedure for those working in the mental health unit, the seasoned providers couldn't always spot a serious issue bubbling up. They didn't know everyone intimately enough to recognize a subtle problem. One person's *strange or unusual* behavior might be perfectly normal for someone else and visa-versa.

Normal is person dependent she was told by Dr. Feinberg. It will always vary and depend on the person being assessed. She knew Steven wasn't behaving as he normally did, even with his PTSD he had acted strangely at home. She knew—and it seemed like common sense—that families and friends were usually the first ones to witness odd behaviors. And she had. Certainly, her sense that he was *losing it*, qualified as an odd behavior, if that was indeed what was happening.

Earlier in his counseling sessions, you could see it unfold in Steven's body language, in the way he paced the room. You could see the look in his eye. He became more irritable, jumpy, and hypervigilant. Numerous times stress seemingly triggered his PTSD, which caused him to unravel with visual and auditory hallucinations. Light undetectable symptoms at first, and then full-bore. Yes, real things that he had experienced were being subconsciously conflated with his distrustful PTSD symptoms and caused him to hear and see things like the inspirational quote morphing and mishearing *You Can't Trust Marlina.* That was, by far, the worst thing that he had experienced since the war. Now, even though he could move about in the psychiatric unit lounge and kitchen area, it was still unfamiliar and confining. For once in his life he couldn't run.

Dr. Feinberg reexamined her sessions with Steven Scott and noted that he had suffered mild symptoms when he received pain medication for his battle wounds. And that through the years, he also suffered bouts of depression, anxiety, and problems with concentration—most likely the residual effects of sleep deprivation and the morphine highs he had experienced in uniform. He never told anyone, but he had also experienced hallucinations a couple times during a non-stop battle—one that lasted 114 hours straight in the Helmand Province. A lot of guys did. Things that had been buried long ago with his childhood memories—the good, the bad, and the ugly. But memories are a funny thing—just like shadows, they're with you even when you're not thinking about them. No one saw the onset of his mental health condition or dreamed that it had reared its psychotic head, but it did.

So now, Steven was being treated, as per their agreement, for the PSYCHONIX project. As he was being treated and tested, he once again recounted some of his wartime experiences with his counselor. It seemed to help him, and it provided Peggy with valuable insights.

"There isn't always a rhyme or reason to the problems in our human neurology," she told Steven Scott during their next session, this time in his room on Unit-B. "Things misfire in the brain, for one reason or another, or for no apparent reason at all."

He found it interesting that doctors called what he had *episodes,* like it was just another show in a television series, and that he would be starring in the next one.

"The *episodes* could have been brought on by a lot of things," Dr. Feinberg told Steven soon after he was able to resume regular counseling sessions.

"I'd call it *a terrifying and all-consuming psychotic rollercoaster.*"

246

"It's pretty scary, isn't it?" She asked.

He furrowed his brow and pursed his lips. "Yeah—it is." He knew that odd things were happening more often, but up until now he had maintained decent control and kept it mostly to himself. He wasn't the kind of man who liked to criticize, condemn, and complain about life's circumstances. To his inner John Wayne, it was a sign of weakness. At first, he reasoned: *it's not real—I can deal with it.* Until he couldn't.

Marlina prayed.

Treatment and testing were going well. Dr. Feinberg had zeroed-in on Steven's issues and knew that it was partially related to his PTSD. It was a problem, but a manageable one. The real matter at hand was an unusual ability slowly being discovered by ITL.

Steven was somehow prescient or clairvoyant or whatever you wanted to call it. He knew things and it seemed to be driven by his extremely high amounts of natural PSYCHON radiation. Fantastically, his childhood ability had slowly, but exponentially, increased after losing his right eye in battle and riding a few morphine highs. Now, with him being weaned off of unnecessary meds, it was becoming keenly acute.

Steven's childhood ability to sense things happening had evolved. He could hear the voices and images of others—and it wasn't a hallucination. More and more he could sense what happened to others, where they were, and what they were thinking or feeling. It was truly overwhelming to learn the news.

"I have a gift?"

He wasn't sure about whether the gift was a good thing or not, but he was certainly relieved that the voices and flashes of images were mostly true. *I have a gift?*

He certainly never thought of it as possessing a skill that others didn't have. However, his natural and apparently unrestricted PSYCHON ability was indeed a gift. Enough so that ITL immediately recruited and vetted him for their PSYCHONIX project. He thought that meant extra testing—and it did.

At first the ability was slow and gradual, but it was patently obvious that Steven Scott could communicate *mind-to-mind* without the PSYCHONIX *MDSL-1* processor. Brad started to jokingly refer to him as the Oracle. For now, Dr. Starr, Dr. Feinberg, and Brad Manuszewski were the only ones at ITL who knew about his incredible ability.

Mark shook his head. *I'll be darned. So that's how he knew things growing up and what allowed him to sense that I was hurt and communicate with me when we were being chased.*

It became clear that there was more to the *Mind-Body Problem* and consciousness than they had ever imagined. *God gave you a precious gift* is what his brother Mark told him. *You will need to use it responsibly.*

Steven and Marlina laughed—and cried.

CHAPTER FORTY-SIX

"The most incomprehensible thing about the world is that it is comprehensible."
~ Albert Einstein

TUNED-IN

ADVANCES IN ROBOTICS, neuroscience, and medicine over the past twenty years has paved the way for the development of bionic body parts that function much like natural parts of the body. Parts that provided sensory feedback like bionic ears and eyes do. Significant technical and quality of life developments that PSYCHONIX tapped into.

"We're developing a staggering range of bionic organs: everything from lungs, hearts, and kidneys, to pancreas—and astoundingly artificial *nanoblood,*" Todd Lopez said. "Who knows what we'll be capable of when that comes to fruition." He changed the subject quickly, as he was prone to do and continued with a knowing grin. "Did you know that we now have the ability to replace eighty-five percent of all human body parts with bionics, and AI may improve on that number soon?"

The research interests and breakthroughs had mainly revolved around how to integrate bionic parts with our nervous system, but it was a new age. Quantum computing techniques were now on the horizon and being innovated, tested, and adapted by ITL. Although currently a top secret project, history would record that they were the first to integrate the *MDSL-1* processor into the brain and a bionic eye.

"I never dreamed it possible," Todd said. "But Brad's a freakin' genius. He came up with the whole idea of linking and transmitting human thought through a cerebral CPU." It still blew their minds that they had something which could receive and transmit conscious and subconscious communication—measuring what had previously been unmeasurable.

Todd Lopez liked the attention that he was getting and happily explained and re-explained the PSYCHONIX *MDLS-1* processor to the team. "It's basically like a new kind of radio and television transmitter for the mind." He went so far as to create snazzy new graphics for the briefings. He pointed to a slide. "You simply isolate the frequency for your favorite station—in this particular case the human mind." He argued that these briefings would be great explainers pieces and archives for future research.

He described to everyone that in the 20th Century listeners had to use a round knob or dial to tune-in AM and FM radios. You had to tune-in limited signals that radiated from tall metal towers. Whether you were at home or in your car—you would have to dial back-and-forth for the desired frequency. The receivers and oscillation were often unstable and depended on your location and the strength of the signal. So, you would hear a high-pitched AM electronic squeal, as you tuned-in to hear broadcasts from Russia, China, and Germany that skipped across the night skies—some signals were clearer than others.

"That's what we're trying to do with the mind," Lopez said. "We're searching for clear channels of transmission or other minds skipping across the universe that we can hear. I just wish I could be the Fessenden of PSYCNONIX—I've planned a speech and everything." Todd bowed and smiled as though he was receiving an honor at this moment. He still hinted and pushed to be the first to get the implant—and it was being considered.

Canadian Reginald Aubrey Fessenden was recognized as the first person to transmit the sound of the human voice without wires. Perhaps Todd Lopez would be the first psychologically bionic person to transmit his thoughts without wires.

CHAPTER FORTY-SEVEN

"A hallucination is a fact, not an error; what is erroneous is a judgment based upon it."
~ Bertrand Russell

PLAYBACK

AFTER STEVEN SCOTT was fully vetted, Brad Manuszewski got him on boarded as quickly as possible for the PSYCHONIX project. ITL was excited about having him on the team and after he spent a few days in *Unit-B* making colorful macaroni art and clay figures—he was glad to have his freedom back.

The staff worked him hard, but it was a regimen that he gladly welcomed. Steven was doing well and back to his jovial old self. Once he realized that he had really seen and heard something, it no longer frightened him and became easier to manage his PTSD. Improvement was ITL's primary focus, as they ran Steven through a gamut of drills, quizzes, scans, and potential scenarios. He had improved and excelled in every way.

The next time he was counseled by Dr. Feinberg, Steven saw portions of his previously recorded sessions. It disturbed him. He glanced up and watched his image appear on a *46* inch, *16*K hidden mirror TV with *132.7* megapixels, which vanished back into the mirror when they were done. He watched curiously with an arched left eyebrow and pursed lips, as the video was played back. He was focused and silently re-mouthed the words that he had said. He moved his lips, but never said anything audibly. It interested him but was also difficult to watch.

"That's enough."

"Okay," Dr. Feinberg said. She made a stop motioned with her hand toward the control room."

Steven stood up to stretch and get a bottle of water. "You know, when I was in the Army—I thought about becoming one of you guys and trading in my OCP or *Operational Camouflage Pattern* uniform, for a nice white coat and stethoscope." He mimed how one would put on a doctor's coat and put his hands into the imaginary pockets, as he admired his own reflection in the mirror. "Now, that guy puts the *hot* in psychotic," he said, modeling playfully. He turned sideways and sucked in his middle-aged paunch.

Dr. Feinberg noted: *He hasn't lost his sense of humor and has a vivid imagination. Not presenting any obvious signs of psychosis—and certainly not afraid of the mirror any longer.*

"There are a few things that I probably need to clarify," Steven said. "Things that I'm still not completely sure about myself. You see, I've been wrestling with—or let's say, trying to figure out—what's real and what's not real in my mind in regard to PTSD."

"—and how to decide which is which," she added empathetically.

"Yes," he nodded. "Some of the stuff that I've experienced seemed true enough at times, but where is the line?"

"The line?"

"Yeah, between—a PTSD hallucination and the truth." It was a deeply philosophical question that perhaps only a professor or a person who thought that they were losing their grip might think about. "If I have an ability—and can hear and see things that others can't, then how do I know if it's the *real McCoy or not*?" he questioned.

"Steven—I can't tell you definitively—but on its face I would say that you try to discern the truth in the same way you are now—by what's warranted."

He nodded.

"Also, I don't think that your uncertainty is necessarily a problem. The truth is often difficult to discern."

"What do you mean?"

"Well, it doesn't always emerge with clarity, where it's easily apparent to all. I would say you just have to ask enough questions and think it through with the evidence and good reasoning. You have to let your feelings be grounded in truth and reality—not the other way around."

"Easier said than done. I was feeling like an emotional seesaw—teetering back-and-forth." His discomfort was exacerbated by the uneasiness he felt and knew that it had created in Marlina. In the beginning he found that it was a lot easier to be alone—and avoid people who may not understand his condition, but now he appreciated the discoveries that had been made and the support of his new team at ITL. "It has been eye-opening—I'll say that."

It was indeed eye-opening to be placed in a mental health unit and for Marlina to spend a few boring days reading literature about *Ignorant Mental Health Myths and Stereotypes*. It was meant to tamp down fearful imaginations, fueled by Hollywood and ignorance. But sometimes it raised questions you never thought of. However, the literature clearly revealed that people with mental health issues were less inclined to cause criminal problems. They were actually more vulnerable to being hurt by someone else, than causing a problem.

Earlier, while waiting, Marlina read the statistics from the U.S. Department of Housing and Urban Development: *More than 124,000 homeless people across the USA suffer from a severe mental illness. They're gripped by schizophrenia, bipolar disorder, PTSD, or severe depression*

— all manageable with the right medication and counseling but debilitating if left untreated. It went on to say that those suffering from psychosis were more likely to commit suicide than homicide and that there were only a small number who weren't diagnosed and properly treated.

Early on, when Marlina was more fearful, Dr. Feinberg told her that those who were untreated seemed to run a gamut of psychotic behaviors. "Some want to protect themselves from a world where nothing looked real and no perceptions could be trusted, or felt that they must right some egregious wrong—and save the world," she said. "Those with mental illnesses are often experiencing an intolerable world full of voices, distorted images, and cryptic messages from beyond reality. Left untreated they often become afraid—and aggression is a natural response to fear."

"I could see that," Marlina said.

"So, stopping the hurt sometimes means ending it all." She empathetically held Marlina's hand. "Fortunately, he's going to be fine now."

CHAPTER FORTY-EIGHT

"You have brains in your head. You have feet in your shoes. You can steer yourself any direction you choose." ~ *Dr. Seuss*

CAFÉ NOUS

"PHILOSOPHICALLY, the *Mind-Body Problem* concerns the relationship between consciousness and thought, between the mind and the brain," Mark Starr began as he ate a chocolate espresso biscotti and sipped a frothy double cappuccino. His favorite. "The way I see it, one must be controlling the other."

The open-ended café discussions with Peggy Feinberg, Gus Kahn, and other staff members had become legendary around ITL. It resembled the way information might have been shared in Athens at Plato's Academy, perhaps with Aristotle studying at his feet in 367 B.C.

"Let me be clear, I believe in human free will and the ability to choose, because we are, no doubt, more than just our physical brains," Mark continued. "I think it's demonstrable that we have a metaphysically rational *soul* that animates us and controls the *brain*."

He stopped talking and took another drink of his coffee, while it was still piping hot. During their get-togethers, everyone would occasionally drop a topic like that to see who picked it up and ran.

"So, let's get this straight—you really, truly think that our conscious mind is some *invisible* thing that exists separate from our brain?" Gus asked. "Something that's there, but we just can't see it?" His skeptical smirk made it obvious that he wasn't buying into it and you shouldn't either.

Mark gazed kindly at Gus with a knowing look. They had been down this road before. "There are those who believe that the *soul* is an embedded element of who we are—our brain—but I think it's totally separate."

"A soul?" Gus repeated, with even less enthusiasm if that was possible.

"Yes—a soul. A soul like most people have believed in throughout most of recorded history."

"Yeah, well, they also believed the Ptolemaic model of the sun rotating around the earth," he sparred.

"Right…" Dr. Starr said, unamused and undaunted by his practiced skepticism. "…which was a *fact* touted by the Aristotelian philosophers and leading scientists of their day."

"Okay?"

"And, unfortunately concordism was adopted and used by the Church to interpret scripture in light of modern science—which is always changing." He paused and gave Dr. Kahn a moment to let that sink in.

"Science made many immature conclusions. One hundred and fifty years ago, scientists said that the universe was eternal," Dr. Starr went on to say. "But now we know better, thanks to Einstein, Freidman, Lemaitre, Hubble, Penzias, and Wilson. Because of their work, we know that our universe had an absolute beginning, *out of nothing—not…any…thing*. And until this day, there is no serious model that has indicated otherwise. So, the simple question still remains: *who or what made it?"* It was a question that he had thought about since he was eight years old, so he couldn't imagine why others didn't share his curiosity.

"The world was made by the laws of gravity in a space vacuum," Kahn said smugly. "—absolutely devoid of matter. Fluctuations of energy, spontaneously created mass, out of *absolutely nothing at all*."

"Listen to yourself—and the contradictions," Mark asserted.

"No, you're wrong, there are no contradictions."

"Laws and *energy create*—aren't they something?"

"Yeah."

"Okay, then it's *not nothing*—in the strictest sense of the word *laws* and *energy* are something, right?"

"I suppose."

"So, how does one account for the existing material energy?" he asked rhetorically. "Who created your universe?" Mark enjoyed another sip of his delectable cappuccino.

Gus defended, "So—it created itself, no problem—it's inexplicable. It had to, because there's a law, so it did!" He couldn't give up the rhetoric his scientism embraced.

"Gus, you can't lift yourself up by your own shoelaces," Peggy interjected. "It doesn't make sense. First, you've got to exist—in order to do something or create something else, right?"

Gus quoted the late Steven Hawkings, "It's like the man said, *because there* is a *law* such as *gravity, the universe can and will create itself* from nothing." He was visibly pleased with himself for having read *The Grand Design* and coming up with such a quick, evidently show-stopping answer.

"Without a doubt, Hawkings was a genius, but that's still an absurd statement. *Gravity*—is also something, which must be accounted for in creation," Mark said. "Who made gravity and a law that gravity is obligated to follow?"

"Well, at least it's not some special *ad hoc* religious reason for the universe—like God waved his magic wand and made it so."

"Gus, it's not *special pleading* to assert that there's a God, any more than it is to assert that the universe is eternal, or that it spontaneously created itself. It actually makes a lot more sense to posit a metaphysical creator," Mark said. He paused again with a friendly, diplomatic smile. "When you think about it, design makes the most sense—since an ultimate *mind* or God is the only thing that's necessary, philosophically speaking."

He wasn't talking about just any god, but a God with all the *great making properties* that make Him worthy of the title *God*. The notion of *the greatest conceivable being*, not the popular Dawkins definition that atheists had leeched-on to:

'A jealous and proud of it; a petty, unjust, unforgiving control-freak; a vindictive, bloodthirsty ethnic cleanser; a misogynistic, homophobic, racist, infanticidal, genocidal, filicidal, pestilential, megalomaniacal, sadomasochistic, capriciously malevolent bully.'

"Your god is unnecessary," Gus asserted. "I'll stick with spontaneous evolution."

"Even if you embrace evolution, it couldn't be spontaneous out of nothing, nor does it make sense to say it evolved from a mindless, unguided universe."

"That's all that's necessary."

"No, the only thing that's actually necessary is an all-powerful, all-knowing, and morally perfect God.

"Gimme a break," Gus said in a bored, *I've heard it before tone.*

"Yes, because—every physical thing in the universe could be completely different than what it is now—different laws, different looks, and different kinds of beings."

"Great point," Sabrina Killian said, using her finger to make an imaginary score mark. "One for Dr. Starr.

He smiled and nodded. "But God is an eternal mind—what philosophers call an *uncaused, timeless, transcendent, space-less, exceptionally powerful and personal being.* A being powerful enough to make the known universe the way it is.

"And wonderfully made at that—I might add," said one of the more religious interns hanging out with them and doing a Groucho Marx impersonation. He attempted to show support and, at the same time, lighten up the conversation.

"I'm just saying that, to me," Mark continued, "theism provides a fuller, richer view of our wonderful vast universe and people. Think of it like this—there are only three possibilities for creation: necessity, chance, or design—and our universe isn't necessary."

"Meaning, it could be something different," Peggy happily followed along.

"Yes, and it couldn't be by chance, because the odds are so astronomical that no one could begin to fathom its fine-tuning. The most likely candidate is that it was designed by an eternal, exceptionally powerful, personal being—capable of creating.

"Makes a lot of sense to me," Peggy said. "If not, then I guess we're just a happy, mindless, unguided accident."

"Right—with no *objective* meaning or purpose," Mark said.

"That's interesting," Peggy said, "I was wondering how that might tie in to our PSYCHONIX project. How those objective aspects would play into our understanding of the mind and body."

"It's an amazing aspect," Mark said. "And, yes—I think it ties in perfectly with our project."

"When we examine the brain, we're primarily concerned with the chemistry and physics," Peggy said with respect to Gus. "That may be the easier part of our study. But the emergence of human consciousness, that's a tough one. I know that we possess it, but I'm at a loss as to what it is, much-less how to go about measuring it."

"Right, it's hard to wrap your mind around," Mark said. "Pun intended."

Peggy scrunched up her face with an, *I get it,* half-smile and frown.

"You guys kill me," Gus said with a knowing air of superiority. "You know good and well that there's no known place for some invisible thing called a *self* or *soul* in your brain or anywhere else. You'll never find it." He paused and shook his head. "It's merely an illusion, which I'd compare to looking for the announcer in your radio."

Peggy interrupted.

"—then I suppose your responses are an illusion too," Peggy said to Gus' expression of annoyance. But everyone knew that she had made a valid point. Sabrina even made another score mark in the air.

"It doesn't seem like you've thought it completely through Gus. If everything is indeed an illusion," Mark said, "then there is no real need to worry, right? If we accept your view, then everything is sort of a dream and there's no ultimate *hope* in this world."

"Okay," Gus said. He was quite willing to accept that view.

Mark's point was that if Gus' inference was true—that *we're merely physical beings*, then we could logically be indifferent about suffering, poverty, starvation, warfare, ecological catastrophes, and fighting for social causes or against global problems. There was no ultimate, objective standard, so it was of no ultimate consequence. That was where Dr. Kahn's worldview led, but not Dr. Starr's. However, like most people in life, Gus lived as though there was objective meaning. It was an obvious contradiction in his thinking, but not one that he recognized or admitted to.

"But there are consequences," Mark continued. "There is a commonsense objective reality that we all share in—and that *you* personally experience every day. We see it in how the brain works, how we communicate with others in the PSYCHONIX project, and I believe in how God directly communicates to each of us, every day."

CHAPTER FORTY-NINE

"You must speak loud to those who are hard of hearing." ~ *Henry David Thoreau*

ARMED AND DANGEROUS

TRIP AND ASHLYNN both worked and made decent money, but they were partiers and poor managers who burned through it fast. They often frittered their hard-earned paychecks on premium liquor and the *MGM National Harbor* casino. They spent many mindless hours gambling—mostly at the slot machines, sometimes seated at the more expensive Blackjack tables.

They usually lost more than they won, but you would never know it from their bragging of free comps for steak dinners, spa treatments, and shows. They expertly boast about it, but no one comped their bank account, when their luck ran out.

It wasn't like they didn't deserve to have some fun. Trip did backbreaking work as a construction supervisor, where he supervised bricklayers on big commercial projects. He also laid brick himself, when he didn't have to settle quarrels or order supplies. Ashlynn painted nails as a manicurist at *About Faces* in the Annapolis Towne Centre. She was good at it. Her creativity attracted many of the local society ladies, who tipped very well. It provided them fun money.

Back at their house Sergeant Ibarra and Corporal Lacdon were still investigating a noise complaint. As he spoke, Trip became more excitable and raised a bit of a ruckus. He was oblivious to both his alcohol and hearing impairments, yelling, "*Look,* Mr. Officer, there ain't no crime—in having a few drinks, right?"

"No," Sgt. Ibarra replied.

"So—*Wadawegottuhtawlkabout?*" What have we got to talk about?

"Sir, you're speaking way too loud and your TV is blaring!" Sgt. Ibarra shouted back to him matter-of-factly and glanced up at the condo windows. "You're disturbing the peace, Mr. Peterson."

It was much too noisy to reasonably talk to a person, supposing you had a reasonable person to talk to. They didn't. The television sounded like loudspeakers that provided entertainment for an outdoor concert. Way too loud. But the only gathering here was a bunch of *looky-loos,* who walked Main Street and looked for a bargain and a nice place to eat.

We've had complaints, sir—about THAT...NOISE," he said. He pointed up toward the windows, "and your LANGUAGE. You need to tone it down."

"*Huh?*" he asked. He looked perplexed, and if it were possible, even more annoyed.

"You—NEED—to turn that—DOWN!" Sgt. Ibarra yelled and emphasized each word loudly as he pointed again and motioned to *turn it down* with his left hand. They waited while Trip dragged himself back up two dozen or so steps, turned down the music, and gingerly trudged back to the street level entrance way.

It was quiet now, except for the muffled screams of children, which wasn't loud enough to be heard at street level. Even so, it could have been tourists. There were a lot of children walking up and down *Main Street,* begging for ice cream and candy and toys, and crying when they didn't get any.

Normal sounds—supposedly.

"You can say whatever you want in private, sir, but the rest of Annapolis doesn't want to hear you," Corporal Lacdon reprimanded. "You got it?"

"*Yeah-yeah*, okay," he said. He avoided giving clear answers and still felt like the COPS were harassing him—and not a clue as to why.

"Hey, I work ALL DAY and Ashlynn is watching some snotty-nosed kids!" he said completely nonplussed. "I don't need this." His blood-shot eyes, and red, wrinkled-up nose fruitlessly pled for a smidge of sympathy.

Those were new pieces of information and Corporal Lacdon wrote it down: *Inebriated male. Hard of hearing. Yelling. Playing television excessively loud. Female babysitting.*

Sergeant Ibarra instructively placed his right index finger to his lips and said, "*Shhh*, let's quiet it down another notch, Mr. Peterson, while we figure this out."

"Oh, SORRY!" Trip said, more conciliatory. He mimicked Sergeant Ibarra's finger to the lips, and then quieted down and said, *"Shhh!"* They were amused at having a drunk man *shhh* them.

He was now behaving like a remorseful drunk who had sobered-up enough to be semi-respectful—at least he remembered that he was speaking to officers of the law, and slowly woke up to the fact that he was probably talking too loud.

"I D—*DIDN'T KNOW*—ah," he paused and adjusted his internal volume down. "I didn't know—how loud I was."

It sounded like they had perhaps reached a peaceful resolution, when a short, thickset woman leaned out of the same window and yelled down to the street.

"*Honestly*, officers, there ain't no trouble up here. *To tell you the truth,* we're just trying to unwind and, *frankly,* just cook some dinner."

The trifecta of deceit: *Honestly, to tell you the truth,* and *frankly.* And amazingly, all in one breath. There was no conspicuous alarm in her voice, but there were noticeable facial markings, which could be seen from the street below. Sergeant Ibarra noticed it. It could have been a scar, birthmark, or even poorly applied make-up, but he thought it might be a bruise.

"We'd like to come up for a minute," the Sergeant said. He opened the door wider—but Trip moved to block his way.

"*Lemme getridda disbottle* and I'll take ya up," he said cradling the bottle between his fingers and taking one last bottoms-up swig. Then he closed one eye and lined up a horseshoe-toss toward a city trash can.

Officer Lacdon held out his hand and said, "Let me take care of that."

"Thanks—there's nothin' worse than a *bitter-lug*, right?"

"Right," he said, rolling his eyes at Sgt. Ibarra.

Trip motioned for the cops to follow him, but moved slowly as he frisked his own pockets, and tried to bum a cigarette from Sergeant Ibarra.

Stalling.

Not stalling because he knew anything about the children being held hostage, but worried about Ashlynn throwing him under the bus for the *teeny-tiny black-eye* that he had given her for gambling-away his liquor money.

He moved slowly and fumbled with his door keys, then put them away as he remembered that the door was unlocked.

More stalling.

They slowly followed Trip up the stairs and entered the second level living room and scanned for any signs of trouble. That's when they first noticed Ashlynn. You couldn't help but notice a morbidly obese woman with large belly rolls of fat, under a tight tee-shirt.

Next, they noticed that she had a bruised right eye. It was clearly a shiner. Corporal Lacdon wrote down: *Periorbital Hematoma.*

They needed to see more of the environment and make sure that Ashlynn and the children Trip had mentioned were safe. The children were there, sitting on the sofa with a ring-side seat, but unusually quiet. Ashlynn had quickly removed the Duct tape and given them life-threatening instructions: "If you don't listen to exactly what I say, then you'll get hurt—and never go home or see your mommy again, ever!—UNDERSTAND?!" It startled them terribly and made them jump. "That would be sad, right?!" she asked with a sideways look of contempt. They nodded fearfully because they had no reason to doubt her.

Earlier on, Ashlynn had frightened the children by waving a butcher knife around. She demonstrated exactly how sharp it was by sticking it in the coffee table as she removed the tape from their mouths. The knife landed with sharp *thunk* and stuck straight up—slicing a pencil on the table in-half in the process.

"Those could be your little fingers, if you don't obey your mommy, right?" she threatened, without expecting an answer from their quivering lips. Eight year old Elizabeth whimpered all the more, as the boys sat beside her and held her hands in stunned silence.

Children know. They know when they're loved, and they know when they're in deep trouble. They wearily rose from the sofa with surrendered, drooped shoulders, and marched somberly toward Ashlynn. That was just as the officers made it to the second floor landing and entered the room. It was a brief, intentional parade for law enforcement to witness.

The officers were happy to see no signs of bruises or broken bones or burns. Everyone appeared to be okay, but nothing was okay. Ashlynn stood directly behind the children, next to the master bedroom door with the pistol tucked in the rear of her expansive waistband. She had threatened to hurt the children if they breathed a single word—and she would do it. She hadn't really thought it through, but whispered to the children that she would kill them first and then herself—so that they would *never, ever, ever make it out alive*. They had *no choice*, or *hope* of escape.

Ashlynn pointed the children toward the bedroom and said, "We just need a minute to speak to the nice officers. So, watch some TV and then we'll go for the ice cream that I promised you," she said, in what she imagined was a motherly or parental tone. It was something that any normal parent or babysitter would have said to shield their children from adult situations and complicated conversations.

These are the police and we have something serious to talk about. They quietly shuffled into the bedroom and didn't make a peep.

"How did you get the black eye?" Sergeant Ibarra asked.

"Well, *frankly*—it's silly," she said, as though she were too embarrassed to repeat the story and had to search her memory to remember exactly how it had happened.

"I fell," she said, pausing an awkward five seconds, "I fell, coming up the steps." Then paused again as she thought about it. "I was running down, or I mean—I was walking up the steps too fast with two bags of groceries in my hands, and the bottom of my shoes slipped. They were slippery from water—because—it had been raining," she said awkwardly. It was nearly incoherent the way she plodded through her extemporaneous lie.

Yes, that sounded reasonable, she thought.

She repeated herself, stuttered a bit, re-explained, and expanded details. It all sounded fishy. The officers asked follow-up questions and had her repeat herself again, to see if the story changed. It was obvious to both officers: *She's lying. Her husband most likely gave her the black eye.* It happened every day, somewhere. It usually started with disrespect or jealousy. Impatient tempers flared and fists flew—ignited by misunderstandings, agitation, worry, fear, liquor, or drugs. People said things and did things that they would never say or do if they were in their right mind. The walls of inhibition started to break down and false courage took over. It led to hurtful words and sometimes blows being exchanged.

Yeah, Trip hit me, but I won't tell them. I've got other plans for him, she thought.

The officers saw the three children get up and make their way across the room. They shuffled from a tufted brown leather sofa by the window to the bedroom. Two young boys and a little girl with her arms tightly wrapped around a *Mrs. Beasley* doll.

The boys protected their little sister on the front and back end of their brief parade to the bedroom. They kept her surrounded and as safe as possible in the middle. The officers noticed that she was crying.

Not abnormal, they're children after all.

CHAPTER FIFTY

"I intend to live forever or die trying."
~ *Joseph Heller, Catch 22*

TODD LOPEZ I

"TODD LOPEZ DIED last night," Dr. Lui said. "His roommate found him wearing the PSYCHONIX goggles at twelve-thirty this morning. He must have taken them home after the test."

"Yes sir, he took his computer but he said he was coming right back—he just needed to run home to take his insulin and get something to eat," Sabrina said.

She didn't see a need to mention their embarrassing moment from earlier that evening. Todd was caught looking at her legs and it had certainly raised his blood-pressure and triggered the first issues with blood-sugar. It also prompted him to abruptly leave, but *that surely wasn't the cause of his death,* she thought. "He called around ten and said he would return after a test that he was in the middle of—in this case beating a new gaming level. You know how Todd is."

"Is that all?" Dr. Starr asked.

"Yeah—at the time he sounded alright to me."

"Well, the medical reports this morning showed that he wasn't alright. He had a heart attack."

The report also showed that he had a history of high blood pressure and was a *type 1 diabetic*. His insulin bottle and a syringe had been found on the floor beside him."

"Crap," Sabrina uttered under her breath. She didn't know anything about his health concerns."

"Todd was likely in a *Catch 22* where his hypertension complicated his diabetes and his diabetes increased the hypertension—which led to his heart attack," Dr. Lui surmised. "Sabrina couldn't have known that. He was probably dead for an hour or so before his roommate discovered him," Dr. Lui added. "And it took just under 30 minutes for the ambulance to arrive."

"And—you may be interested to know," Brad said, "—he had the PSYCHONIX goggles on for the entire time. The medics are the ones who removed it, to check his eyes."

Everyone sadly nodded.

"Why did you make a special note that he was still wearing the device?" Dr. Starr asked.

"Because—I just checked the playback video and he continued to send and receive signals for almost 90 minutes—after he died.

CHAPTER FIFTY-ONE

*"*Atheism is for people who are afraid of the light."
~ Dr. John Lennox

AFRAID OF THE LIGHT

MARK STARR DIDN'T believe that humans were strictly biochemical machines or, as some have said, *wet robots*. That caused him to think a lot about metaphysics and spiritual matters, as they pertained to the PSYCHONIX project. Just last night he read that two-point four percent of people in the world were atheists. Twelve-point five percent were not affiliated with any religion at all, but 85 point one percent of the world believed in a God that heard and answered prayers. *It isn't evidence that there is a God*, he thought, but it was certainly a strong personal indicator that something real was going on. Something that strongly impelled people toward New Age Spirituality, Hinduism, Buddhism, Islam, Judaism, and Christianity.

Why is that?

Prior to one of their daily IPRs or *in progress reviews,* Dr. Starr brought up the subject and asked, "Are 85 percent of those people being heard by a higher power or are they just talking to themselves?" Those that had been to the café with him weren't surprised by the spiritual question.

"They're talking to themselves," Dr. Kahn quickly asserted. "Religion—or the idea of a god, is nothing but a delusion, *Band-Aid, crutch or wishful thinking,* to make you feel better and play nice with others in the herd—until we die."

"That's a pretty gloomy outlook, if not a delusional view itself," Dr. Feinberg commented. The inner-office conversations were often entertaining and eruditely parsed, but Peggy wasn't fond of controversial conversations in large groups and especially at work—that were, in her estimation, too riddled with tension.

"Don't get me wrong," Dr. Kahn said. "I don't think that they're all bad people, just ignorant—superstitious people—who are afraid of the dark."

Peggy sighed.

Mark smiled. It wasn't the first time he had heard that type of uninformed comment. He wasn't the argumentative type, but he couldn't let it go unchallenged. "Okay Gus, that's really a simplistic *meme,* not an argument for atheism," he parried. "I could just as easily say that atheists are *afraid of the light*—and quickly remind you that neither one of us has said anything of great value—at least in supporting our beliefs."

"*Touché,*" Gus acquiesced. "But I'll choose the hard sciences, thank you—that's something I can get my arms around."

It was small talk, banter, and a little benign sparring amongst fellow physicians with opposing worldviews while they sat around a large metal workbench in the Innovations Tech-Lab, still waiting for their morning meeting to get started.

"Sure, but you don't have to make a choice between them—science and religion aren't mutually exclusive categories. I, for one, am a successful scientist—and also believe in God, for many very good reasons."

"Yeah, like what?" Dr. Kahn said with an incredulous tone.

"Like God being the best explanation for the beginning of the universe—the best explanation for fine-tuning—the best explanation for objective morality and much more. As a scientist, I can appreciate all the great works of science, but I've also gained some critical knowledge through other areas of study."

"Such as?" Dr. Kahn continued to prod him.

"Such as history and philosophy and theology," Mark listed. "Our greatest thinkers, from the time of the Middle Ages, were required to pursue the Aristotelian philosophies of physics, metaphysics, and moral philosophy for their liberal arts university degrees."

"That was hundreds of years ago, Mark—we're a lot smarter now because of science," he said with a triumphant nod.

"You may not realize it, but you're confusing two vastly different categories of explanations: *Mechanisms* and *Agency*."

"What?"

"Science, as you know, deals with natural laws and the physical descriptions and effects of mechanisms. It's the study of the natural world based on facts that we've learned through repeated experiments and observations—even touching on cosmology—the study of the *origin* of the universe. Those are the metaphysical studies that lead us down philosophical trails— helping us come to grips with the *cause* of the *Big Bang*—the very beginning of our finite universe."

"Finite?"

"Yes, finite. You know, as well as I do, that Georges Lemaître proposed what later became known as the *Big Bang Theory* of the origin of the universe." Dr. Starr didn't have to repeat it.

274

Dr. Kahn knew that the term was initially derisive and meant to disparage the idea of the universe being created. I know—I know," he conceded. "I teach it. Lemaître was the first to identify and propose the recession of nearby galaxies. It was explained by a theory of an expanding universe, which was—might I add—*observationally* confirmed by Edwin Hubble's discovery of the redshift he saw looking out at the galaxies."

Sabrina chimed-in, "Not to mention that Penzias and Wilson were awarded the Nobel Prize in Physics for discovering a cosmic microwave background radiation—accepted as important evidence for the *Big Bang*." Impressive trivia that only a young science engineer would probably know.

"Gus—all I'm saying is that when you seriously consider how we got here—it's either by chance, necessity, or design—and it strongly leads one to believe it couldn't have been an accident. Some eternal mind with the wherewithal to create made the universe—and other minds," he concluded, but promptly added. "I believe that's the deep well from which we draw objective meaning and purpose in life—and discover God."

"Nonsense," Dr. Kahn said, "It was nonsense when you mentioned it at the café and it's nonsense now." Just then, his cell phone rang loudly with a funky-science ringtone that he had downloaded: *Where the Higgs at? Where the Higgs at? Go! Go! Go!* He ruefully smiled, answered, and started talking as he walked toward an adjacent, empty office. He turned and said, "It won't take a minute—I've got to take this call."

Dr. Lui quickly popped up and followed him into the office.

Mark, Peggy and a few others from the ITL team continued to make small talk and sip coffee from their Styrofoam cups, until Gus and Lui returned—inconspicuously without their phones.

CHAPTER FIFTY-TWO

"You only lie to two people in your life, your girlfriend and the police." ~ *Jack Nicholson*

REPORT

SERGEANT IBARRA AND Corporal Lacdon got back in their cruiser and radioed, "Officer 727—we're clearing. No crime committed." Their warnings had been heeded and no one filed charges, so in their minds, the job was done. They eased back down the stairs, scooted into their cruiser, and slowly maneuvered toward the City Dock to file their long, boring, bureaucratic police report: Neighbors complained.

- Tyrone "Trip" Peterson; half-deaf, excessive drinking. Talking and listening to TV at high volume. TV turned down. Compliant.

- Ashlynn Peterson; bruised right eye – potential domestic abuse. No complaint filed. Compliant.

- Three children: 12, 10, 8. Two boys and an unusually quiet little girl crying. Mr. Peterson says his wife is babysitting them. Mrs. Peterson says their parents work long hours in D.C. and this is a way for her to earn extra money.

- '*Lively*' domestic incident, deescalated.

Ashlynn and Trip could perhaps be adjudged as a *dysfunctional couple* at best, but the court system and jails couldn't begin to house all the dysfunction in Anne Arundel County. Besides, there were no laws broken—at least nothing actionable. Nothing obvious or provable. No ongoing complaints or criminal actions identified in their database. Yes, neighbors had reported a domestic disturbance, but it was the first time a problem had been reported to the police, even though the neighbors were quite fed up with their shenanigans. It was the first time law enforcement had been called in to investigate what was really the tip of the iceberg.

In all probability, it was an unhealthy relationship. It was full of verbal abuse and there appeared to be physical abuse. Maybe there was emotional abuse too. There was likely a combination of it all, but they were cops not counselors. An imperfect relationship, yes, but a private one, unless charges were filed.

A textbook domestic abuse case, thought Sergeant Ibarra.

He had lectured on this type of abuse for the department. He knew that domestic abuse wasn't always an obvious problem or one that went away quickly nor quietly.

It was a Friday night and there was another insidious family problem, deeply rooted in our culture—and the statistics proved it. The officers expeditiously engaged, assessed, de-escalated, and departed.

By the book.

Sergeant Ibarra and Corporal Lacdon lingered a while longer in their blue and yellow-striped *Ford Crown Victoria* cruiser, across from *Mission BBQ*, in the crowded Annapolis City Dock parking lot. When evening events settled down, they passed the time talking about their families, politics, religion, and sports… like they usually did. They settled all of life's *little problems* with their off-the-cuff opinions of how the world should be. It made their shift go by a whole lot faster.

"You gotta believe the Redskins are going to the Super Bowl this year!" Corporal Lacdon would say.

"Oh, and you think you've got what it takes to make detective someday?!" Sergeant Ibarra laughed.

They patrolled, in-place, for nearly 45 minutes. That meant they sat and listened to the police radio, as they finished their report. They also drank coffee and enjoyed their panoramic windshield view of Spa Creek and the Annapolis Harbor. Folks on vacation strolled about and enjoyed their day in rustic restaurants and on touring boats. It was a far cry from the City Dock 250 years ago, when the African slave ship arrived with Alex Hailey's forefather, *Kunta Kinte*.

After they completed their paperwork, they exited the vehicle to stretch their cramped legs. They looked around at the bustling herds of tourists, got back in the cruiser and rolled out north. Cautiously they drove across *Market Space*, by the *Middletown Tavern*. It was a tavern often frequented by the likes of George Washington, Thomas Jefferson, and Benjamin Franklin. Right now, there was a history and political law student from St. John's College outside waiting tables.

They cautiously hooked a left, past the *Iron Rooster*, and *City Dock Coffee*, when they heard the high-pitch *crack* and echo of a gun being fired. It was immediately recognized as a gunshot, echoing up and down the colonial streets of Annapolis—followed by two other shots. Their vehicle came to a dead stop, in the middle of the road, as they fired up the red, white, and blue flashing bar lights. Both officers exited quickly, pulled their weapons, and ran bravely toward the sounds—on foot, toward Main Street.

As they rounded the corner, a person coming out of *Buddy's Crabs & Ribs* pointed and shouted, "It came from the direction of *Kokopelli's*."

It was the exact three-story building that the officers had responded to earlier, but this time there was someone laid out on the sidewalk.

Our tests aren't conclusive, but it seems obvious to me that the brain can easily be manipulated by the mind—and that it's a different sort of thing. I'm hopeful that my upcoming media interviews will shed more light on the matter.

Clinical trials have demonstrated that some people who believe that they are getting an effective medication, but are in fact being given a sugar pill, will get better. This is called the "placebo effect" and applies to a wide variety of conditions. Scientists have even shown that if someone is given decaffeinated coffee, but believes it is caffeinated, the scans will show that their brain has been activated in the same way as if it had been real coffee.

Many studies have demonstrated the power of having hope or holding on to a hope of something that is greater than yourself. Where does the idea of hope come from? Maybe it's as foolish as asking, "Where does the idea of hunger and thirst come from?" Hope seems like something our body and soul desires. A desire that can be satisfied in some way.

CHAPTER FIFTY-THREE

"We all make choices in life, but in the end our choices make us." ~ *Andrew Ryan, Bioshock*

GONE

WHILE AT HOME Todd Lopez had engaged in a strenuous two-player video game called *Street Racquetball*. Not a wise beginner's routine for an overweight, sedentary engineer with diabetes and high blood pressure. Never-the-less he played his heart out. In his mind he was still a strong high school athlete, but in reality, he was now considered unhealthy on the *BMI*. Even though the game was played via the mind, it still activated all the normal physical and pulmonary reactions in his body.

As soon as he got home, Todd should have immediately taken his insulin and had something to eat, but he was so engrossed in the project and having fun that he decided to hook up the game and keep testing. He pressed START and the next thing you know it was an hour, two hours, and etcetera. He ignored or didn't hear incoming phone calls and his voicemail filled up.

Todd, if you're there pick up. Todd, are you coming back? Todd, this isn't funny!

He was getting into the interactive video game. The character that he had designed was buff, agile, and handsome. He was not. His character had to run, jump, and fight for survival. So, Todd's mind was fully engaged, and it caused him to become quite weary. He soon felt tired and had trouble concentrating, then his head hurt, and his vision started to blur. It came on gradually. He was so excited about the game that he lost track of time and sense of where he was. His blood pressure skyrocketed, and he had a high blood sugar level of 600. He kept up with the game as his character learned how to make difficult slams, lobs, and drop-shots—until he keeled over. At first, he passed out, but then he was gone.

The bewildered ITL staff watched and re-watched Lopez's video. Everything he had tested was recorded on their network server. He was still connected and playing, when his heart rate flatlined and there was no blood pressure. There was zero brain activity, yet he continued to play. Astonishingly, there were still 90 minutes of video signals being produced from the grave. Dr. Starr was just as mystified as anyone else. "How's that even possible?!"

"We're not sure, but apparently a *psychomorhic algorithm* spontaneously emerged within the telepathic transport conditions—animating his PSYCHONS within the *MDSL-1* processor," Brad rattled off. "It literally became a part of his mind as he died."

"Like in Tron!" Sabrina said. "How cool is that!" Excited for a moment but was chastised by the multiple looks that reminded her Todd had just died. "Sorry."

"Sort of like Tron," Brad said, "but not quite. This time instead of a person being transported into the mainframe of a computer—the computer processor morphed a mental substance—PSYCHONS.

"I can't believe it," Dr. Kahn said.

"But it appears to be true," Dr. Lui stated as he closely examined the computer screen. "He communicated with us until the moment the goggles were removed by an EMS member, 90 minutes after he died. Listen to this!"

They were all glued to the playback monitors again and watched Todd Lopez's recorded thoughts with great interest:

Wow—that was a tough game, but I'm not even breathing hard, Lopez said looking around. He felt strong and light on his feet, like he had just woken-up from a refreshing nap. He looked in the mirror, astonished at not seeing his reflection. He double-checked and blinked his eyes, but still didn't see anything. *Whoa—that's weird.*

He waved his arms around and tried to pick up his reflection. The phone rang in the background. He walked over and tried to answer, but his hand passed right through the receiver and it kept ringing. He looked down. *What the heck?! Who's that guy lying on the floor?* To get a closer look, he crouched down on his hands and knees, between the TV and the sofa, up close to the immobile guy's face. *He looks just like me, but he's not breathing. He's NOT breathing—oh $#!t, it's me!* The phone stopped ringing; the team at ITL had given up.

I don't feel dead, he said on the recording. Todd Lopez stared out the apartment window at his car and fumbled in his pockets, for his key. *I've got to get out of here.* That wasn't going to be a problem. He was leaving sooner than he knew.

What the—something! Something is moving me up—and out of the room! You could hear a running commentary as it happened. *Wow, I'm floating in the air—and going right through the damn ceiling. Hey, there's the orange Frisbee I lost on the roof last summer. This is freaky, man. I'm moving so fast now that I can see the whole neighborhood. I know—I must be dreaming.*

He tried to pinch himself, but that accomplished nothing. It didn't feel like a dream to him, mainly because it was really happening—and then there was a brilliant flash of light—and he saw someone standing in the distance.

A calm moving figure with dark, curly hair, and a beard appeared. He was a regular looking guy with a sad face and aura of light that radiated from him. The light faded as Todd drew nearer. It was unmistakable. Even with just a brief glimpse of the person, Todd knew who it was, but he wasn't acknowledged.

It's me, Todd Lopez! Again, Todd shouted, *help me!* –as the man turned, and slowly walked away. He yelled after him again, louder, *It's me—Todd Lopez!* One could only imagine the sick feeling he had in his stomach, after being approached and then left all alone. Just then the video showed two *Light beings* whisk him away. They escorted him through a wide, dark ravine, where they passed through a thick, grayish fog—headed toward an even bleaker landscape.

It's getting darker—where am I?

The ones in this realm, who knew—didn't answer. They moved about as ghosts, uneasily toiling, but not doing anything to assist him. They popped in and out. Each passed from his sight and others appeared with long looks of dread and misery. Not tortured souls, but tormented beings—without hope.

I really hope that this is just diabetic distress. But it wasn't.

There's a group that just noticed me. They're swarming—pushing, shoving and yelling and fighting. What are they fighting about? It's too difficult to watch, but I can't turn away. Everyone's stressed and crying, but no one seems to care. It's getting darker. I feel the presence of other souls, but no one is communicating. I'm alone, but I feel the grief, misery and isolation of a legion.

The audio-video transmission ended.

CHAPTER FIFTY-FOUR

"No, I'm not a good shot, but I shoot often."
~ *Theodore Roosevelt*

BIG BANG

ASHLYNN PETERSON CLUTCHED a fully loaded .38 double action revolver in her clammy right hand. She had endured enough of Trip's abusive ways—and her jumbled brain was comfortably numbed by heavy drinking and a wide assortment of licit drugs. A combo that made her feel happy and sad—and then like her life was completely *hopeless*.

So, she fired the gun.

The first shot entered the dark bamboo floor, next to her intoxicated husband's splayed feet. The next bullet fired when he had an ill-advised thought about being a hero. He couldn't be the hero—he couldn't walk a straight line. Trip had trouble forming coherent words, from all the alcohol he had consumed. At this point, being a hero was simply out of the question, but that didn't keep him from lunging at her gun.

He ungracefully pawed in the direction of her pistol, but it was a futile attempt.

Ashlynn held the .38 double-action revolver by her side and raised it again, slowly. She shouted at Trip to *Shut-up* and motioned for him to sit down, as she gripped her weapon gangster style with a *flash sight* picture, sideways. It was a fast, but inaccurate tilt-style that never actually allowed you to take the same shot twice. It looked good in the movies, but wasn't practical. She didn't know that.

Your clothing is often a form of communication and there are *rules* for putting your best foot forward. Ashlynn had never learned them. She wasn't a stylish girl that fit into the petite, regular, or tall categories. Her taste and wardrobe were unstylishly sloppy and that's the way she liked it. She was dressed in a pair of red *Lane Bryant* stretch pants and a black tank top. Her hair was a sweat soaked, untamed mop.

There was also a simple rule for guns: never ever let the barrel point at *anything* you don't intend to kill. She didn't follow that *rule* either. Guns treated carelessly could and would kill people, whether intentionally or unintentionally. They don't discriminate.

The entire scenario was a bad accident waiting to happen. Trip stumbled forward awkwardly, swiped at Ashlynn's pistol again. He missed, fell forward, and his momentum sent him straight to the floor. It was a foolish move that caused her arm to jerk away fast and the pistol with it. An instinctive flinch. Down and to the left, causing her to pull the trigger. The third round exploded from the pistol and traveled through the only closed window on the second floor. *Down to the left.* It shattered the glass windowpane at 900 mph and ricocheted off an old, quintessential American gas streetlamp, before it came to an abrupt stop in seven year-old Chelsea Croxon's head.

It slammed into her hard and she was now lying face down on the sidewalk—clutching her recently purchased giant swirl lollipop. Her princess tiara and magic wand were strewn between the street and iron gutter drain. Her mother screamed—her father didn't believe it yet. Streaks of blood streamed down her long blonde hair—and pooled toward the top of her tiny head.

Paralyzed with shock, they knelt on their knees beside her, with blotchy specks of blood sprayed across their faces.

The roaring twenties, of the last century, ushered in a new modern age. Bootleggers, booze, flappers, jazz, and verificationism! A seeing is believing philosophy. If you can't observe it with your senses, then it's nonsense. That's the word I keep hearing from Gus: *nonsense*.

After the ordeal of World War I, people were eager to enjoy life—or perhaps they just didn't have time to think it through in all the jazzed excitement. No one considered that the statement itself was nonsense.

Most scientists agreed that consciousness is irreducible. That's a fact and it can't be categorized as an illusion or delusion like the color red. As Descartes may have said—if he was presenting a lecture today: *there is still 'me' consciously having this thing you call a delusion.*

Physics requires evidence. Metaphysics requires a different kind of evidence, but it's still evidence. Evidential facts that fall into a scientific and philosophic array of explanatory scope, explanatory power, predictive power, plausibility, simplicity, accord with accepted beliefs, superior to rival hypothesis, disconfirmed by fewer accepted beliefs, low change of an incompatible post-hypotheses, nesting, track record, and fruitfulness. Based on facts, not bias and hocus-pocus.

CHAPTER FIFTY-FIVE

"Build me a son, O Lord, who will be strong enough to know when he is weak, and brave enough to face himself when he is afraid, one who will be proud and unbending in honest defeat, and humble and gentle in victory." ~*Douglas MacArthur*

PTSD PLUS

COLONEL STEVEN SCOTT wore a black polyester mesh eyepatch to occlude his missing right eye. An unwelcome souvenir from his last deluxe, all expenses paid tour of Afghanistan. A single 7.62 mm AK-47 round from the jihadi terrorist weapon of choice had traveled through the right frontal lobe tip toward his forehead. One of the few places that he didn't have body armor.

"I was pretty sure that I was going to die," Steven said. It was another counseling session and he wanted to talk about his injuries and experiences as a Soldier. "They said that it hit me in just the right place—angled well above my skull and passed through without causing permanent damage to vital brain tissue or vascular structures." Not a great consolation prize since his traumatic brain injury (TBI) had developed into PTSD.

He continued, "I was honorably retired from the United States Army three years ago, after serving twenty-six years as a *Combat Infantry/ Special Forces* Soldier. My final deployment was with the 10th Mountain Division, as part of the *Spartans* of the 3rd Brigade Combat Team at Fort Drum, New York, now deactivated."

The Spartans' motto of *"With Your Shield or On It"* was the kind of mindset that Steven fully embraced as a warfighter. Values embraced by their ancient namesakes, the most fearsome military force in the Greek world—the *Warriors of Sparta*. It meant Soldiers who came back from battle had only two ways to do so with their honor intact: either on their feet with their shield in hand or upon their shield, as a casualty. He fell into a different modern category, still honorable, but not dead.

His Soldiers lived up to the reputation of their Greek brothers in arms. *The Tribe of the Crossed Swords* is what the Afghan people dubbed them, for their heroic counter-insurgency operations.

For a veteran like Colonel Steven Scott it was sixteen grueling months of fighting the nation's Global War on Terrorism in support of Operation Enduring Freedom and in what he called, "*A bassackwards 3rd Century hellhole—with all due respect!*" But little respect was intended.

Combat leadership imbued the patriotic fiber of his being; physically, spiritually, and psychologically. He was an intelligent, highly trained, and well-equipped man on the battlefield. It was clear that he knew what he was fighting for—*to Win America's Wars and Protect Freedom.*

He had witnessed death and dying up-close. It didn't shake him outwardly, but inside, in his subconscious mind—it left its mark. He had seen life at its inspiring best, and at its bitter, disgusting, and morbid worst. It was strongly imprinted on his mind and unfortunately, the insidious wake of combat stress had caught up to him.

After Steven retired, he bought a house in his hometown of Walla Walla, Washington. That was where he grew up in the late 70's to the mid-90s. Initially, he ran with a pretty rough crowd, had an undisciplined youth—and his communication style reflected it. So, he spoke frankly, bluntly and with the candor of a well-seasoned, cantankerous Soldier. In the heat of battle, he had a warrior-face and an even coarser texture. He commanded and communicated with operatic bravado and bluster. They were the earthy raw emotions of an intense warfighter spewing vulgarities, acronyms, and *perverse imaginative recommendations*—to get his people motivated. It stemmed from his pure unadulterated passion for freedom.

When he was asked about his colorful language, by Christian friends back home, he would merely say "I'm a strategic curser—and fire for effect." It wasn't an excuse, just a fact and it was something he still worked on.

Colonel Scott fought for America, but when pushed to explain his feelings by family or the media or a counselor—he was punted to: "I fight for the guys next to me—that's all. The guys who engage death on a daily basis. I fight to keep the other person beside me alive and he fights to keep me alive too."

It wasn't something that he liked to talk about much. It was common knowledge that most veterans who had witnessed the horrors of war didn't like to intentionally revisit it. They would just as soon forget about it, but PTSD took care of that. The decorations on his chest told his military story; *Distinguished Service Cross*, two *Silver Stars, three Bronze Stars with Combat V,* and the *Purple Heart with two oak-leaf clusters*—meaning he had been wounded in battle three times. He didn't want credit. What he saw in those awards was the blood, sweat, and tears of heroes.

"One of them is a bit embarrassing to mention—the million-dollar wound," Steven Scott revealed to Dr. Feinberg. "I didn't realize it at first, because I was laying down some *hellacious* ground-fire, just before I dove behind a HESCO MIL for cover."

The HESCO MIL was a military fortification, used as a blast wall against explosions and small arms. It had originally been used to control beach erosion and reinforce levees around New Orleans between Hurricane Katrina and Hurricane Rita, but now it stopped bullets and shrapnel.

"I didn't feel anything at first, but I swiped at the blood seeping from the wound with my left hand—*not good*, I thought. So, I told my XO, the Executive Officer; *I think I just got shot in the ass.* He verified it with an affirmative nod and later we both laughed, until we nearly cried—and laughed even harder after I started tripping on the *Morphine-Ketamine cocktail* that the field medic gave me."

Later, Steven Scott learned about the hallucinogenic side-effects the hard way—likely the genesis of his current mental health issues.

During his deployments, Colonel Scott earned a wide assortment of medals for leading his fellow soldiers. The military distinctions given to him as a mark of honor were for military achievements, meritorious service, and heroism. It was just one of the first. The second incident took out his eye during an overwhelming attack on his unit's position.

He humbly reiterated to Dr. Feinberg that he didn't believe he had earned the big medals. It seemed to be a code among heroes—none of them ever believed that they had earned it.

"The heroes that I was fortunate enough to lead, wrote a blank check and made it payable to the United States of America—for an amount up to and including their life—and it was cashed by some. My *boys* were the toughest when it came to hand-to-hand combat. It was what we were trained for and we refused to back down from a fight—wouldn't have it!" he said with a glint of pride in his eye. "The rules of an infantry Soldier are simple, survive to fight another day or minute or second."

During one violent conflict, his fellow Soldier, Sergeant Justin Daily came face-to-face with three brawny insurgents. Not an easy hand-to-hand scenario for anyone. So, he opened fire at close range with his M249 SAW and immediately killed two of them, before his weapon jammed tight—too hot to fire.

"The best solution would have been a M240B, but he didn't have one. So, he grabbed the third Taliban Soldier's rifle-barrel with both hands and beat him to death with it. It was amazing—he completely stunned the guy, when he snatched it out of his hands and swung it around like a *Louisville Slugger*." Those are the stories he told with a smile of pride, on the edge of gritted teeth.

Steven Scott told of another member of the 10th Mountain Division, Specialist Velasquez, who took out a house full of insurgent fighters with his M9. "When he ran out of ammo, he took down the last remaining fighter with his combat knife. It was a mighty reverse diagonal strike at a 45 degree angle, slicing the guy's neck, severing his carotid and jugular, rendering him incapacitated almost immediately, as the blood supply to his brain was cut off—and then he stepped into him with a forceful thrust," he acted it out. "Right in the lower-stomach with a half-twist." Steven paid homage to his brave Soldiers, whenever he mentioned *the war*—you could see the great veneration in his eyes.

"It was much better than a *Ginsu* knife," he gave a half-laugh, which spoke to his mixed feelings. "It could cut through a nail, a tin can, a radio hose, a tomato and drop an insurgent before he could yell, *Allahu 'Akbar*," Scott said analogizing the story in his mind, as only a soldier who's *been there* and *done that* could.

Two of the other special Soldiers he memorialized in his war stories were Master Sergeant Gary Shaw and Lieutenant Charley "Chaz" Anderson. "They were on a night recon and killed four enemy fighters firing on Americans through the window of an abandoned storefront. Shaw returned fire and dropped two immediately—one more with his Sig Sauer P320 after they kicked down the door and began clearing," he said, to their wide-eyed interest. "Lt. Anderson or LT had an M4, but it was no good when one of the enemy fighters jumped from a rafter and landed on his back. It dislocated his shoulder on impact and broke his brand-new *WO-PVS-7D* night vision goggles.

"The $3,500 goggles could be replaced, but it pissed him off really bad," he said. "So, LT leaned hard into the stone wall and popped his shoulder back into place. It was a loud crackling-pop, punctuated by an agonizing groan, a slight grin—and a look of utter determination on his face when he turned and confronted the enemy. He surprised his Afghan opponent with a quick, step-in, forehead strike to the nose, and a whip-around that snapped his arm, before dropping his opponent to the floor. To his utter dismay, the guy jumped right up and continued to fight with him. *Are you kidding?* We thought that he had to be juiced on something. But no matter—LT proceeded to kick the fighter's broken arm, causing him to shriek in pain, before twisting him around and strangling the no-good piece of—*huh*—guy to death with his bare hands."

No kidding was the usual response when he told that story.

Dr. Feinberg listened and nodded but didn't reveal her disgust. *It's no wonder he has bad dreams.*

Steven Scott smiled and nodded back and kept talking.

"LT stood there choking him, a little longer than necessary. Frozen. I had to actually unclasp his fingers from the *raghead's* limp neck."

Soldiers were trained to execute assaults under any possible circumstance and knew that the forehead and the elbow were the hardest and sharpest points on the human body. When applied with the right momentum and a calculated angle of attack, it was devastating.

Steven explained, "The power largely comes from staying centered and rotating the torso with the elbow or ulna centered and stationary. It's a blade-like bone that runs through the forearm. Sharper and deadlier—if the hand is open and the muscles relaxed as it crushes the throat, temple, or chin. The palm heel strike would be a good secondary *go to* in hand-to-hand combat, if delivered in a straight-forward thrusting motion with the hand flexed backward and fingers pointing upward." He demonstrated.

"The fingers shouldn't make contact with your target during the strike, only the palm delivers the force." He could see it all in his mind and it had been useful to Staff Sergeant Austin on that day of battle in January 2010.

"I wasn't there," Steven said, "but I read the reports. Another one of my Soldiers, Sergeant First Class Karl Feld, was clearing a village and stumbled on an insurgent hiding under a pile of rolled-up Afghan rugs. He severely beat the guy with palm strikes to the nose and throat, before he grabbed his *8-inch Matrix Extreme,* trigger-assisted, trench knife and cut the guy's throat. His Captain described the event that day, saying *Sergeant Feld casually cleaned-off the knife on his pants-leg, put it back in the sheath, and walked away like it was all in a day's work.*

Sadly, moments later Feld stepped on and detonated a pressure-plated, improvised explosive device (PPIED), which was placed under another rug in the middle of the room. It was a lethal snare that killed him and six other men in his unit—who rushed to his aid." He paused and blew out a slow, deep breath before he said, "Those are the men that earned medals, not me. No, not me! I'm here because of them. I'm here for them! He remembered all of his troops and had repeated those humble words, when he was honored with his second Silver Star. Many of the words were replaced with silence and tears.

His men, the *Spartan Soldiers,* had broken the insurgent's undisciplined grip through lethal combat. Colonel Steven Scott and his troops applied immense, continuous pressure on the enemy, advancing farther south than anyone had gone before. That's when it happened. That's the moment that would be forever etched on his mind—the day he lost his eye. This is how his Silver Star citation read:

"During operations against the Taliban at Combat Outpost Keating, Kamdesh District, Nuristan Province, Afghanistan Colonel Steven Scott was awakened to an attack of more than 350 enemy fighters. The insurgents had the high ground, firing into a fishbowl for all intents and purposes. Scott and his unit were taking concentrated fire from rifles, rocket propelled grenades, anti-aircraft machine guns, mortars, and small arms fire.

Scott moved around and through the battlefield uncovered, providing reconnaissance, and seeking reinforcements. He took out a five-man machine gun team and, while engaging another group, was hit by an incoming rocket-propelled grenade. With complete disregard for his own safety, Colonel Steven Scott continued to fight with multiple shrapnel wounds, exposing himself to throngs of fierce Taliban fighters who had breached his outpost. Scott confidently mobilized his five remaining Soldiers and provided cover with a sniper rifle that he secured from Sergeant Carl "Red Feather" Hetzenauer's dead hands."

Sergeant Hetzenauer had been the first to die that day. It was strategic on the Taliban's part. Eliminate the sniper first and give your unit greater mobility and flexibility on the battlefield. It freed them from the paralyzing psychology of an efficient killer, at-a-distance.

The longest confirmed shot during the War in Afghanistan had been a twofer at 2,707 yards. It hit two Taliban fighters consecutively. It caused the Taliban to have a healthy fear of our *Night Vision* capabilities and our snipers. It was an edge we needed, because the Taliban had been trained by us as a counter power against the Soviet Union. "We taught them," Steven would remind people.

Steven took one of the dog-tags and the small *red feather* Carl wore as a necklace. He had learned that it symbolized his courage, good fortune, and vitality. The irony wasn't at all lost on him, as he crammed Carl's personal items in his left OCP cargo pants pocket and took cover. Perhaps it would bring him better luck. The Silver Star citation continued:

"`Colonel Steven Scott attended to three wounded Soldiers and orchestrated his unit through the ferocity of a three-hour battle. He secured and reinforced key points and maintained radio communication with the tactical operations center. He directed air support to destroy more than 45 enemy fighters.`

`His team pushed forward under overwhelming enemy fire to prevent the abduction of fallen comrades to be used for propaganda and demoralization. Colonel Scott's heroic actions suppressed an enemy that had far greater numbers. While severely wounded from a headshot, his extraordinary efforts gave the Spartans the opportunity to regroup, reorganize, account for` personnel, prepare for counterattacks, and secure Combat Post Keating.

Colonel Scott's discipline and extraordinary heroism above and beyond the call of duty reflect great credit upon himself, 3rd Brigade Combat Team, 10th Mountain Division and the United States Army."

It was another interesting counseling session and Dr. Feinberg didn't have a lot to say. She listened, made notes, and learned gruesome details about Steven Scott's life. Details gruesome enough to warrant a debriefing session of her own to vent the repulsion. Yes, Colonel Steven Scott was a hero, but he was now fighting a different sort of war with PTSD—and no got a medal for that.

CHAPTER FIFTY-SIX

"Once you choose hope, anything's possible."
~ *Christopher Reeve*

CRACK

MOST BULLETS TRAVEL faster than supersonic speed, and what you hear is a mini sonic boom, simultaneously with the explosion of the gunpowder and gas from the barrel, after the bullet leaves the gun. That was the sound that everyone heard up-and-down Main Street, just before Sergeant Ibarra and Corporal Lacdon dashed toward Kokopelli's—with weapons drawn.

There were multiple gunshots—and now a little girl laid dying from the impact of the third stray bullet. Her skull bled rivers of bright red blood down her pale little face. The tiny piece of *jacketed lead* traveled into her head, before it lodged in her spine—and paralyzing her.

The two officers were still on location, doing paperwork—and had also received a notification about three missing children. Important yes. Connected? No one knew yet. There was no time to wait on back-up. They had to move now. Corporal Lacdon radioed for help while they ran. He quickly gave his assessment and established an open line with their Special Operations Division. In the small town of Annapolis, that meant a part-time SWAT or Quick Response Team, kept on call for such emergencies. They were the gung-ho types that thrived on adrenaline and having their fortitude tested.

Within minutes, they rolled in with their mobile command post bus. It was a souped-up RV, loaded with TV's, a round table, and coffee—always plenty of coffee. The *big wigs* each operated on their own channels. They directly communicated and coordinated movements with the Police Commander on the ground, who planned and tried to figure out the situation. They also stayed in direct contact and coordinated with the Deputy Sheriffs, SWAT, and the Crisis Negotiation Team (CNT). The Police Commander immediately used the Deputy Sheriffs, from 8 Church Circle and 199 Taylor Avenue, to systematically cordon-off the local streets. He would personally see to it that an ambulance was staged two blocks away that he could quickly call in. He also became noticeably agitated, when he saw the CNT by-pass him and take up a position directly across the street from *Kokopelli's*. He knew that these *touchy-feely* negotiators wanted to be first on the scene to prevent any hostile perceptions, but covering them and setting up a parameter was paramount.

The area from Main Street to St. Anne's Parish and down the hill to Buddy's Crab & Ribs was systematically cordoned-off with local media outlets referring to: *an unknown gunman firing a weapon into the busy downtown district of Colonial Annapolis and striking a child in the head.* There was no official word on whether the little girl was dead or alive.

The Annapolis Police Department mobilized their Specialized Operations Division and provided the necessary fire power to get the job done efficiently and effectively. It included the Quick Response Team (QRT/SWAT TEAM), K-9 Unit, Safety, and Aviation Units needed for response to a hostage situation. They were being dispatched at this very moment to assist. All at the Police Commander's disposal.

All the overly inquisitive and terrified tourists had been escorted to the City Dock, near the *Kunta Kinte-Alex Haley Memorial*, located at the junction of Compromise and Randall Street.

They were aptly secured behind statues that memorialized *hope* and the *triumph* of the human spirit in very difficult times.

Indeed—they were in difficult times today. Mostly due to the trouble that was brewing inside condo 249 on Main Street. It was there that three recently abducted children sat—and watched in sheer terror. Ashlynn had completely silenced them again, by tightly binding duct tape around their faces, hands and ankles. But not tight enough—the eldest had wiggled a hand free—and was looking for a way of escape.

Senator and Mrs. Croxon's world stopped turning as a tactical medic outside the line of fire swooped in, picked Chelsea up, and moved her inside Kokopelli's. These pararescue guys moved without fear and were considered the craziest of the crazy on the SWAT team. He had moved around the danger zone with nothing but a bag of medical supplies for protection. After securing Chelsea, the medic laid her on Kokopelli's sales counter and went straight to work triaging. Emergency treatment was necessary. Immediate medical attention saved lives and the medic was doing everything that he could do to stop the blood flow. He saw the entrance wound, but there was no exit wound. Her skull was deformed with sunken areas of visible bone fragments and exposed brain. He knew not to elevate her legs, move anything more than necessary, or apply too much pressure. His only choice was to temporarily seal the wound.

Surviving a brain injury would greatly depend on how quickly they could get her moved to a hospital.

"We've got to get her out now," the Police Commander said into his radio. Just then the staged ambulance silently rounded the back loop of Gorman Street—behind Kokopelli's—and acknowledged their position to the commander.

The Senator and his wife, Missy, sobbed tears of grief and hopelessness as they gingerly boarded the back of the ambulance with their wounded daughter.

CHAPTER FIFTY-SEVEN

"Steve Austin, astronaut: a man barely alive. Gentlemen we can rebuild him. We have the technology. We have the capability to make the world's first bionic man. Steve Austin will be that man. Better than he was before. Better, Stronger, Faster." ~*Oscar Goldman*

BIONICS

THE SIX MILLION DOLLAR MAN was no longer a science fiction pipedream, created for

television entertainment. "We've entered an age where those lacking bionics are considered

disabled," Brad said. "The aesthetics match the engineering in nearly every area of biology."

It was true. There were robotic replicas of the heart, lungs and the likeness of your face.

Also, neural implants that regulated memory and communicated with DNA. It has increased and

optimized brain function with a variety of sensory feedback.

Dr. Lui worked closely with Brad and Sabrina. He painstakingly documented the test

feedback and findings—and filed confidential reports to ITL leadership—but not everything.

There was a sanitized version for ITL and a more complete version that he shared with his

counterparts in China. He was quite subtle and clever in his movements. His ability to obtain

secret information wasn't obvious to onlookers. He used malware and cellphones as couriers

and had recruited someone from within ITL to assist.

If the sensitive intelligence information got into the wrong hands, it could potentially derail

the U.S. PSYCHONIX project. Dr. Lui was a new American citizen and a patriot—for China.

As a mole, he was conspiring against the U.S. Government in a classic case of electronic espionage. For two years he had been a sleeper agent who waved the U.S flag, all the while communicating with the motherland.

Initially it was a solo act, but he persuaded an engineer to install *upgraded* software on the lab computers. It was really a piece of complex malware designed to mine and relay information to other systems and communication devices.

That's where Dr. Kahn came in.

He was recruited and employed as a courier to transfer phone files back-and-forth. From the computer, to a phone, to a USB and repeat. Dr. Kahn didn't think of it as cyber-enabled theft of intellectual property or helping the Chinese government, but he knew exactly what he was doing.

Dr. Kahn had read and signed the *SF312*, The Classified Information Nondisclosure Agreement. It was so critical that no digital or electronic signatures were accepted. It had to be hand signed. But that didn't matter to him. He needed a lot of money, fast. Badly enough to carry out his treasonous acts without a hint of guilt.

Dr. Kahn and Dr. Lui worked fluidly and in tandem. Both of their cellphones were capable of mining the ITL files and ultimately transferring it to a black 4TB USB with a single 2TB SD card slot, which Dr. Lui kept in his lab coat pocket.

At this point they had only passed along *Alpha Testing* level information, but it was undeniably a serious crime of espionage. No one at ITL had noticed their well-orchestrated transfer of cellphones, but it was quite the logistical dance. Dr. Lui would take Dr. Kahn's cellphone when he left it face-up on the conference table and Dr. Kahn would exchange it for his. It was a sign that there was new data available. Dr. Lui made the transfer, dumped the data from the USB, and mailed the thin SD card to his home in China. It was usually disguised as a special gift for a distant relative. In the meantime, it was business as usual.

Brad and Sabrina shared briefing duties and annotated findings in the database. Within their reports they outlined historical accomplishments and advances in the *mind-body* research.

Sabrina was still intrigued about bionics and asked the group, "Did you know that archaeologists found ancient Roman and Egyptian replacement body parts? Crude wooden legs, strap-on toes, and hinged joints?"

"That's interesting," Brad said patronizingly. "But these days we have fully articulated bionic hands that allow you to feel through sensors, amazing cochlear implants, and bionic eyes that transmit a mosaic of impulses connecting the eyes to the brain."

"Well, they will no doubt be dug up by archeologists in the 24th century and have their crude technology put on display in some local museum too," she said to amused head-nods.

"Today, microelectrodes in the eyes and ears are giving us a broader range of conditions to explore," Dr. Starr said. "Our ITL team should be very proud of their *Mr. Watson, come here* moment—without a doubt an even greater discovery than Alexander Graham Bell's voice transmission."

"A momentous discovery," Dr. Lui added.

"Or an innovative accident," Brad said humbly, "like the telephone."

On June 2, 1875, while working in one room with their experimental harmonic telegraph, Watson tried to free a reed that had been too tightly wound around the pole of its electromagnet. He inadvertently plucked the reed, which produced a twang that Bell heard on a second device in another room. That discovery or *happy accident* led Bell to change his focus from improving the telegraph to figuring out a way to realize the potential for voice transmissions.

"Yes, I think that's an apropos comparison—many great discoveries have been made by *accident*," Dr. Feinberg said.

"At the time I was simply looking through a lens and attempted to adjust frequencies with a new quantope-crystals lattice that I was developing," Brad said. "It was intended to fix problems related to *DNA healing* and reading blood-flow patterns in the brain—but I faintly heard something new. A sound that we now recognize as the neurological code produced within PSYCHON radiation. I also understood that Sabrina was working closely with an *SGD speech-generating device* and that gave me some new ideas." He looked at her. "So, your work inspired me."

She nodded with a delighted smile.

"An *SGD*...what?" Dr. Kahn asked.

"It's a machine like the one Stephen Hawking used to talk through his computer," Sabrina said. "Although, he spoke through the voice synthesizer by simply twitching his cheek or painstakingly blinking through letters on an alphabet board."

"But this is completely different with the new *ocular-based biometrics in the goggles or implant,*" Brad said. "As Sabrina says, biometrics that read your soul."

"Yeah, don't let Apple or Samsung get a hold of that," Sabrina said, "or your soul will be made in China.

Dr. Lui scowled inside but ignored the comment.

I've been amazed at all of the multiple prosthetic devices being used nowadays. Necessity has no doubt been the mother of invention. It provides our wounded warriors with a better quality of life—and it has quickly propelled our technological advances. I didn't realize it, but prosthetic devices have been around for thousands of years, helping us interact with the world around us.

What we're doing now is unbelievable. It would be like magic to time travelers from the past, but what we're doing isn't a ritual to please the gods. We have scientifically bridged to the mind with an amazing prosthetic device, which allows us to communicate telepathically. I can't mention it in my diary, but it will change the world.

It seems obvious that the mind is more than a residual physical effect of the brain. It's more that the interactions of chemicals between neurons. As I've heard it said, a computer can replicate every aspect of water yet never be wet. It could also produce the effects of a brain and never have a soul.

CHAPTER FIFTY-EIGHT

"I cannot think of any need in childhood as strong as the need for a father's protection."
~ *Sigmund Freud*

POLITICS

THE PRINCESS WAS down. A pretty, petite angel, dressed-up like a princess for her seventh birthday. She was holding hands and skipping across the street with her daddy—Virginia Senator, John Croxon—when the bullet struck her in the head. It was like a hot needle that drove into her skull and dropped her to the pavement, *bam*. Her world went dark and so did her parents'.

The staged ambulance quietly rounded the back loop of Gorman Street with its lights off. On cue, they guardedly backed in behind Kokopelli's—and got as close as they could, using the vehicle for cover. The SWAT paramedic scurried out the back of the store and loaded Chelsea in the back of the ambulance—which sped off in a blur of blue lights and pulsating sounds. They urgently weaved through the traffic, carrying precious cargo to Anne Arundel Hospital—where a helicopter whisked them off to Johns Hopkins. Flight Time: 12-15 minutes.

In the intensity of the moment, John and his wife, Missy, rode along silently in the ambulance, scooted under the chuffing whirl of the rotors, and boarded the helicopter. Missy touched the top of Chelsea's little hand and prayed. Moments earlier, they had been strolling down the sidewalk of Main Street, enjoying the day and then, suddenly, they were kneeling over their daughter's torpid body.

The Senator replayed the day's events over and over in his mind. What could he have done better? At the sound of the first gunshot, his world froze in *bullet time*. He had instinctively yelled: *DOWN!* –and whipped out a concealed *Glock 17* from under his suit jacket and scanned a 360 with the nose of the pistol. By law, he had carried since he was the Mayor of Richlands, Virginia—and still carried on holiday and on all his senatorial travels. On Capitol Hill he had *24* hour police protection, but not while on family vacation.

He urgently instructed his family—*RUN!* —but the third bullet came faster than his instructions and Chelsea's ability to flee. Now, her brain had been severely damaged by a 9.07mm bullet. Her excited bright blue eyes dimmed, and her long blonde ponytail now encrusted with blood. It was supposed to be a family vacation, a boat ride, and ice cream kind of day, but it was abruptly terminated by someone else's bad choices and a reckless bullet. Chelsea died on the way to the hospital—but they were able to revive her. It was touch-n-go and she was holding on for her dear sweet life.

CHAPTER FIFTY-NINE

"The best date is to be with someone who can take you anywhere without touching anything but only your heart." ~ *Unknown*

LOVE AT FIRST DANCE

"I WAS RUNNING a little late and super nervous," Peggy Feinberg said, updating her best girlfriend on the last few engagements with Mark Starr. "Our first date was like being dropped into the middle of a Nicholas Sparks novel." She explained that since they were colleagues, they had decided to meet at the Chart House, a local Annapolis restaurant, on the water. "But when I entered, I couldn't find him. I panicked for a moment, thinking that Mark stood me up. But finally, I saw him waving from a corner table at the river window."

"I would have been a nervous wreck too," Pam said. "He's quite handsome."

"Ha! My nerves were running a million miles a minute, but when I walked up to him, he gave me a welcoming and affectionate hug. Mark was charming and handsome—as you say—and made all of the nerves melt away quickly with his gentle manner." She paused a long moment and thought about their evening talking, eating, and the positively stunning view of Spa Creek.

"Hello, you there, Peggy?" her friend said at the other end of the phone.

"Yeah, well," she said as she snapped back to reality. "We've mostly known each other professionally, but you know—I instantly felt comfortable with him and we talked for hours. It was like we were the only two people in the world. He wasn't pushy, but after dinner I invited him over for a drink."

"You what?" she chuckled at her friend's brazenness.

"Oh, get your mind out of the gutter girl. It was cocoa—and it was a genuinely nice, romantic evening. We stayed up to 2 a.m. Saturday and shared stories about our families and life. Honestly, we didn't realize how late it had gotten, but you know—it felt like we could talk forever."

"Did he kiss you?"

"Pam, please!" she said with faux shock. "He never tried to kiss me—not once. It was our first real date, but I thought he was going to when he leaned over close and asked, *would you like to dance?*"

"Wow, a Hallmark Movie moment."

"Yeah. We slow-danced in the middle of my living room as Andrea Bocelli softly played in the background: *Besame, besame mucho. Como si fuera ésta noche La última vez.*

"Later, before he drove home, we stood on the front porch holding hands."

"And?"

"...and with a lingering look he said, *I really enjoyed our time tonight...*"

"And?"

"...and we said, *good night*—that's all."

"Oh wow, he's a keeper."

"Yeah, well, wait until you hear this. On our second date he was even more thoughtful and romantic. He picked me up and we drove to the Annapolis waterfront again, on the city side. We walked along the pier and sat on a bench overlooking the Severn River. It was a special time," she paused. "He opened up and told me how he felt about me. And I told him that I've had a crush on him—from the beginning."

"That's huge!"

"Yeah—so, we sat on a bench, under the stars, and he gently kissed me—once softly and a little longer the second time. When we noticed the time, it was starting to get late. He asked if I wanted to go somewhere to grab a bite, so we drove down the road to *49 West*. It's a traditional European style coffee house with a lively rhythm and blues band. We found a small table with the *just right* ambience. He ordered a bottle of my favorite wine from the bar, a *Northern Italian Friuliano* and told me to order anything I wanted from the menu. Then, he stood and said he needed a minute to do something. Pam, you won't believe it. Mark walked over to the band that was performing and grabbed a mic. It turned out that he was friends with the owner and had arranged to sing a song for me."

"Wow."

"I didn't realize it, but he's a great singer and said he often sat in with the band. I had no idea, but it was wonderful."

"I bet."

"Mark sang a 1930's *Ink Spot* song called *If I Didn't Care,* while he slowly walked around the cafe. At one point he handed me a rose, sat down at our table, and serenaded me. I smiled into his eyes and for the life of me—I tried to keep it together. Then he held out his hand and led me to the dance floor."

"Honey, I'd call that love at first dance."

CHAPTER SIXTY

"Yet you do not know what tomorrow will bring. What is your life? For you are a mist that appears for a little time and then vanishes. ~ *James 4:14*

SURGERY

CHELSEA MARIE CROXON was immediately triaged and stabilized at Anne Arundel Hospital. She was then airlifted to the Johns Hopkins campus in Baltimore, Maryland, where Dr. Mark Starr and a team of neurosurgeons were called-in to begin a *seven-hour* operation. They worked against the clock since edema or severe swelling had developed in the left portion of her brain and on her spine.

A high level of sophistication would be required for such a delicate surgery—and he was the best that money or a decent insurance plan could buy. That was of little consolation to an overwrought mom and dad who paced the waiting room in tears. Her chance of survival was at best 70 percent—and that dismal number decreased by the second.

With a quick prayer, the Croxons apprehensively signed off on a *decompressive craniectomy*—not knowing what it really meant. They didn't understand the five dollar medical words or the procedure, but they knew that Chelsea would die if they didn't do something now. They would have signed their lives away to save their little girl.

Surgery would be done promptly to control the bleeding and attempt to salvage as much spinal function as possible. There was no doubt some direct damage to the spinal cord by the bullet and blood, which had accumulated in what doctors called a hematoma. It could have been applying pressure to the spinal cord—which would have made things look worse than they were. Dr. Mark Starr would remove the bullet, if possible, without causing more injury.

The recovery depended on the nature of the injury, the effectiveness of the surgery, and luck. If things went well, she might be in an ICU for a few days and a regular hospital surgical bed for another week—and then transferred to an in-hospital rehab unit for a few weeks. But, right now she was, once again, on the verge of death.

For seven-hours the doctors worked to remove the 9.07mm bullet, which had traveled through Chelsea's head and lodged in her shoulder—near the sensory and motor nerves that made up her tiny spinal cord. The bullet lodged in the spinal cord at the *C1* level and there was no way to know yet, whether she would suffer a temporary paralysis or at worst be rendered a quadriplegic. She was on a ventilator and a minimally invasive approach was used to limit the perioperative complication risk—and expedite Chelsea's recovery. Dr. Starr used an expandable retractor system and with the aid of a microscope, the posterior arch of *C1* was removed, the dura was opened, and the bullet fragment was successfully removed from the spinal cord.

They removed the bullet, but the *Beep, beep, beep* of the monitor alarms activated. Chelsea stopped breathing. A nurse yelled: *CODE BLUE!* Dr. Mark Starr systematically ran through all the lifesaving protocols. He worked with the highest sense of urgency and pulled out every trick in the book—but, still she didn't make it. Chelsea died on the operating table—pale and lifeless.

CHAPTER SIXTY-ONE

"For he is God's servant for your good. But if you do wrong, be afraid, for he does not bear the sword in vain. For he is the servant of God, an avenger who carries out God's wrath on the wrongdoer." ~ *Romans 13:3*

SWAT

IT WAS A late August evening in Colonial Annapolis with many of the windows flung wide open. Being located next to the water allowed bay breezes to ease the stress of the heat. It also made it easy for eyewitnesses to see events unfold at 249th Main Street.

There wasn't much privacy on the romantic streets. Town houses, stores, and restaurants were scrunched side-by-side. The narrow 18th century brick-paved streets were laid to make it safer for horses that pulled heavy loads, and to get rid of the mud, muck, and abundant manure deposited in the good old days. A street once anchoring horses to convenient hitching posts was now lined with modern vehicles and greedy parking meters.

The streets of Annapolis were planned in 1696 and laid out in a *Baroque* urban style; much like they were in Europe, during the 17th century. Governor Francis Nicholson laid it out to accentuate the city's two most important buildings: The Maryland State House, located on the downtown's highest point of land and St. Anne's Parish, located on the second highest spot. That would be the spot scouted and chosen for one of two snipers, who now lined up his sites, prepared to get the bad guys.

"I saw them as clearly as I see you," Martha Jackson, a witness and neighbor from across Main Street said. "We live in the third floor loft on the corner of Main and Francis Street with a direct birds-eye view of the condos above *Kokopelli*, where the shot came from."

"We looked out when we heard a bunch of kids crying," Martha's husband clarified. "—and we saw it."

They had witnessed an abused woman, on drugs, and with mental health problems. There was nothing more they could add. She had abducted the children out of a displaced need—to be called *Mommy*. It was a sad situation. She didn't have a plan, or hope, or much else of her mind left.

The Annapolis SWAT Officers & Crisis Negotiation Team threaded their way through the winding historic streets and deployed their support and forces tactically around the downtown district. They had practiced rescue operations here and knew exactly what to do.

The Special Operations SWAT police officers were trained and ready to perform high-risk maneuvers, things that fell outside the capabilities of regular forces. The Police Chief's elite tactical unit set about to bring this incident to a safe and successful conclusion. The goal as always: *to serve mankind, safeguard lives and property, and go home at night.* That was the real main goal. Go home, alive and well.

They arrived quickly, set up a cautious perimeter with two snipers strategically positioned in the old church tower and one prone, above Buddy's Crabs and Ribs. The one inside the dark, narrow space of the St. Anne's steeple, Corporal Greer, disappeared up a rickety ladder, ringed by a metal cage with a narrow plank stretched across it. It was a tactical position, high above one of the four-sided clocks. He was nestled-in near the top of the 155-foot spire and watched patiently from a wooden ventilation window.

Corporal Greer peered out through the slatted window, stabilized his Colt M16A2 and took careful aim with his scope. With a *Nightforce Optics 5.5-22×56 NXS Riflescope* he could see the Main Street apartment clearly. Usually he would have a spotter helping him determine distance, telling him the necessary info to dial on the scope, making wind calls, and necessary adjustments to bring the round on target—if he missed. Today there was no room for an extra in the clock tower. He was on his own. Greer was the best on the force—quick, efficient, and *by the book*—a sniper's MO, which is his *modus operandi* or work habit. He knew that he had to be in a good support position, ahead of time, and use breathing to control the heart rate, so he could shoot between breaths.

Safety-off, in-case talking doesn't work.

CHAPTER SIXTY-TWO

"The darker the night, the brighter the stars. The deeper the grief, the closer is God!"
~ *Fyodor Dostoevsky, Crime and Punishment*

NDE

CHELSEA MARIE CROXON stopped breathing and lost all brain functions. Dr. Mark Starr removed his surgical mask, sighed heavily, and pronounced her dead at *9:45* p.m. Telling the parents that she had died would be even more daunting than the hours spent trying desperately to save her, but he knew that he owed it to them.

Death was an inevitable part of life on earth, and yet it was one of the hardest things to contemplate and deal with. Mark was about to change their lives forever. In about five minutes, he would pass on heartbreaking news that their child hadn't pulled through. They would never be the same again, they would never be as happy again—because they believed that all *hope* was lost.

He hung his head in exasperation and felt a huge sense of responsibility to his little patient as her parents fretted in the waiting room, not knowing. Children brought a completely different perspective to coping with death. They weren't supposed to die first. They were young and innocent and full of vitality.

Dr. Starr came out of surgery immediately to break the news to Senator Croxon and his wife Missy. It was unbearable. They hugged and wept and hung on to the only things that seemed to matter, each other.

Counselors sometimes tried to put things into tidy boxes. They say that everyone goes through *five stages of grief*. It was something that Elisabeth Kübler-Ross, a Swiss American psychiatrist, came up with in her book *On Death and Dying*. She said you go through denial, anger, bargaining, depression, and acceptance, but that didn't describe how Mr. and Mrs. Croxon felt at this very moment.

"The only way I can describe it," Senator Croxon would later say, "is that there was no feeling. It was as if my heart had been ripped out and stomped on. There was nothing left, but a complete numbness."

Chelsea Marie Croxon was dead. A medical certificate had been filed that showed the cause and time of death. It would be sealed in an envelope and given to the family later, but for now her little body had been laid out and covered by a sheet in the room. It would be transported and kept in the hospital mortuary until arrangements could be made with an on call funeral director. There was nothing else to do—no one made advance plans for the death of a seven year old little girl.

It took time, depending on the circumstances, before a body was transported to the morgue. The most common practice was for the mortuary team to go to the room with a specialized stretcher, which looked like it had an extra fabric frame over the top to hide it from view.

That was the stretcher being used to transport Chelsea to the morgue now. You would never know that it was anything other than an odd looking laundry cart or stretcher. Those handling the body came in with a reverential calm and showed solemn respect for the body and the mourning family.

They moved her body out of the room, slowly and deliberately, to an elevator and into a basement walk-in cooler.

CHAPTER SIXTY-THREE

"Anyone who can be replaced by a machine deserves to be." ~ *Dennis Gunton*

HOOPTIE

DR. STARR FELT a great sense of responsibility to his patients and their loved ones. He became an early believer in the value of a condolence letter. It helped him cope. Not only did it serve as a tribute to the patient and source of comfort to the family but helped him get a grip on his own mind. Substituting distress with more useful thoughts. He was thinking about life deeply today. That's why he wrote the Croxons a letter and delivered it himself before pressing on with the business of the day. It was a small but significant token.

Later that day, he sat alone at lunch, or at least tried to. It was a useful distraction to have an unscheduled synapse of neurologist residents ask to sit with him. They found him pondering the meaning of life.

"Everybody philosophizes and speculates about meaning and purpose these days. Think about it. Even so-called logical and mathematical truths can't be proven by science. They *presuppose* logical and mathematical truths, so to try to prove it *by science* would be circular reasoning."

"You've lost it, Doc!" said one of his more vocal protégés. They knew he was still reeling from the loss of the little girl, so it was merely an attempt at a lighthearted poke.

"So, how can we know that we know anything?" One of the more inquisitive interns asked.

"I don't know how we know—but I believe that you can know certain basic things—through something that philosophers call a *properly basic belief*," Dr. Starr said. "Those are the things that we're all justified to believe. Things that don't need more evidence than our physical and moral experiences give us."

"Like what?"

"Like it's wrong to murder someone for sport," he said. "We don't need more reasons to believe something like that—we instinctively know it's true. Or, like that wall is blue." He pointed. "You believe that, don't you?"

They nodded.

"You can believe that it's blue, unless there's some overriding factor to warrant a different answer—like you're color blind."

"Interesting," another said. "But, if we were formed through a mindless, unguided process, then I guess we can't really know anything, right?"

Dr. Starr laughed. "If that were the case—then you're right. We couldn't know anything for sure. It would be at least a 50/50 chance."

"How's that?"

"Well, if you were created by a mindless, unguided process, then how could you trust any of the thoughts that you have?" he asked. "Your thoughts would be left to chance—and what you think is a thought, which is merely your synapses reacting to chemicals." He smiled and waited for a response that never came.

"How do you know that?" one of them asked.

"I can't say how I know anything if I don't have a trustworthy *objective standard* outside of myself to compare it to. Something objectively responsible for rationality. You would have to make subjective conclusions as to what that standard is, and one guess would be as good as the next. But to be clear—I believe that God is our objective standard for *origins, meaning, morality, and destiny.*"

There were a couple nods and a couple raised eyebrows—and some who could care less.

Mark enjoyed explaining his theories in class and in small, after class, group discussions like this. He had their full attention.

"As scientists we explore *how* things work, every day. But an equally good, if not better, set of questions is *why are we here* and *why does it work*? If you're just a mixed bag of selfish, predetermined chemicals, then why do you think you can really know anything?"

It started to make sense to a few, and a couple took their coffee and left. To others it didn't matter, or they were just too intimidated or polite to engage.

"If your brain is made up of only matter, then there's no separate conscious mind—and you can't have a true or false belief—it's all a *mechanical process*. In this case, your only meaning or purpose is to exist for a short time, adapt and survive," he said. "You can't find *objective morality* in a chemical."

They considered his words and nodded.

"So, then maybe we're not all that special," Dr. Starr said, "Maybe we're more like an old *hooptie* that outlived its value, any economic viability, and got hauled off to the junkyard at the end of its usefulness."

"I agree—you've lost it, Doc!" They all laughed, including Mark, as he quipped, "Yes, but there's still *hope*, even for my *hooptie*."

CHAPTER SIXTY-FOUR

"The two most powerful warriors are patience and time." ~ *Leo Tolstoy*

TIME FOR ACTION

THE FOUR FACES of the clock that encircled the spire of St. Anne's Parish registered *1:27* p.m. That was exactly *1727* hours Zulu for the Annapolis SWAT team. Zulu time is used when they deal with a team in a 24 hour operation that may cross different areas and time zones and frames of reference. The military uses it and the police use it for the same reason. It simply eliminates an area of potential confusion when timing was critical.

The church clock was originally built to give *Annapolitans* the proper time to set their pocket watches by. An older fashioned practice, from a bygone day, when the exact time wasn't as important to the residents. Up until the 1800's, clocks were exceedingly rare, and people usually guessed the time. But now, the timing was critical. Seconds mattered. It had been 17 minutes from the time SWAT was notified until they had settled into their positions.

From the top traffic circle, one sniper could see clearly to the Annapolis Harbor and Chesapeake Bay. As he looked up from *Memorial Circle*, next to *Spa Creek* and the Annapolis City Dock, one of their other snipers had a clear view of St. Anne's Parish. The street was covered from both angles.

A radio bleeped. "Streets secured; perimeters set!"

"Copy," the Police Commander said.

Locals, tourists, and Naval Cadets dressed in their white uniforms were corralled to safety—they scurried behind cordoned off sections of living history, from West Street and College Avenue, to the Naval Academy. It's not every day you see yellow police tape rope off historic buildings.

The Annapolis Police Chief, his Special Operations Swat team, and the Crisis Negotiation Team were on the scene to communicate, tamp down trouble, and de-escalate tensions. They were prepared and heavily armed with specialized weapons and equipment, but first they wanted to talk. Talking and negotiating were always the best first steps, when there were hostages involved. They had learned that children were being held hostage and knew that the rescue could be touchy. However, they were highly trained negotiators, artfully using persuasion, communication, and rapport building. From 30 yards across the street, Sergeant Shepard, a well-trained CNT officer, made her plea from a 50 watt megaphone bullhorn.

Ashlynn and Trip could hear her loud and clear.

"Let's figure this out, so no one gets hurt—let the kids go and we'll talk about it." The megaphone boomed, then gave a feedback squeal.

Ashlynn was devilishly enraged. She mentally pushed back and cast aspersions on the circumstances of their birth, along with some crass hall of fame, four letter descriptions of what they could do with it. The CNT stayed at it, but nothing seemed to work. Ashlynn suddenly and erratically unraveled, becoming even more delusional than before. She made her senseless demands clear, especially that she would not go peacefully:

Leave me alone—I just wanted to be a Mommy!

One couldn't help but to feel sorry for her, but she was long past the need for empathy.

She had taken three children and shot at her husband in an attempt to fulfill her wish to be a mommy. Trip passed out, drunk on the floor. The Police Commander, Captain Dickerson, gave another nod and the Crisis Negotiator got back on the bullhorn and repeated her standard spiel:

"Ashlynn, you don't have to do this. You have other choices." She repeated. "We can work this out together, so that no one gets hurt, right?"

There was no answer. *Radio silence*: however, she heard the officer and was shaking her head from side-to-side with a disturbed smirk on her face.

"Are you there?" the CNT Sergeant asked.

"I HEARD you!" she shouted came from just inside the window.

Contact...

Communication was paramount in these situations. Get them talking. Get them to care about something—friends, family, future, life, and hope. You humanize yourself. You remind them that you're a Grandma, a Navy sports fan, and a person who also feels, loves and hopes. That was the kind of person that could walk another hurting person back from the ledge of destruction. That was what Sergeant Shepard was good at doing—so, she stayed at it.

"I just want to make this work for you, Ashlynn."

In the meantime, other SWAT Officers coordinated. They had arrived with a 17 member, stand-alone team prepared for this type of emergency rescue operations: One Team Commander, two Team Leaders, two Snipers, and twelve Operators. Peace Officers locked and loaded, and now in sync with all support elements. They were prepared, but Ashlynn remained barricaded in her Main Street apartment.

CHAPTER SIXTY-FIVE

"We are never trapped unless we choose to be."
~ *Anais Nin*

DEATH AND DYING

THE FEMALE GUNMAN, as she was being called on the news, had succeeded in shutting down Annapolis. She was large and in charge, still holding court on Main Street. But, not for much longer.

Unprocessed, repressed anger wreaked havoc in her mind and on everyone in her wake. Stored up negative emotions from her dad, husband—and for all men, everywhere. Her impulses and emotions raged in an eruption of blame for things that she had played over and over in her head, until she began to believe them.

Words that echoed in her insecure mind. They were mean-spirited, inconsiderate, and unsympathetic words that Trip spewed, every day, especially when he drank too much.

I could have been somebody if I hadn't married him! she raged in her mind.

Counselors would have had a *Freudian field day* with her, scratching their collective chins, and dispensing their academic wisdom: *She's projecting. Defending herself against her own unconscious impulses, denying their existence, and blaming others. Even willing to die for it.*

It didn't matter now. Shots had been fired and hostages had been taken—and in the end, a small girl had died on the operating table.

Trip was coming out of his stupor. He had passed out cold while trying to save the day. Now he was more concerned about saving his own skin and going to the bathroom.

"I've got to pee!" he declared with no worldly care about the children tied up on his couch or Ashlynn pointing a pistol at him. *When you gotta go, you gotta go.*

She rolled her eyes and motioned him toward the bathroom with the barrel of her pistol. It was permission and he didn't wait around for a second opinion. Trip scurried his fat bottom to the rear apartment bathroom, locked the door, and started to climb out the small window. He grunted and struggled as he wiggled himself up and into the narrow window.

He no sooner felt stuck than he started to panic. Just then he heard a SWAT Officer yell, "Show me your hands!" The officer who yelled at Trip was one of four officers who crouched and waited on the back ledge of the apartment. He was the Sergeant that communicated and received play-by-play instructions from the command post bus and Police Commander. The Sergeant was ready to *make entry* but had the flexibility to change the call—and that's what he did when he saw the top of a man's head poke out the bathroom window. He didn't have time to relay the situation and receive permission from *the Bus*. It was a curveball, but they adjusted the plan and apprehended him.

One of the four officers was considered *lethal* and pointed an AR-15. The second, *less lethal* and held a pepperball launcher and Taser, ready to engage if necessary. The third held a shield in place for their protection. The fourth stood prepared as *hands,* ready to apprehend, handcuff, and lead the person away—to be interviewed.

When Ty Peterson heard *Show me your hands*, he yelped, "Don't shoot!" The fourth officer grabbed him by the shoulders and expeditiously hauled him out the window.

CHAPTER SIXTY-SIX

"I don't need an inspirational quote. I need coffee."
~ *Unknown*

COFFEE BREAK ACADEMY

WHEN LIFE GOT tough and the pressures were greatest, it was perhaps more important than ever to breathe and take good care of yourself. Todd Lopez's passing had been a tough pill to swallow for everyone. It caused some to fixate on *Near Death Experiences* and what that meant about life after death. If the video was accurate there was cause for great alarm. They had just witnessed their colleague and friend get dragged to what they could only imagine as hell.

Others went about their business as normal, as though nothing of major consequence had happened. Dr. Mark Starr's office was open, and he was happy to discuss anyone's views or concerns. Some people took him up on it, but others like Dr. Gus Kahn wrote it off as an echoic and iconic memory. "If it's a residual biological stimulus, then recording Todd Lopez's death merely allowed us to see a projected aspect of his brain's imagination—that's all."

It was a possibility.

Dr. Starr also brought in an outside counselor to help his team process recent life and death events and have an opportunity to talk about it. Although he was greatly saddened by Chelsea's death and Todd Lopez's recent passing, Mark's faith was strengthened by what he had witnessed on the video. For many reasons, he already believed that there was an afterlife, but the video provided greater validation. It also gave him more *hope* and brought him a greater sense of peace.

Mark continued to meet with colleagues at Café Nous to talk about events. He, himself, enjoyed decompressing at good cafés, where he could savor a mid-morning *Café Lungo* or velvety cappuccino and relax with friends. He used it as a time to provide insights to those needing to talk about whatever was on their mind. In this case incredible events that they had witnessed.

Dr. Starr had a peripatetic teaching style and treated his students as friends. He sat or walked and talked about a wide range of ideas—history, philosophy, religion, or anything to get his mind off the pain of losing someone.

The nuances of thought seemed to pop with clarity, as he sipped his cappuccino: two shots of espresso, equal ratio of foamed to steamed milk to produce a light layer of crema. He always told the barista: *I'll have a rich cup of caffeinated goodness. The stronger the better.* They knew his order by heart.

Dr. Starr comforted and challenged his protégés with his metaphysical questions and answers. Today it was Brad, Sabrina, and a couple of their peers. Sitting. Relaxing. Learning. No curriculum or membership fees—just a vigorous intellectual volleyball while savoring their drinks.

"All religions basically say the same thing," one of them asserted. "It's mostly social pressure and doing things that your community wants you to do. That decides what's right and wrong. I know—I did one of my undergraduate term papers on Bertrand Russell."

Mark found it humorous the late Russell's name was invoked as an authority. Many of his arguments had been addressed during the Christian apologetics reformation of the 1970's and

1980's, but he never put anyone on the spot, nor did he embarrass them. It was all about the journey of learning and growing.

"How or where we learn something doesn't make it true or false. One of the ways we discover things could be through the herd," Dr. Starr said. "But that doesn't make the herd right or all religions wrong."

Today, smart friends were in a cozy atmosphere, talking about *hope*, meaning, and the purpose of life—not everyone agreed and that was okay. Death caused people to ponder life and ask deeper questions. Mark offered reasonable answers. It was up to them to believe it or not. He understood that some folks had planted their flags and that no one changed their minds through angry exchanges. He knew very well: *It's a personal decision.*

He also understood that it was a broad subject since *all religions conflicted on the major issues and weren't at all alike.* He knew that objective truth wasn't determined by groups, cultures, or polls. He had learned those philosophical lessons early.

Most of the young technicians, who sat with Dr. Starr, weren't educated in philosophy but enjoyed rigorous thinking. They also enjoyed their own roasted blends, double chocolate biscotti, cannoli, and some lemon or vanilla *Pizzelle.*

Not all of them embraced the *God Hypothesis* he put forward but were still respectful and definitely awake, thanks to their newly caffeine packed and sugar induced energy. Today, Dr. Starr gave them something extra to chew on, an intellectually rich perspective.

Tonight, I'm thinking about religions and the fact that they can't all be true. Common-sense seems to dictate that. They aren't the same. They make completely opposite claims about the nature of God, Christ, Redemption, and life after death.

It is, however, safe to say that there is always a unique combination of factors—or steps—that move us toward belief in God. Evidence. Family, friends, tradition, literature, philosophy, science, and reason. The mind can be changed when it's willing to follow the warranted evidence—wherever it leads.

It's the intellectual sensibility and tradition drawn from theology and an enriching experience not found in the Velcroed propaganda of Atheism. God is the only one who can unlock a stubborn brain and provide them with the spiritual oxygen necessary for their existence.

CHAPTER SIXTY-SEVEN

"Hold on loosely but don't let go. If you cling too tightly, you're gonna lose control."
~ *.38 Special*

.38 SPECIAL

EVEN IF ASHLYNN had seen the little girl lying on the street bleeding, it wouldn't have phased her foggy mind. She had mostly separated from reality—with hallucinations and voices becoming more assertive, dangerous, and in control. Nothing mattered to her more than motherhood—not even being a good mother.

It dawned on her that Trip hadn't returned, so she crept back to check on him, just as he was being hauled out the bathroom window by the cops. It inflamed her, all the more, as she saw him flopping in the windowsill. The insane control knob stuck on high, she was now a swirling cauldron of psychotic emotions: Agitated. Hostile. Hyper. Restless, and racing paranoid thoughts!

He's leaving me!

It's a trap—but I won't let them get me!

If possible, her paranoia and delusions had intensified with even more mistrust, suspicion, fear, anger, and betrayal.

I know what they're up to, and I'll get them all!

She cocked the hammer of her .38 special, a museum piece really. *Boom!* Ashlynn's shot ricocheted off the bathtub and into the tiled bathroom wall, just as Trip found freedom on the outside ledge. His dangling legs and feet barely escaped the successive two shots: *Boom! Boom!* The bullets chaotically busted up the white porcelain pedestal sink and sprung a leak in the commode water tank—but coming nowhere near hitting Trip.

Trip was quickly uncorked from the windowsill, just in the nick of time. He fell to the ledge, slipped and cut his hands on the broken window glass below. However, there was no time to stop and worry about that. The cops dragged him to safer ground, just as Ashlynn remembered that the kids were left alone.

The children saw her leave the room, heard the commotion, and took advantage of the situation. It was their first opportunity to make a run for it. The twelve year old Gary had wiggled out of the Duct tape, cut the others loose, and pointed them in the direction that they should go. All three of them swiftly edged their way along the wall and got about halfway down the stairs, when an infuriated Ashlynn trudged back into the living room and discovered them missing. When she didn't see the children on the sofa, she was provoked to an out of control wrath, firing one shot after another toward the door and down the wall of the stairs. She barely missed the children as the shots hit the wall just above their heads.

Panicking! Hallucinating! Driven to madness!

The time she spent in the bathroom and firing at the door—it was enough. Enough time for someone to escape. It was just the diversion that the children needed as they ran for the blue-framed, glass entrance door below—too shocked and terrified to breathe.

Ashlynn pursued them as outrageous voices screamed in her head:

Her unraveled brain told her that there was only one way out of this mess: *Kill the Kids, Kill the Cops, Kill Yourself!!!* She repeated in her mind over-and-over, as she clumsily ran down the stairs—chasing after the children. Moving as fast as she could, uselessly pulling the trigger, dry firing, as it ran out of bullets.

CLICK! CLICK! CLICK!

She spent all six of her .38 Special rounds. The gun was completely empty, but still pointed at the children, as she ran out and into the middle of Main Street.

CLICK! CLICK! CLICK!

The children barely escaped the building. They ran and were swiftly scooped up and guided by three SWAT Officers and immediately escorted to safety, behind the SunTrust Bank on Francis Street. They were too scared to cry, but the little girl screamed when she heard the woman shout: *Come to mommy!*

It was *0100* Zulu—sundown in Annapolis. Ashlynn ran with her pistol still aimed at the children. The sniper would have to make a split-second decision, since there was no way to cuff her. Who knew what else she might have? She had taken only three steps onto the brick-paved street below her apartment. *ONE, TWO, THREE*, and it was halfway through the word *MOMMY* that she lost everything.

Ashlynn was the exception to the rule because most sufferers were peaceful and found hope in their mental health treatments, but years of addictions and an untreated psychosis caught up with her.

It was a one-in-a-million, one round, one-kill headshot. There was a three-second target window, from sidewalk-to-sidewalk, using thermal imagery. About as close to impossible as you could get for an expert SWAT sniper, but he still pulled it off. No *hope* of survival. One minute she was running and the next she was nearly decapitated—her neck opened-up like a zipper.

CHAPTER SIXTY-EIGHT

"If my body is enslaved, still my mind is free."
~ Sophocles

PLAY-BY-PLAY

"HOW DOES A dead man communicate?" Dr. Gus Kahn wouldn't drop it. "I'll take another stab in the dark—he didn't. They were, as I said, residual memories or dreams winding down in his brain."

"I don't think so," Sabrina said. "The PSYCHONIX processor in Todd's goggles allowed him to communicate throughout the entire evening. That was him talking after he died, not a memory."

"You can't prove that," Kahn said with his ever-present skepticism flowing as freely as a good wine.

"You can't prove he didn't! But—yes, I think there's plenty of evidence," she said to Dr. Kahn's rigidly raised palm-hand that outright dismissed her follow-up. He held little to no respect for a medical technician.

Dr. Starr stated, "It's enough evidence for me. We have a conscious stream of thought, recorded from before the time of his heart attack until the PSYCHONIX goggles were removed—we saw it."

"It was his soul," Sabrina Killian said. She had become more spiritual about the entire project and started to listen more closely to what Dr. Starr had to say about it.

Brad found her *transcendental stupor* to be quite humorous. He spoke up to distract and diffuse the conflict. "Well, I'm not sure that our PSYCHONIX roaming plan covers transdimensional communication—for souls." But he was still open for discussion on the matter.

Sabrina gave a contemplative smile and added, "I wonder how many *quantum-gigs* you'd need for that?"

Everyone was giddy with excitement and with the implications. They had mastered a form of telepathy and now a real person had provided them a play-by-play—from the grave.

CHAPTER SIXTY-NINE

"To know that we know what we know, and to know that we do not know what we do not know, that is true knowledge." ~ *Nicolaus Copernicus*

COPERNICUS

THE LIGHT-MINDED COPERNICUS questioned the status quo of the universe. He formulated a crazy model, which moved the Earth and stopped the Sun, placing it at the center of the universe. At that time, Christians were reluctant to reject a theory that seemed to agree so greatly with Biblical passages. They discovered later that it did not line up with Scripture, but up until then the layperson had been admonished not to trifle with such sacred things.

It was a day and age when the Ptolemaic scientific consensus was that the Sun, Moon, stars, and planets all orbited Earth. It was quite obvious to any observer that the Earth was unmoving, solid, stable, and stationary—until the truth was discovered.

Information came to light at ITL in a similar fashion. They made a new discovery, perhaps greater than that of Copernicus. In the course of their experiments, they unexpectedly found a metaphysical, telepathic bridge or a form of communication that transcended and bound us all together in a mental or spiritual way. Like *heliocentrism,* it was a truth that needed to be discovered and explored. Now, it has been tested multiple times in the lab and once from a man who had died. This seemed to put the soul at the center of man. Everything else revolved around it.

That aspect alone piqued their interests and spurred all their imaginations and conversations during IPRs. That was where they discussed the next best steps. The possibilities and questions were endless. *What If* and *Why Not* became their modus operandi as they sought more answers. They now knew that they could communicate with other minds, but what about other beings in other universes, realities, or dimensions? *Why Not?*

The discovery held *unlimited possibilities* with each person functioning as a communication hub. Brad even raised the notion of time-travel. "If one subscribes to the B-Theory of time, then perhaps it would even be possible to speak to people in the past or from the future. Since we live in a space-time block, it could be that every moment of time is equally real. So, maybe we can communicate to them from here."

For the moment, it was all systematic conjecture. From a religious perspective, Dr. Starr had philosophical objections to the *B-theory*:

"It means that at some point in time, Christ is still on the cross and sins haven't been forgiven, once and for all. And that the execution could be repeated on repeat visits. It means that everything was pre-determined and that nothing was contingent or depended on anything else to exist—it was all here, somewhere, simultaneously from the beginning—like a film."

Films are already made, but he didn't believe that our freedom of choice had been determined. *It's a contradictory statement,* he thought.

He also noted a strong scientific objection related to evolutionary biology. "For instance, if evolution is simply explained as *change over time* and there really isn't any genuine change of time on the *B-theory*, then biologists should reject it, because evolution requires a real sequence of events. No, I think that the common-sense view is that things are really coming into existence and passing away."

His brain was working overtime.

Dr. Mark Starr was not one to leave his brain at the narthex of the church door. He thought deeply and pondered the major communication achievements of PSYCHONIX in relation to personal prayer: *We can cognitively connect with others, but biblically we've always been able to connect with God—and He with us.*

Had they just climbed another technological mountain to find out that God was sitting there all along? Science had only determined in the last one hundred years, or so, that the universe had an absolute beginning, something taught by Jewish believers more than 3400 years ago. He contemplated whether PSYCHONIX was really connecting them to the heavens now. It seemed so.

Earlier, Dr. Mark Starr humbly expressed to his staff what he thought:

"I believe that there is a higher source of wisdom, knowledge and power—that connects and directs us all. A God who hears from us—and us from Him."

"Amen," said a new janitor mopping up by the break room door. "Sorry—I heard ya talkin' and well, I don't know all the stuff you fellas do—but I talk to that God each and every day."

Mark smiled and nodded. "Me too." He didn't *feel* like a guy who knew *all the stuff*—quite the opposite. As a scientist and person of faith he made discoveries every day. It brought to mind another verse that meant there was a lot which is unknown: *For now, we see in a mirror dimly, but then face to face. Now I know in part; then I shall know fully, even as I have been known fully.* It was a divinely promised capability, Mark Starr thought: *to know fully.* But it surely didn't mean you know everything, or that you were omniscient.

That would make you God.

He took a sip of coffee and allowed others to say what they wanted to about the topic. Again, not everyone agreed and that was okay. Mark listened and then continued, "And—now, for the first time in history it seems that we've actually heard from another dimension. Because of the *Lopez video* we may have a better understanding about how we're all tied together."

The IPR wrapped up and Dr. Kahn muttered to himself as he stood up and walked out of the room. It was clear how he felt and what he was muttering as he left: "Idiots. What we heard was a residual delusion playing out in his dying brain."

Mark thought *he's not the only one with a dying brain* but held his tongue. He sat at the conference table, finished his coffee, and continued to think about the situation. *We heard from Lopez, but wouldn't it be amazing if we could get a glimpse of Heaven like the Apostle John?* He flashed back to a message he heard on the radio, while driving to work one day. *Wouldn't it be amazing, if like John, we could see beyond the universe that we see with our telescopes and technology, and actually see and communicate with Heaven? It happened before.*

Theories had been bandied to-and-fro as to what PSYCHONS were made of. It was a non-material substance being radiated that they started calling a *mental substance*. That was the life-changing, scientific discovery that allowed for mind-to-mind communication. No one really knew what it was made of, but Mark's brain continued to process it.

"This entire project has shifted our way of thinking, much like Nicolaus Copernicus did during the 13th and 14th centuries," Dr. Starr said. "So, for the time being let's just say that PSYCHONS are made of *Copernicus particles*. It's totally made up but sounds pretty cool."

Everyone nodded.

The philosophical implications were vast: *It now seemed clear that the universe wasn't the center of reality.*

CHAPTER SEVENTY

"He said, Leave; for the girl has not died, but is asleep. And they began laughing at Him."
~Matthew 9: 24

AND WE'RE BACK

CHELSEA ELIZABETH CROXON had been dead for nearly six hours, when she woke up shivering and screaming in the morgue. One moment she was lying on the metal bed, cold and dead with a white sheet pulled tightly over her body—the next moment she was alive.

For six hours there had been no heartbeat, no brain activity, no anything, despite extensive attempts to revive her early on. Family members had braced for the worst and prayed. Dozens of friends were gathered at the hospital. Many of them were still on their knees in prayer circles. Doctors said that her skin had already started to harden, her hands and toes were already drawn up and starting to curl.

"There was no pulse, blood pressure or measurable brain activity," doctors told them. "And there were no signs that she had neurological functions." The family had agonized—and said their goodbyes. John and Missy both took turns and kissed her sweet little cheeks, before they started the onerous task of making funeral arrangements.

At 7:43 a.m. Chelsea's heart suddenly restarted. She took a huge gulp of air and began moving her limbs—alive but trapped in a walk-in cooler in the basement of the hospital. It was a real life nightmare. She was scared, and banged and screamed as loud as she could. It more than terrified a couple of nurses, as they came on shift.

In less than 24 hours Chelsea had gone from being a carefree seven year princess, to dying from a bullet wound, and coming back to life. Who got to make that phone call and what would they say?

We thought your daughter was dead, but it looks like we were wrong. It happens all the time, can you come pick her up?

They were in shock. The fact was that she was alive and well, and it didn't matter why. It was a miracle. They couldn't explain it, maybe they never could. Doctors tried desperately to spin and categorize it, simply calling it the *Lazarus Phenomenon.* They didn't know. But, just as with the resurrection of Lazarus, the family was ecstatic. They broke land-speed records as they tore back to the hospital and abandoned their car at the entrance.

Still in disbelief.

They had seen her lifeless. They stood by her bed for an hour and grieved her passing, but now she was alive and talking.

"I saw mommy speaking to a lady in a wheelchair," Chelsea recalled. "It was a lady with gray hair and a red sweater. She patted mommy on the back while they were praying together." Everyone was astounded because it had happened just as Chelsea described—but she couldn't have known.

"I felt like—I just kept going *up, up, up* in the air, like a balloon. I saw the doctor touch my neck and then there were two angels who held my hands and told me not to be afraid," she said. "They took me to a really pretty place Mommy."

The family called it a miracle, because how else does one explain an event that was so inexplicable, by natural or scientific laws? It was *divine* and she was healing from the bullet wound. It had been removed from her spine before she died. Now she sat in bed and responded well to the reconstruction and treatment. Doctors said she had a good chance at a full recovery, without brain damage. But the things she recalled still baffled them. Things she had seen when she was *asleep*. People she had spoken to.

If you believed any of it, then you had to believe it all. You would have to believe that she floated toward heaven, traveled to another dimension, and talked to angels and to people who had died long ago.

"Daddy, one man said I was brave and put a *Red Feather* in my hair—is it still there?" Chelsea asked. She felt around her head, but there was nothing but bandages. Her hair had been shaved off and her head was bandaged from ear-to-ear. There were no signs of a feather—red or otherwise.

Her hair was gone, but her memories were intact. Some thought that perhaps it was a delightful part of her young imagination. However, one thing was irrefutable—the story of the red feather was remarkable. It had circulated through the hospital faster than PSYCHON radiation and eventually reached the ears of Steven Scott.

CHAPTER SEVENTY-ONE

"No distance of place or lapse of time can lessen the friendship of those who are thoroughly persuaded of each other's worth." ~ *Robert Southey*

REUNION STORIES

CHELSEA WAS ALIVE again! They were still in disbelief, but John and Missy could barely contain their joy as they kept watch and cried the happiest of tears. Still relieved and numb, they passed the boring hours telling her hopeful stories from their childhood. Stories that they never thought they would get a chance to share with her—about family, friends, and special times with family and neighbors, who were like family. She listened attentively. As soon as possible, maybe even Christmas, they would try to get back home and recapture the good things that they remembered.

For now, Chelsea needed to lie still and recover. So, what better way to pass the time than to watch TV, color, and hear stories about the magical, faraway towns of Richlands, Cedar Bluff, and Grundy? Places near and dear to the Croxons. John called it their refuge from life's troubles. Although it certainly had its own small-town troubles, John said, "When I'm there, I feel at peace."

"You used to say it's so beautiful that it's not enough to have two eyes," Missy said with a wink toward Chelsea.

"True enough," John patted her little hand. "I think it's probably where God started making Heaven." Chelsea beamed a broad smile as she considered God actually making Heaven with a hammer and saw.

In their retelling of growing up, the hometown stories and expressions sometimes seemed bigger than life, if not fictionalized. In Richlands we say, "*Way over yonder*, which means way over there and *Madder than a wet hen.* Have you ever seen a wet hen?"

Chelsea nodded.

"If so, then you'd know being madder—is mad indeed."

Chelsea giggled and her tiny facial expressions lit up before she requested, "Tell me more, Daddy."

Some of the nurses taking care of Chelsea heard the stories and asked their own questions. It was a useful distraction for the Croxons and an opportunity to educate Chelsea about her southern family heritage. And it fondly reminded John and Missy of where they came from and of simpler, tough times.

"Although money was in short supply," John said, "we always found ways to occupy ourselves and made Christmas a fun time at *The Grundy Mountain Mission Home.*"

"Why were you there at Christmas, Daddy?"

"Because it was the place that God provided for us kids and our mommy, when we needed help—when we didn't have anywhere else to go."

It was enough of an answer for a seven year old. She didn't need to hear about his Daddy dying in the coal mines of black lung and Missy's parents' unfortunate accident. Her parents had died in a terrible house fire and the home had taken her in as a six year old.

"It's a good thing that people loved you—wasn't it, Daddy?"

"Yes, it was honey. That first Christmas we were mostly happy to have love and still be together. But being there, gave us the *hope* we needed, when we needed it. We were warm, well fed, and each of us got a few gifts: toy animals whittled out of wood that were left by the buck stove in the dayroom, new shoes ordered from the *Sears & Roebuck* catalog—and an orange, an apple, a few nuts and peppermint candy sticks stuck in a sock. Larger gifts and hand-me-downs were sometimes provided by local churches and the limited resources of *The Home*."

"But what about Santa," Chelsea asked. "Did he get there too?"

"Ah yes, somehow Santa invariably found us," he said gently squeezing Chelsea's hand, as she leaned forward, and he continued to paint pictures of long-ago memories.

"On our tree at *the Home,* we always made our own Christmas decorations," Missy said. She remembered it like it was yesterday. There was a lot of sadness, but it was also how she had met John. They enjoyed making the Christmas crafts together and took turns pushing each other on the playground swing, when they were small.

"We usually strung popcorn, didn't we?"

"Yep, snowflakes, paper chains, and candy canes, if we were lucky. I'll show Chelsea how to do it this year at our Christmas reunion—everyone is going to be so happy to see you," Missy added. "You just keep heal'n up and we'll be on our way in no time." That was her hope.

Chelsea smiled.

"I had forgotten all about that," John said.

"Me too, but your Grandma Keene reminded me, when she called to check on Chelsea. It'll sure be sweet to have everyone together this year—we've been away too long." It was a much-welcomed conversation that relieved the anguish they had undergone the last few days.

"Your mom decorated our rooms and windows at *The Home* with scraps of cloth, apples, and cotton that made it look like it had snowed," she said.

"And the smell!" John remembered. "We used to make a hand-poured homemade pine cedar candle in a mason jar—that reminds me of *The Home* to this day," he said reminiscing.

As they spoke and told stories, Steven Scott began his hospital search for Chelsea. He strolled the hallways looking for the right room, then he stopped, checked the room number, and knocked. There was only one seven year old little girl in the hospital, so she wasn't hard to locate. He had spoken with John Croxon over the phone, earlier that morning, and let them know who he was and why he was so interested in meeting and hearing Chelsea's *Red Feather* story.

It piqued their interest, so he briefly spoke to Chelsea on the phone and had asked her too—if it would be okay to visit. *On the phone she had an encouraging Shirley Temple type of optimism,* Steven recalled.

"We both have to be brave now, Mr. Steven—Sergeant Red Feather said so."

He couldn't believe the words coming out of her little mouth and wanted to hear more about it, in person.

"Knock-knock," Steven Scott said, as he rapped lightly and cracked the door open. He peeked inside. "I heard that there's a little girl here with a red feather?"

He was cheerfully greeted by Chelsea's broad smile, freshly minus that top right front tooth still waiting under the pillow for the Tooth Fairy. He was promptly motioned in and shook all their hands and introduced himself again, before being asked to take a seat in one of the hospital chairs. Steven told her that he knew all about the *Red Feather* and that he would love to talk about it some more. "The Sergeant was a good friend of mine," he said.

Chelsea sat up straight away and looked intently at him, as she relayed the story of her unusual journey. It strangely comforted Steven to hear about his old battle-buddy, Sergeant Carl "Red Feather" Hetzenaur. Hetzenaur was the sniper mentioned in his *Silver Star* military citation. It comforted Chelsea, too, that an adult truly believed her story about seeing someone, when she was *asleep*.

Steven tried not to take up too much of Chelsea's time, since she was still in recovery. He knew that there would be plenty of time, over the course of the next few days or weeks, to share stories and compare notes, but she was eager to talk. "I went to heaven! That's where I met him."

He believed her and talked up, not down to her as a child. He also listened and waited on her to talk. Chelsea and the family liked him instantly and after a month of visits she started referring to him as Uncle Steven.

During one of the visits, Steven was fortunate enough to hear the much anticipated news. A doctor came whistling into the room with a big smile and a special announcement for the Croxons. "You're making great progress. And if you keep it up, you can continue your rehab at home this Christmas," she glanced down at her clipboard, "but it says here that you've got to be good for Santa Claus and eat a lot of cookies too."

It was great news. In its truest sense, it seemed like Christmas this year would be a sweet, wonderful time of refreshing.

Chelsea shook her head up and down saying, "Oh, I will—I will."

"Yeah!" came the shouts from everyone in the room. From sheer relief and joy, Missy placed her hand over her mouth and started to cry. John gave her shoulder a gentle squeeze and held her hand, his eyes teared up as well.

"Just no rough-housing," the doctor said. "Your bones are still healing." Chelsea had undergone a cranial reconstruction. Parts of her skull had been fragmented. She also required a Cochlear implant to restore some of her hearing. She didn't seem to mind.

"Do you really think she's ready for all that?" her mother interrupted.

"She'll be here for another six weeks," the doctor said, looking at the chart, "but yes, I think she's healthy enough. Being home will do her good. And you can follow-up in the New Year."

Chelsea waggled her arms in the air and gyrated with silly glee.

"And lively too," John said as he leaned down to kiss her on the cheek.

"Yes, and *very* lively," she trumpeted back.

"She's doing much better than expected," the doctor said. "—and so, with the necessary precautions, I see no need to keep her trapped during the holidays."

"Can *Uncle Steven* come visit us for Christmas," Chelsea asked with a hopeful, faux pout on her tiny face.

"Well, that's up to him and his wife," John said. He looked at Steven. "It's a six-and-a-half-hour drive from Baltimore to Southwestern Virginia, but you and Marlina are *more* than welcome."

It wasn't at all an odd request to Steven Scott. Having served around the world in the military, he had grown used to making fast friends with strangers. Everyone attached to his unit became a *mandatory* friend. It doesn't matter if you *like* them, *hate* them, or think they are the *dumbest* person ever, they have just become your *salvation* and destruction, and you may spend more time with them than your family. This was obviously a much better circumstance.

"I think we're going to visit our son in Bluefield, Virginia, this Christmas," Steven said.

"Well that's right in our neck of the woods," Missy replied.

"Why don't we plan a get together," John said.

"I'll mention it to Marlina."

"Please Uncle Steven," Chelsea begged.

He winked at her. "It may be just what the doctor ordered."

She scrunched up her face and tried to wink back, but all she could do was force an adorable blink.

CHAPTER SEVENTY-TWO

"It does not end with mortal death; it just begins."
~ *Boyd K. Packer*

VISIT

OVER THE COURSE of the following weeks, Chelsea shared the most unbelievable stories with her family and Steven about what had happened while she was *sleeping*. That was her family's euphemistic way of talking about death to a seven year old. But she didn't mind the word *death*, it had a different, pleasant meaning to her now.

"It's true—not only did I see *Red Feather* when I was *sleeping*, but—" she looked up at Missy, "I saw your mommy and daddy too. They told me to call them Gramsy and Poppy and hugged me *sooo* tight—that I nearly popped!" She smiled her sweet innocent smile. It made Missy tear up to hear it. "They said that I was *too early* and that I'd have to come back and visit another time."

It was an incredible story and Missy didn't really know what to think about it. She hadn't seen them since she was a little girl, before the fatal fire.

"I was taken to the home shortly after they died," Missy said.

John and his wife Missy wiped away a great deal of tears that day, as they listened to her sweet stories. Things that she couldn't have known, like the color of the dress that Missy wore on that fateful day and that her mother used to call her *Little Missy Mae*. Chelsea wasn't even alive then, so it was beyond incredible. They were simply agog to hear more. Chelsea didn't usually make up fanciful stories like that, and even if she did—they knew that she couldn't have been so accurate about those details. She had never known her mom's side of the family.

"It was like a fun dream, except it was really real," she said looking expectantly, wanting them to believe her. Their eyes revealed that they also wanted to.

"I ran all around Heaven and touched the trees and flowers and butterflies—and I danced with Gramsy. She held my hands out and swung me around in circles and made my legs and feet fly in the air. Then Poppy took me for long walks in the woods and told me all about the trees and the flowers and all their names. Did you know that they all had names Mommy?" she asked. "He's quiet—but he sure smiled at me a lot."

Her account of Heaven and the people she met were beyond astonishing. There were too many uncanny things that had never been told to her—that she couldn't have known, unless she had actually died and gone to Heaven.

"I was there all day! I even got to have an *ice cream*! I'm so glad that they have ice cream in Heaven," she said, shooting a thankful look around the room. "Just before I came back, we were all sitting on the front porch—of a big beautiful pretty house and they both gave me messages for you, mommy. They said, *don't worry! We love you and we're proud of you and the woman you've become!"*

Tears flowed down Missy's cheek.

"They waved bye and then I was pulled away through a *funny white rainbow tunnel*. It made me so sad, Mommy, and I reached my hands out, but I couldn't hold on to them no matter how hard I tried." As Chelsea spoke, she held out her hands like she was reaching. "They didn't seem sad though. They just blew me kisses."

354

CHAPTER SEVENTY-THREE

"Everyone comes with baggage. Find someone who loves you enough to help you unpack."
~ *Ziad K. Abdelnour*

EMERGE

PHYSICIANS CARRY THE same emotional baggage that everyone else does. Like everyone else, they can embrace false views and assumptions tainted with their bias, or even deny the plain facts staring them in the face. That was Dr. Gus Kahn's predicament—for whatever reason, he denied plain facts. He would argue that a belief was false, if it implied something that he'd rather not hear.

"All anyone can do is to show him *the price he has to pay* by holding an absurd view," Dr. Starr shared with Dr. Feinberg. He knew that the cost of maintaining a false view was too high a price to pay for someone dedicated to finding the truth. Dr. Kahn didn't care. He was ill-fatedly on the verge of bankruptcy and his mounting bills trumped everything. *Truth be damned.*

So far, there was little doubt in anyone's mind that Todd Lopez had communicated from beyond the grave and that a seven year old little girl had a *Near Death Experience*. The evidence of a direct link between the *mind, body,* and *consciousness* was also piling up, and it would have many physical and metaphysical ramifications. But Dr. Gus Kahn didn't buy it.

"This is all nonsense," he said responding in private to Dr. Lui. "We will eventually disprove this life after death and eternal soul stuff that religious people cling to."

355

"…with their Bibles and their guns," Dr. Lui added. He remembered hearing President Obama say that and thought that it would make him sound more American.

He nodded. They both dismissed what they considered as the silly metaphysical nonsense, but eagerly embraced the idea of making a fortune.

Together, they developed a cunning plan to delay ITL's progress and sell superior PSYCHONIX technology to China. It was irresistible. Dr. Kahn would run interference for a sizable pay-off. Maybe millions. Dr. Lui, on the other hand, still had strong loyalties to his motherland.

"This technology could be even greater than the most powerful nuclear weapon ever created," Dr. Kahn said. "And I'll bet your contact will pay big bucks for it."

Dr. Lui nodded his agreement. "But only if we can decipher the PSYCHON radiation codes." They were becoming fast friends and allies.

CHAPTER SEVENTY-FOUR

"God crowns us. Most people crown their Christmas tree with either an angel or a star. God uses both." ~ *Max Lucado*

CHRISTMAS ANGEL

CHELSEA'S INPATIENT REHAB took longer than expected. There was a cerebral edema, known as brain swelling. It was a life-threatening condition that causes fluid to develop on the brain and increases pressure inside of the skull. It was frightening, but they had a lot of options. Everything from medication, ventriculostomy, to surgery—but it seemed like the best prescription now was rest.

After more worry and prayer, the swelling seemed to be under control. The interminable poking, prodding, and rehab took its toll, but they tried to remain thankful. Since the time of the surgery, recovery, and edema, nearly four months had passed. Now the Croxons eagerly waited for insurance claims and paperwork to be completed. She probably wouldn't get out until after Thanksgiving, but at least she's being released.

As she passed the time, Chelsea laid in the hospital bed and read a new *Berenstain Bears* book that her mother had loaded on the iPad. *The Christmas Angel* had totally captivated her mind to the point that she nearly forgot where she was. Her seven year old imagination ventured to *Bear Country,* where the family could make a *snow bear* and *snow angels* and drink hot cocoa, while Mama and Papa Bear talked about some very special angels and the work that they do for God. She was in deep thought about that, when the iPad lit up and interrupted story time with an expected call from Steven Scott. Her daddy told her it was okay to answer, because Uncle Steven had something to show her.

Chelsea heard the call coming in and saw Steven Scott's name prominently displayed on the iPad's screen. She was young but had learned how to navigate the iPad from plenty of video chats with her grandparents in Richlands, Virginia. She knew what to do and instantly tapped the screen to answer the call. There he was:

"Oh, hey! How did you get in there?" Steven teased her.

"It's FaceTime," she said with a giggle. "We're not in it."

"Oh, I see. So, then how do I give you a hug?" he asked, extending his arms toward the screen.

"You can't," she said dragging out the words to express just how silly she thought the idea was. *"You caaaan't.* I'm in here and you're out there."

"Oh, I see—you're very smart Chelsea. Are your mom and dad there?" She turned the camera and they both waved. "Hey Steven!"

"Hey everybody—I talked it over with Marlina and she liked the idea of visiting you guys at Christmas, on the way to see our son. He'll have precious few days off from the Bluefield Regional Medical Center, so we're not sure exactly when."

Missy poked her head in front of the screen. "Well then, why can't he come down, too—everybody can spend Christmas together with us?"

John added, "That's a wonderful idea. We've got a big place and we would love to show off our small town and the Christmas festival."

"You don't have to ask me twice, but first let me huddle with the family again and I'll let you know. Oh—I almost forgot—Chelsea?"

"Yes, Uncle Steven?"

"I wanted to show you the necklace that belonged to my friend Sergeant Hetzenauer."

"Which friend is that? Sergeant Het-zen—." She struggled to say the name and looked over at her dad for help, but Steven quickly pronounced it again as he held up a feather and necklace beads. "This is Red Feather's."

"Ooh my, that's pretty!" she said.

"Yes, I guess it is." Of course, *pretty w*asn't exactly the way an old Soldier like him would have described it, especially considering the amount of death associated with it.

"Oh, and Mr. Steven—I almost forgot to tell you—*Red Feather* said to say thank you for bringing him home!" That completely flabbergasted Steven, because Sergeant Hetzenauer had returned home to Delaware on a C-5 Galaxy with the other dead Soldiers.

Now it was Steven with the lump in his throat. It was a military thing—*no man left behind.* He was just doing his duty and no one outside of the U.S. Army knew any details of that battle. It was a deeply personal and tragic part of his military history, which was occasionally conjured up in his PTSD. In the throes of fighting, Sergeant Carl Hetzenauer had been gunned down. He was a sniper, taken out by an enemy sniper at the start of the conflict. He would spare her all the gory details.

He felt his emotions well up in his throat and stopped talking…but then found the words he said, "I found him and this necklace of feathers and beads around his neck after the smoke had mostly cleared. I said a prayer, took it off of him, and thought I could return it to his family. It was a good thought, but to no avail. I never had any of my calls returned—and after a while I guess that I just forgot about it."

"He said it brought you both good fortunes," Chelsea said.

"How so?" he asked with a puzzled look, still trying to process everything. He still remembered from his research that a red feather symbolizes good fortune for some Native Americans.

It all happened so long ago—before she was even born.

"The Sergeant said you're a brave man and that you should wear the *Red Feather* now. He also said that his death had been a gift—they both did."

"I don't understand. A gift—what do you mean that they both did?

How in the world could it have been a gift?

"He got to be with his wife again."

"Lynn?"

"Yes, sir—she died from cancer, but now he was holding her hand again."

CHAPTER SEVENTY-FIVE

"All things are bound together. All things are connected." ~ *Chief Seattle*

THE GREAT DEFENDER

ARMY MASTER SERGEANT James *"Blue Crow"* Bay was a 95 year old Penobscot tribal elder and highly decorated veteran of World War II, awarded the *Silver Star* and the *Legion d'Honneur* (French Legion of Honor). He served proudly as a combat medic with the *Big Red One* and had landed on Omaha Beach in the first wave.

Today, like many other days, he demonstrated why he was a member of the Greatest Generation as he scouted the hospital and made his daily visitations. Without exception, he brightened the days of patients as he meandered from room-to-room spreading kindness. There was a special visit on his mind now, as he strolled toward Chelsea's room.

Steven Scott was already in her room for a short, early morning visit and wanted to discuss their upcoming holiday plans. He and Marlina talked it over and decided to accept the Croxon's hospitable offer. It would be fun to visit them at Christmas. First though, they would spend a day with their son Vito in Bluefield, West Virginia and then head down to Richlands. It wouldn't take long, since it was only thirty-six miles from the Bluefield Regional Medical Center.

"From everything you've told us, Christmas in your hometown sounds great," Steven commented.

"Oh, it is," added Chelsea.

"Well, it's our little slice of Heaven," Missy said as she hugged up next to Chelsea. "And now an oasis of *new hope* for our little family."

"That sounds even better," Steven said. "I could use an oasis like that in my life."

"As children, my brother Mark and I loved Christmas and living in a small town where the neighbors all know each other. I suppose most children do."

"I do," Chelsea volunteered.

"We love the way our grandma celebrated it," Steven said.

"Good memories," John said.

"Yeah, one of few. We loved the lights, parades, and the candy."

"Me too—I love candy," Chelsea volunteered.

"Well, invite your brother too," Missy said. "The more the merrier."

"I'll mention it to him."

They nodded and Steven smiled. *They're such nice people.*

Christmas in the South sounded delightful—a restful getaway for the entire Scott Family. Mark Starr agreed and said it sounded like a great idea, if he could get the time off. They spent a lot of time planning and knew it would be fun. They were excited about spending Christmas together; however, a friendly disagreement arose as to where everyone would stay over the holidays.

"Oh no! No one pays for a hotel—we won't hear it," John insisted.

"There's plenty of room at the *Old Perry Mansion,* honey," Missy said. "Of course, y'all will stay with us—Mark, too."

"The more the merrier," John added.

Steven held his hands up in mock-surrender, but then for no apparent reason sensed that something was about to happen. He looked around, at the Croxons, and asked, "Are you expecting another visitor today?"

It wasn't unusual. People had visitors in the hospital all the time. But the timing was odd since *Blue Crow* almost immediately knocked and poked his head in the door. Missy waved him in, and he introduced himself with, "The Spirits are strong here today."

Not exactly what they had expected to hear in a hospital room in the middle of Baltimore—or anywhere else for that matter.

"The what?" Steven Scott asked.

"I was drawn on this path and as I was passing by—I heard your spirits," Blue Crow said to a roomful of sideways pursed lips and skeptically furrowed brows. He smiled wisely. "My ancestors have long communicated with the souls of the living—I often hear them whisper." He looked up for a moment and gave a knowing nod to those in the room.

Now, Steven Scott really questioned whether or not this guy was a *nutcase*. He didn't say anything, but Chelsea in her complete child-like innocence asked, "Mr. Blue Crow, what did my spirit say?"

"Your spirit has walked with my brother *Red Feather* and from him—you have learned the Way."

"That's right." Her eyes lit up.

John was suspicious, too—thinking, *what's his angle?* Perhaps inappropriately, wondering if this tribal elder had smoked Peyote. The word had obviously been passed around the hospital and had made its way to him. How else could he know about *Red Feather*?

It's a con, Steven thought.

Blue Crow didn't need to hear spirits to know that his words weren't trusted, so he continued to gently share. "My connection is strong, since I have cleared my mind to see."

Steven raised cuckoo bird eyebrows at John.

Blue Crow gave Steven a friendly, open-handed pat on the shoulder. "You, my dear friend, have survived, but are deeply-wounded in your spirit," he said, not having been told, but somehow knowing of Steven Scott's battle scars.

"Like me, you have lost friends in war and strong medicine cannot ease your pain. It is only in the power of the Spirit that you will find rest."

How could he have known that or anything about the Red Feather? He likely heard it or he could have read my citations, but why?

There was no deceit in Blue Crows voice, and he wasn't asking for anything—*so what then?* He continued, "Our friends have passed on before us as we must, also—in time. You may think me a foolish old man, but I am forever linked to the souls of the men I have fought with—and other men of honor like yourself." He nodded upward and sat back down slowly as he reflected on his words, drinking in the universe with his deep set dark brown eyes.

It was an utterly inconceivable claim, but not one that could be disproven. Although Blue Crow never tried to prove anything. *He only came to share his story.* Much later ITL requested that Blue Crow come in for PSYCHON testing. He wasn't interested. But if they had been able to measure his PSYCHON radiation, then they would have found that it was also off the charts. He was truly connected in ways that he never understood.

"I came only to say—you will be okay. The *Great Defender* has prevailed in your life, so that you may walk in peace forever."

It was an inexplicable, spiritual, encounter with Jimmy *"Blue Crow"* Bay. *He seems competent and he knows a lot,* thought Steven.

Steven Scott wasn't sure why, but when Blue Crow was around, he felt a peace that completely surpassed his understanding.

My Blackwell Companion book on Science and Christianity is so marked-up that it resembles a "*My 1st Animal ABC*" coloring book but twice as difficult to decipher with all the yellow, green, orange, and blue highlighting and notes. My *Philosophical Foundations for a Christian Worldview* and *Blackwell's Companion on Natural Theology* books are just as dog-eared. Necessary reading if Bobby and I are going to take another Pfister Award in Psychiatry and Religion.

I'm enjoying a John Lennox book; *God's Undertaker: Has Science Buried God?* In the book he mentioned categorical differences within our thinking about God and science and how they truly don't conflict. He categorizes God as an *Agent* and the physical world as a *mechanism.*

He said, "Think about it in the terms of Henry Ford the person as an *agent* and the Model-T car engine as a *mechanism.*" He made insightful points. "No one would claim that Henry Ford was unnecessary, simply because he had figured out everything, he needed to know about how the combustible engine works. The car falls into a different category than a person."

Note: Some scientists think that any attempt to reintroduce God [in our work] is an impediment to science. When the truth is that theism fits more comfortably than naturalism, which doesn't support rational intelligibility or irreducible complexity at all. So, it's just the opposite of what we've been told. Go figure!

CHAPTER SEVENTY-SIX

"Care about what other people think and you will always be a prisoner." ~ *Loa Tzu*

STARR AND SMITH

"SOME PEOPLE BELIEVE that we each have a soul and that when you die, your soul leaves the body. I believe it too," Mark Starr said, but I can't say that I really understand it. Most of my colleagues believe that death is the end—that's it. Maybe they're right. Maybe I'm missing something, but I can't get past a few things."

"What's that?" Dr. Robert "Bobby" Smith asked. He was in town on business and had dropped by for a short visit with his old friend from youth group days. Maybe they could even toss around a few more book ideas.

"The simple fact that we can think about ourselves in first person," Mark answered. "That seems to be pretty strong evidence of a mind, but if our thoughts and memories are somehow unified in our brain, how do we distinguish the brain as being different from the mind or soul?"

They were deep questions, but he was talking it over with a friend and professional apologist that he greatly admired while indulging himself in another dark roast cappuccino at the *Baltimore Coffee & Tea*. Two shots of espresso. Lots of foam.

Bobby rocked back on the hind legs of his metal café chair as Mark maneuvered into his seat—skillfully balancing his coffee cup and a plate of blueberry-lemon cake. He set his food down with a clunk and wiped off his chair with a napkin before sitting down. He then pulled out a small notebook pad and pen, before finally scooting up close to the table.

"Aristotle would have yawned at the question."

"How so?"

Bobby shrugged. "Of course, the mind is not wholly material. Abstract thought is immaterial by its nature and can't be generated by the brain." He took another sip of cappuccino.

You would have never known it from his humble, approachable manner, but Bobby was touted as one the top twenty philosophers in academia. A man loaded with scholarly accolades and impressive doctoral degrees in mathematics, philosophy, *and* quantum physics. Not to mention years of intense research at multiple European universities. Munich. Edinburgh. Oxford. He was also fluent in German and French.

But then, Mark was no slouch himself.

"It's more or less obvious to most of us that there's something else—a soul that's different from our body," Bobby said. "So, from the beginning you pretty much believe that, unless you're taught something else. At least that's been true throughout most of history. Just look at all the societies that have believed in a soul."

Bobby had straight black hair, graying at the temples, which he kept closely cropped and neatly parted to the side. He wore a gray tweed sports jacket, light denim jeans, with a black and white Bob Dylan t-shirt. Sharply dressed, but very casual. He stirred the foam of his cappuccino as he waited for Mark's next question—the one he saw hanging on his furrowed brow.

"But what's the evidence that we have a soul—something that's separate from our body? And how do we know that it's not just some far-fetched religious notion?"

"Those are great questions, Mark. The first thing to note, for guys like us, is that the Bible teaches it—and there are great reasons to believe the Bible. But I'm not saying—just because the Bible says so, makes it so. There are also other incredibly good deductive reasons to believe that we are made up of two broad components—*mind and matter*. Body and soul. They are typically parsed into those two main views."

"Physicalism and dualism," Mark said."

"Yes."

"Okay, I get that."

"Physicalism, as you know, claims that humans are entirely physical beings," Bobby said. "Dualism claims that we are both physical and mental beings—and they both come in different varieties. I'm what you'd call a *substance dualist*. Meaning I believe that the brain is a physical object with physical properties and that the mind is a mental substance that has mental properties—I think it's demonstrable."

"For instance?"

"For instance, I believe that when you're in pain, your brain produces electrical and chemical properties, which are physical—and that your soul or *self* is the thing that is consciously aware of the pain."

"Okay."

"In essence, the *soul* is the possessor of your body's experiences. It surrounds them and remains the same throughout your life. The way I see it, the soul and the brain were made to interact with each other, but they are different things with different properties."

"There's a name for that."

"Yeah, the interaction of the brain and mind is referred to as the centrencephalic integrating system. And since I believe the *soul* is not a part of the *brain*—it can survive the destruction of the body."

"I've heard stories of near-death experiences and have often wondered about their validity," Mark said. "Until I recently—I saw it for myself."

"What do you mean?"

"Sorry, I wish I could talk about it, but it's a classified part of our ITL studies." He had information that he couldn't talk about in detail. He had witnessed a death and a resuscitation with Todd Lopez and Chelsea Croxon, respectively.

Bobby nodded and spoke at length about the reasons to believe that there's a *soul* that can survive separately from the *body* and provided Mark with some very good reasons for it.

"If we can find one thing true, or even possibly true of the *mind* and not the *brain*, then some form of dualism has been established. Meaning—the mind is not the brain."

"Got it."

It was just the tip of the iceberg and needed to be explored more extensively. The new Innovations Technology Laboratory, *Mind Over Matter* educational program would be the place perfectly suited for this technical discussion. Before saying their goodbyes, they pulled out their phones, and scheduled an interview time.

CHAPTER SEVENTY-SEVEN

"There is hope, even when your brain tells you there isn't."
~ *Turtles All the Way Down, John Green*

MIND OVER MATTER S1E1

"WE'RE ON IN 3-2- ," the television studio director instructed. The floor manager held up her fingers to indicate the countdown, then she silently swept her hand down and across the front of the camera lens to indicate that they were live *on-the-air*.

The sound booth turned on the lavalier-lapel microphones, as the camera Jib crane swept over and across the studio and produced a dynamic wide-shot of Dr. Mark Starr and his special guest. A quick cut to camera-two set up a close-up of Starr, who sat in front of a green screen. A quickly pointed finger was the floor manager's signal that Mark could start speaking.

ITL had spared no expense in their development of a virtual studio to interview subject matter experts. It was a medium sized studio with lights, tripods, cameras, cables, monitors, and other set decorations. This created a realistic talk show setting in front of a green screen. The green screen allowed for a variety of slides, scenery, photos, and video to replace the real background of a video with a digital background.

It came with pre-rendered 8K-images for video editors to use as background and green-screen *Chroma key* materials. None of which Dr. Starr understood anything about, except that he had picked the interviews and named the show, *Mind Over Matter*. That was as involved in the production aspect of the show that he cared to be.

"Hello, I'm Dr. Mark Starr. Welcome to *Mind Over Matter*—a program dedicated to the *Mind-Body Problem*. I'm delving into a topic that you hear little about—and that is the nature of consciousness and the soul. Throughout our time together, I want to explore what sort of thing consciousness is and ask other questions about whether or not we have a soul, and if so—ask—is it different than our brain? In other words, is consciousness a *physical state* of the brain or is it something *immaterial*?" He asked turning to look at a different camera with an over-the-shoulder graphic appearing. Each related to the topic at hand.

"Why should we care and what difference does it make? It's a good question. *First*, it's an important topic for some religions, because their scriptures teach that we have a soul and that it survives the death of the body. However, the fact is—and I hate to be the one to break it to you—but if there is *no soul*, then the teachings are false."

His guest hadn't been introduced yet, but you could see him nod and mouth the word *true*.

"*Secondly,* from a spiritual perspective, a *soul* seems to make it more plausible for belief that you could survive the death of your body." A variety of peace, love, life, and balance symbols popped on the screen, including *the Cross, Peace Sign, Egyptian Ankh, and Daoist Yin & Yang.* "Because, if I'm not my body, then that at least opens-up the possibility for life after death."

The other pictures faded out one at a time, finally replaced by the white-bearded Darwin circa 1880. "The *third* reason the existence of consciousness and soul are important is that—if they're real, then there will never be a scientific or an evolutionary explanation for the origin of consciousness and the soul. Evolution can't, in principle, explain the origin of the mind or consciousness and the soul—because it seems to deal strictly with *matter* or the body. You see, until the time of Darwin, most of the world believed that we have an immaterial soul. And even though he was a strict materialist, he clearly understood the need for a different kind of explanation if something non-physical about us was ever discovered."

The screen flashed up his quote:

…if there is anything about living beings that is not physical, it would require another explanation, namely a theistic explanation, and that would render my own theory superfluous in other areas.

"In Darwin's M&N notebooks he made the claim that if his theory was true and God does not exist, then it follows that materialism about living things must be the case. Because if you start with matter—and you say *in the beginning were the particles*—and all you do is rearrange particles according to the laws of chemistry, physics, mutation, and natural selection, then you're going to end up with a *more complicated arrangement of particles. Not something conscious, or a soul!* You will not get a mind popping into existence, because that is to get something from nothing."

"But if your belief starts with the existence of an ultimate mind or mental substance or God," Mark added, "then there's no difficulty in explaining where your mind could come from." Behind him an animated brain magically popped on the video screen with a speech balloon that said, *what am I supposed to think about this?*

"Right, because on the theistic view, the fundamental entity isn't an electron or a string—it's a mind."

"Hmm, so as you can tell, this hasn't quite been settled yet." He looked at the camera. "That's why we're digging into it on *Mind Over Matter.*" That was the cue for the technical director to intersperse a five second video piece with the show title and fifteen seconds of music for Mark to continue speaking over. It made for a nice looking introduction.

"In this three-part series I'll be asking:

What is consciousness?

What reason do we have for thinking it's not physical?

What are conscious states and physical states, and how are they different?

What is the thing that has consciousness—the brain, or is it the mind, or a soul, or something like that?

The questions were being immediately superimposed on the screen behind him, as he read each one from the teleprompter. Then the studio director took a wide camera shot to prepare for an exchange between Dr. Mark Starr and his guest.

"Those are all questions that our guest will help us navigate in our series," Dr. Starr said as he turned to greet Dr. Robert Smith. "Glad you could join us today, Dr. Smith." His name and title were superimposed just below him on the screen:

Dr. Robert W. Smith
Research Professor of Philosophy, Houston Baptist University.

"If you don't mind, let's dig straight into it."

Smith nodded. "First, thanks for having me on your program," he said shifting comfortably in his chair. "I needn't remind you that the brain is a very interesting *chemically-electrolyzed cut of beef.*"

"Indeed," Dr. Starr said. He enjoyed the depictive metaphor. "Perhaps we should have titled the show *Where's The Beef?"* referring to a classic 1980's catchphrase, born out of a Wendy's hamburger commercial.

"Hmm, yes, perhaps so," Smith said, with a contemplative tone of amusement in his voice, but then transitioned quickly to address the serious questions at hand. "This very complicated question of how our mind, consciousness, and brain are aligned and cooperate isn't one that we can fully answer today." It was his way of managing expectations. "But I'd like to begin with three preliminary remarks, if I could."

"Sure."

"After that I'll describe what consciousness is and argue that it's not physical. Then I'm going to define what a soul is and argue that it's not physical either."

"Sounds fascinating."

"The first thing to keep in mind is that our topic is not a scientific question."

"No?" Mark asked, curiously.

"No. Neurobiology can't answer those types of questions—and here's why…I want to educate your audience on the notion of *Empirically Equivalent* theories. It's just a big word that means: *if there are two theories that are consistent with the same observations, then one is not better than the other.* For example: the claim that I am my brain, *physicalism*, and the claim that I am a soul that uses my brain, *dualism*, are what we call *empirically equivalent* claims. There's no scientific test, or empirical observation to decide which one is true. So, they are empirically equivalent."

"You're saying that this debate can't be solved by scientific argumentation?"

"Correct, it is fundamentally a philosophical and theological question and not within the purview of the hard sciences."

"If you don't mind, can you break that down for us?"

"Sure, but first I'd also like to draw a distinction between a *thing* and a *state of a thing*. Water for example is a *thing* or a *substance*, which is capable of existing in three states: *solid, liquid, and gas.* The solid state obviously differs from the liquid state and the same can be said of the liquid state—it differs from the gaseous state. We could take a cup of water and turn it in to a solid, liquid, or the gaseous state, but what we see is that there are distinctions between the *states* of things, right?"

"Right," Dr. Starr agreed.

"And —what is it that has those states?"

"H2O!"

"Yes, and I believe that we're going to find out the same things are true of consciousness. There are at least five-states of consciousness. We'll go over them in the time we're allowed, but let's quickly change gears for a moment to make sure that we're laying the proper groundwork and following the rules of logic. Something all good scientists do," Dr. Smith added with an astute nod to the camera. Let's write down a *rule* that we can all agree upon."

"Okay."

"It's called *The Law of Identity*. You break it—then I'd have to call the philosophy police and have you arrested."

Mark laughed.

"The law basically says that if *A* is the same thing as *B*, then they are the same thing," Smith said. "Simple enough, right?"

The technical director called up a Leibniz's Law graphic from the Chyron generator and put it on-air as they spoke.

"You can see here that Leibniz thought about it in depth, more than three-hundred years ago," Dr. Smith pointed to a graphic that popped up.

Leibniz's Law: The Indiscernibility of Identicals

$$(x)(y) [x=y \rightarrow (F)(Fx \leftrightarrow Fy)],$$

For any x and y, if x is identical to y, then x and y have all the same properties.

Dr. Mark Starr agreed with another affirmative nod of his head. "For example, if I say *the snow is white* and *die schnee ist weiss*, then I'm saying the same thing, correct?"

"Yes," Smith replied. "One is in English and the other is German, but they mean the same thing. That means I'm using two different words to say the exact same thing—so how many colors do we have, one or two?" he asked, belaboring the obvious but sparing no detail in his practical explanation. "One, right? Yes—of course!" he asked and answered his own question to keep from putting Mark on the spot and maintain the explanatory momentum. "So, what is true of *A* is true of *B*, and the opposite is also true."

Mark nodded his head as he followed along.

"Just for grins, let's use one more example. If the color of my brand-new *Ford F-250* is my favorite color, then whatever is true of the color of my truck is true of my favorite color— *Lightning Blue.*"

"Interesting," Mark said. "Because we're not talking about two different colors. We're talking about one color—and one really cool truck."

"I think so," Dr. Smith said. "The point is that this is a *test of non-identity*. That means that if I can find one thing that is true or possibly true of *A* that is not true of *B*, then *A* can't be identical to *B*."

"Let's move the ball forward a bit now," Dr. Starr said. "That's a nice philosophical take on propositions, but what about *real* causes and effects? It seems to me like we can make our brain do things."

"Sure," Smith said. "That's right, but remember that *identity* is not the same thing as *cause and effect,* is it?"

377

Before continuing to speak, Dr. Smith crossed his legs and slowly stroked his philosopher's beard. His body language perpetuated the stereotypical view of a philosopher, going all the way back to Socrates and Plato. "Because A causes B it doesn't follow that A is identical to B. This is how I think about it—just because we know that fire causes smoke, it doesn't mean that fire is the exact same thing as smoke, right?

"Right," Mark said.

"Or, for example, just because my car depends on a key to make the engine start, doesn't prove that my engine is the same thing as my key, does it?"

"No, but is that a good analogy for the brain? Dr. Starr asked. "Scientists have already demonstrated, by probing certain regions of the brain that it can cause a conscious event to happen—for example in epileptic patients, neuroscientists have touched certain regions of the brain that caused the person to have a memory of their grandmother frying chicken or making biscuits."

"Yes, but when their probe touched that part of the brain, there was what we call a brain event," Dr. Smith answered. "Let's call that event B. Then we had a memory event, call that M. Just because the brain event B caused the memory event of your grandmother frying chicken, M, that doesn't prove that B is the same thing as M. Those are different events, right?"

"Okay," Dr. Starr replied.

"So, it doesn't follow that that brain event is the same thing as the memory or that fire is the same thing as smoke, just because I can cause smoke by lighting a fire. And it doesn't follow that thoughts or memories are physical, just because I can cause a thought or memory to occur by stimulating a certain area of the brain. All that established was cause and effect. To establish *identity* then, whatever is true of a thought must also be true of that brain event. If there's one thing true of a thought that's not true of a brain event, then even if they always go together or one causes the other—they're not the same thing."

Mark nodded. "Wow, this is pretty heavy stuff—but I think I'm keeping up!"

"Yes, it is, and we've still not answered why she fried chicken and made biscuits," Robert said, to distract from the heavy logic. It was sort of a mental swish, swirl, move it around, spit and rinse technique you would do after sipping a good wine.

"Well, she probably knew that you love that kind of food!" Mark said.

"Ah-hah! So, now we've found the cause," Robert said. "My grandmother made fried chicken and biscuits because she knows I love it. The effect or outcome was that I enjoyed it very much."

"Well, we know what's on everybody's mind now," Mark said, patting his belly. "And speaking of what's on our mind—we'll address more of these interesting, complex questions about the mind-body problem and consciousness, in future episodes."

Just as he verbally signaled the end of the show, the program name was superimposed at the bottom-middle part of the screen for the viewers to see. "That's all the time we have today. I'm Dr. Mark Starr and I would like to thank our special guest, Dr. Robert Smith, for appearing on this three-part series concerning the mind-body problem. This is *Mind Over Matter*—see you next time."

"*And* we're out!" the floor manager said.

They unclipped their lavalier microphones from their ties and proceeded with their after-show dinner plans. It became a short-lived tradition, after each of the three episodes they filmed, to take turns finding a nice place to eat in Baltimore. Tonight, they headed down to the Capitol Grille on 500 East Pratt Street for some of the best steaks in Maryland. Mark ordered the

Gorgonzola and truffle crusted dry-aged New York Strip and Bobby ordered the sliced Filet Mignon with Cipollini onions and wild mushrooms. The show had been a lot of hard mental work and called for a celebration.

CHAPTER SEVENTY-EIGHT

"The news and the truth are not the same thing."
~ *Walter Lippmann*

THE RIGHT CHOICE

"THERE'S GOOD NEWS…and there's good news," Mark said to Steven, as he came to visit his older stepbrother and inform him of his medical condition.

"Okay, then I'll take the good news first," he flashed a half-grin.

"Since we've ruled out any serious mental illnesses—other than mild *PTSD* and general weirdness—."

"Thanks." The brothers were drawn to humorously poke each other, even as older men. It was part of their unique bond.

"—we can lean into and really explore this…*ability* you seem to have."

"I know crazy, right? It's like I've got some superpower or something. And—the other good news?"

"Well, as you now know—there's a mental substance, which we call PSYCHON radiation."

"Right."

"And we ran an extensive panel of tests on you."

"Yeah. I even surprised myself."

"Steven, you were off the bloom'n charts and it seems to still be increasing. Brad said that you were able to tune in and hear someone's thoughts—from more than a block away."

"Meaning?"

"Meaning—we don't know. You naturally generate high levels of PSYCHONS, so that seems to make you an extraordinarily strong transmitter and receiver. Our team had to wear goggles to get a similar effect, but you can hear and talk to our team without it."

"I know, that was wild."

"However," Mark continued. "I don't want to *unveil* your ability until we get to test it more."

"Lest I become a freak show."

"Exactly."

"So, we won't tell this to anyone—especially the *Nous* Secret Service agents or Dr. Kahn, okay?"

Steven looked at him questioningly.

"I have my reasons—but mainly it's for your safety. So, let's keep it hush-hush, until we can get our arms around this better."

"Can you believe I'm a freak'n *walkie-talkie*?" Steven asked.

"Yep, and with a *who knows-what* range—that's likely why you've always experienced connections to the people around you. I assume Peggy told you, but some of the earlier stuff you experienced, like the graffiti, was likely triggered from your PTSD—and exacerbated by the new meds."

"Yeah, thanks."

"Okay, but who could have known?" he shrugged. "And that it would've reacted on you like it did. But the good news is that a lot of the stuff you saw and heard was real."

"Wow, I couldn't have imagined that in a million years."

Even though the developing project issues hadn't been fully discussed with Steven Scott yet, his viability as a candidate for the PSYCHONIX implant was now a major topic of conversation. Steven knew a little, and knew that it required a surgical procedure, but he didn't fully understand the implications or *requirements* of the project.

Brad was the first to broach the issue. He mentioned that Steven's unique physiology made him perfectly suited to the project. "He's already missing an eye—so the procedure would be relatively simple. All the PSYCHONIX technology could be packed into an *ocular prosthesis* or artificial eye that would replace his missing right eye—and then fused it to the nerve centers."

"I agree, he would be perfect for it," Dr. Starr said. "Steven mentioned it himself, but he doesn't yet know the full extent of the project."

Dr. Feinberg, Brad, and Sabrina nodded.

Steven was a brave man and easily bored. He had been that way since he was a kid; but used to getting out of his comfort zone and trusting his instincts for survival. Throughout his life he had serious risk-taking tendencies toward excitement and thrill-seeking.

"He might embrace this as *an opportunity to advance science*," Dr. Starr said.

Once they brought Steven into the PSYCHONIX conversation, they gave him many encouraging examples: *Christopher Columbus exposed himself to harm and sailed into dark mysterious ocean waters, the Wright Brothers into the air, and astronauts have taken fiery-rockets for a spin to the Moon. That was what some of the most adventurous risk takers in history did—and they changed our world forever.*

That was how they wanted Steven to think about the opportunity.

He certainly had the right temperament and personality type. As a boy, he and his stepbrother loved the sensation-seeking hustle and bustle of being pursued by an angry landowner. He enjoyed the exhilaration of making a clean getaway, after what he considered benign trespassing, and meeting up with his neighborhood chums to joke about it later. He enjoyed being chased out of a neighbor's yard, a farmer's field, or an unguarded warehouse when discovered or the alarms went off. He never stole anything, but always came up with a cunning plan to make a clean getaway. He planned out and plotted escape routes that they had cleverly named: *The Chase.*

Before being asked to participate in the PSYCHONIX project, Steven had nearly every detail explained to him. "The optic and auditory nerves will wirelessly transmit visual information between the bionic retina to the brain," Sabrina said. "It will bypass physical routes and tap directly into the cerebrum's nerve center—the obvious choice for interpreting touch, vision, hearing, speech, reasoning, emotions, learning, and fine control of movement."

"Oh, it sounds lovely," he said facetiously.

"The process would be like by-passing your home television and tapping into the city power plant between the monitor, and the water or coal plant powering it." It was a simplified explanation that he understood without all the scientific mumbo-jumbo.

Only they left out one important detail.

CHAPTER SEVENTY-NINE

"You do not know what will happen tomorrow. For what is your life? It is even a vapor that appears for a little time and then vanishes away" ~ *James 4:14*

BLANK CHECK

MARK HOPED TO discuss the details of the PSYCHONIX project with his brother in private, but Sabrina got over her skis—and was less diplomatic. She blurted it out in her devil-may-care manner, "The biggest challenge would be flatlining you and bringing you back to life." It sounded more like she was describing a colonoscopy, instead of a potentially lethal implant.

"Are you insane??" Steven objected and shot Mark a wicked sideways glance. "There's no way! Sure, I thought it was a cool idea to get a bionic eye, but, *ha*—I'm not dying to do it!" He stood up and paced the room as he spoke excitedly with his hands. If there was a time for his PTSD to be triggered again, then this might be it. "Tell me—how do you even know that resuscitation is possible?"

"We've tested the deamination process on animals—a rhesus monkey and a dog," Brad said, as his words trailed off. "Like they did for the first rocket launches."

Steven shook his head. "*Unbelievable.*" That's all he could say. For twenty-six years of his life he had written a *blank check* that was made payable to *The United States of America* for an amount up to and including his life. It was honorable but he was retired now, and ready to live. *"Unbelievable."*

"We need your answer by the end of the week," Dr. Feinberg said. Mark thought that it would be better coming from her.

"Oh, by the end of the week, no problem! Tell you what—I'll have my people call yours." He made the telephone sign, by extending his thumb and pinkie, and holding it up to his ear and mouth. "That gives me just about enough time to mail my Christmas cards, finish my will, and kiss my butt goodbye," he said in a faux nonchalant tone. He exited the lab, still shaking his head. Mark followed him out, but Steven waved him off. "I need to be alone." He paced halfway up the hall and then came back, to loudly discuss the new requirement with Mark.

It was mostly a one-way conversation. Mark was conflicted, but tried to explain the safety protocols, processes, and successes that they had had with the project up until this point.

"As your brother I don't want you to do it but, as the Director of ITL, I have to ask. You're our best shot—especially with your newfound gift. But in the end—it's still your choice."

Steven walked away, still shaking his head.

For the next few days Steven's emotions fluctuated worse than a bumpy stretch on the Stock Market. He exhaustively pondered the risk—including the fugacious aspects of life. He didn't know what tomorrow would bring, no one did, but he had long ago realized that life was short: *It is even a vapor that appears for a little time and then vanishes away.*

He mostly was mostly trying to consider Marlina's feelings and tried to discuss it with her a couple times. But it was a tough topic to raise and he couldn't quite bring himself around to it, as it played out in his head:

They asked me to die for this project, are you good with that?

Why yes dear, when will you be home for dinner?

But he couldn't say it.

He tossed the idea back-and-forth in his mind and lost sleep—until he finally talked about it. And then he got the kind of response that he thought he would.

There's no way! She was adamantly against it, just like he was—initially. But now, after hearing Mark out, he considered the possibilities. His adventure-seeking side wanted to continue, but it was a serious gamble. Marlina couldn't believe that it was even on the table.

"The only other person to *supposedly* communicate from beyond the grave was that guy Todd Lopez," Marlina reminded him. "And he didn't come back, Steven! Do you understand that—you might not come back?!"

"We all die," he nodded with a sympathetic wink and an affectionate hug. He opened his Bible and pointed midway down the page. "Remember the verse we learned at youth camp?'

"You do not know what tomorrow will bring. What is your life? For you are a mist that appears for a little time and then vanishes. James 4:14."

She gave him an inconsolable and tearful nod. "Don't bring the Bible into this Steven."

"You know, there's really nothing to fear," he said as he pulled her close. "Even in death we'll be together one day," he brushed her hair back and kissed her on the forehead. "Besides, they said I wouldn't die forever—this time. They've already tested it."

"Yeah, on monkeys."

Steven scratched under his arm and bobbed his head like a monkey, but it wasn't funny to her.

"They'd monitor me closely from a *special tank* that they put me in. Then they would cause me to slowly flatline, see what happens, and have me back before you know it. Think about it, *Mar*—I could be the Chuck Yeager of the afterlife."

Marlina stared off into the distance with a contemplative, and deeply troubled, look on her face. She tried to muster a smile, but wasn't as optimistic as Steven. In her mind, there was no bright side to this risky deal, but she knew that her thrill-seeking husband was certainly thinking about doing it.

They hugged, talked, and weighed the pros and cons before they made the decision—to sleep on it. Then he pulled her chin up and said seriously, "If you don't want me to, then I won't."

CHAPTER EIGHTY

"Translation is that which transforms everything, so that nothing changes." ~ *Gunter Grass*

這是個錯誤的號碼
THIS IS A WRONG NUMBER.

EVERY PROFESSION HAD a specific vocabulary that is used in its field of operation. Jargon. Mostly developed as a means to effectively and efficiently communicate with another person in the same field. If you couldn't decipher the code slang, then they could talk a lot of crap about you behind your back.

The code words ranged from darkly funny, to rude, and downright racist. Whether they were being used by spies or professionals, they helped to keep secrets that might have otherwise caused problems, if exposed. That was the case with Dr. Lui Wei. However, if he didn't want those around him to understand what he was up to, it was easier for him to speak his mother tongue Mandarin, Chinese.

Dr. Lui was the only one in his office that spoke Mandarin, so he felt emboldened to talk privately on the phone, even when the office was full of people. He was in America now and enjoyed our ways, but had developed a false sense of freedom that made him careless and incautious with his secret agent scheme. His phone rang at 7:30 p.m., and when he answered, there was a foreign sounding lady on the line.

"你有消息吗?" *Do you have any news?*

He responded: "不, 还没有" *No, not yet*, and hung up quickly. He then placed his phone upside down next to Dr. Kahn's phone.

"Who was that?" Sabrina asked.

"It was a wrong number," he answered curtly.

Brad glanced furtively back toward Dr. Lui, and then without breathing a word, continued to work. But something didn't sit right with him. *A wrong number—in Chinese?*

CHAPTER EIGHTY-ONE

"So, we do not lose heart. Though our outer self is wasting away, our inner self is being renewed day by day. For this light momentary affliction is preparing for us an eternal weight of glory beyond all comparison, as we look not to the things that are seen but to the things that are unseen. For the things that are seen are transient, but the things that are unseen are eternal."
~ *Apostle Paul*

INTERSECTION

MARLINA RAN ERRANDS and took care of family business while Steven was undergoing all of his new testing at ITL. The medical facilities could be cold and boring places, and it was an understatement to say, "*the cafeteria food isn't appealing.*" After a couple months of their food, she needed to find something a little better to eat. That pursuit sent her down the road, in the direction of Ellicott City for a leisurely bite and some small talk with a middle-aged waitress named Debbie. She was on a double shift, loved to talk, and kept coffee cups filled. What else do you need?

Marlina discovered that she had two kids and needed the extra hours. *Nice lady*, she thought. Marlina respected hard workers and tipped her well. She grew up poor and knew what it was like to struggle, especially as a woman.

After she ate dinner, she sipped another cup of coffee and answered a few emails and text messages from Vito and Donna:

Yes, I'm okay. Dad is doing much better. He does have mild PTSD issues, but some of the problems were due to the medicines they gave him. No, we're not sure how much longer it will be. Can't wait to see you at Christmas Vito. I'm running errands now. Love, Mom.

Marlina walked out, got in the car, and turned on an upbeat radio station, before making her way back down the road and to the lab.

First, she stopped at their *Holiday Inn Express* to freshen up a bit and change blouses—then headed straight back to the hospital to pick up Steven. He was just as tired as she was and wanted to get back to the hotel as fast as possible. Marlina took the *East* route on the Baltimore National Pike to Edmondson to Franklin Street. She then got on West Mullberry and merged on MLK with a drop-off at the university. Easy to miss if you're not from the area and closely watching the signs. She drove past old row homes with bars on the doors and windows—not certain whether they were to keep people out or keep them in. It wasn't something that she was used to, or ever saw on the windows in Walla Walla, Washington.

Trash was piled in the street and there were no other cars driving on the road. That was a bad sign. It was getting darker by the minute and her feelings of nervousness mounted. As Marlina made her way slowly down the road, she could tell that she was being eyeballed by young thugs, posted on the stoops of their dilapidated townhouses. In her mind it seemed that they were postured to sweep down on their prey. She focused and looked straight ahead. She sped up a little—all the while her heart raced. At some point she passed a well-lit fire station. Two older firemen wearily shook their heads as she passed by, like she was trapped in a burning building with no way out. It wasn't comforting.

She felt a bit on edge, and in her state of mind—*wasn't going to stop for anything*. Her eyes were glued to the *GPS display* that tracked her location, when suddenly out of nowhere, a few men sped by on scooters, yelling and weaving all over the road. They barely missed her car. It wasn't a great situation. And, as if that weren't scary enough, there also appeared to be a dealer and a prostitute on every second or third corner. She wouldn't have taken her foot off the gas to save her life, but of course *Murphy's Law* kicked-in and she hit every single red light possible. Marlina glanced at the clock. *Steven is going to wonder where I am.* As she drove, she tried to distract herself by praying and singing along to songs on the radio. It helped—a little.

A few blocks up it appeared that this worn-down street was coming to a dead-end, so she double-checked her door locks. *Click-click. Okay, that's better!* Marlina wasn't given to panic, but she started to panic. But then she noticed that the road she was on, was merely a kiddy-cornered cross street—and that she wouldn't be stuck or have to maneuver her way out. She felt relieved and excited by her newly discovered prospects. So excited, in fact, that she completely missed the stop sign and barely had time to scream before the airbags knocked her back—and everything went silent.

It was in that distracted instant between stepping on the gas, taking her eyes off the road, and removing her right-hand from the steering wheel to turn up the radio—that another high-speed car collided with her Honda CR-V. The police report said that there was an extremely sharp blow to her drivers-side door, before the vehicle bounced and her vehicle was shoved under the metallic grip of an on-coming tractor and trailer. That sent the car grinding and tumbling over and over, before it came to a sliding stop on the median strip.

The smashed car had flipped so many times that Marlina had already drifted out of consciousness, before she had time to feel pain or see the flicker of ambulance lights racing to the rescue. There was no *hope.* The EMS pronounced her dead at the scene of the accident.

CHAPTER EIGHTY-TWO

"The easier you can make it inside your head, the easier it will make things outside your head." ~ *Richard Bandler*

CHANCE

RUSSELL MORENO ALSO volunteered for the *Mind-Body Problem* study. He agreed to be a guinea pig for their clinical research study while under hypnosis. It was a personal choice. He had no obligation to do so and could have terminated participation at any moment. He, like many others, sought gratis medical attention with ITL, which his insurance didn't fully cover. He felt it was a small price to pay and was willing to surrender his will while under hypnosis to get it. It would be an interesting experiment on how the brain and consciousness, or subconsciousness worked together.

Russell had a bipolar condition that plagued him every day. In the interview he expressed it well, "My emotions bounce between tempestuous madness and soulful melancholy." To get to the root of the problem, he was undergoing regression-based hypnotherapy and other residual tests related to the consciousness aspects of the project.

Hypnotherapy was still a controversial form of therapy within mental health and it might take several sessions to see results. However, given his chronic mental health issues—it was recommended and agreed upon by him and his family. Even in his dogged determination that he didn't have a problem, out of curiosity he relented and gave ITL consent. For whatever reason, they were moving forward with the hypnosis. It wasn't a panacea—but, given his state of mind Russell thought, *what do I have to lose?*

Russell's altered state of consciousness would be explored using a relaxation technique—induced by the power of suggestion, key words, guided imagery or some combination thereof to bring about positive changes in his behavior. Given the right conditions, the doctors at ITL believed that they could subtly alter the effects of his unconscious mind and help him relax, change his perceptions, and hopefully bring about positive changes.

Dr. Kahn monitored Russell's brain activity with an EEG to note the physical changes that occurred. As he was hypnotized, it would be incredible to watch the brain orchestrate a symphony of 10 quintillion neuro-receptors and distributed across 500 trillion synapses, which connected 100 billion neurons. If you counted.

They began the experiment. He was hypnotized and instructed to walk straight across an empty room without stopping. When asked he replied, "Yes, the room is completely empty." He couldn't consciously see anything, except for an empty room. However, unbeknownst to him, a small plastic desk chair with metal legs had been placed exactly in the middle of the room. It was positioned in his path, but his hypnotized brain continued to tell him that the room was completely empty.

Russell was then given instructions to walk straight across the room, so that was what he did. He walked directly across the room without stopping but swerved to step around the plastic desk chair in the middle of the room and then continued to walk to the opposite side of the room.

"Look at these readings," Dr. Feinberg said as she glanced at the EEG monitor. "While under hypnosis, the activity decreased in his frontal lobes."

"It could have been a computer or brain override, because of faulty instructions," Dr. Kahn said.

"Or it could be an indicator that his actions are being generated from someplace other than the normal brain centers," Dr. Starr said.

"I lean toward the latter," Dr. Feinberg weighed-in with a smile.

Throughout the test, Russell was triggered to speak and say certain things—and to forget other things. He was asked to forget simple things like the seventh letter of the alphabet. So, when he repeated the alphabet back to the team he said, "A, B, C, D, E, F, H, I…" It was an amazing demonstration and seemed to clearly indicate that you could override the brain with suggestions.

In the end, it became obvious that the mental gymnastics they ran him through—had overwhelmed him. It triggered severe anxiety and unleashed a nightmarish hallucination in his mind. They hadn't anticipated that. It caused Russell a lot of mental anguish—enough so that he started throwing himself against the wall. It was unexpected and sad.

Russell Moreno had to be given an emergency shot of haloperidol and restrained with the help of a *Posey 5th Point* restraint due to the constant bucking up and down. No one liked using it, but it kept him from hurting himself worse. There would, no doubt, be an in-depth ethical review board to assess the future use of regression-based hypnotherapy within ITL. It didn't seem likely.

CHAPTER EIGHTY-THREE

"The soul cannot think without a picture!*"* *~Aristotle*

MIND OVER MATTER S1E2

"HELLO I'M DR. Mark Starr. Welcome to *Mind Over Matter,* a program dedicated to the *Mind-Body Problem.* Our second episode in this three part series asks more in-depth questions about the mind and body—specifically we'll discuss consciousness. During the last program we reviewed a lot of terms, but today let's get down to the nuts and bolts and review where we're headed!" A graphic overlay of the review flashed over his left shoulder, as he mentioned each one in turn.

What is consciousness?

What reason do we have for thinking it's not physical?

What are conscious states and physical states, and how are they different?

What is the thing that has consciousness—the brain, or is it the mind,

or a soul or something like that?

"We also welcome back our esteemed guest, Dr. Robert W. Smith—Research Professor of Philosophy at Houston Baptist University."

All the shows were being produced and recorded *live-to-tape,* a term still used in the digital age. It meant that the recording never stopped, and they would make minor adjustments and edits in post-production, if necessary.

"The only way to enter this cerebral pool is to just jump in head first, so—with that in mind—what is consciousness?" he asked.

"Okay, that's fine. Let's do it." Dr. Smith said. He pressed his hands together as though he was ready to take a dive. "The only way to adequately define consciousness is to *illustrate* what it is. Philosophers call that an *ostensive* explanation. For example, I would say that by the word *argyle* that I mean this," he said and pointed to his argyle pullover sweater. "If you've never seen an argyle sweater, then you wouldn't know what it means—so you point to one, by way of an explanation. That's an *ostensive* explanation. Let me give you another illustration. Suppose there's a middle-aged man named Jimmy that's just been in surgery and rendered unconscious with an anesthesia. While he was knocked-out he had his gallbladder removed and is now in the recovery room. While lying there, he starts coming to and tries to shift his weight. When he does, he begins to *feel* an unpleasant sensation—a throbbing pain around his abdomen. So, he says to himself: *Hmm, I don't think I'm at home.* Followed by the *belief* that: *I just had gallbladder surgery and I'm in the recovery room.* Now, he has the sudden *desire* for something to drink. So, he uses his *free will* to shout out to any nurse that's available, "Hey, can you bring me something to drink?"

"That's the first thing I'd ask for too," Mark interjected.

Bobby smiled. "So, Jimmy recognized that he was thirsty. He's regaining consciousness—and that is what consciousness is—*recognizing it.*"

"Okay, that sounds simple enough."

"Yes, and by the way, the brain and the states of the brain can't be defined that way. The states of the brain are defined by neurobiology, physics, and chemistry. Consciousness is defined *ostensively*, so—it follows that the *brain* and consciousness are not the same thing.

"That clearly falls in the area of the *Law of Identicals* that we discussed in the first part of the series."

"Correct, and I defined it by giving you an example of it. Again—it's when you pay attention to what's going on inside of you and what you're attending to—that is *your own consciousness*. He has been conscious before, so as he was coming to, he recognized it.

"I see," Dr. Starr said. "No one had to say: *Hey Jim, you're conscious now! You can make decisions*! You clearly know that it's—you."

. "Exactly!" Dr. Smith said. "It's *you* that realizes there is a *you* that senses, thinks, believes, and desires something."

"Okay, I'm with you so far."

"Most of us are vaguely familiar with Descartes' proclamation, *I think therefore I am!* "

"Yes."

"He once made an argument for there being a *self* to be referenced. When you can do that, then you're conscious."

"But couldn't you be fooled?"

"Sure, but he said that even if you were being deceived by an external being—that *you* recognize that it is *you* being deceived."

Mark held up his hand and waved his finger in a questioning gesture. "Okay, but maybe that's just slick linguistics Dr. Smith. Let's drill down further on this state of consciousness thing that you've introduced us to," Mark said. "How many states of consciousness are there?"

"There are at least five states of consciousness—maybe more—maybe there are states and dimensions that we aren't even aware of yet," Robert said, "so I'll leave it at that."

"Let's explore the ones we know."

"Okay, First, I think we all recognize a state of consciousness called a *sensation*. A sensation is purely a state of sentient awareness. Like the feeling you get after hitting your finger with a hammer, tasting a bitter grapefruit, hearing loud music or even a variety of emotions—like happiness, anger, disgust, sadness, surprise, and fear." He elaborated more about the fact that sensations were neither true nor false. "It doesn't make any sense to say that that feeling of pain I'm having is *true* or that the taste of grapefruit, having been bitter, *true*, but they can be *accurate or inaccurate*."

He gave a more pleasant example of an award-winning breakfast his grandmother used to make back home in Mountain City, Tennessee: *homemade apple-butter, buttermilk biscuits, country ham, and Red-Eye gravy.* "Oh, it used to smell so good, as you woke up early in the morning."

"Is that an invitation?" Mark asked.

"We'll see. That sensation might just overwhelm city folks," Robert chuckled, "but first let's think about the experience of waking up and smelling that wonderful country breakfast."

"That experience is a *sensation, right?*" Mark prompted.

"Right, a sensation that can't be judged by whether or not it's true or false. Let me give you another example:

"Say you're admiring my *Lightning Blue F-250* truck and because of the lightning outside it looks *black* to you. You would be having a *blackish* experience of something that was actually blue in color," Robert said. "So, it doesn't make sense to say that your sensation is false, but you could say that your sensation is inaccurate, because it doesn't match up with the actual surface color of the truck."

"Okay, I see. What else?"

400

"The second state of consciousness is a *thought*," Robert said. "That is the mental content that can be expressed in a sentence as a simple statement of fact and can be either true or false. Take the statements we used before: *It's snowing* and *es schneit*. Those are two sentences that express the same thought in English and German. So, you see—a *thought* is not the same thing as a *sensation*, because thoughts can be true or false, but sensations can't, so they're different kinds of mental states."

"It's either true that it's snowing or it's false—it's not snowing," Mark added.

"Correct."

"So, if there was no consciousness in the world, then there would be no sensations or thoughts," Mark said.

"Right, I think that's a true thought. And remember your thought was different than a sensation. You can have thoughts that you're not sensing and have sensations you're not thinking about. Make sense? Or have I lost all your listeners Mark?"

"Yes, both of them, including me," he said smiling. "Not really, but this is heady stuff."

"Well, yes, at first it can be a little tough to wrap your mind around—pun intended," Robert said. "Just re-listen to this program again, a few hundred more times, and I think you'll have it down."

"Thank you—good promo!" he added. "Fortunately, this will be linked for everyone to hear on our ITL website and YouTube channel." He paused. "Okay—enough promotions, let's move on. Is there a third mental state?"

"Yes, as I said there are five mental states all together—maybe more. But, the third kind of consciousness mental state is a *belief*. A belief is the mental content that I take to be true between 51 and 100 percent certainty. Beliefs are what I consider true, and your beliefs can be different than mine. For instance—I have some beliefs that aren't as certain this year, like the Washington Redskins will make the Super Bowl," he said with a mixed expression of hope.

"So, a belief is not a thought," continued Dr. Smith.

"No, because I can have thoughts that I don't believe, and I can have beliefs that I'm not thinking about—like, a moment ago, I wasn't thinking about unicorns."

"Because a thought only exists while you're entertaining it, but a belief doesn't go away when you stop entertaining it."

"Yes, I think that's the simplest way to explain it," Dr. Smith said.

"Great information—but unfortunately that's all the time we have for this show. Let me conclude by summarizing the three states of consciousness that you've mentioned," Dr. Starr said: "You told us that *beliefs* aren't the same thing as *thoughts* and they're not the same thing as *sensations*, because beliefs and thoughts can be true or false, but sensations can't. So far, in our program, we've talked about sensations, thoughts, and beliefs that are different states of consciousness—different from each other. You've told us that they are analogous to the states of water—like solid, liquid, and gas."

"Yes, well said."

"Thank you for your insightful analysis—we'll get to talk to you one more time in this three-part series. I'm Dr. Mark Starr with our special guest Dr. Robert W. Smith. Please join us for the next installment, as we continue to discuss the mind-body problem and specifically consciousness. Here on *Mind Over Matter*."

"And we're out!" the floor manager said. "Lunch!"

Prior to the morning rush of going into the studio, Dr. Smith inhaled a Green Chile egg-white breakfast and a quick cup of black coffee at Einstein Bros Bagels inside ITL's Cobblestone Cafe.

He was on a tight schedule, so there wouldn't be time for a leisurely meal today; however, on the way out he did offer Dr. Starr an invitation.

"I have a speaking engagement—a debate really—at Harvard next month," Bobby said as he slipped on his jacket and headed toward the studio exit. "The topic is: *God vs. Science,* and I thought it would tie in well—perhaps give us some ideas for our book proposal." They were still bouncing ideas for their psychiatry and religion book but hadn't settled on anything. If nothing else, it was a great excuse for old friends to see each other again.

"Sounds interesting," Mark said. "Just let me know when and where—and hey, what if I brought Peggy along as a date?"

"Sure, I'll reserve two prime seats and text you the info," Bobby said. "I'm out of here—see you for the last part of the series next week."

CHAPTER EIGHTY-FOUR

"We are hard pressed on every side, but not crushed; perplexed, but not in despair; persecuted, but not abandoned; struck down, but not destroyed"
~ *2 Corinthians 4:8-9*

IN THE NAME OF SCIENCE

STEVEN SCOTT HADN'T taken the news of Marlina's fatal accident well—and unfortunately, he wasn't given much time to process it all. He was much too busy making the funeral arrangements, dealing with vast amounts of paperwork, and well-meaning but sometimes awkward phone calls from family and friends who sent their love and prayers and told him how sorry they were for his loss. It was nice, but it was numbing. He felt like his head was in a fog and that he was walking in quicksand. He hadn't slept well and wondered if he would ever be okay again. For now, he needed a little space and time to grieve his lost love.

His grief was much bigger than any sadness he had ever experienced. He tearfully mourned her loss but didn't blame God. Every strained movement and thought took its toll on him now, but his PTSD was well under control—hardly even noticeable. However, the smell of grief still hung thick in the air.

"It's—overwhelming."

"I'm here for you, Steven," Mark said. He shared in his grief. "So, don't try to do everything on your own, okay? He decided it was best to drop his brother from the PSYCHONIX project.

404

He's too upset. That's for the best. Instead, Mark would do everything in his power to comfort Steven and be there for him during this difficult time. Steven needed to go at his own pace.

Mark himself was deeply reflective about her passing. She had been a wonderful sister-in-law—the best. He thought about the love that we all have for each other and the love that still lived in our hearts and minds when our loved ones departed. He understood that showing love to yourself and others was one of the best ways to honor the love you had shared—and it facilitated healing. He contemplated those things, but never said it out loud. Now was a time for hugs, not words.

"What about the PSYCHONIX project?" Steven asked.

"Let's just forget about it Steven."

"No, I'm okay. *Really.* I'm in. I'm really in now, Mark—just give me time to wrap things up—a few more days, maybe a week at most, and we're a go!"

Mark was surprised and in listening mode. He knew that Steven was still emotional—maybe even suicidal. He didn't want it to be used as a way of escape. To him family was way more important than a project—regardless of its impact or pressure from the U.S. Government.

Steven needed time to think—to work it out. The horrendous news of Marlina's death hit him like a ton of bricks and his energy level was down the toilet. It was awful.

How can I bear it? Steven cried on Mark's shoulder.

He didn't enjoy being alone in his thoughts anymore. In the next counseling session, he told Dr. Feinberg, "I'm angry—mostly angry at God." He was a believer but still had many questions on the shelf that he couldn't answer: *Why her? She was a good girl. She was still young. Why would God let her suffer and die like that?*

Mark didn't try to answer him. Pat answers weren't helpful and there was no orderly progress of emotions, when someone was full-on grieving. Everyone was different. He didn't try to make sense of it or accelerate closure for his brother. His advanced counseling education made him want to facilitate—to nudge Steven in the right directions or at least in the direction he thought it should be, but no, he would leave that in Peggy's capable hands—and allow time to heal.

Mark believed that God was in control. Steven did too, but he was in a lot of emotional pain. Even when he didn't understand why, he still believed that God was in command—and that He was loving and just. They both believed that ultimately *all things worked together for good* within God's providence. But now wasn't a time to say all that. It was a time for him to listen, cry, embrace, and love his brother. *That's what family does.*

"I'm sorry, Steven—I really am." That was all that he could say. That was all that needed to be said. Rarely does one's grief have a clear beginning, middle, and end, like hiking a trail up and back down a mountain, but it was always nice to have someone with you.

To Steven, his life seemed like an accelerating, vicious cycle of tragic episodes. Out of one problem and into another. A downward spiral of financial, physical, and mental health stressors interspersed with brief moments of peace. Exacerbated by his head wounds and PTSD, which was the likely culprit of his mental health issues.

He bowed his head. *"Lord, I can't go on like this!"* is how he started his prayer. *"God, I know I sound like a broken record—annoying you with all my needy prayers, but sometimes I feel like you're not listening. I was told in church that you cared about me, but lately it doesn't seem like you do! Really—it doesn't seem like you've been paying much attention at all. Things are sure tough down here since you took my lovely Marlina—and God—I'm feeling lonely tonight,"* he said with tears streaming down his cheeks.

"Please help me—that's all I ask. Give me strength, and tonight—give her extra kisses for me." He sniffed and wiped his face with a tissue. Then he picked up his phone and called Mark.

Mark picked up on the third ring. "Hello?"

"Hey, let's get started."

"The PSYCHONIX Project?"

"Yeah—I'm ready."

CHAPTER EIGHTY-FIVE

"It is during our darkest moments that we must focus to see the light." ~ *Aristotle*

FOCUS

STEVEN SCOTT FOCUSED on the PSYCHONIX project as much as he possibly could, because it distracted him from the sadness that he felt deep inside. Waking up with something to do helped to quickly improve his emotional state and kept his depression at bay. On paper he was doing totally fine, yet he didn't feel fine. The love of his life was gone and that had greatly affected his thinking, emotions, perceptions and sometimes his behavior.

He still felt conflicted, because Marlina was against him volunteering to have the *MDSL-1 processor* implanted, but she was gone now. *So why does it matter?* He felt a sick hopelessness in the pit of his stomach and needed a distraction, *so why not?*

On the plus side, the project was educational. It gave him something new to focus on and look forward to in his dreary life. He was also excited about the possibility of getting a new *bionic* eye for the project. As a child he had watched Lee Majors play the *Six Million Dollar Man,* Colonel Steve Austin, on television. How he crashed and burned and was rebuilt. *Now it was Colonel Steven Scott's turn to be faster, better and stronger,* he thought.

The thought of having a bionic implant intrigued him a lot and got his risk-taking adrenaline pumping. It made him feel alive, even though it would kill him in the process. He was briefed and learned the specifications of the PSYCHONIX advanced technology, inside and out. It would help him see images better and clearer and farther than ever before, and perhaps experience things that no one else has ever witnessed. *I wonder what I'll see?*

The powerhouse was an *MDSL-1 processor,* the size of a grain of rice, that would be implanted into Steven Scott's central nerve system, wirelessly linked via his new prosthetic eye. When used, they believed it would amplify, transmit, and receive PSYCHON radiation. That remained to be seen. ITL master control should also be able to coordinate and record Steven's movements—at any range. Brad and Dr. Lui had already proven that capability with their PSYCHONIX goggles, months ago. In their earlier tests, they communicated instantly via deep space satellites.

Steven's new eye would be an easy fit, and a relatively safe procedure to fuse the tiny processor to his central nervous system. It would then communicate wirelessly and provide the *Holt* data stream necessary for monitoring and recording each step of his soul's journey.

"I'm jealous—I almost wish I could replace one of my eyes with that thing," Sabrina said.

"You're going to love it," Brad said. "We've bioengineered airtight and waterproof seals of synesthetic materials that are perfectly integrated with the bionics. If needed, it would allow you to change out your eye without ever breaking the link between us and the processor. And its capabilities are unbelievable. The zooming magnification alone provides a 10400mm focal length."

"It's like you're upgrading from a Fiat to a Lamborghini," Sabrina continued.

The ITL team tested, demonstrated, and explained the power of the technology to Steven Scott, as best they could. They also introduced a bright new, trusted member to the ITL team, Stanley Norris. He previously worked with Brad and Sabrina on projects and would assume Todd Lopez's duties. He knew nothing of Steven's innate psychic abilities. *Maybe later.*

Without delay, he jumped right into the briefing pool and amazed Steven with details and specifications about the PSYCHONIX eye.

"The new eye is a state-of-the-art learning machine, linked directly with your mind," Stanley said. "It contains a *96* megapixel microsensor capable of zooming into objects clearly from ten miles away, shooting stills, and streaming video with a resolution of *15,864 x 11864*."

"Is that a lot?" Steven asked.

"Is that a lot?" Stanley and Sabrina asked at nearly the same time. It was quite amusing to their nerdy-technical-minds. No one in the world had come close to discovering, much less reproducing this kind of technology for human use.

"But the most spectacular affect that we theorize," Stanley said, "is a *psychomorphic algorithm* that spontaneously emerges in the system." It was impossible for them to wrap their minds around that aspect, because no one understood all the telepathic transport conditions. Neither did they understand how it could morph physical objects like the *Multi-Dimensional Spatial Lattice* (MDSL-1) into a mental substance, but they believed that it would. In their lab tests they had breached the speed of light, punctuated with a luminance boom and transported animals and objects. Now, it had to be tested on a human.

"It's not just a state-of-the-art learning machine and camera," Sabrina said to Stanley. "It's a *Soul Machine*."

CHAPTER EIGHTY-SIX

"The most incomprehensible thing about the world is that it is comprehensible."
~*Albert Einstein*

PSYCHONS BY ANY OTHER NAME

EINSTEIN WAS THE one who said that *everything is energy, it can be no other way.* It was clearly a philosophical assertion—*it can be no other way.* And true, perhaps, depending on how one defined the word energy. To the ITL team it appeared as though PSYCHONS were a metaphysical energy or substance that could bridge minds. They amplified something that had always been present in humans from the beginning of time but was scientifically undetectable— until now.

Since no one had ever heard of PYSCHONS—they had to be ostensively defined. That meant that you would have to point out examples of how it worked, in order to show what it was. For example, defining "red" by pointing out red objects—apples, stop signs, roses—was giving an ostensive definition. It was the same with PSYCHONS. But now that they had been harnessed, you could point to its effects.

"For better or worse, similar concepts of energy or life forces or animating principles had existed in various forms, fashions, and cultures since the beginning of time," Dr. Starr said. "Including: the Latin *anima*, Islamic and Sufi *ruh*, the Greek *pneuma*, the Chinese *qi*, the Polynesian *mana*, the Amerindian *orenda*, the German *od*, the Hebrew *ruah*, or what the Hindus call *prana*. Are those the same things—like referencing snow and schnee? Who knows?"

411

Dr. Feinberg shrugged.

. "Time will tell," he said. Dr. Starr reflected on many other terms and concepts that he had learned through apologetics that also caused him to ponder.

"In Neoplatonism the *hypostasis* of the soul, the *nous* or intellect, and *the one* was addressed by Plotinus. A combination of *hypo,* meaning *that which stands under,* and *ousia* meaning our true being, essence, or substance." The terminology was useful in establishing the early Christian Church's Doctrine of Christ and the Trinity. "In 325 A.D. the Nicene Creed used the word *hupostasis*, which referred to the human and divine natures of Christ—like *hypostasis* it denoted *being* or *nature*."

It was thought by theologians to be the underlying substance and the fundamental essence of reality. From Mark's point of view the most interesting thing was that the essence of reality could be amplified by the *MDSL-1 processor*, the primary driver of PSYCHONIX.

The religions disagreed on most major doctrines but had one thing in common. They believed in a unifying force. ITL considered that unifying force to be PSYCHONS, but there was still significant disagreement as to exactly what it was and where it came from. Dr. Starr believed strongly that their discovery was *a bridge—a physical and metaphysical connection between people and God.* Others saw it as a fundamental connection to each other, which required no further explanation—it was inexplicably there as a residual material energy.

If it could be explained, then it would be in some naturalistic way that only an *M-Theory* physicist could understand. But then, even Edward Witten thought the *M* should stand for *magic* until more about the theory was known. There was a lot that was unknown but what they did know at ITL was that two people had recently died and communicated their experiences.

It could be that we're all connected to God, the source of all power and knowledge. That made the most sense to Dr. Starr. He believed that the truth of the universe had to be grounded in something immensely powerful and personal. In an ultimate mind. *If not, then how else does one account for the intelligibility of human knowledge or the universe for that matter?*

"It's a substance of some sort. I suppose we could call our discovery—energy," Dr. Starr said to his team. "But it's a different type of energy. If the word energy was defined to mean that which goes beyond its kinetic, thermal, chemical, or nuclear forms and linked our mind or soul to each other and God, then yes, perhaps Einstein was correct, *energy is everything*. And perhaps the *Theory of Everything* isn't held together by magic—but PSYCHONS."

CHAPTER EIGHTY-SEVEN

"Don't downgrade your dream just to fit your reality. Upgrade your conviction to match your destiny." ~ Stuart W. Scott

MIND OVER MATTER

DR. MARK STARR left no stone unturned as he elaborated on other aspects of PSYCHONS and spoke to the team about the *Mind-Body Problem,* and the impact that our mind has over our body.

"When we worry, we can get ulcers, right? When we're discouraged, our immunities are often lowered to the point of making us sick. When we're afraid, our eyes dilate, and we sometimes get stronger and run faster. During times of adversity, optimism is good for our health. It has been of significant help to those who suffered health-related setbacks—helping them to recover faster."

Having a positive mindset was called *disposition optimism.* If you had positive expectations for the future, then you would likely make better psychological adjustments, if not physical improvements. Dr. Starr believed that optimism was a good thing. It helped. Believing in something greater than yourself, provided you with more than just a good psychological outlook—it gave you hope.

Dr. Starr entertained religious and social ideas—and some cultural usage of language and radical claims amused him. He chuckled as he pondered the notion that *perhaps the hippies, in the 1960's, got something right about people having positive vibes.* "It wouldn't be fair to dismiss their claims out of hand, when there may possibly be a golden nugget of truth."

People have long searched for a higher power or reality, especially in the drug culture. Some people took drugs in an effort to reach *God.* The hippies were urged by Timothy Leary to *Turn on, tune in, drop out*, and to embrace cultural changes using psychedelics, by detaching from the existing conventions and hierarchies in society. It was also the motto of his League for Spiritual Discovery.

Turn on meant to go within, to activate your neural and genetic equipment. To become sensitive to the many and various levels of *consciousness* and the specific triggers that engaged them. Drugs were supposed to be one way to accomplish that end. *Tune in* meant to interact harmoniously with the world around you—externalize, materialize, express your new internal perspectives.

Drop out suggested a detachment from unconscious commitments, with a goal of self-reliance and a discovery of one's singularity, a commitment to mobility, choice, and change. Leary was on record as saying his explanations of personal development were misinterpreted to mean: *Get stoned and abandon all constructive activity.*

As misguided as some of the hippies or drug culture was, Mark Starr believed that the desire for a religious connection and the hippie usage of the word *vibes* was on to something spiritually real. Mark thought *there must have been some drug induced PSYCHON interactions being transmitted in SoCal.* It was certainly a theory that he had ever so briefly entertained with a smile. He even theorized that instead of *pheromones,* it was *PSYCHONS* that actually attracted us to one another.

CHAPTER EIGHTY-EIGHT

"For where two or three gather in my name, there am I with them." ~ *Matthew 18:20*

LOGISTICS

"RESISTANCE IS FUTILE," Steven Scott joked as he admired his reflection in one of the large lab mirrors. His new PSYCHONIX eye made him look like a cybernetic organism ready to join a collective consciousness. Unlike a character in his favorite TV show, though, he would maintain his individuality and self-determination. Even from across the room, he could see the gleam of a red light emerge, blink, and swirl out from the synthetic retina. It was converting PSYCHONS into *Holt* impulses, which could be measured as they were being transmitted between the mind and the body. It was for all intents and purposes a mental fingerprint.

A superhuman eye, cool! He thought to himself. *I'm really going ahead with this! Worst case scenario—I get to see Marlina earlier than expected.* That was a good thought, and not a suicidal wish.

He was in, all the way—totally committed to the project—so there was no turning back now. As he sat in the lab and they began to run more advanced tests he would sometimes play *Ride of the Valkyries* on his phone—to psych himself up. That and *Black Dog* by Led Zeppelin. It was a weird iPod mix of Classic and Classical. *No room for the faint hearted.* He had to do something for fun, since the lab was pretty much his home now. But it was a great distraction. If you gave yourself too much time to think, you might start to second guess decisions and capabilities, and get cold feet. ITL didn't want to risk that either, so they kept him busy. They understood that timing was everything.

As a retired Army infantry officer, Colonel Steven Scott knew a lot about timing and commitment. He wasn't about to back out. He had always been a disciplined man, who worked and played hard. He enjoyed his downtime on R&R and knew how to remain calm in a chaotic, combat environment. It was how they trained and how they fought. In sustained battles he had learned to relax and breathe when taking his shots. It was critical. *Your reaction time is slower, and your aim will be off, if you're too tense.* There was no doubt, Steven Scott was the perfect person for the project.

For the upcoming experiment he was doing all the right things: meditating, focusing on his breathing, and practicing mindfulness. Fully self-aware, but not overly reactive or overwhelmed by what was going on around him or who he was speaking with. He played a variety of virtual video games that helped him develop a heightened sensitivity to his surroundings. If his soul survived death, he would need it. The growling sounds he heard in the background of Todd Lopez's recording haunted a couple of his nightmares. He felt sure that he knew what it was and that he wouldn't have the same fate.

He was still being counseled and monitored closely by Dr. Feinberg. She was happy with his progress. He had gone a year and a half without any problems. His therapy and the low dose of meds kept it in check. There was some anxiety and depression, but he no longer experienced hallucinations or the need to run. For the most part, he had resumed a normal, healthy life.

Maybe it was Steven's sense of the end or a new beginning, but he felt elated, a bit giddy, and quite animated as they prepped him with the new PSYCHONIX eye. He felt somehow revitalized and alive, but still mildly nervous and more chatty than normal. It was the same type of nervous adrenaline he had experienced as a kid, being chased—and he liked it. He read and understood all the grisly details and possibilities but didn't want to think about it anymore. He didn't need to hear more about what could *possibly* happen, any more than one would want to hear about all the side-effects of new medication that they had to take. *What good does it do to read about all the negative possibilities?* He knew that the PSYCHONIX project meant succumbing to a highly monitored clinical death. How could it be any plainer?

"We will gradually cool your body and slow down your heart until it stops and all breathing ceases," Dr. Lui said. "You won't be legally alive, but we will keep you on a ventilator after being declared brain-dead by our doctors."

"Brain-dead?! Steven asked. "I didn't think there was any coming back from that."

"That's right, typically if you're brain-dead, you're dead, and the brain will never work again, but we believe that because of the biological and metaphysical transport conditions we can maintain a *psychomorphic link* and pull you back."

"Resuscitate me?"

"It worked on the monkeys," Sabrina said.

Steven shot her an incredulous look. "Yeah, so I heard." He had heard enough about the damn monkeys.

"If all of the criteria for brain death are met, then it's pretty clear that there's nothing left to do but support your bodily processes: gastric, kidney, immune, thyroid, blood pressure, and body temperature," Dr. Lui said. "Today, with ventilators, blood pressure augmentation and hormones, the body of a brain-dead person could, in theory, be kept functioning for a long time, perhaps indefinitely. The critical part is your brain."

"No kidding."

There had been brain-dead patients who recovered after doctors gave up on them. Hours and days after there was *no hope of recovery.* Those patients showed that doctors and hospitals were sometimes dead wrong.

The fact that they didn't know everything was the part that stirred a little anxiety in Steven Scott. That's when he'd start humming Ride of the Valkyries again. *I'm going to relax and rely on these brainiacs to initiate death, monitor my mind—and bring me back—no sweat.* He walked over and spoke into the Rhesus monkeys cage. "No big deal, right?" *If things go south, then they do.* It was good self-talk, which he nearly believed—but felt drawn to pray. Steven Scott bowed his head, folded his hands and whispered a prayer to himself. He punctuated it with a loud *Amen!*

A few members of the ITL team repeated after him. *Amen!*

CHAPTER EIGHTY-NINE

"The mind is the key; the heart is the door; the soul is corridor; the universe is the destination." ~
Matshona Dhliwayo

GREATER POWER

MARK STARR BELIEVED that the *hope* of having a meaningful and purpose-filled future was the one thing that drove us and spurred us on to recovery-oriented and redeemed lives. It took us beyond merely meeting our physical needs. It supplied us the motivation to explore and dream of something better. Of brighter days full of new discoveries, dreams, and lasting relationships.

"We all desire meaningful connections, so doesn't it seem like hope should exist in an ultimate way?" Mark asked rhetorically. He knew that Peggy believed it as well. It was small talk while they once again took a short coffee break and chatted. Afterward, they headed back to the lab. "In our over-communicated world of social media, a lot of people are searching for value and significance."

"Tell me about it," Peggy said, "But there doesn't seem like much value or significance in anonymous voyeurism."

"Right—peeking into people's lives can be strange, and how many mundane meals and cat videos can one endure?" he said, flashing a grin.

"If you're sharing precious moments with your family, then I can see the point, but heated conversations with strangers are borderline pathologic."

"Agreed," he nodded. "We have something ironically called social media, but in many ways, we couldn't be more disconnected and lost in this big universe. Perhaps our new way of connecting through PSYCHONIX will bring us together in ways we've never dreamed of."

"Yeah, could you imagine a social media company called *ThoughtBook?*"

Dr. Starr and Dr. Feinberg settled around the lab conference table as Dr. Lui began the next IPR. "In our beta-test last night we discovered that the person wearing the PSYCHONIX processor could connect with the minds of others not wearing the chip—as long as they were within a five-meter radius."

Dr. Starr nodded and thought. *It's similar to Steven's situation, except there's a limited range with the use of goggles, and Steven is capable of so much more.*

"So, in essence, the person wearing the goggles amplified the radiation field enough to become a conduit for those not wearing them—if that person granted them access."

The permissions aspect frustrated Dr. Lui. He had searched tirelessly for a way to bypass personal permissions and had failed. The code may as well have been the Liber Primus provided by *Cicada 3301*. Fortunately, he didn't know—and would never know that Steven Scott was a natural conduit, superior to any of the testing he had done. As far as Lui was concerned the PSYCHONIX implant within Steven was merely an embedded version of the goggles, which established the necessary link.

That was the only way to explain today's test with Steven Scott. There were a few preliminary adjustments that needed to be made and two chairs were set up on a dais in the middle of the room. The rest of the team viewed the demonstration from the four rows of lecture hall seating.

"Today—with Steven's help, we will conclude one of our final tests and once again demonstrate that there is an energy connecting us all," Stanley Norris said. "That we are, in a sense, one. To demonstrate that we have a special connection as human beings, I will blindfold Sabrina and Brad and have them sit down. Steven will stand in the middle of them."

He explained that Steven would be using the power of his PSYCHONIX EYE to establish a PSYCHON radiation link. It was greater than they imagined because of his ever-increasing ability. Dr. Lui and Stanley Norris still didn't know that. "Again, just as Dr. Lui indicated—we now know that the other person doesn't have to be wearing goggles if they're within five meters and granted access through mental assent. It worked with the goggles, so we believe that it will work with the implant as well."

The mental assent was merely a subconscious checkpoint that limited and sustained the amount of information shared. They weren't quite sure how it worked, but it did.

"Are you ready?" he asked everyone.

"Yes sir," Steven said.

Dr. Lui nodded.

"Very good. Now, I ask each of you to pay close attention to the sensations or thoughts that you feel—a touch, a pinch, a pat, or whatever. And I'll ask you to sustain a state of mental assent, and to share the thoughts and sensations that you sense amongst yourselves—that is key. We'll create a clear channel, so to speak. Will you allow that?" he asked.

They nodded.

"First, I'll begin by having Steven follow my directions," he looked at Steven. "Okay—then touch one of them now and think about touching the other in the same way." Steven turned to his left and tapped Brad lightly on his right shoulder.

"If you felt a touch raise your right hand." Brad and Sabrina both raised their hands. It was a bewildering sight since Steven had only touched Brad on the shoulder.

"Now lower your hand, and again—pay close attention to all sensations or thoughts that you feel. Steven, touch one of them again and think about the other." This time he patted Brad on his stomach.

"If you felt a pat, then raise your right hand." They both raised their hands. Others watching were astonished into silence, as they sat silently, some with their hands over their mouth.

"Now point to where you felt that pat." They both pointed to their stomach.

One person audibly gasped. *How could it be?*

"This time I will ask you to remember how many times you felt a touch."

Steven had been given instructions not to touch either one of them, but to only think about touching them. He closed his eyes to concentrate and mentally tapped Sabrina and Brad on their shoulders three times.

"If you felt a touch raise your right hand." They both raised their hands. "—and now with your fingers indicate how many times you were touched." They both held up three fingers.

"Is that right Steven?" he asked.

"Yes."

"Your connection is incredible." PSYCHONIX had united their minds and bodies. Mentally, Steven tapped them both. Through the amplification of their PSYCHONS it had allowed both them to sense what the other person was sensing—and thinking.

423

"Now—for the ultimate *mind-body* test I will give you each a marker and a small dry-erase board," Stanley Norris said. "I ask that everyone in the lab remain silent so that they're not distracted. I also ask that Steven Scott think of a word now and that each of you sustain the connection. I will give you five seconds to write down the word that he is thinking. Begin!"

After five seconds Brad and Sabrina were asked to remove their masks and flip over the dry-erase board, so that everyone could see the words that they wrote. To everyone's disbelief and amazement—the same exact word was written on each board and in Steven Scott's handwriting. *Marlina.*

"You see—when two or more people are connected, the truly impossible is possible." No one else outside the circle of Mark, Peggy, and Brad yet realized that his PSYCHONIX ability was naturally supercharged, so the circus display amazed them beyond belief. However, Steven was tiring of the show—fortunately, this would be the final test before they launched the ultimate part of the project.

To distract himself from the risk, Steven focused more on his upcoming vacation in Southwestern Virginia. It would be a time of refreshing that he looked forward to with new friends. He mentioned it, and Mark agreed to come as well and asked to bring Peggy. It would finally be that special *small-town reunion* and Christmas that they had talked about for years.

John and Missy Croxon were good people and had invited everyone—Steven, Mark, Peggy, and Vito. It was a good plan. No one would be alone this Christmas—except his daughter who was still deployed to Afghanistan. They would brighten her world and send a care package right away.

This time away from ITL would be a much-needed time of rest and recovery for his weary soul. The PSYCHONIX project had him wound tighter than a drum. He knew that no one who was legally declared brain-dead had ever recovered. Relaxation in a small southern town, on the other hand, had never hurt anybody.

CHAPTER NINETY

"He that has eyes to see and ears to hear may convince himself that no mortal can keep a secret. If his lips are silent, he chatters with his fingertips; betrayal oozes out of him at every pore. ~ *Sigmund Freud*

SECRETS

FOR ABOUT TWO years Innovations Technology Laboratory was privy to classified information, which many in the tech world could have only dreamed of. The technological inner workings of the National Security Intelligence Agencies secretive operations was astonishing.

The government developed psychological operations tools used within the National Security Division. They believed that the PSYCHONIX project showed potential as an untraceable cyber-espionage tool. They had good reasons to believe that it could help the *Director of National Intelligence* and the *Department of Defense* better coordinate activities and guard the U.S. against terrorism, cyberattacks, and espionage in the future.

It would be used for good, or so they said, for *U.S. National Defense*, even though it had the potential to be one of the most evil weapons of all time. Even though its intrusive boundaries into the mind had not yet been fully realized.

Little did ITL know, but a CIA van was parked across the street, monitoring activities, and they had one person working on the inside—recently hired as a janitor. He had discreetly installed and hacked ITL systems with a *zero-day* piece of his own malicious software. It allowed those in the van to surreptitiously attack and exploit the network vulnerabilities of the *black hat* hackers.

When you've got the CIA, NSI or some other powerful government organization so interested in you that they're coming into your office to clandestinely install spyware on your computer, you may have bigger problems to worry about than you think. Dr. Lui and Dr. Kahn had no idea what they were up against.

The new janitor wore a throat-mic and had just communicated some valuable Intel to the team in the van. "It probably means nothing, but I've noticed two ITL doctors playing a strange game of phone tag."

"Keep an eye on them," an agent in the van replied.

CHAPTER NINETY-ONE

"For now we see in a mirror dimly, but then face to face. Now I know in part; then I shall know fully, even as I have been fully known." ~ *1 Corinthians 13:12*

WELCOME HOME

IN THE FIRST moments of her tragic car accident, Marlina didn't have time to close her eyes, worry about a family problem, or even wonder for a moment, whether or not her heart was still beating in her chest. At the time of the collision, she merely exhaled. It was as though a candle had been blown out. For an instant she felt as though she couldn't breathe and then as an unembodied spirit, she stood by her lifeless body, and watched the ambulance arrive.

Time ran thick and slow in the same space but in a different time. She turned her head and saw the glow of a passing firefly, nearly frozen in flight with its light still on. It was glorious, as though she was engulfed in the bioluminescence of its glow. But she was in some kind of synchronic distortion, between heaven and earth. Then time sped up and she dissolved into flecks of spotted light. The maddening speed swallowed Marlina, as she hurtled toward pirouetting beams of light. Everything that defined her life peeled away, like the mummified silk of a cocoon, to uncover and transform her soul.

Then suddenly, before being whisked up and away from the wreck, she knew that breathing didn't matter anymore. There was a split second of blackness, a flash of light, and she just as suddenly inhaled. It was as though a swimmer had recovered from drowning, but instead of gasping, she felt relaxed, euphoric, and less inhibited. Her senses were opened and there was an indescribable harmony with everything around her. She had entered into a divine collective of contentment, love, and joy, to become her truest, best self.

That's when Marlina found herself in what could only have been described as a dream—with a one-way ticket to the Land of Oz. In the beginning, she honestly didn't know where she was headed, as she passed through a spinning burst of wispy clouds, planets, stars, and galaxies. However, she was conscious enough to believe that it was actually happening.

Throughout the unexpected journey, she felt an incredibly soothing inner-peace, which couldn't have been explained in earthly terms, but she wasn't worried or burdened or anxious. Thought and personality had been replaced by an uncharted harmony. Then there was another burst of brilliant lights, which left her rubbing and refocusing her eyes, as one might if they were surprised by flashing paparazzi cameras. *I'm out of my mind,* she thought. No, that wasn't it. She was completely out of her wrong mind and moving into the light.

As things became clearer and took shape, Marlina walked under a diaphanous *fogbow* and found herself standing at the edge of a sun-dappled forest in a field of tall, wavy, green and silver-white grass. It was as though the blades had been coated with feathery streaks of ice and sprinkled with powdery snow, except that they gently swayed. From the East there was a warm peaceful breeze that blew through the fine grass and multi-colored flowers. It produced a comforting and welcoming melody.

"Where am I?"

At that moment, I felt as though I could see and feel with more than just my eyes and hands, she later recalled to friends and family, *My heart, mind, and soul were merely absorbing, reflecting, and praising God!* Those already in Heaven smiled and laughed. Stories like that were a unique pleasure and everyone had their delightful experiences to share. They loved hearing all about her arrival and discoveries. They nodded and smiled and assured her that the comforting feelings of love and encouraging praise were a forever thing. *Just wait*, they told her with broad smiles.

If she knew anything at all now, it was that she was loved and completely safe. There was no doubting that. *Next to the field, just a few short yards away, I saw a Hansel and Gretel path, like you might see in a Brothers Grimm fairytale. I walked toward it and slowly beside it, not thinking it was a footpath or an ordinary sidewalk that you could walk on. It had uneven emerald and sapphire stones lining each side and tiny ruby and diamond gravel ground into a type of clear asphalt. I timidly stepped onto the path and the music from the fields drew me forward. It seemed to be the only way.*

In the distance, there was a cottage that glistened in the sun. Marlina noticed that there was no front door. Later, it dawned on her that there was no need for doors in heaven with everyone being safe, comfortable, and always welcome. You could have them for decoration or privacy, but they were unnecessary. No one bothered you in Heaven.

I felt so peaceful that I laid down for a short while in the inviting soft squashy grass, closed my eyes, and unhurriedly soaked in the music that swished through the majestic rolling fields.

It was magical. The ears of wheat, rye, and barley changed tunes as she walked and gently rubbed the palms of her hands across their tops. The sound coming from each field was a beautiful, high adagio that floated up and piped through heaven.

I had no words to adequately describe it. The sights, sounds, and smells surrounded and embraced me. So, this is Heaven! Ha…I couldn't believe that the fields orchestrated such a beautiful melody. Just then I heard a calming voice—and was reminded that all things were possible.

"Hello, Marlina—*rise* and *open* your eyes."

She knew that voice—and obeyed. "Jesus?!" She momentarily froze in place as He strolled forward with arms opened wide. His smiling eyes painted in rings of gold light. In one hand, he held a long bundle of wheat, which he used as a baton to orchestrate the sounds that flowed from the fields.

Oh my—I could see the joy radiating from His face—and I knew that He loved me and had been waiting for this day. "Jesus," she cried out again. It was all she could say. It was all that needed to be said. Those sorts of testimonies never grew tiresome in Heaven. Everyone, including the angels had a special, unique relationship with the Master that was shared like the daily news, on the far corners of Heaven: *Did you see what Jesus did? I was with Jesus when...or look, I learned this from Jesus today.* Those were, of course, the best topics of the day.

Marlina skipped forward and suddenly dashed headfirst into His outstretched arms. He gently squeezed and pressed a loving kiss to her forehead—and she cried for joy as she was embraced. Jesus smiled, wiped away her tears and said, "Welcome home my daughter!."

They walked along the edge of a glimmering clear lake that reflected the sky and tall cedars flanked by its edge. It wasn't a lonely place. Many people sat along the banks to soak their feet and greeted Jesus as they walked by. They spoke for what seemed like hours or days or months—who was to say in Heaven. He wouldn't leave her side until most of her questions had been answered—at least the ones you might think of on your first day in heaven.

Is my family here? Where will I live? Is sleep necessary? Do we eat regular food? Is my dog here? Can we travel? Are we all angels now? Do we have sex in heaven?

Jesus gave a hearty laugh. "Slow down." Those were questions that everyone had and Jesus was happy to answer her. "There are greater joys that await you than you have ever known of, my dear. What God has designed outweighs all your desires. You'll see!"

"I can't believe it—I mean I've always believed it. *Sheesh,* I'm in heaven," she said. She reeled from the new information and waved her hands in praise. "I'm really, truly in Heaven!" Even in Heaven Marlina's Italian exuberance bubbled over. Again she asked, "Where will I live, Jesus?"

He took her hands into his. "My little one—you have always known my teachings."

"Yes, Lord—you've prepared a place for me!"

"That's right," he said as he turned and continued to walk. "There's plenty of time—and so much to learn, my love."

It crossed her mind again that she might be dreaming, but she didn't see a Scarecrow, Tin Man, Cowardly Lion lurking in the distance. It was all too real and she was conscious of everything that had happened.

I cant' believe that I was driving my car, and now I'm talking to Jesus, she thought.

"Yes, you are," Jesus said.

He even knows my thoughts.

"Yes, I do," he smiled broadly again. Jesus enjoyed watching His children make new discoveries and see how connected they were with Him and each other in Heaven.

Is Steven here?"

"No, Marlina—but he's safe and will join us soon. He still has other things that I need for him to do, but there are others here to see you—others who've joyously waited for you!" He motioned toward *The Eternal City*.

He called me by my name—Marlina. Hearing her thoughts, Jesus smiled again and directed her attention toward a charming stone cottage on the horizon—just west of *The Eternal City*. Seated on the front porch were two familiar people who smiled and waved vigorously. It was Papa and Mama Millie. They spotted her and came barreling down the steps as fast as they could carry themselves into the yard. What a reunion! They were running eagerly down the path with their hands in the air, motioning for her to come quickly. Marlina ran and met them halfway in the yard—and they embraced with a dance of hugs and tears and laughter.

"The family is together again—*con un sacco d'amore!" with a lot of love*! Mama Millie shouted. In Heaven you could speak any language you wanted to and had plenty of time to practice. *God must love all the languages and cultures,* she thought. *Of course He does, he created them.* They all repeated Mama Millie's words together: *un sacco d'amore!* and laughed heartily as they continued to celebrate their happy eternal reunion.

"You're-ah-home, right on time," Mama said. It was just the way Marlina remembered hearing her—except somehow, she seemed younger, healthier, and more vibrant.

"Home—on time?" Marlina asked. "For what?"

"We knew you were coming today," Papa said.

"You did?"

"Of course—everyone's arriving right on time," he smiled.

"And we have-*ah* a big party at-*ah* your house," Papa said.

"My house?"

433

"Yes, Jesus," Mama said. "He made this wonderful place. It's-*ah* just for you Marlina—and He let us help—so it's extra special."

Papa nodded.

Marlina smiled. Everything was *extra* for mama—but now there was no exaggeration. They would have an extra-wonderful forever-after together. "It's an extra special place for you—that you will-*ah love, love, love*!"

They walked Marlina up the steps and into this special, radiant home. It was full of singing and laughter with the words *Love, Love, Love* painted above a roaring stone fireplace.

"Oh, this is such a beautiful place of joy and contentment. I can feel it. It was more than worth the wait!" She wept tears of joy.

Marlina's soul was happy—and still somewhat stunned. She was briefly lost in her thoughts, as she walked through her new home. It was only for a fleeting moment, but she thought about all the evil, suffering, and pain experienced in the world. *It was a vapor. It's not forever, but this is.* She smiled again. The past troubles weren't important anymore. *This is joy. This is ultimate happiness. This is our hope.* She couldn't stop smiling and it seemed that Heaven was full of the most beautiful people—who smiled back. No big surprise. It wasn't a group of white clouds with angels and harps and lists of rules. Loving your neighbor came much more naturally now, and it was the most spectacular place she had ever seen.

It's no wonder that the Apostle John had such trouble describing it, she thought.

It filled one's senses beyond the scope of dreams or imagination.

Like the rest of Heaven, her *home* was a lot more than met the eye. Yes, it appeared to be a simple stone cottage, but that would be like calling the wardrobe into Narnia a simple piece of furniture, or the Tardis a police box. It was everything she needed and everything that God knew she desired. This little cottage was both quaint and quite magical at the same time. Marlina was dumbstruck as she surveyed her delightful new home.

She discovered, as she moved from room to room, that the seasons and landscape shifted too, depending on which window or doorway she gazed out of. The scenery illuminated and transfigured depending on which direction she turned her head—and each room was fashioned to meet her heart's desire. So much so, that in the following days Marlina gasped with joy as she rushed to-and-fro and from window-to-window with multiple giddy double-takes. Hearing her say, *oh my, did you see that?* —became a daily occurrence.

The grand living room was a cozy mountain lodge, tucked into a spectacular winter wonderland with mid-mountain access to the slopes—something that she had always dreamt of. It was an incredible getaway where she could while away her days and watch snowflakes fall outside her window, as she enjoyed the warmth of a roaring fire and a soothing warm drink. The pristine snow-covered landscapes provided breathtaking views and a magnificent wildlife habitat. Just at that moment, Marlina spotted a herd of Elk frolicking at the edge of the forest and a rabbit hopping toward the house in search of the carrots placed by the decorative French doors.

God is taking care of the animals too.

From a different part of the house she could sit in a wingback chair or recline on a chaise lounge and read, as the wind whistled, and a gentle rain tapped her windowsill. There was also a large king-sized bed to enjoy. Sleep wasn't necessary, but still possible in Heaven. It was a refreshing and creative experience for the mind, where one could still enjoy entertaining aspects of the impossible and dream.

In the kitchen, there was the smell of cinnamon buns lofting from the oven. "We'll come back for those later," Mama Millie said, smacking her lips. "And we'll put on some coffee."

Marlina nodded.

It was nice to hear that the smell and taste of coffee was still valued in Heaven. From the picture window view of her country kitchen it was perpetually springtime, and beautiful flowers bloomed. There was also an abundance of fruit that grew on the trees and an assortment of vegetables sprouted in the garden. From the den, one could take in the gold and red fall leaves, which hung on the mature autumn trees. And one could amble through the Mediterranean grand arches, dripping with blooming flowers, to exit the house and find a perfect pumpkin or challenging corn maze nearby.

"It's beyond anything that I could have ever imagined in life," Marlina said.

Life.

The irony wasn't at all lost on her; she was dead. Not such a bad deal. During her earthly life, she remembered hearing people say, YOLO. *You only live once.* They were obviously wrong—*you live forever.* To those on Earth she was a dead person and they sadly mourned her loss, but she felt more alive than ever.

"Isn't it interesting how your perspective changes?" she asked while talking it over with Mama Millie. In half an instant, her mind, senses, and perspective had been divinely expanded. She had barely stepped her toe into eternity, but still heard things that she had never heard before and saw colors that she had never seen.

As Marlina walked through her cottage, she immediately noticed that each room or suite had its own distinctive touch and came complete with a variety of decorations and furniture, well beyond her expectations. Even the bathrooms were something to behold—Roman, rustic, and royal baths—one with an old-fashioned clawfoot tub like her grandmother used to have during the *Great Depression*.

You could also soak in the great outdoors from a hot tub gazebo with a panoramic view of the distant valley and glacial lake below. Inside, this heavenly cottage featured every imaginable convenience. A gourmet kitchen with a fully stocked pantry, walk-in closets, recreation rooms, spa, and comfy terry cloth robes to lounge around in, if you chose. The letter *M* was cursively sewn on the pockets, for Marlina. Not that one had to dress up or wear anything at all for that matter, but as with most other things in Heaven, it was one of the unlimited options. As she felt the texture of the linen, she had the flicker of a funny memory. The robes, sheets, and pillows were so soft that she imagined *Mike Lindell* popping in to tell her about the ultra-soft *Giza Dream* cotton found in them.

One could travel to Marlina's home in a variety of ways, but her favorite was by a horse-drawn sleigh. The horse, of course, was treated with the utmost kindness and love in their well-stocked barn, where he was rubbed down and fed oats and apples. As visitors arrived, Marlina would greet them with a heartfelt, welcoming smile and a toasty cup of *Nana's Old-Fashioned Hot Cocoa*. It was a special recipe that she had been given by Mama Millie, whom everyone in the family knew as *Nana*.

Sometimes guests relaxed in the largest room, which was basically a snow lodge with large leather sofas, wingback chairs, and comfy rugs. It was the place to settle in with their drinks and enjoy homemade *cocoa, cookies*, and *conversation*. Marlina had affectionately founded what would heretofore be known as the *3C Club*. They snuggled cozily around the warmth of her enormous stone fireplace, which ran up the middle of spectacular floor-to-ceiling windows.

From there you could catch a glimpse of the awe-inspiring beauty and peaceful vistas, which even outshined the Rocky Mountains.

From this side of the house one could only arrive on foot, skis, or by a horse drawn sleigh. There were no loud engines. No pushing. No pressuring. Just plenty of time to get where you wanted to go and to do what you wanted to do, for days or months and eternity. There was also a *pay-it-forward* kind of attitude that permeated all of Heaven. It was a world where everyone was treated as a king and behaved as joyful servants.

Marlina would spend endless millennia acquainting herself with her intriguing new home and blessing of friends. Painting. Swimming. Reading. Cooking. Dinners out. That was one of the most surprising parts of heaven. She hadn't given much thought, but Heaven had the best restaurants and you couldn't gain weight. It wasn't possible. To her amazement, there was a delightful economy in Heaven too, where gifts could be expressed to their fullest. Many Angels and people loved to cook. It was never boring. Everyone created, accomplished, set goals, and fulfilled them—to God's glory.

Although time or amounts of time were never a worrisome concern, Marlina would spend a great deal of it in the front part of her home, where she enjoyed the silky white and pink-sand beaches, accompanied by the frothy, rolling waves that crashed rhythmically to the shore. She and her friends, old and new arrivals swam, surfed, and soaked in the sunshine for large parts of forever.

Marlina was in the most perfect place you could ever imagine with the colors deeper and the tastes richer. A place filled with more love than you could ever dream of and where you don't just feel your joy and happiness—you sense everyone else's too. She understood more than she had ever known, and still loved Steven with a deep and unwavering affection. It was beyond description, but since she had been upgraded from economy to first class, there was a pure, unconditional, and infinite love in her heart. Time no longer mattered. She knew that when he graduated, that they would meet in Heaven someday.

CHAPTER NINETY-TWO

"God is our refuge and strength, a very present help in trouble." ~ *Psalm 46:1*

MOUNTAIN MISSION HOME

MAGGIE CROXON CARRIED a rag mop with a long wooden handle over her left shoulder and pushed along a hot bucket of soapy water into whatever room she started scrubbing. She churned her mop in the gray water, splashed it into the metal squeeze wringer, and thoroughly pulled the handle. Then she flung it forward, and dragged figure eights, as she slowly and methodically backed down the halls of the Grundy Mountain Mission Home.

That was a vivid memory that Senator Croxon held of his mother, from their time at the orphanage in Southwestern, Virginia. The Grundy Mountain Mission Home or the *Home* as they like to call it. It reminded him of where he came from and the *hopes* that she had for the family. Day-in and day-out his single mother worked hard to earn their keep. It barely supplemented room and board but provided them a safe environment. That was a big deal when you painstakingly raised six hungry kids alone. Still, she felt blessed and so did the children, even though between classes they, too, had to do their own chores—served food, took out trash, watched after smaller children, and helped with homework.

As far as they were concerned it was a fair trade-off, in order to have a non-leaking roof over their heads, and warm food in their bellies. At the *Home* they were all treated well, for the most part, and taught the value of hard work and getting up early, whether you felt like it or not—and always doing your best.

Sometimes they were visited by their Mom-Maw and Pop-Paw Keene, who lived less than an hour away in Richlands. They weren't well to do but loved the children and helped out as much as they could. Mostly they provided used clothes and shoes that they collected and sold from large wooden bins in their root cellar. They meagerly managed what one might call a *Goodwill*, before there was anything other than actual goodwill. That's where Maggie rummaged to find the right sized pants, shirts, and shoes for the kids.

"If it fit, I got it," John Croxon said.

Weekends and school breaks were special because each of the children took turns visiting their grandparents. They spent many of their lazy summer days chasing fireflies and a few delightful white Christmases looking for Rudolf in the night sky. They spent hours playing hide-n-seek and disappeared under mounds of old clothes in the musty old storage bins.

John often reflected on those carefree times. Even though his family was poor, he felt tremendously blessed and rich in love. The family was together, and they were healthy. That was all that really *mattered*—and that was the legacy that he wanted to pass down to Chelsea.

"It won't be long before we leave for Richlands," John told her. They were still at the hospital, but had most things packed up and in the car, ready to roll. Steven and the gang would follow on shortly and he would return for a couple tests prior to Christmas.

"That's our hometown isn't it, Daddy?" She knew that it was, but loved hearing about it.

"Yes, it is sweetie. That's where we're going for Christmas this year." As a Senator he didn't get to spend a lot of time in Richlands now. The fact was that during Chelsea's seven short years of life they had spent more time in the District of Columbia.

441

"With Uncle Steven too?"

"Of course—and his son Vito and brother Mark."

"And his *girlfriend*," she giggled."

"Yes, we'll be their hosts!"

"What's a—host?"

"Well, let's see—I guess you could say that we'll be the ones that make him feel welcome and at home during his visit."

"And showing him all around?" she hoped.

"Yes…and showing him all around our small town—if you're feeling up to it. Would you like that?"

"I'd love being the host, Daddy," she nodded with a happy grin. "I think I'm feeling better and better already, and I'll bet they've never seen where God first started making Heaven." Just then there were *three rapid knocks* and she spotted Steven peeking through the crack of the door. John waved him in, and Chelsea leaped from the bed, anxious to tell him something that obviously couldn't wait a moment longer.

"I think you'll love our hometown, Uncle Steven," she said, standing directly in front of him.

They hugged and he picked her up in his arms. "Oh, I know I will, especially since I'll be with my favorite new friends—and your newest little friend," he said. He pulled a small toy stuffed animal out from behind his back and the overjoyed look on her face revealed that the tiny gift was a much-welcomed surprise. "This little guy doesn't have a name yet, but he said he'd like to meet you."

Chelsea giggled, "He can't talk." Steven made the toy dog's ears flop around and give her a pretend kiss on the cheek. "Aww—he's so cute. I love him. I think I'm going to call him Baby."

"Well, you and Baby can show Uncle Steven what Christmas is like in Richlands this year," John said. He stood up to stretch. "Like Chelsea said—I think you're gonna love it. And we can't wait to show it off during our Winter Fest—"

"—with Santa Claus on the firetruck!" Chelsea said, bursting with excitement.

"Yes, that's how he arrives each year at our Christmas parade," Missy said.

"As a kid, I always enjoyed the parades in Walla Walla too," Steven said.

"Oh—and you see all the lights on *Christmas Tree Hill*!" Chelsea beamed. "With the big tree and star!"

"Yes, and all the lights…" John added. He looked toward Steven to explain her enthusiasm about the tree, "You see, the lights are attached to a *70* foot metal tower and spread out to look like a big Christmas tree. It's sort of an iconic Richland's tradition."

Steven nodded. "I love Christmas lights."

"We'll be heading down just as soon as Chelsea is cleared by her doctor," Missy said.

"I can't wait!" Steven said.

It would be a happy diversion, if he survived the first phase of the PSYCHONIX project.

CHAPTER NINETY-THREE

"Neither a borrower nor a lender be…" William Shakespeare

FULLY STOCKED

JOHN CROXON WASN'T born with a silver spoon in his mouth, but he had made it big in U.S. politics. He was a Virginia Senator now. He worked hard for it—harder than most because he had farther to climb and fully understood what it meant to be poor. For a short period of time in his life he had actually lived in a local cave and gone hungry. It didn't get much worse than that.

The earliest parts of his life were difficult; however, it had molded him into the man that he was today. It taught him to work hard, take care of people, and that nothing in life was free. It taught him lessons that he eventually took with him to Congress.

"I'm just a simple country boy at heart," he often said. And it was true, but he was also exceptionally smart and a fierce fighter. There was no doubt that his upbringing made him one of the wisest Senators' that Virginia had ever known. It was clear that he loved the people he served, and they loved him.

John put in long hours, but there was nothing quite like going home and reuniting with old friends and family to refresh one's soul. He believed what he told Steven.

"Christmas in the Mountains is about as close to Heaven as we'll get down here."

As Chelsea steadily recovered, it would definitely be a holiday to remember.

"Well, if you're not completely better by the time we leave, then Mom-Maw's cooking will surely do the trick," he sniffed the air. "I can smell it already—can't you?" he asked. John walked over to Chelsea and they both sniffed the air together and pretended to smell cornbread and biscuits, smoked ham and pinto beans. But just then they were interrupted by a cafeteria server, who arrived with tray of bland hospital food: a Styro-foam cup of watery broth, orange Jell-O, meat, bread, unsalted green beans, a juice box, and generic saltines, neatly lined up on a dull gray hospital tray.

"I guess this will have to do until then," he said. Everyone contorted their faces in mildly amused disgust. John pursed his lips sideways as he stared at some type of thick, yellowish gravy poured over a slice of white bread and something else that resembled meatloaf. Chelsea giggled as he pinched his nose and poked at it with a plastic fork. "Is it dead?"

As the doctors and nurses made their final assessments and finished paperwork, it gave them plenty of time to visit and share more stories. John missed his Mom-Maws's cooking, but remembered plenty of the same, hospital-style slop and glop being served at the Mountain Mission cafeteria. He laughed and said, "We use to call this stuff S.O.S.—Sausage and Stuff on a Shingle." It had a more colorful name, but he edited appropriately for a seven year old.

John looked off into the distance, finger-combed his hair, and thought back to less prosperous times, when he would have welcomed almost anything on a shingle.

His mother, Maggie, and the kids never considered themselves poor since they had everything that they needed—love, shelter, and food—all provided by their mother with a lot of help from God and the Grundy Mountain Mission Home.

John Croxon, or *Little Johnny* as he was called back then, was twelve years old when they were first taken into *The Home*. His earliest memories were of wearing hand-me-downs, and having to borrow pencils, paper, and lunch money. It was forever etched on his brain. As a man he had grown to disdain that word—*borrow*—and never wanted his children to borrow anything, ever. The thought brought tears to his eyes.

In the early 1960's, John was hardly old enough to work, but did whatever he could to get a bottle of pop or see an afternoon matinee. He cleaned out sheds, cut grass, and carried and shoveled coal for older folks or shut-ins who needed to have it dropped in their coal chute or stocked near their furnace in galvanized coal buckets for cold mornings and extra cold nights.

Those weren't stories that he liked to tell, but through the years he would often remind Chelsea:

Sweetie, I'll get you whatever you need, when you need it. Just let me know, okay. I'll make sure you have what you need." He would say that at the beginning, and throughout every school year without fail.

Chelsea wasn't old enough to understand biblical metaphors, but she knew that she had a father that loved and cared for her.

CHAPTER NINETY-FOUR

"Faith is the radar that sees through the fog."
~ *Corrie ten Boom*

RADAR

DR. LUI'S PLANS were riddled with discernible missteps that included suspicious conversations, a cleared desk, and locked out computers. He became anxious and overly eager to get back to China. But before he did, he had to arrange for Steven Scott to be kidnapped and the rival developers at ITL to be killed. Those were the orders he wrote down in Chinese, wadded-up, and threw in the trash after it was memorized.

The first part of the plan involved hiring kidnappers. It called for Steven to be taken off the street or from a car, the next time he ventured out. He would be blindfolded, sedated, and beaten if necessary. That might be the easy part. Dr. Lui also attempted to subcontract a hitman for $400,000. One hundred and fifty thousand would be paid upfront and the rest when the murders were completed.

It took a CIA operative posing as a janitor to discover the wadded-up plans and have them translated. That accelerated the entire investigation. Now there was a full sweep of ITL, which resulted in the discovery of the malware, maneuvers, and Near Field Communication transfer logs that happened between Dr. Lui's phones and computers. It was a type of short-range wireless connectivity, which enabled communication between devices when they're touched together or brought within a few centimeters of each other to make payments or, in this case, share files. Drs. Lui and Kahn were now a blinking red light on the radar of National Intelligence, and it would surely prove to be a gripping weekend.

A black sedan slow rolled past Steven while he was out taking a morning walk. Two tough-looking guys in dark suits, sunglasses, and black leather gloves got out, and Steven froze. He immediately turned to walk away, where he was met by two more dark suits who blocked his path. The one on the left motioned him in the car with his pistol, where he was cuffed and blindfolded, before they sped away.

The early Sunday morning papers indicated that *an Innovations Technology Laboratory engineer, Dr. Lui Wei, was arrested by U.S. authorities at Dulles International Airport while preparing to board a flight to China. He was charged with stealing proprietary information related to a special government project.* Of course, it was the PSYCHONIX project, but that couldn't be released in a public affairs statement.

The men in the black sedan aggressively secured Steven and drove him to an underground garage before they revealed that they were Federal Agents, and that this was completely for his safety.

"I'm Agent Yarymovych, CIA." He flashed his badge

Steven sighed, "Great, what'd I do now?"

"Nothing, sir. You were in imminent danger," a second agent said.

"It was for your safety," said another, who seemed to be in charge and had just strolled in with a cup of coffee for himself and Steven."

"Safety?"

"Yes, there was a contract hit out on you. In a matter of moments, they would have had you, and the chip too, so we had to move fast."

"Can I make a phone call?" Steven asked.

"Of course, sir, you're not under arrest. As soon as I get the all-clear, we'll drive you home."

Investigators revealed that Dr. Lui was scheduled to go over a few test procedures with Sabrina Killian the night before, but failed to show up. She said that she had tried to access the project files while she waited on him. That was when she first knew that there was something wrong. She was denied computer access and locked out of the ITL network. Sabrina rechecked her password, but still couldn't get in. It was then that she also noticed that Dr. Lui's desk was completely cleared off. *That's not normal.*

She called Brad in and he attempted to log-in as well. He was nearly locked out, but remembered that there was an override code built-in for just this kind of worst case scenario. It was clearly unusual and they both found it suspicious—especially coupled with the unusual communication that Brad had witnessed and the fact that Dr. Lui had cleared out his desk. Brad immediately inspected the *PSYCHONIX* project files and noticed that there were multiple unauthorized data dumps and deletions. Everything had disappeared and the files were wiped. He even checked back up files and recycle folders—they were gone. Brad alerted Dr. Starr and he contacted the Director of National Intelligence. The Feds were already waiting on Dr. Lui when he arrived at the airport.

At the time of his arrest, he said he had worked for a Chinese company that also developed interrelated communication technologies and that the data and equipment was theirs. However, according to a criminal complaint filed in federal court in Washington, D.C. on Monday, the CIA and the U.S. attorney's office, it was a cut and dry case of intellectual property theft, if not outright espionage.

The files were recovered and Dr. Lui no longer attempted to deny his culpability. It was a felony and he wouldn't be returning to ITL or China any time soon. He said he was working alone, but they knew better. Not only was Dr. Kahn being closely surveilled, but he would spend the remainder of his life in a Federal Penitentiary, as an American citizen. From there they will limit his communication, use him to nail Dr. Kahn—and catch bigger fish.

CHAPTER NINETY-FIVE

"It is the mark of an educated mind to be able to entertain a thought
without accepting it." ~ *Aristotle*

MIND OVER MATTER S1E3

"I'M DR. MARK STARR. Welcome to *Mind Over Matter*—a program dedicated to the

Mind-Body Problem. This is our third installment in the series, asking questions about

consciousness." Again, they reviewed intriguing topics that they would talk about, and had

discussed previously, as the questions flashed on the screen.

What is consciousness?

What reason do we have for thinking it's not physical?

What are conscious states and physical states, and how are they different?

What is the thing that has consciousness—the brain, or is it the mind,

or a soul or something like that?

"Once again we welcome our esteemed guest Dr. Robert W. Smith—a research Professor of

Philosophy at Liberty University—to talk all about consciousness. Welcome."

"Thank you, Dr. Starr, it's great to be back."

"You've discussed three out of the five brain states that folks can familiarize themselves with

on our website. What's the fourth one?" he asked.

"It's a pleasure to be on your new program, Mark—where we can discuss important things with such an open mind," Robert said with a polite nod to the camera. "The fourth state of consciousness is a *desire*. A desire is a person's natural urge or inclination for or against something. I very often have a desire for pistachio ice cream and simultaneously a desire to avoid the dentist. That's the conflict I endure to enjoy food and protect my teeth. You're probably ahead of me, based on the last program—but a desire is neither true nor false. They can be appropriate or inappropriate—and a desire is not the same thing as a sensation. A sensation is just a state of awareness without you being drawn away or towards something."

"And the fifth brain state?"

"This mental or conscious state is an act of volition or *free choice*—endeavoring to bring something about. Suppose I was admitted to a Psychiatric unit, after this unbelievably awesome interview, and one of my disgruntled students came into my room while I slept and injected my muscles with some type of paralyzing *pancuronim bromide and sodium thiopental*, a strong barbiturate intended to render me unconscious — you know the stuff they use on death row. But I don't know that they used it on me, at least I don't know it until I wake up, and realize what my students have done."

"You're just lying there in the dark," Dr. Starr added.

"Yes, I'm paralyzed and I'm waking up thirsty again. Fortunately, there's a tray next to me, with a glass of water on it that I'd really like to drink now. So, I look at the water, and attempt to get the water, but my body doesn't move. So, mentally I've performed a *conscious* action. I make every effort to lift my arm to get that glass and drink the water. I exercised my freedom of will, to do it, but my body doesn't cooperate. That is exercising my freewill—in that I tried to bring it about, that my arm moves, so that I could grab the glass of water." He explained that that was an act of free choice.

"So, what you're saying is that thoughts of consciousness are sentient states of one kind or another, but not physical," Mark said.

"Correct! And another example of their differences is what philosophers call intentionality. Intentionality is the *of-ness* or *about-ness* of a mental state," Robert said. "For instance, my thought is *of* or *about* World War II. My sensation is a sensation *of* tasting a pepperoni pizza. My desire is a desire *about* a new car, and my belief is a belief *about* John F. Kennedy.

"So conscious-states have an *of-ness* or *about-ness*?"

"Yes, that is directed toward an object. Brain-states don't have intentionality. There is no *of-ness* or *about-ness* of a brain-state."

"So, the physical brain is described in physical terms," Mark said. "—neurons, synapses, axons, dendrites, etc."

"That's right," Robert said. "And all the other things that go on in the brain. The problem is that there are a small number of conscious states, like a pain state or an itch, that don't seem to have intentionality."

"So that sort of destroys your argument," Dr. Starr said.

"No, not quite. It just proves that there are rare secondary-order states of consciousness."

"Like awareness?"

"Yes, an awareness *of* the pain state," Robert said. "There may have been an object that caused it, like a kick in the knee. In this case the resulting effect—the pain event—was caused *by* but not *of* or *about* the kick."

"In that case the pain state does, in fact, entail a state with intentionality—namely that *you* know *about* the pain," Dr. Starr continued.

"Yes, so, it seems safe to say that the overwhelming number of conscious states do have intentionality, and the few that don't still entail secondary states with intentionality." Robert told Mark that from the time you wake from a dream, until this very moment, you could think of your consciousness as a flow of various states. You're dreaming or you're awake. You're in one state and then you're in another state. You're thinking about a lot of stuff. You have sensations, thoughts, desires, and beliefs.

"So, in essence, as you've gone through multiple conscious-states there are also activities going on in your brain, separately," Mark stated to demonstrate his full understanding. "You have conscious-states going on and you have brain-states taking place. The question is, are these the same?"

"Right. And I don't believe they are. I ask you—is the sensation of pain that you're feeling, identical to a certain *neuronic C-fiber* event going on in your brain, or is it different? I have good reasons for thinking that conscious-states are entirely different from physical-states of the brain. Because there appears to be those things that are true of my conscious-states that aren't true of my brain-states. And if that's the case, then they can't be the same thing, can they?"

Dr. Starr nodded in agreement. "The Law of Identity," he said.

"Exactly Mark," he said. "Suppose that you're thinking about the Super Bowl and the fact that, prior to tonight, the Redskins were down seven games to none and you're wondering whether or not they'll play in the Super Bowl. While you're having the thought about the Super Bowl, there is a thought event that's going on in your brain that we can actually measure with magnetic resonance imaging."

"So, the event that's going on in your brain while you're thinking about the Super Bowl..." Starr asked, "...has mass?

Dr. Smith skootched toward the edge of his studio chair. He steepled his fingers, and briefly glanced toward the television camera as he vigorously maintained his insightful train of thought.

"That's correct!" Dr. Smith said. "However, the thought you're having about the Super Bowl doesn't have a size, shape, and location. It doesn't make any sense to ask, *"How big was that thought?* You see—there's no need for Nobel Peace Prize winner neck braces to support their heavy thoughts."

"So, the answer to *do your thoughts have spatial properties*," Starr said, "is no. But brain states have spatial properties."

"Yes, so they can't be the same thing."

"The Law of Identity."

"Right."

"I'm following as best as I can."

"You're doing great. Now—when you hold a certain belief," Dr. Smith said, "it makes sense that the belief could either be true or false. But brains can't be true or false, they just exist as organic mechanisms. They don't seem to be *about* anything, right?" he asked.

"That's what you just taught us. Brain-states aren't capable of being true or false, but the state of your consciousness — namely the thought that you're having now—could be true or false."

"You've got it. Okay, now—consider this. In your conscious life, there is a thought that only you can have. *What it's like* to be Dr. Mark Starr. That's a state of consciousness that only you can ever have, and only you can tell us *what it's like* to be in that state.

Starr nodded his understanding. *It's complicated, but easy to grasp the 30th or 40th time you hear it,* he thought. "Can you drill-down on that for our audience Dr. Smith?" he requested.

"Okay, let's go deeper: So, if you get hurt, then there's a *what it's like* to be in pain. If I marry a wonderful woman, then there's a *what it's like* to be happy with her. When I'm eating my favorite ice cream, there's a *what it's like* for me to taste pistachio ice cream—and trust me it's heavenly.

"I understand. That's how I feel about Rocky Road."

"All of those things that I've mentioned are different *what it's like* statements. The difference between a pain and a feeling of happiness is that they have different *what its likes*. Including *what it's like to be you*. And think about this—we all experience pain differently, too. We say that pain hurts physically, but we experience happiness in a non-physical sense."

Dr. Mark Starr could see that Dr. Smith had pounded it in: *Law of Identity.* "Okay, so tell us about your cake analogy," he said. He wanted to nail down the explanation and communicate it in less complicated terms.

"My birthday cake—which will need to be ordered each year, prior to July *11th*, makes a great tasting example. But it doesn't make any sense to say *what's it like* to be my birthday cake. *What's it like* to be mixed in a bowl, poured into a pan, baked, and covered in chocolate ganache? Why is that—because, cakes are the kind of things that can only be described in the language of chemistry and physics, like the brain. There is no such thing as *what it's like* to be a large slice of delicious sugary matter arranged and baked into my birthday cake. It seems to be different because it is different.

"Although there are some half-baked ideas…our brain isn't a cake, Dr. Smith. So, I have to ask—if we imagined that science has discovered everything that there is to know about our brain, does that mean that we would know how consciousness works?" he asked.

Dr. Robert Smith stroked his graying goatee as he considered the notion. It wasn't the first time he had heard the question or thought about it. "Mark—there are so many *ifs* and *buts* in speculation and imagination that we could span an imaginary river, if we had an imaginary bridge, just big enough to get over it. So, let's address the question with a thought experiment: suppose we lived in the year *2561* where neuroscientists knew everything that there was to know about all matter, brains, and the central nervous system."

"They had a *God's-eye-view* of matter," Dr. Starr said.

"Yes, and suppose that my Great, Great, Great, Great, Granddaughter Elizabeth Smith, is the leading neuroscientist in the entire universe. She knows every material fact about the brain. She knows all the physical facts that there are to know about hearing, but there's one interesting thing about Elizabeth—she was born deaf. Suppose that through the miracle of modern science that one day, for the first time, she gained the ability to hear sounds. At that time, what would happen?" he asked, looking at the camera, and then inquisitively back at Dr. Starr, waiting for an answer.

Starr contemplatively pursed his lips, squinted his eyes in thought, and shrugged. "I don't know."

"Think about it," Smith said, "for the first time she would now gain an entirely new realm of facts and knowledge. Those facts would involve *what it's like* to hear people, animals, and machines produce sounds."

457

"A blind person would have a similar, *what it's like,* sensation to seeing the colors red, white, and blue."

"Yes—but let's stick with Elizabeth for the moment. So, if she already knew all of the physical facts before her hearing returned, then afterward she learned new facts—that can't be physical, right? So, what are they?"

"Consciousness!"

"Yes! I think so."

"Fascinating stuff."

"Yes, it is, but let me give credit to one of my mentors, Dr. J.P. Moreland. Much of what I've mentioned in our series was extracted from his illuminating work on consciousness."

"We'll link his work to our video."

"It's worth your time."

"I'm sure. This has been very insightful," Dr. Starr said, looking toward the camera. "What a great series. I'd like to thank Dr. Robert W. Smith for providing us with his valuable philosophical knowledge here on *Mind Over Matter.*" He reached over to shake hands. "Dr. Smith is speaking from the Sander's Theatre, Memorial Hall, next Friday night at 7 o'clock. He invites you to join him online, or at Harvard Yard, Boston, Massachusetts, as he debates the topic *God vs. Science.* Hope to see you there."

CHAPTER NINETY-SIX

"When I die, I want to die like my grandfather, who died peacefully in his sleep.
Not screaming like all the passengers in his car." ~ *Will Rogers*

SPARE PARTS

"I WON'T HAVE any spares with me, right?" Steven Scott asked, knowing he wouldn't, but in his heightened mental state, felt that he needed to say something, even if it was silly. Although a pretty tough guy, at times he could be a nervous talker who rambled endlessly. Some people shut down when they were anxious, others couldn't find the mute button. He was the latter and had once joked that they would have to put a period on his tombstone to let people know he was done.

ITL continued to test the PSYCHONIX eye as he was poked and prodded and wired up for the project. The wireless technology connected well and communicated just like it was supposed to. They had it down now. All of the components were self-contained and computer-linked, much like it was done with modern pacemakers. Minimal surgery and no wires. A *megasonic test tone* undulated across the newly discovered *Holt Scale*. If you were looking directly at Steven, you could see it. A red light swirled and blinked all around the bionic retina, much like a spectrum analyzer or volume indicator, but this signal registered his unique *Holt* frequency.

It was a new measurement in search of an appropriate title. The name was chosen in honor of *Henry Holt*, who believed in Psychokinesis or *mind over matter* and the motion of the mind, soul, spirit, or breath.

"He was a little whacky in some of his practices," Brad said, "but then again so were Freud, Einstein, Tesla, and Benjamin Franklin, who started his days with an air bath—half an hour each day in his birthday suit, in front of an open window—to read, write, and get his mental juices flowing."

"Seriously," Steven asked.

"Yep, but even though *Holt* didn't air bathe in his birthday suit, he did have some unusual beliefs: "*I believe we can move objects by supernatural forces, including spirits and ghosts*." For whatever reason, *Holt* seemed like an appropriate name for a supernatural frequency, even though it wasn't about moving physical objects. And they didn't use it because of any pseudo-scientific psychic practices he may have held, but merely because it had measured a *mental substance* called PSYCHONS. In their minds, *Holt* was an aspirational naming convention and an admission that there was something out there that could be manipulated. Something personal, transcendent, and accessible to the eyes and ears. As far as some of the ITL engineers were concerned, it expressed a new dimension of radiation signatures. One that couldn't be expressed in *hertz*, because it wasn't a matter of air particles being disturbed by a physical energy—but nevertheless a communication channel.

It was a completely different communication capability. Not one that science fully understood. It was akin to the technological leap between the use of chalk and an extraterrestrial gamma-ray burst used for communication in the S.E.T.I. project, where they monitored electromagnetic radiation for signs of transmissions from civilizations on other planets. Nothing had been discovered with that project.

Now with the PSYCHONICS *MDSL*-1, it was arguable that alien life had been discovered. There was no easy way to describe it, but people could speak with each other telepathically.

"The system panels are responding and communicating correctly with the PSYCHONIX processor, his bionic eye, and our lab," Brad Manuszewski confirmed. He stared at his monitor with a raised eyebrow, slid the faders up, tweaked monitors, and made all the necessary adjustments. Even he had a hard time believing what he was saying, "The Holt or HT Router is connected and applying his PIP applications. *Psychon Internet Protocol.* If all goes well Mr. Scott will continue to communicate with us during the final stage of life and his transition."

That was how they tried to diplomatically phrase it—not a flatline, but transition. It sounded somehow less invasive and calming. Steven however, heard everything going on as he laid still in the *Amaranth* isolation tank, enveloped in futuristic technology with wires up to his bionic eyeball. *Why can't doctors just talk like regular people?* He thought. *Final stage of life— really? You mean when I die!?*

"Yes, when you die sir," Brad said with an amused smile.

Oh, I forgot for a moment that you were monitoring me with the goggles! Steven said. He was strapped into the tank, barely able to budge. *I feel like I'm in a spaceship.* Everything he said registered in the goggles. He was swaddled in a silky high-tech cocoon spun with tubes, apparently ready to emerge one day as a techno-butterfly. It was how ITL monitored him and would continue to be his only lifeline, as he transitioned.

Looking at Steven in the tank, Mark said, "*Command and Control* here. I'll be carefully monitoring you with the team and—."

"Yeah, yeah, just make sure I don't get unplugged."

"No worries—we've got extra batteries," Mark said. He embraced the much-needed levity.

"Yeah, I'd appreciate that!" Steven said.

"No worries, sir," Stanley Norris chimed in, not realizing that they were joking. "We're actually on an independent back-up power supply. We have enough fuel on-site to keep our generators running for a total of 96 hours or four days."

Mark and Steven stifled worried smiles and nodded their heads. It wasn't exactly comforting to know that one's potential lifespan could be computed in miles per gallon.

What could go wrong?

CHAPTER NINETY-SEVEN

"Be generous to the poor orphans and those in need. The man to whom our Lord has been liberal ought not to be stingy. We shall one day find in Heaven as much rest and joy as we ourselves have dispensed in this life." ~ *Saint Ignatius*

DOUBLE-SHIFT

WHILE WORKING A double-shift, Senator Croxon's daddy died in a coal mining explosion. It was devastating. With no welfare programs or pension available to the family, they were forced to endure a dehumanizing poverty in Appalachia. They were already in debt to the mining company for train rides and back rent in their company house.

How could we ever catch up? His mother restlessly contemplated.

When his daddy started working, he was required to open a line of credit at the company store to buy rations of food, clothing, and the equipment necessary to mine coal. That immediately put him in debt. He was paid in *scrip*, a form of currency usable only at company-owned establishments, so his mother Maggie had a lot of debts and no money—and eventually no home and *no hope*.

She and the children were left homeless with no money in the bank and little to nothing for food. If it hadn't been for the Grundy Mountain Mission Home, they might have frozen to death in *Chimney Cave*. Because they weren't able to pay the back-rent for their rusted out 1953 Silver Star company trailer, they held-up in the cave—just seven miles from the nearest family. Too proud to ask for any help, they spent three long nights huddled in a section of

Chimney Cave, before being discovered by the Richlands County Child Welfare Board or RCCWB. They were worried at first, when they saw bright lights at the entrance of the cave, but fear faded to joy as their rescuers led them out of the cave by flashlight.

"Being led out like that was nearly a spiritual experience, if you can imagine—just how dark our life had become. That night we got hot showers, a much-needed meal, and warm beds with a real roof over our heads. "I can't explain it any other way—it was like angels had met us at the gates of hell and pulled us back into heaven. I still donate to the RCCWB to this day," John told Steven.

The RCCWB was established in 1883 for orphaned, abused, and neglected kids who needed a home. But the Croxon children weren't orphaned, abused, or intentionally neglected—just desperately hungry and cold. Unfortunately, not one single person or local family could be responsible for the care and feeding of seven new mouths. "No one knew our plight, because momma was proud—and the rule for most country folks was *never* accept handouts or charity. It was considered begging. You just didn't do it." John believed that if his grandparents or local churches had known, they would have gladly shared what they had—but no one knew.

"Momma didn't want to be beholden to anyone and charity meant people knew your private business," John Croxon said. "Pride is a powerful thing—it keeps people from seeking help." It was powerful enough to make her self-conscious and protective. "It was hard to see the upside when you were at the end of your rope," John said in defense of his mother. He often thought about his early circumstances, whenever he wrote Senate legislation bills aimed at protecting the less fortunate.

Welfare and Foster Care hadn't been invented yet, or at least it hadn't made significant headway into the hollers of Tazewell County. Maggie prayed hard and often with the kids, because they took to heart the old adage that: *the family that prays together, stays together.* That meant something real to them. They loved each other and couldn't stand the thought of ever being separated from their mother and placed in the Richlands Children's Home. It was a place, in the past, where children were called inmates, and worked the farms that supported the agency.

They loved each other but, by definition, they were a *State Social Problem.* They prayed and cried, and cried-out to God for help every night. They started to think He had abandoned them. Being discovered by Child Welfare was scary for the family, but it ended up being a godsend. Even though they didn't realize it, it was the *hope* they had been looking for. Being relocated to the Grundy, Virginia Mountain Mission Home was the answer to all their prayers.

CHAPTER NINETY-EIGHT

"Any day spent with you is my favorite day. So, today is my new favorite day."
~ *Winnie the Pooh*

YES

"ONE OF MY college friends waited eight years and five months for her proposal. It had become a running joke among us all that she would marry someone else and invite her fiancé as a guest to the wedding. That's not going to be our case," Peggy explained to her girlfriend Pam, as they sipped tea at a local cafe. "We didn't fall in love over time; we were in love from the beginning—at least from the time we began dating." They had truly fallen head-over-heels for one another. "After six months of knowing that we were right for each other, Mark proposed. We scheduled a cruise to St. Michael's and had dinner reservations at the *Inn at Perry Cabin* with beautiful fire pits on the back lawn." It was an old romantic town with colonial dinner taverns and views of the harbor at sunset. In her mind, the picturesque moment under the late evening sky was as perfect as life got. "After dinner we walked to a white gazebo nestled close to the shore. Mark stood next to me and pointed to a sailboat that danced across the wind-tipped waters. It took my breath. On the billowing sails were written the words, **Marry Me!**

"Oh, how beautiful," Pam sighed.

"Mark immediately got down on one knee, took my hand, and held out the most stunning, glistening ring that you've ever seen. A *Marquise-cut diamond*, exactly right for my slender

466

fingers. I didn't know whether to laugh or cry—but I immediately said *yes,* put the ring on, and sealed the proposal with a kiss." The guy on the boat applauded and gave us two thumbs up, as he sailed toward the dock."

"You must be the happiest girl in the whole world now"

"Yeah, it was quite wonderful. He remembered how much I love St. Michael's and made it a forever memory."

"You found your soulmate."

"Yes, I did. You know, I've heard people say *it was worth the wait*, but given that we only dated for six months—I'd have to say it was *worth the rush*," she chuckled a giddy laugh with Pam.

"Well, when it's right, it's right."

"We spent the rest of the evening walking along the bank of the river, talking about everything—our wedding, children, *hopes*, and dreams. It was a beautiful time together."

Peggy and Mark celebrated one of the best days of their life on the shore of St. Michael's. It was lovely that just the two of them knew about the engagement—at least for the first few days. Everyone else got to know when they arrived home and returned to work the next week.

CHAPTER NINETY-NINE

"Love begins at home, and it is not how much we do…but how much love we put in that action." ~ *Mother Teresa*

THE HOME

THE HOME, AS they called the Grundy Mountain Mission, was founded in 1921 and resembled a small college campus; except it was for children eighteen months to twenty years old. It was really an *oasis of hope run by angels.* It included an educational, vocational, and fine arts building, campus chapel, cafeteria and plenty of cooking, mending, and cleaning work for Maggie Croxon.

"Our time there got us ready for life, but they also required us to go to church. I guess, in a way, that got us ready for life, too but, at the time we just accepted it as part of the deal. Most of us did. It didn't sit too well with our little sister Judy, though. She thought that she should be allowed to do whatever she wanted to," Senator Croxon remembered.

It was fun not to have U.S. Government business that he had to rush off to. With the Senate on Christmas recess, he had time to sit in his pajamas, eat a leisurely breakfast, and chat with the family.

"You see, we had a time to go to bed, a time to eat—and they even made us attend school, too, if you can believe that. Judy was okay with everything, except the religious parts. "I tried to explain to her that it was a mission school. That the word *Mission* in Mountain Mission Home represented Christian missions being done all around the world."

It was a place that rescued kids and provided them with clean residential care, education, shelter, clothing, meals, and love. In many ways, it was like attending a Christian elementary, high school, or college with biblical studies, worship, devotions, and prayer.

"I can understand some of her disillusionment," John said. "It's an eye-opener when you first realize that Christian organizations, like secular organizations, have nearly as many fallible people on their staff as other organizations. Back then, I told her something that took a few years to understand—that *God's truth doesn't change*, just because people are lazy, ignorant or hypocritical. Truth isn't something that we invent—it's something that we discover. Yeah, sure—sometimes it's certainly distorted, but truth doesn't change based on people messing up." It was a principled way to look at the world and one that he had never forgotten, along with many other things he learned there.

"It was life changing for me when I first heard *B.R. Lakin* speak in chapel," John said. "Newspaper articles called him a divinely sent human meteor that showed up on a mule with his Bible in saddlebags, but he arrived in a car when he came to visit us. He and most of the speakers told us all about Christ and His cross."

The Mountain Mission Home's goal was: *In all things offer the best of our efforts to Jesus Christ for the glory of God the Father through the help and good offices of the Holy Spirit.*

"The Home never claimed perfection or expected it from us, which was good, because none of us came from perfect homes or led perfect lives. And I remember most of the people like it was yesterday," he said, recalling their names and faces. "Some that I've stayed in touch with through the years, like twelve-year old Johnny Hudson. His mom was a heroin addict and was always too high or drunk to take him to school. So, he shut down—and became bitter and distrusting, but at *the Home* he felt safe, attended school, and was able to dream of his future as a veterinarian. Occasionally, he worked on broken stuffed animals worn out by much use."

Then there was also seven year old Roger O'Shaughnessy, who was homeless and said it was a blessing not to worry about where his next meal was coming from. He knew what it was like to have an empty belly, too. He said, *I want to be a farmer, so I can feed the world—and no one will ever go hungry.* He did it, too. Then there was little Bobby Jamison who got a soccer ball one Christmas.

"It was his best Christmas ever. Now he coaches the D.C United professional soccer team. He never has to worry about wearing poor-fitted hand-me-downs again," John said.

"I also recall a little girl named Becky Worthington, who studied and read everything she could get her hands on in the MMH library. She loved science and wanted to be an astronaut. Her advanced college prep classes, and the older kids who helped her with homework, inspired her to realize those dreams. That little girl with dreams is now a civil servant with NASA's Goddard Space Flight Center in Greenbelt, Maryland and works with innovative Earth Science, Astrophysics, Helio-Physics, and Planetary Science teams. She helps other young women reach for their goals—and could, perhaps, become the first person to walk on Mars."

Senator Croxon enjoyed reminiscing and could see that it captivated Chelsea. "I remember that they could barely keep her supplied in *Galaxy Girl* books. Books filled with amazing true stories of inspirational women who helped fuel some of the greatest achievements in space exploration."

"Could I get one of those books, Daddy?" Chelsea asked.

He nodded. "Well, let's be sure to tell Santa Claus that tomorrow, okay?"

The testimonials of Mountain Mission successes were nearly endless. It was the only true home that many of the children had ever known and the friendships endured. It delivered them from tragic circumstances and struggles to sustenance, stability, and success. Mountain Mission Home was a *lighthouse* that answered the plea for help when all *hope* seemed lost.

"It was tough on us at first," Senator Croxon said, with a reflection of sadness in his eyes. "Not long after our daddy died, we were brought to the MMH. I was twelve, Jerome was fifteen, Deana thirteen, Bobby eleven, Ronnie nine, and Lisa was just six-years-old."

In many ways, John and Missy thought of the Grundy Mountain Mission Home as their childhood home. Even after he graduated from the Air Force Academy and went into U.S. politics, they always referred to it as *back home*.

Now, just up the road, the people in the small town of Richlands would be looking out for his family as his daughter Chelsea continued to heal from her head wounds. They would of course stay in their Cedar Bluff home, but a fair amount of the Christmas holiday time would be celebrated at Mom-Maw and Pop-Paw Keene's house. It was a tradition. They would arrive with warm hugs and kisses and expressions of *My haven't you grown* and *Lawd, honey you haven't changed a bit. Is anybody hungry?* There were always snacks for everyone to feast on before supper.

John flashed back, in his mind, to the cozy country guest rooms with their feather beds and the overly packed basement, which had been the perfect place for hide-n-seek with his cousins. It wasn't an elegant or flawless structure, but nevertheless a home full of perfect childhood memories. John had explored every nook and cranny of this 1920's-style home as a child—and looked forward to spending more time there with Missy and Chelsea. They would arrive the week before Christmas. *Lord willin' and the creek don't rise,* he thought. It was mountain slang that implied his strong intention to be there if it wasn't frustrated by unforeseeable events.

CHAPTER ONE HUNDRED

"The sky vanished like a scroll that is being rolled up, and every mountain and island was removed from its place." ~*Revelation 6:14*

LIFT OFF

THE THEORY WAS sound but complicated. First, they would put Steven Scott to sleep and fuse the *MDSL-1* processor into his central nervous system. Once he came to, they would let him snugly fit the prosthetic eye with a short metal suction rod. He was given instructions: *Lift the upper lid with your index finger to create an opening and slide the top edge of the prosthesis under the upper lid.* Done. It fit directly into the eye socket. Instantly, the processor wirelessly linked to the bionic eye and the ITL network.

"Now all we have to do is induce clinical death," Brad muttered to himself, as he worked. "In some ways simple. The heart stops beating, and blood circulation terminates, breathing ceases, but let's keep our fingers crossed. Hopefully, he regains consciousness."

"You know I can hear you too," Steven said.

It was tedious, nerve-wracking work for everyone assigned to the project, and a man's life was potentially at stake. On the first attempt, he would be legally dead for up to one minute. That was all. *We're all going to jail for killing this man,* Dr. Kahn thought. Fortunately, he hadn't put his headset on yet. And little did he know how true his thought would be, after agents finished pumping him for information.

As the lights dimmed and the machinery hummed, Steven felt his left eye twitch and his hands trembled slightly from the nervous adrenaline. That worried him.

Oh no, not now! It wasn't a good time for a mental breakdown. No time was a good time to unravel, but fortunately, in this case it was nothing more than a bad case of the nerves. *Enough already, let's do it!* Steven communicated through the PSYCHONIX system.

"Roger, sir. We're ready, in 5-4-3-2…" Brad and Sabrina initiated a two-person security protocol and punched in their individual launch codes. This was an anti-espionage protocol initiated after Dr. Lui was arrested by the CIA. As Steven prepared to temporarily die, Dr. Lui sat and stared at the wall of his jail cell, awaiting trial, charged with stealing proprietary information related to ITL's PSYCHONIX project. He wasn't going anywhere.

Everyone else put on their headsets, as the anesthetist induced sleep and began Steven's lengthy cooling protocol with an injection of cryoprotectants, well-regulated chemical kinetics, and a precisely timed bursting freeze, to initiate cryopreservation.

By the time Brad said *two*, Steven was out cold. In due time, he wasn't breathing at all. He was gone—flatlined, no breathing, no circulation—nothing was working on its own. There were absolutely no electrical activities in the heart or brain that could be detected. There were a few tones and beeps and chirps as his PSYCHONIX EYE swirled and pulsated the red digital patterns.

They saw an illuminated glow within the *Amaranth* Dewar and were seeing something unbelievable on their monitors. Over the whir of the machines they heard a retracting soundsnap that descended from a high pitch to low quiet hum. It banged and jarred the room with a gentle shockwave of light.

"His soul jumped," Dr. Starr commented. As Steven transitioned the team saw it too. He was immediately lifted from his body and could see himself lying cradled in the *Amaranth*. Steven heard familiar, distant voices—none of them from ITL. It was intoxicating. He turned his head and saw Sabrina break a nail, while frantically typing data into the computer, and heard Brad mention that the Washington Capitals beat the Pittsburgh Penguins 1-0 in last night's hockey game. "Ovechkin is amazing!" It surprised Brad seeing himself say it on the monitor. "What the heck?!"

In the monitors they could see and hear everything that Steven experienced. "We've got a Steven's-eye view," Dr. Starr said.

Steven gave him a tip-of-the-hat salute. "Steve-o-vision…it's the latest thing," he chuckled.

Everyone applauded.

It looks like you're prepared for a NASA lift-off. Everyone nodded or gave a thumbs-up. They saw him scanning the room and as he started to talk again, his movements accelerated, and he was lifted up and out of the room. Thirty seconds in—they lost video and panicked, feverishly working to restore the connection. Fortunately, they could still clearly hear him talking:

"Wow, I've never experienced anything like this before. I'm being drawn toward streaming blue and white lights—it's like a foggy tunnel." And then he was just as suddenly in the ITL room and returned to his body.

"We got him," Sabrina said. "At exactly one minute." It would take some time before vital signs registered as normal, but he would eventually be reanimated during the warming protocol. "We've detected some ever-so-slight molecular movements, but it will be a while before he breathes on his own."

They methodically adjusted the *Amaranth* and waited patiently. "Body temperature is 37 degrees Celsius," Stanley Norris said. He stared at his monitor, worried. "Come on, man—we need you to start breathing on your own." Just then there was a slight gasp, followed by others, the kind of breaths a newborn baby might take, or the sound of someone being resuscitated after a drowning incident. "We've got him. Blood pressure a little high, 130/70 with the heartbeat and brain activity registering normal."

"It could just be an autonomic reflex," Sabrina said, usually more positive, but she had never brought anyone back from the dead before.

"Can you hear me, Steven," Dr. Mark Starr asked. Steven was breathing—but barely. Then he began to move his mouth. He also pursed his lips in a visible effort to form words, but not making any sounds.

"Steven, are you with us?" his brother Mark asked again, still worried about the residual neurological effects of the experiment. Even though it wasn't long enough to do brain damage, it was still dangerous. "Can you hear me?"

"Copy," he said with a deeper breath and sputtered coughs, a signal that the lungs were fit for breathing again. "Sorry, I was just watching my life flash before my eyes. You'll be happy to know that universe is safe—*Over,*" he said with a weak smile. Mark knew that he was referring to their use of walkie-talkies as children.

"Must've been some trip." Mark reached in the Dewar and patted him on the shoulder. "It's good to have you back, *Over!*"

The team monitored and observed Steven for the better part of the night. They ensured that he got plenty of fluids and that all his vital signs and faculties were up and running correctly. After that, he was cleared and ready to talk about it.

"I know it was only for a minute, but it was a satisfying, peaceful escape, greater than I've ever felt. And my mind was crystal clear. It was like someone plugged me into a ginormous battery. For the first time in my life, it felt like every light in my soul had been turned on.

I heard Brad say, *Ovechkin is amazing!* And I saw Sabrina break one of her nails on the keyboard, and I saw you all applaud before I left."

"We know," Dr. Starr said.

"Yeah, we saw that much on the monitor too!" Dr. Feinberg said. "But we lost video. The last thing we heard was you thinking, *there's something like a foggy tunnel.*"

"Well, that was about all there was, except that at first I got that melty, tranced-out feeling that comes over you, when you've had a glass of wine. Then I remember looking away, because I felt as though something was pulling me back."

"But what was the tunnel like?" Dr. Feinberg asked.

"It was so fast. I saw it for all of seven seconds."

"And?"

"And it was like an indistinct opening or tear in space. A fissure, but it was expanding or maybe getting closer—I don't know. That was pretty much all I saw, before you brought me back."

"Right! I'd lay odds you saw things from your imagination." Dr. Kahn had to put in his skeptical two cent worth.

"Mmm, I don't think I would have ever imagined what I saw or even how I felt. Also, you guys didn't mention it, but as I was going up and out of the ITL building, I saw a pair of floral nursing shoes on the ledge of the *South Wing* roof."

"We'll have to investigate," Dr. Kahn said.

They did. It was true. A pair of floral nurse's shoes had fallen from a window and were hanging on the ledge."

"And another thing. I could swear that I heard familiar voices. Like a party, but voices of people who've been dead a long time."

CHAPTER ONE HUNDRED-ONE

"Qigong is more than a set of exercises.
It is an attitude that works to restructure one's perspective on life, leading to balance and harmony with the world around us. ~ *Garri Garripoli*

CHI

DR. LUI WEI started work at the Innovations Technology Laboratory in September 2017. Sadly, he was accused in court of downloading, sending, and transporting *top secret* files that included equipment, engineering schematics, and technical reports. Prior to immigrating to the U.S. and becoming a U.S. citizen he had worked as an engineer for the *Lumni Gongsi, Qigong Lab* and did research and development on artificial intelligence and robots. His connection to China had never been severed.

Legal documents read in detail that, "The U.S. considers Lumni Gongsi (*Qigong*), like Huawei, TicToc, and all other communist owned companies, an arm of the Chinese government."

The Qigong Lab also researched similar psychological bionics projects like ITL. The name *Qigong* itself referred to the practice of cultivating qi or chi, believed to be a *material energy* or *life force* forming part of any living entity. It was the underlying principle in Chinese traditional medicine and in martial arts—that if nothing else, led to palliation.

The official statement from *Lumni-Qigong* denied any sensitive information being communicated by Dr. Lui Wei. The Chinese lab also added, "We are working with local authorities on the probe and will do everything possible to make sure that this individual and any other individuals involved are held accountable for their actions, as they are released into our custody."

That wasn't going to happen.

CHAPTER ONE HUNDRED-TWO

"A near-death experience is more about living than it is about dying." ~ *Pat Johnson*

GOING BACK

ON THE SECOND trip Steven flatlined for 1.5 minutes, no more and no less. It was necessary to slowly increase and regulate the limits, to better understand their capabilities and ensure his safety. The PSYCHONIX systems power was exponentially increased, which allowed Steven to make it through the foggy tunnel of lights that he had described the last time. Not everything could be seen by the team, so his descriptions were enlightening. "It was an opening into another dimension—*Heaven*. And it wasn't a bunch of fluffy clouds with stereotypical angels playing harps and lyres. No, Heaven seemed real and beautiful—and I was met by a spirit guide or guardian angel, if you will."

"And you knew this how?" Dr. Kahn asked.

"Easy—he told me."

Dr. Kahn raised his eyebrows and nodded as though he was speaking to a crazy person. "Hmm, I see."

"At first there was a brilliant flash of multi-colored lights, and then he just appeared—and started to approach me. I was shocked when he introduced himself and said that he had been a Soldier, like me:

"Hello, my name is *Malchus*—maybe you've heard of me?" He looked hopeful.

"No, sorry," Steven said.

"That's okay, I'm not one of the more famous people here. I'm known as the guy who got his ear cut off trying to arrest Jesus in the Garden of Gethsemane."

"No kidding! I remember you."

Malchus was an Arab Chieftain slave of the high-priest Caiaphas, and the individual among the party charged with arresting Jesus. When Malchus tried to do his duty, however, Peter jumped to Jesus' defense and cut off the servant's right ear. But Jesus immediately touched the ear and it was healed. Malchus looked at him with a knowing nod, like that probably wasn't the best thing to be remembered for.

"I became a believer at the very moment Jesus reattached my ear—*ha.*"

"Oh, okay—I remember that part too"

"Peter and I still have a good laugh about it from time-to-time. He was quite the hothead, back in the day. It's interesting, though, none of those things divide us or matter here."

"What do you mean?"

"I mean that here in Heaven, all of our mistakes, pain, and suffering are inconsequential."

Those listening to the video feed at ITL were speechless. They had been listening for one minute and thirty seconds. Because of dimensional time differences that was an entire day for Steven. It would be the third or fourth trip before Dr. Starr started to make the—*a day is like a thousand years,* calculations.

"That entirely blew my mind. How cool was that?" Steven Scott asked later. "God had someone welcome me into Heaven with someone who could relate to what I did in life. We were both wounded Soldiers. I was missing an eye and he was missing an ear. Go figure."

Steven continued to relate the adventures of his journey:

"Malchus walked along, beside me, apparently shielding me from an angry mob that I faintly heard from somewhere just outside the gates—maybe another dimension. I asked about whether they were trying to get in."

"No, just the opposite," Malchus said. "They hate this place."

"Can they get in?"

"I suppose so, they've had the key all along. They just don't look for it anymore."

"The key?"

"Yes, they were originally made with hope, but they've long forgotten where they put it."

The lab monitors didn't do justice to the recording, so Steven had to more clearly describe what it was that he had seen.

"I was being escorted forward and around an undulating country path. It wasn't like one of those books you read about Heaven or movies that you see on television. Everyone was perfect, younger, and healthier. Except there was no endless horizon of white clouds or anyone wearing an illuminated halo who needed to earn their wings, like Clarence Odbody from the *It's a Wonderful Life* classic. But it was still majestic and marvelous, exceeding explanation and comprehension." He was frozen in a reverential awe as he told the story.

"I guess you could say that it was everything that was beautiful about Earth, but a lot more than I understand or have the words to express." Steven tried to, though.

He told them about the crystal-clear rivers that flowed from majestic mountains toward lush fields, and a sparkling city adorned with what we would consider sparkling jewels. The trees had indescribable colors and an abundance of delicious fruit ready to pluck and eat. The paths along the way were a pale-white and as transparent as gold in its purest form—and *it was surprisingly soft to walk on.*

"As I was led toward *The Eternal City*, I saw a beautiful cottage across the rolling meadow and there were a few people that I could see from a distance—you must've seen it."

"We could hear you and some of the people but couldn't see anything whenever you gazed toward the city, or angels," Brad said. "I think we were divinely censured or something."

"The voices that I had heard before came back to me, and one soft voice became clearer than before. I recognized it and shouted—*Marlina, is that you*? It had to be, I'd swear it, but there was no response! I could somehow sense her presence and I wanted to run toward her, but *Malchus* stopped me short:

"This is a far as you can go now, Steven," Malchus said.

As it happened, everyone in the ITL control room watched silently with their mouths agape. No one dared remove their goggles, since it was PSYCHONIX that linked them. They all saw the shiny path, the rolling hillside, and the cottage. They also heard the buzz of other beings but couldn't see or hear them.

"Maybe they're angels too," Mark speculated.

Inexplicably, the control team could see Malchus, the cottage, and the countryside. Conjecture ran the gamut. Dr. Feinberg surmised, "Maybe you could only see people who had previously died like Malchus." Others said, "Maybe the camera couldn't pick up angels or it wasn't allowed." Those were all plausible theories.

At one and a half minutes, Steven's time was up! They began the egress procedures to expeditiously bring him back. Steven resisted and looked at Malchus with distress as he was being drawn back. "I don't want to go home!"

Malchus gave him the Roman *across the chest* salute and said, "You are home, Steven—but God has another assignment for you." Just then a sweeping, rolling wave of light enveloped

Steven Scott, like on-coming headlights. It pulled him rapidly backwards, through flashes of brilliant lights.

Later he recalled to Mark that it was as though a series of multi-colored curtains had closed behind him.

Next thing he knew, he was above the laboratory room watching everyone working, and saw his lifeless body lying in the *Amaranth* tank. He found himself beside his body, right before his soul positioned itself for reentry.

"One minute, thirty seconds," Sabrina said. "We got him!"

Resuscitation procedures were being followed to the letter and he was doing fine. Vitals detected. *Heartbeat, brainwaves, and respiration are all good.* Brad called Dr. Starr over and pointed at the screen. Somehow a couple of near-death cycles in the Amaranth accelerated a sharp increase of PSYCHON radiation.

Mark shook his head in disbelief. It had more than doubled.

As soon as Steven could speak, his first words were, "I heard Marlina's voice! I know it was her, but he wouldn't let me go to her. I've got to go back—I've got to find her!"

CHAPTER ONE HUNDRED-THREE

Jesus said to her, "I am the resurrection and the life. The one who believes in me will live, even though they die; and whoever lives by believing in me will never die..."
~ *John 11:25-26*

RICHLANDS

RICHLANDS, VIRGINIA IS my home. That was how Senator John Croxon thought about it. It was where his mom and grandparents lived now. Maggie lived there now and attended to them. It was a perfect situation when they were in town, because John and Missy's house was only two and a half miles up the road in Cedar Bluff.

While they waited a bit longer for Chelsea's official hospital discharge, John told more stories and set the stage for their journey south. "Richlands has always been home, no matter where I laid my head."

While sharing one of his fondest back home memories, he lost himself in reminiscent thoughts of the little town, the people, and a special Christmas in 1967. It was a cherished recollection that often comforted him, while going to sleep at night or whenever life got a little rough around the edges. Over the next few weeks, John wove stories about the Appalachian heritage he had grown to revere. He knew that when they arrived, his visitors, Steven, Vito, Mark, and Peggy would love staying with them and hearing about these salt-of-the-earth people.

Steven Scott had already been to Heaven and even though John said it was wonderful, he still wasn't quite sure what he would find in the Blue Ridge Mountains; *Li'l Abner* or another character from *Hee-Haw*. Pleasantly, it was neither. It was exactly as the Croxons had described it: *A heavenly oasis, where God must have started His work on Heaven.*

He soon realized that they were mostly a hardworking, blue-collar lot like the people he grew up with in Walla Walla. He would also find that Richlands was one of the prettiest places he had ever seen.

He loved hearing Senator Croxon recount their life in the country. As a retired military guy who had traveled the world, he had become somewhat of a chameleon and learned to rapidly adjust to his new environments. This time, it would be a pleasure to adjust, relax, and embrace the ways of the South. He did it more quickly than some. They continued to reminisce while waiting on Chelsea's discharge from the hospital.

"I like the way *y'all* talk down there," he joked in a faux southern accent.

"It's nice and I know—perhaps I have some sappy, misplaced or romanticized memories," John said. "But I don't care. It's a part of who I am—the people, places, and traditions." Times changed and people changed, but he knew that his Southwestern Virginia memories and identity would never fade away.

Perhaps it was due to his unpredictable childhood and military career, but Steven was drawn to the calm, casual, and unpretentious culture. He liked hearing the stories, nearly as much as Chelsea did.

"Let me tell you about the *best Christmas ever*," John said to Chelsea and his curious visitors. He spoke with childlike excitement in his voice. "It all began on the snowy hillside of *314 Grove Street* with the family preparing food, cookies and candy in the kitchen, and a stack of Bing Crosby, Elvis, Frank Sinatra, and Supremes records playing on our walnut RCA credenza. Pop-Paw enjoyed it all from his recliner—watching football with his eyes closed…," he winked at Chelsea. "You know—the way I do." She sat on the floor, still as a mouse, and listened to the bigger than life tales about where he had his best Christmas ever.

"Why do we call them *Mom-Maw* and *Pop-Paw?*" Chelsea asked.

"It's just what we were taught to call them as kids—like we taught you, sweetie," he said. Other than tradition, there had never been a consensus on where the names came from, but the prevailing theory was that *Mom-Maw* comes from a Lowland Scot term *Ma Maw*, meaning, *My Mother*. There was no satisfactory answer for the word *Pop-Paw*, except dozens of internet articles about Appalachia's forgotten fruit tree, the *PawPaw*.

"Regardless," John said, "it's an exclusively Southern term that describes the best man I've ever known." His grandfather was a respected patriarch in Richlands, known as an honest, tough, hardworking man. He remembered him as a tough-as-nails farmer who knew how to fix things—when he wasn't plowing, feeding the chickens, or slopping hogs."

That's how he described his grandfather as they sat around relaxing—still waiting in her hospital room to be released. Then, right on cue, the doctor zipped in with the good news and most of the nursing staff trailed behind her. They surprised Chelsea with a spontaneous going away party; chocolate cake, balloons, and one nurse dressed up like a clown, doing an assortment of funny tricks for her. The staff became close to Chelsea, and fell in love with the little princess who had died and come back to life, even the ones she scared in the mortuary.

After the party, they said their temporary goodbyes. Steven helped the Croxons load up their car and he gave Chelsea a tight hug. "That'll have to hold you until we're reunited at Christmas."

"You've got the directions?" John asked.

"Yep," he held up a piece of paper that read: *Down 81 South to Wytheville, 77 North through the East River Mountain Tunnel, 460 West past Bluefield, and take a sharp right turn at Claypool Hill.*

"Okay," John shook his hand, "that'll lead you straight to our house in Cedar Bluff."

"I'll be on my way soon," he waved to Chelsea through the back of the car window." He looked at John, "But I'll probably have to bounce back and forth a couple times, as I go through the last part of my program."

"Let's discuss some other arrangements—I'll call you," John said.

"Other arrangements?"

"Yeah, I got a Cessna parked in Edgewater—that'll taxi you back-and-forth in about *45* minutes."

"Sounds nice," Steven said.

Missy hugged him. "Safe travels!

CHAPTER ONE HUNDRED-FOUR

"Most of my best memories come from some old dirt road."
~ *Unknown*

PLAY-BY-PLAY

A COTTONY SNOWFALL mocked the inaccuracy of the WRIC weather forecast as the

Croxon SUV unhurriedly crept and meandered along the twisting *Cedar Valley Drive*,

descending *417* feet down into the City of Richlands. That would be the first stop, so his mom

and grandparents could see Chelsea, and see just how well she was doing. As they gingerly

topped the ridge, Chelsea pointed out the rear car window at the beautiful snow, swaddling the

tall mountain cedars.

"That looks just like the fogbow I saw," she said, "when I went to Heaven."

The *Governor George C. Peery* Highway didn't exist when John was a little boy, so he still

liked taking the old back roads, winding his way down from Claypool Hill, through a series of

hollers. John couldn't help but do a play-by-play for Chelsea, as they snaked through the hills.

It was an important family heritage lesson for her, since she had spent most of her young life in

their Washington D.C. condo.

"That's the *Old Mill Road* where the *Woolen Mill* used to make blankets during World War I

and II—and back twenty-five yards, across those railroad tracks there used to be a boarding

house. When it stood, the building bunked close to fifty people and had a large hotel-style kitchen. At least it did when it supported an active woolen mill. For years, it was infamously referred to as the *Titanic*, because of its size and the way it teetered over the steep banks of the Clinch River—ominously poised to go down. The sunken porch supports were starting to give way when I was a child and the railing bowed and listed to the left."

Everyone leaned and strained their necks to peer down a barren, and overgrown yard, that was abandoned long years ago.

"It's gone now," John said. "Years ago, the old place eventually took an awkward tumble into the Clinch River, down there." He pointed below as they passed over the dual car and railroad bridge. "When it did, the remnants of antique lumber could be seen in bits and pieces, strewn along those banks."

"Was anyone inside?" Chelsea asked, with sweet concern in her little voice.

"No, no one was hurt when it collapsed, because it had been condemned and was avoided by nearly everyone but ghosts."

"There were ghosts there, Daddy?" Chelsea asked.

"He's just kidding dear," Missy replied with a *don't go there* look at her husband.

"I often wondered what that old house would say if it could talk," he said, shaking his head: *When I was a young hotel, one of the richest men who ever lived, named Cornelius Vanderbilt, stayed here while bringing in the railroad. They called him the 'The Commodore.'* "The old place provided a few generations of post-Depression Era housing for many of my folks, after the mill closed down."

Without going into more detail, John changed the subject and spoke of better times at the house. He told Chelsea about his playful sleepovers with his cousins; fishing, walking the winding mountainside trails, and playing on the steep mountainside of the woods. He playfully

491

shuddered as he remembered watching older cousins get up with the roosters and stoke the furnace with coal after long winter nights. He and the other smaller children stayed tucked under their blankets until the oldest trudged out and warmed up the house.

"We took turns bathing in a round, galvanized wash-tub. You see—not everybody had bathtubs back then, so it was used, sparingly, a few times a week. They kept it heated-up from multiple pots and kettles of water that they boiled on the stove."

"That's a funny way to take a bath," Chelsea said.

"Yeah, I guess it was, but the old *Titanic* was actually quite modern for its time. It even provided the occupants a luxurious indoor toilet," he said tongue-in-cheek to Missy's cackle.

"Well—it was actually an outhouse that was butted up against the kitchen, but it worked just fine. At least you didn't have to venture out in the snow or rain—or find it with a flashlight in the middle of the night."

"Didn't it smell?" Missy asked. "I don't think I'd like that—especially not next to the kitchen."

"No, as I recall, they kept everything spic-n-span. Poor didn't mean dirty and it was always clean and tidy—even with all the coal that they had to bring in for the furnace."

John soaked in the memories as the tour continued. That was the primary reason why he chose the older, slower route through Cedar Bluff, so that he could enjoy the familiar sights.

"Oh, look!—that's the Cedar Bluff Elementary school, where I attended first grade. The front window on the bottom right was my classroom. I remember Mrs. Elswick started us out reading *Tip and Mitten*—and then *Dick and Jane.* I loved to read everything that I could get a hold of…just like you, Chelsea."

She smiled and nodded.

492

"Oh—look over there!" he said, pointing again. "It's the old red Grist Mill by the river—and if you look directly through the woods and across the river, there's our house." They could see it clearly now on the left with a low, narrow concrete bridge, which crossed the river and led up to their home. "It used to be Governor George Peery's old home place. Reading about him in high school is what first got me interested in politics."

George Peery was born in Cedar Bluff, and became the 52nd Governor of Virginia, from *1934-1952*, and created unemployment insurance, Virginia State Parks, and Virginia's Alcohol Beverage Control board after prohibition ended.

"He set up the ABC board but could never stop the moonshiners—even to this day," John said. His expression made one believe that he was still keeping a few family secrets.

"What's a Moon—shiner?" Chelsea innocently asked.

John shot Missy an *oops glance,* and came up with a sidetracking distraction, from something else that he noticed on the right-side of the road. "Hey—there's Richland's High School, home of the *Blue Tornadoes.* I played tight end and linebacker there." Then he pointed out the *Tastee Freeze* directly across the street. "I used to binge on footlong chili dogs there, every Friday night after the football game. And I loved them with onion rings and a thick strawberry milkshake, Mmm-mmm!"

"Why didn't you go to the Dairy Queen?" Chelsea asked. That was one of her favorite places for ice cream.

"Well—that's a good question, princess! It was a whole lot different here in the 1960's. And a lot harder to travel here. There weren't any tunnels going through those big mountains or major highways leading to Richlands. You had to patiently zig-zag around the winding mountain roads—up and down and around," he said swaying back-and-forth. He acted like he

493

was getting seasick just thinking about the tedious journey. "And there weren't any franchise restaurants—no Burger King, McDonalds or Dairy Queen either. We had the local places like the *Claypool Hill bus depot*, *Wimpy's Place*, *King Kone*, and an old-fashioned soda fountain inside our local *Rx* drug store. That was where folks stopped by for a rich-tasting malt, a bag of candy, a scoop or two of ice cream, and to hang out with your best friends."

He kept the car crawling through the light snowfall, toward Richlands. Eventually, Cedar Valley Drive became Front Street, as they traced the Clinch River, and descended from Cedar Bluff and down to the *Dalton Edition* Bridge on the bottom left. They turned left across a rusted metal bridge that occasionally flooded-out during rainstorms.

"I used to stop there at Cordell's, on the right bank, for pop, candy, and a box of fishing worms," John said, as Chelsea scrunched up her pretty little face in disgust.

"*Yuck,* you ate worms?"

Missy cracked up.

"No, the worms were for fishing," he chuckled. "I guess it didn't come out right."

They headed the car up Virginia Avenue, turned right at Crawford Ave, and then right on Grove Street. The family's old home place was still standing on the steep side of the hill, in the *Farmer Heights* part of the *Dalton Addition*. He knew it so well; he could find it with his eyes closed. The address was fondly etched in his memory: *314 Grove Street*.

"Yep, this will be another Christmas to remember," John concluded.

As they pulled the car up to the rear driveway door and got out, Mom-Maw, Pop-Paw, and his mother Maggie smothered them with hugs—and all the kind, familiar words that they had expected.

My haven't you grown little lady!

CHAPTER ONE HUNDRED-FIVE

"The 50-50-90 rule: Anytime you have a 50/50 chance of getting something right, there's a 90% probability you'll get it wrong." ~ *Andy Rooney*

TWO-MAN RULE

ACCORDING TO THE Department of Justice's complaint and affidavit, Dr. Lui Wei had been granted broad access to secure and confidential internal databases that contained trade secrets and *top secret* intellectual property. Not only that, he was the lead engineer on the PSYCHONIX project.

In one of his follow-up interviews with the DOJ, Dr. Mark Starr reiterated, "We had authenticators, but we didn't have our two-man rule in place at the time. Regardless, I really don't think Dr. Lui could have breached our security on his own."

He was right. According to the government investigators, there were suspects, but nothing that they could share. It alarmed everyone in the office and had them all on edge, especially Dr. Kahn. ITL went to great length to secure their research projects, which left many to speculate about the nature of their highly classified work. But not everyone could know. If the information got into the wrong hands, it could have potentially been used as a weapon—not enough was known about its cognitive power.

"Information about our *Mind-Body Problem* project is close-hold," Dr. Starr said. He never mentioned PSYCHONIX outside of work, to anyone. "It's strictly on a need to know basis and only eight employees were currently *disclosed* or *whitelisted* on the project. That meant that they were working on the project or had limited information related to their specific assignments."

"Whitelisting" was the practice of explicitly allowing privileged access. The reverse of blacklisting. The report also noted that they all had access to the project's databases.

Dr. Starr trusted his team but suspected one person.

"That's the greatest comeback since Lazarus."
~ Sid Waddell

ON ICE

"DON'T PULL ME back until I tell you to!" Steven commanded.

"But, Mr. Scott," Sabrina said. "You'll only have five minutes—ten minutes at the most, before anoxia causes irreversible brain death."

"I want ten," Steven said.

"It's too close—and there's no such thing as surviving total brain death," Brad added. "There's no return."

"But Chelsea survived for hours and Todd Lopez communicated with us for ninety minutes after he died. How do you explain that?" he asked. It was a good point and irrefutable. Within a few months several people at ITL or nearby facilities had been declared clinically dead, communicated, and/or returned to life within hours.

"We can't," Dr. Starr said. "It's the *Lazarus Effect*, at least that's what we call it. And that's all we know—it's an inexplicable miracle, but it happened."

"But we might be able to flatline you a bit longer in the *Amaranth*, if we reduce your body temperature—closer to a deep freeze," Brad said. "It will slow the rate of injury to your body and sustain your brain for a longer period."

"Given the trans-dimensional time differential, you'll be there for at least 3 ½ days," Stanley Norris added.

"Good," Steven said.

"I heard that a woman in Mongolia survived after spending eighty minutes trapped in ice," Sabrina said. "And I know that some animals have been resuscitated after three hours of clinical death."

"So, it's possible?" Steven asked.

"Well, yes, it's happened over longer periods of time too, but it's not sensible," his brother Mark chided. "And it's too dangerous, to say the least."

"The whole thing is dangerous Mark," Steven said, staring at him incredulously. "But all I'm asking for is ten minutes. Just give me ten minutes on ice to talk to Marlina—is that too much to ask?"

"Maybe…it might be the last thing you ever ask."

CHAPTER ONE HUNDRED SEVEN

"It's better to debate a question without settling it, than to settle a question without debating it."
~ Joseph Jubert

DEBATE

IMMEDIATELY NORTH OF Harvard Yard in Cambridge, Massachusetts the skeptics, atheists, and believers—as well as the plain curious—shuffled into Memorial Hall. Sander's Theatre was a High Victorian Gothic auditorium, often used on the Harvard campus since 1876 for concerts, conferences, ceremonies, and lectures—and debates, like the one being hosted tonight between Dr. Robert W. Smith and Dr. Stephanie Csornock. They were two eminent philosophers with opposing points of view.

Bobby invited Mark to attend and he in turn had asked if Peggy could come along, as a date. They would make an evening of it in Boston, starting with dinner at Aqua Pazza on the North End, before heading to the forensic debate. Upon their arrival, they slowly made it to the orchestra, greeted esteemed faculty, and took their place—closely seated toward the stage; row C, seats 7, and 8. Peggy commented on their elegant accommodations and breathtaking views, which were steeped in history, tradition, ambience, and more importantly—cushioned seats.

Tonight, this intimate, sumptuous, red oak, timber-covered chamber with solemn historical portraits and stained glass windows was a refectory of scientific and religious ideas. It was small—churchlike—and majestic. The Sanders Theatre quickly swelled to its 1166 seating capacity, with many people seated along the walls and many others who watched in the overflow.

Those from around the country, unable to attend, listened on local radio, tuned-in via Facebook Live, or streamed it some other way. The media support team was engaged, Tweeted, and provided input for the question and answer segment, which followed the debate.

Dr. Smith wore silver reading glasses halfway down his nose. He studiously flipped through his notes and scribbled last minute thoughts as he hydrated himself with a small bottle of *San Pellegrino* mineral water. He sat in a green room, provided for each of the speakers, but his debate partner hadn't arrived yet. The waiting room was nestled snugly behind the grand, wooden stage and ornate three-tiered auditorium, from where he could easily see the swelling crowd.

The time of the debate was approaching fast, so he poked his head out to look around. What he saw were sections, framed by private boxes and walls, decorated with intricate patterns like those found in great opera houses around the world. He also saw the sponsor and host for the evening coming on stage, prepared to make introductions.

CHAPTER ONE HUNDRED EIGHT

"Generally speaking, espionage offers each spy an opportunity to go crazy in a way he finds irresistible." ~ *Kurt Vonnegut*

SLEEPER

THE CHINESE CORPORATION *Lumni* was sorry to report that *all American scientists serving as exchange researchers were being returned to the U.S.* According to a company spokesman, "This is a sad day, but pending the *judicious* release of Dr. Lui Wei we have no choice but to suspend our collaborative research programs." They went on to say, "We take confidentiality and the protection of our intellectual property seriously." It was public relations 101 and the Chinese were experts at lying with ambassadorial flair and jargon.

The Department of Justice believed that Dr. Lui Wei was part of a massive clandestine campaign to steal national security secrets from the U.S. government and, in addition, industrial and technological secrets from American technology companies across the United States. That was what espionage looked like. In fact, they now knew that Dr. Lui wasn't just an engineer, but a high ranking agent within the Chinese Ministry of State Security (CMSS)—the principal intelligence agency of the Chinese government. He was a spy and he was guilty—never mind that he attempted the kidnapping and solicited the murder of Steven Scott and other ITL scientists.

A CIA agent debriefed Dr. Starr. "The CMSS is roughly like the CIA and the FBI put together. Their capabilities are world-class. Not only cyber capabilities, but they have a mature expertise in turning people into cooperators. That's how they got to one of your physicians—Dr. Gus Kahn." The wiretaps, phone records, massive debts, and large bank deposits were sufficiently incriminating, and would prove him roundly culpable.

Scientists and engineers that worked in the United States were increasingly likely to be foreign-born, primarily because the U.S. continued to attract large numbers of skilled workers from abroad. There was, however, an intensified scrutiny of those with alleged links to Beijing over fears of espionage. In some cases, like the stealing of ITL research, it had a chilling effect on long-standing collaborations.

As was often the case, timing was everything. Two years ago, Dr. Lui Wei immigrated to America, ostensibly to further his research and provide a better way of life for his family, who were still living in China. He got a green card as soon as he arrived in the U.S. and applied for citizenship as soon as he could, immigration was none the wiser. And since immigration was such a huge contributor to U.S. science and innovation, his application was expeditiously placed on the front burner.

Dr. Lui entered the U.S. on a post-World War II policy, which started allowing 105 Chinese people each year to immigrate and permit those present to become naturalized citizens. "He said he loved America," Mark recalled, "He was one of us." But no one knew that he was also a Chinese penetration agent or a mole.

In China, everything belonged to the state and that included Dr. Lui Wei. Early on in his career, he had been recruited by the CMSS as a long-term clandestine spy or informant. His government knew that he may eventually have access to secret intelligence. The only thing he had access to now was a free lawyer and a phone call.

CHAPTER ONE HUNDRED NINE

"The best of all gifts around any Christmas tree: the presence of a happy family all wrapped up in each other." ~ *Burton Hills*

CHRISTMAS TREE HILL

IN HONOR OF Christmas, it was common for the Croxon family, and for everyone else in Richlands to participate in *Winter Fest*, a week-long series of holiday events on and around *Christmas Tree Hill*. The metal tree at the top of the hill was an eighty-five year old, iconic landmark symbolizing that the Christmas season has arrived. Its lighting and the red light atop other radio towers stirred an occasional reindeer sighting and prompted reminders that: *Santa Claus is watching you*. The tree was often a reminder to the children as they rushed off crayoned letters to the North Pole.

Steven Scott became fast friends with John and Missy Croxon at the hospital. He missed Marlina and he could relate to the immense sadness that they felt when they thought that they had lost Chelsea. They had rallied for each other. It was an unexpected friendship and a comforting familiarity for an old Soldier. Surprisingly, this seven year old girl was a kindred spirit who, like him, had suffered a serious head wound, knew his friend *Blue Crow*—and had traveled to the other side and back.

They called often, texted, and sent photos as they prepared for Steven Scott's holiday visit. They also prayed for him often as he prepared to finish up his tests.

"Let's pray for whatever he's going through at the hospital," Missy said each night.

As a U.S. Senator, John was on the Intel Committee. He now knew what Steven was involved in, but couldn't talk about it and wouldn't interfere. He tried to stay focused on the holidays.

To prepare for his visit, they sent website links for the *Towns of Richlands* and *Cedar Bluff*, and *The Visit Tazewell County* site, so Steven, Mark, and the rest could read up on the local history. It helped them to pass the time, in between PSYCHONIX projects. Today, Steven read an article about *Christmas Tree Hill* and looked over the interesting historical photos and local folklore:

The hillside and the path leading up Christmas Tree Hill is turned into a winter wonderland with a magical explosion of twinkling lights, enchanting sounds, mouthwatering flavors, and lots of Appalachian crafts, food, fun and laughter. The tree isn't an evergreen conifer like a spruce, pine, or fir, but an artificial metal tree decorated by colored lights extending from and around the 75 foot tower, on a small hill overlooking the community of Richlands.

Since 1936, the tree, and the ten-by-ten encircled star topping, is lit and can be seen from many miles away. It was first powered by a gift from President Franklin Delano Roosevelt, ten years after the Depression, as a gift that brought electricity to many parts of rural Virginia for washing machines, refrigerators, cow milking machines, and Christmas trees.

John shared Steven's return messages with the family and let him know that he had grown up enjoying the lights on *Christmas Tree Hill* and that, yes, the lights around Richlands would definitely remind him and Mark of the displays they enjoyed so much growing up in Walla Walla, Washington.

The family, especially Chelsea, looked forward to the visit and were excited to share it in person. John texted: *It makes us so happy to be home again—and I hope they keep the traditions going for many years to come.*

Steven texted back a message with a DIY emoji picture of Santa and the reindeer, "Sounds like fun. Tell Chelsea to save me and Santa some cookies!"

```
              __     _ __
  | \__ `\0/ `--  {}     \}     {/
  \    \_(~)/_____/=____/=____/=*
   \=======/    //\\  >\/>  || \>
   ----`---`---   `` `` ```` `` ``
```

Each weekend before Christmas, Senator Croxon brought the whole gang down to visit. When Steven, Vito, Mark, and Peggy arrived they soaked in every moment. At sundown, the tree lighting ceremony was hosted by the newly elected Mayor James Franklin. He stood on a platform in front of Town Hall, counted down, and pushed the button as families and friends treasured their time together and sang carols. Steven carried Chelsea on his shoulders, and everyone sang as loud as they could.

To those attending, Christmas Tree Hill was more than a tall metal Christmas tree stuck on a hill. It was a beacon of hope—that celebrated the birth of Christ. It was also the signal for *Winter Fest* and the *Richlands Christmas Parade* to begin. For the couple weeks, the city streets would be livelier than ever, as shoppers bustled in and out of stores—never offended by a hearty *Merry Christmas*.

"I always loved this parade," John commented as he and his visitors stood on the sidewalk. "The cars, trucks, motorcycles, and homemade floats are fully decorated to show off our Appalachian heritage, high school band, football team, and local celebrities."

"And that's one of our DJ's from WRIC standing in the back of the monster truck."

"Mommy, he's throwing out candy," Chelsea squealed.

"I see. I see."

Vito caught a piece for her.

John shared that his earliest parade memory was from what he considered that incredibly special Christmas season of 1967. Perhaps that's what helped make it one of the best Christmases. The parade evening started with millions of floating snowflakes that fell from the sky, eliciting *oohs* and *aahs,* and the squeals from children anxious to see Santa and build their first snowman of the season. The enchanting Richlands streets were decoratively lit, and the sky was getting darker, as the moon drifted higher and the stars began to glint in the darkness overhead. The star on Christmas Tree Hill had also been lit and the band started to march, playing *Here Comes Santa Claus*.

John explained, "The view from across Railroad Avenue and Front Street up to the library and old Farm Bureau looks much as it did eighty years ago, architecturally." But today the buildings and streets were decorated with lit garlands, Christmas trees, wreaths, and smiling faces. The parade would lead the way, straight into a month-long celebration.

"Not bad for a small coal mining town," John said.

His visitors nodded.

"Winter Fest is one of our oldest traditions," Missy said. "It dates back to the hard-working German and Scotch-Irish settlers who began their first Richlands Christmas market traditions by candlelight and lantern in the 1890's. The ladies would cook for weeks and then have a progressive dinner and celebration that moved from house-to-house and church-to-church—and usually ended up at the hub of the town, the *Hotel Richlands*."

"Always with an abundance of Christmas delicacies and a toy collection for the needy among us," John said. "Besides *the Home*—that's where I got most of my toys. "

"Sounds like things were pretty slim?" Vito asked.

"Well, no one had much back then, but everyone gave what they could."

Vito nodded.

"And they always celebrated like this might be the last Christmas before Jesus returned."

Years ago, the first event of *Winter Fest* was the Coal Miners Christmas Dance. It was lit by lanterns and candles because it was held long before there was electricity or a tree lighting ceremony. At that time there was nothing too fancy, other than a neighborly potluck with a simple speech from the mayor, a prayer from a pastor, and Bluegrass Christmas music picked until late into the night.

Perfect. That's all that he could think of this special time at home and his treasured memories. Most importantly, Chelsea was healing, and they were home with family and friends at Christmas.

CHAPTER ONE HUNDRED TEN

"A little bit of mercy makes the world less cold and more just." ~ *Pope Francis*

POLAR PLUNGE

ON THE THIRD trip they once again induced a type of hypothermia inside the *Amaranth*. Steven was secured into his thermal cocoon and immersed into something that resembled liquid nitrogen. This time it was a slow and more meticulously cooling of his body temperature.

"First, we will do everything we can to protect the brain and organs," Brad said, "We will chill the body to 89.6° Fahrenheit and continue to slowly lower the body temperature through a cold fluid, 39.2° Fahrenheit infusion."

"Wow, that's a real *Polar plunge*!" Steven said. That was his way of coping with the stressful process. He had survived twice already. On the third go, he still needed humorous distractions, not the statistical odds of surviving. It was practically irrelevant at this point.

"Do I really have to hear this?"

"Yes, we have to let you know exactly what we're doing and the risk that's involved," Mark said. "So, listen—at a certain point you will be, for all intents and purposes, frozen and sealed into a secondary, reinforced *Cryogenic storage Dewar*. It's a double-walled flask of silvered glass with a thin vacuum between the walls of the *Amaranth*, used to hold liquids at well below ambient temperature.

"Cool!"

"Yes, to say the least—and it's for your protection. The second and third phases involve the maintenance and slow, controlled rewarming. That will be a lengthier process, since you'll be submerged and breaching dimensions longer."

"But at that point, I'm dead—so I won't know, and it won't *matter*."

"Well, yes and no," Mark said. "You're not technically dead until you're warm and dead."

"We'll know when we thaw you out, in the next twenty-four hours," Sabrina said looking at her watch.

It was a scary proposition if one contemplated it for too long. Just prior to Steven's anesthesia taking full effect, he felt his body temperature drop—causing a prickling feeling and tingling numbness on his skin. It was like he had been playing out in the snow too long, but that was all he remembered as his muscles and waxy skin grew cold and stiffened. At the molecular level he was now lifeless, but still detectably conscious through the PSYCHONIX monitoring systems. Tubes and devices were attached from head-to-toe, tracking his thoughts—even though he was confined in the *Amaranth*.

"Poverty is the mother of crime." ~ *Marcus Aurelius*

HE WAS SELLING

"THEY HAVE ALL the tools of a very capable intelligence organization," was how U.S. agents described their counterparts in the Chinese Ministry of State Security.

During their investigations, agents discovered that the PSYCHONIX project had significant safety protocols in place, but not impenetrable if you went rogue or had a trusty sidekick. Dr. Lui Wei had most certainly not been *The Lone Ranger* and had easily infiltrated and transmitted valuable research to his home server. The malware had been surreptitiously installed on ITL computers and was remotely accessible whenever no one was engaged on their computer—some files automatically downloading and sending during each log-off or when triggered by code. The shocking reveal was that they had zeroed-in on Dr. Lui's partner in crime. No one could believe it.

"Why Kahn?" said a mildly astonished Dr. Starr. He felt that Gus was a suspect and knew that he had been acting strange, but still didn't want to believe it. "I don't understand. He had his own opinions and we disagreed about a lot of things—but he was no traitor."

"I agree. He resisted nearly every approach on the *Mind-Body Problem* project and never seemed convinced by our breakthroughs, but…an opposite view was always welcomed. Besides, he was mostly a good person," Dr. Feinberg said.

The agents nodded. Even in Dr. Kahn's initial defense of himself he had pleaded, *but I'm a good person*. It was a normal response. The agents could have told you many similar stories. Without exception offenders regarded themselves as good people. No matter how long their trail of carnage, no matter what suffering or pain that they sewed or caused others, they retained the view that they were a good person.

"We've heard it all," one agent said. "One murderer we convicted said, "If I thought of it as evil, I couldn't live with myself.""

The agents continued their *out brief* to Dr. Starr. "You see, Dr. Gus Kahn was ripe for this type of recruitment. Our investigations revealed that he had deep financial troubles. Not only did he own too much home, but he was paying alimony to his ex-wife, and had serious gambling debts."

"So, he was desperate for money," the agents concluded. "It's not an uncommon situation. People become spies or give away secrets for a variety of reasons like extortion, financial pressures, ideology, or greed. At first, they do something small and may think that it was too benign to be considered spying—but they're wrong. In Kahn's case, it seemed that his ego and financial commitments played a large role."

It was true, Dr. Kahn was in debt up to his skeptical ears.

CHAPTER ONE HUNDRED TWELVE

"The more I study nature, the more I stand amazed at the work of the Creator.
Science brings men nearer to God." ~ *Louis Pasteur*

EVENT - INTRODUCTION

"WELCOME LADIES AND gentlemen! I am Dr. Armando Selby—representing *Metanoia*, the student organization that's hosting tonight's Harvard debate forum. Metanoia literally means *Change of Mind* or to turn in a new direction. However, our goal this evening is a bit more modest—if we can't change your mind, we at least want to give you something worth thinking about. Here at Harvard, we endeavor to stimulate research and conversations—connecting experts, students, and the world with avant-garde ideas. That's why I think you'll be particularly interested in the subject at hand."

Dr. Selby continued, "Tonight, we're debating *God vs. Science.* Its limits and boundaries regarding metaphysics and physics because we think that's where the rubber meets the road. Why does it *matter*? Why is it that I can think at all? We hope that tonight's debate will unsettle you just a little, because that means that you are paying attention and feeling the intellectual weight of these arguments.

Tonight, we ask one of the biggest questions you could ask, are *God and Science* at odds? I'm glad you could make it."

The audience applauded respectfully as Dr. Selby continued the introduction. "The itinerary tonight is rather easy to follow. Each speaker will make a presentation for fifteen minutes with five minutes of rebuttal. Dr. Stephanie Csornock will begin, immediately followed by Dr. Robert Smith. Afterwards, there will be a moderated discussion for twenty minutes, followed by twenty minutes of questions and answers. We are thankful to those of you attending tonight and hope you find it informative."

He explained that their industrious staff would do their best to engage and pass on fair representations of the questions to each speaker. "But, for now—it gives me great pleasure to welcome our guests to the stage. And our moderator for tonight's debate, Kevin Wolf," he said as he applauded and smiled, "to introduce the worthy opponents."

CHAPTER ONE HUNDRED THIRTEEN

"And when I saw Him, I fell at His feet as a dead man."
~ Revelation 1:17a

THIRD TRIP

STEVEN SCOTT LAID visibly frozen inside a giant glass vacuum flask called…the *Amaranth*. It was an aspirational name of an imaginary flower that was immortal or unfading. That was the hope of everyone in the project. Not that he would be immortal, but that it would, at minimum, keep him alive long enough to be reanimated.

In years gone by, hundreds of people had opted for a similar type of cryogenics, in hopes of a second life in the future. There was no known living testimony of it ever being successful. For many good reasons, Steven believed and now knew that there was a life after death, so in that sense he thought, *we're all immortal*. But today he was only hoping for a short metaphysical cruise.

"We are not *bodies with souls*, but *souls with bodies*," Steven transmitted via the open PSYCHONIX channel.

"C.S. Lewis," Mark answered.

"Yep, that's what they say."

Brad Manuszewski punched in the computer commands. "Sir, your PSYCHON radiation code was received and registered strong on the *Holt* scale. We are linked and cleared to

515

proceed." The computer whirred a low hum with a fantastic display of computer lights, which danced to his processor's code. Brad once again adjusted the screen panels, which illuminated the kaleidoscopic bursts of Steven's PSYCHON radiation.

The delicate process was based on hypothermic patients who were accidentally frozen and had survived cardiac arrest. At first, none of them showed signs of life whatsoever. It was a complete flat line, like you could have drawn it with a ruler—no heartbeat and all breathing had ceased. Like you would see at the scene of an accident, but in Steven's case, it was no accident. He had volunteered and was now unconscious with his core body temperature that dipped and then plunged to sub-zero temperatures. He would be frozen solid until clinically dead.

"His brain is slowing down to protect it from damage, before he dies," Stanley Norris said. "Typically, our brains can only go twenty minutes without oxygen before irreversible damage sets in. But as he cools down, his body's metabolism will also slow down, and our new accelerated *Amaranth* processes will—hopefully sustain him."

"Meaning?" Dr. Starr asked.

"The brain can get by with far less oxygen than we ever thought," Brad said, "So keep your fingers crossed."

"Look!" Sabrina said.

In the final moments, there was indeed evidence of his spirit radiating from the *Amaranth*. Their computers sounded with successive harmonic tones and beeps that symbolized elements of Steven's unique radiation code.

Brad gave a thumbs up. "All systems go."

The lab again looked much like NASA's Mission Control Center, but in this case ITL managed a trans-dimensional flight with support personnel who monitored every aspect of the transcendent mission. A large monitor in the middle of the control room stayed focused on Steven's swirling red bionic eye.

The initial process culminated with a series of tones and flashes of light that expanded quickly, swept the tank, and then receded in a split-second implosion. Only Steven's eye and the ITL monitors showed any type of detectable activity. Everyone held their breath...

Hello—can you hear me? I'm rising from my body—and now I'm out.

The leap was once again successful.

I can see you all.

They waved as he ascended upward—everyone except Mark who popped a salute.

Thanks, little brother! See you soon!

"Copy," Mark replied, "Over."

As the words came out of Mark's mouth, Steven's invisible soul hovered above the *Amaranth*. In an instant, there was a flicker of light and he was whisked away. The glow of the tank quickly faded as a smoldering ember. Everyone with PSYCHONIX goggles witnessed the same spectacular sights, sounds, flashes of light, and the bright streaming blue and white light tunnel, which he had previously reported. It was exactly the same.

Again, Steven Scott had been transferred somewhere else—to another dimension. He heard the same familiar voices. It was uncanny how he felt—amazingly alert and aware and healthier than before. He didn't have to ask—he immediately knew where he was. He had been transported from Earth and back to Heaven.

When he arrived, he saw *Malchus* again as he lounged by a small quiet river, patiently fishing. "Hello!"

Malchus looked up, smiled, and said, "Hello, I've been waiting for you."

"You've been waiting...but how did you—?"

Malchus held up his hand. "This is Heaven," he said in his distinct Philadelphian accent. He had been enslaved to the Roman Army in the Aegean region of Turkey, so it was quite noticeable. Even though *this is Heaven* was his only answer, it was certainly good enough. Steven walked over and sat beside him on the edge of the riverbank, as cool water flowed by, eddying around the twigs of a fallen tree branch. It had fallen from a sturdy oak tree behind him, exactly the same as the one he used to climb with his brother as a boy

"How's the fishing?"

"The fishing is always good," he said in a calm, unhurried way, "whether you catch anything or not." He glanced toward Steven with a relaxed smile and then back at his fishing pole. "But today, there's something else that I've got on the line for you, my friend." He gestured with a friendly nod of his head toward an old-fashioned arching walkway bridge that connected the path across the glassy clear, swirling brook. "Over there—someone special is waiting for you."

Steven heard a recognizable voice call for him again and, in his excitement, he nearly shoved Malchus into the stream, fishing pole and all.

"*Hey, hey*—be gone, before you scare away the fish," he said, much amused at Steven's reckless haste.

Steven enthusiastically sprinted up and across the bridge—and down a narrow glimmering stone trail. His eyes, *both* restored beyond normal in his Heavenly state, darted in every direction until he saw Marlina from a distance. She also ran toward him with arms flailing. *Yep, that's Marlina!* It was more or less like an old *1960's* television commercial, where the two lovers ran toward each other in slow motion, held hands, and swung in a circle—they even had the appropriate theme music playing in the background.

It was odd, funny, and beautiful at the same time. In the middle of the field, located directly between Marlina and Steven, there was a good-humored angel sitting at a grand piano, banging out Henry Mancini's *Love Theme from Romeo and Julie.* "I couldn't help but laugh aloud at God's sense of humor, as we reunited in a delightful embrace." It was a very endearing gift from God to Steven and Marlina.

Even though Steven's PSYCHONIX eye had *psychomorphically adapted* to the dimensional transition, he was still aware of ITL notifications. For all intents and purposes, it seemed like he had been there for days, but in the upper left corner of his peripheral vision his timer flashed **3 MIN.** Brain death would have been imminent, if his body hadn't been carefully preserved in the *Amaranth.*

As the ITL teams continued to monitor, they were gobsmacked. Much of what they witnessed was blurred or censored, as though they were looking through a foggy antique mirror.

"I'm so glad you came," Marlina said as though Steven had met up with her for a Sunday picnic. They leisurely walked toward her cottage together, smiling, talking like always, but not really talking at first—but still communicating. "You know we can speak normally here…if we want to," she said."

"Marlina, I've missed you," were the first words he vocally uttered. That was all that needed to be said.

It was a merry reunion, but all she responded with was, "I know." It wasn't a cold or disinterested statement, but a matter of fact statement, from someone blissfully on this side of eternity. No longer was she clouded by worry, trouble, sorrow, or sadness. She knew that Steven would join her in time and in eternity. And there was no rush or anxiety driven need to get something done right now. Since her earthly departure, she had changed, and *loosened-up*. Her whole life she had heard people say don't be so uptight or loosen-up—so her favorite expression in Heaven became, "I'm *loosed-up!*"

Marlina turned her head to look as someone else slowly approached them.

It's Jesus! Steven noticed Him too.

He was walking from the direction of The Eternal City, which was blurred from ITL's view. However, they could still see Jesus and the scars on His hands and feet. It reconfirmed their *theory* that they were being allowed to see people who had human bodies. No one could believe it. They were peering into Heaven and saw Jesus face-to-face with Steven. It was mind-blowing and soul changing.

Of course, Jesus would want everyone to know, Mark thought as he watched the video stream. *He had never hidden who He was.* In life, He had appeared to Mary Magdalene, Mary the mother of James, Salome, the Twelve, and then more than five hundred of the brothers and sisters at the same time. This would be His first digitally recorded appearance.

Later, Steven would recall to the ITL team, "I could identify with how John fell at His feet like a dead man." The surprise meeting had such an awe-inspiring effect on him that his spiritual muscles completely lost their strength, and his knees buckled. "I would have fallen limply to the ground, if He hadn't taken my arm." He shook his head and smiled, mouth agape. "Jesus actually kept me from stumbling."

Back at ITL, Steven told them that it was such a delightful thought that he could barely contain himself. "You can tell from the video that He's a normal looking man with a thin, muscular build and rough hands, but his expressions were gentle and calming—watch this…"

"Welcome, Steven! I've been expecting you."

"You have?"

"Of course," Jesus said with humble, compassionate, yet piercingly powerful eyes. They embraced and strolled along the narrow, undulating path.

As they embraced, everyone in the lab saw Steven's lifeless body re-illuminate the *Amaranth*. His PSYCHONIX eye seemed to generate three spinning, interlocking spoke rings as the entire room was flooded with bright, flecked beams of light. He didn't know it then, but it had somehow changed him, when he touched Jesus. His mind and his body. Not only had his ability been exponentially increased, he was fully and immediately healed of his PTSD.

"Lord, why have you allowed me here?"

"Steven—you, like my brother John, are a disciple that *I love*. First, I want you to take time and enjoy this moment with Marlina, but then—when you return—to let our visit be a sign to others."

"What kind of sign, Lord?"

Back at ITL Command and Control, Brad said, "For some reason we just lost the sound again." He adjusted the faders and barked orders to Sabrina and Stanley, as they feverishly tried to reestablish audio.

"Steven, I have given you a precious gift—an ability to know the mind of man. Through this ability, you will fight for the poor, oppressed, and persecuted. In the power of my name, you will communicate a message of hope for all generations, that—."

"We've got audio!" Stanley quickly announced.

Jesus walked slowly ahead, turned, and gradually faded from their sight. As he spoke, the last few words could be heard in the ITL monitors. "I Am the way, the truth, and the life. No man comes to the Father, except through me."

CHAPTER ONE HUNDRED FOURTEEN

"The secret of change is to focus all of your energy,
not on fighting the old but on building the new." ~ *Socrates*

CHANGES

THE HOTEL RICHLANDS was gone now. It eventually became the *Old Dominion College and* offered education and cultured entertainment to the mountain folk up until 1915, when it burned down. After that, the imposing Mattie Williams Hospital and nursing school was built on the ground. The Victorian structure closed and was abandoned and torn down just one hundred years after the original Hotel had been opened.

"That's where the Town Hall is now," John told Chelsea, as they walked up Suffolk Avenue toward the town center with Steven. The others decided to stay at home, watch TV, and eat cookies.

"What's a town hall?" she asked.

"It's a place where politicians come to listen to people."

"About what?"

"Oh, about whatever's on their mind—things that'll make Richlands a better place for us."

John caught sight of a couple abandoned buildings, on the corner—one he fondly remembered as *Tanner's*. "That was a diner, where Mom and Mom-Maw waited tables. It was a small family run business, where you could get a Coke, a chili dog, and fries for a buck while swiveling in circles on a chrome bar stool, under a loud, rickety, GE air conditioner."

"I'd like to spin in circles, too, Daddy," Chelsea yelled, as she ran ahead and pirouetted with her face to the sky, her arms fluttering above her head like a prima ballerina's.

"Okay, that's nice, but stay with us young lady." Chelsea quickly ran back and took their hands.

"Nice memories, huh," Steven said.

"Yeah, the good memories don't stick as well as the bad ones, so you have to keep counting all your blessings."

Steven nodded, "Tell me about it."

He and John lifted her by her arms every few steps so she could leap through the air. "Look, I'm making my memories, Daddy," Chelsea said.

"Yes, you are, dear."

"That's great," Steven said.

"Our town has seen much better days," John said with a sigh of lassitude. "I just hope I can rally the town council and pump some life back into our community."

 "It's a shame to see Main Street looking so battle-worn," Steven said. "—but we can all recover, look at me—and your little one."

John smiled as he strolled the streets of his hometown with Steven. Chelsea skipped along, in the middle, holding both of their hands. Again, they lifted her with a loud *Wheeeee!* as she once again took giant leaps with a single bound and flew through the air. It was indeed a good new memory and a nice, relaxing stroll after flying Steven back into Richlands.

"Thanks for whisking me away from the clinic for a while," Steven said. "There's not much more that we'll have to do before Christmas."

"Don't mention it. I've got duties in D.C. that constantly keep me in the air and anyways—I enjoy the company."

John didn't like keeping secrets from friends, but as a member of the Senate Select Committee on Intelligence, he had just been briefed about the PSYCHONIX project and learned of Steven Scott's participation. He couldn't share it. It was merely a coincidence of fate that their paths had crossed at Johns Hopkins. He thought that at some point, maybe he could be of some help, but for now he couldn't share or broach the subject.

It's nice to have a Senator as your friend, Steven thought, as they continued their walking tour—*especially one with his own plane*.

"I'm doing what I can to infuse some life and hope back into this weary coal mining community."

"Everyone needs hope—and a worthy project," Steven said.

"I agree, but it's more than just a project to me. These are the people I grew up with." John crossed the street to circle back down Suffolk Avenue and waved at a neighbor getting out of his truck, headed into the Farm Bureau. At the corner of Front Street and Suffolk Avenue there was an old, decorative concrete block, jewelry store that might have been a bank at one time or another. The white blocks were the rage in house building from the 1890's to the 1930's.

"It's a nice day. Let's walk toward the pharmacy and get a Coke," John said.

On their way, they passed a theatre turned church and the *Flannery Theater*, which hadn't shown movies in the last fifty years. It had decayed along with the jobs and the town and was mostly used as a flea market, until it had recently been saved by a church.

"You'll notice that most of the stores in Richlands face the railroad tracks," John informed Steven and Chelsea. "It was by design, since this was primarily supposed to be a coal mining town that needed access to the railroad."

On the way back to the car, they paused outside another abandoned building on the railroad tracks side of Front Street. "See, where I'm standing Chelsea?" John asked, planting his feet between the window and the front door of what used to be the Sears & Roebuck and S&H Green Stamps store.

"I haven't heard of Green Stamp stores in decades," Steven said.

"Not since 1982."

"What are *Geeen* Stamps?" Chelsea asked.

"No…Green, like your pretty shirt," her daddy said. "Green Stamps were stamps that you could collect from local retailers and exchange at their stores for household items—and even for Christmas toys."

Chelsea's eyes lit up when he mentioned Christmas.

"Why, when I was a kid, I lined up right here to see Santa Claus. I could see all the toys right there in the window." He had to use his imagination because, at the moment, he was staring through fogged glass into a large stripped-out room.

Chelsea nodded and moved her daddy forward, so she could stand where he stood. "I'm gonna wait on Santa Claus, too."

John and Steven laughed.

"Why don't we let him come and find you this year," John said, "like he used to find me?"

"Maybe we should go home and make a Christmas list and see what everyone else is up to," Steven recommended.

"Good idea."

Chelsea shook her head, anxious to get started.

In John's special *Christmas of 1967,* his toy list started out by circling pictures in the highly valued *Sears Christmas* catalog that always arrived in the mail, right on time. The cover had a picture of a Christmas tree and a roaring fireplace with a wreath over it.

"I remember that we couldn't wait for the new Christmas catalog to show up. The one I remember best had a *Dennis The Menace* cartoon on the front that said, **I'm going to bed! So, you can come any time now!**" he told Chelsea.

"Sounds like that would be a good plan this year too," Steven added. "I used to circle the toys in the catalogue too, with pencils and dog-eared the pages, so that Santa and my parents could be sure of what we wanted the most."

"It was fun to see all the new toys and go to sleep at night wrapped in *hopeful* dreams."

"Oh, I'd like to do that too Daddy," Chelsea said. "Will you get me a catalogue?"

He shrugged, "Honey, I don't think they've printed those since the early 1990's."

It was a great memory. A small town Christmas in the 1960's seemed so innocent and simple by today's standards. "We wanted toys, I won't lie, but the focus was more on the birth of Christ, sharing a few gifts, and having a bountiful Christmas dinner—oh, and of course Mom-Maw's homemade potato candy."

"What was that?" Chelsea asked.

Steven was curious as well.

"It was a sugar coma waiting to happen," John said with a grin, and licked his lips. "Confectioner's sugar, sweetened condensed milk, vanilla extract—and some people added potatoes."

"Really," she said.

"Yep, I think the potatoes were used as a filler after the *Great Depression,* when folks needed to stretch their food supply. *But* I digress—then you roll it out, spread delicious peanut butter on it, roll it, cut into pinwheel pieces, and chill it in the refrigerator."

"I'd like some, Mommy," she said.

"Oh, yes—we'll absolutely make it together," John said. "It's not Christmas without Mom-Maw's potato candy."

CHAPTER ONE HUNDRED FIFTEEN

"Spies cannot be usefully employed without a certain intuitive sagacity." ~ *Sun Tzu*

GROOMING

"SO, DR. LUI was slowly and methodically fishing and searching, for something and someone he could hook. Someone here at ITL who was willing to work clandestinely with him for one reason or another," Dr. Starr somberly reported to the staff.

"And Dr. Kahn was ripe for the picking. He never believed in our project from the jump. He thought it was merely a way to make a profit," Dr. Feinberg added.

"Right, but it was more complicated than that, I think. He was in a financial bind and thought that it was his way out."

"I was even okay with his skepticism," Brad said. "Every team needs a different, but honest, perspective."

"The honest part is where we lost him Mark," Peggy said, with raised eyebrows.

"I just can't believe that, in such a short time, he had developed a close relationship with Dr. Lui," Dr. Starr said. "And that he thought it was okay to do what he did."

"He thought he was selling Dr. Lui innocuous information," Sabrina added. "Dr. Kahn was willing and probably thought that nobody would get hurt by it. At least, he was convinced that was the case."

"That's how it works," Dr. Starr replied. "The grooming is constant testing, that gets amped up, to see how the person thinks and what they are willing to do. It's a mind game. As psychologists—we should really have seen it coming."

CHAPTER ONE HUNDRED SIXTEEN

"Opportunity is missed by most people because it is dressed in overalls and looks like work."
~ *Thomas Edison*

PITTSBURGH OF THE SOUTH

STEVEN SCOTT HAD a natural curiosity as a Special Forces Army investigator. Wherever he landed, he always acclimated himself to the surroundings. Now, even though retired, he was a lifelong learner and still an observer of people. He enjoyed museums and read everything he could. Now that there were new friends in Richlands that had adopted him, he wanted to know more about the culture and history—so prior to each flight down to Tazewell, he did his homework and asked John about the local industry.

"I thought on this trip that I'd show you all a coalmine—like our families worked in."

"That sounds interesting," Steven said.

"I'm game," Mark seconded.

"How about I stay and help your mom make cookies?" Peggy volunteered.

"You know what, there's an Alabama vs. Georgia game on and—."

"Fine, fine, make yourselves at home. I guess it'll just be me, Mark, Chelsea, and Steven.

"Yay!" Chelsea clapped her hands.

531

"You might find this interesting, too," John told Steven. "The Richlands Land Company came here looking for iron ore and started a business boom in 1890. They wanted to make Richlands, the *Pittsburgh of the South*."

"No kidding."

"But they gave it up after the stock market crash of 1893."

"I didn't even know about that one."

"Not many folks do, but as they say in these parts, *it put a hurtin' on us*. Oh, and that two-story, white house on the corner with the front porch lined with shrubs was the office for The Clinch Valley Coal and Iron Company."

"And when the stock market crashed?"

"Well, then it was transformed into the home of our prominent pioneer and physician, Dr. William Resse Williams, and eventually the Richlands Tazewell County Branch Library."

"What about the little place down Front Street?" Steven asked.

"That was the N&W Railroad foreman's log home section house. It's the oldest remaining residential building in Richlands and stands as a reminder of our *aspirations*. It was an important time here. The industrial cyclone of development brought with it coal mining jobs, and everything else an *Appalachian* community required—farming, a brickyard, logging, hardware store, schools, and *hope*."

"What's *Appa-LAH-chee-uhn* mean?" Chelsea asked.

"*Appah-lat-chun*," he sounded it out for her. "Some folks say *Appah-lay-shin*. That's the name the Spanish explorers gave these beautiful mountains. It's a variation of *Apalchen,* the name of the native Americans who migrated to this area."

"Oh...I think I'll just call it Richlands," Chelsea said.

"That works for me, too," Steven said, giving her a tight hug.

"It apparently worked for our ancestors too."

"Without debate, without criticism, no administration and no country can succeed—and no republic can survive." ~ *John F. Kennedy*

THE DEBATE INTRO

KEVIN WOLF ENERGETICALLY walked from the wings of the auditorium, up a few stairs and took center stage. He adjusted the mic and was ready to provide introductions and get the debate started.

"Dr. Stephanie Csornock is a University Distinguished Scholar and Professor of Philosophy at Brown University in Providence, Rhode Island. She has worked in several different fields of analytical philosophy: language, mind, physics, religion, and the metaphysics of feeling," he said emphasizing the word *feeelings*. "Her focus and most significant contributions are to the philosophy of quantum cosmology. Stephanie's work on the natural selection of universes has had an impact within the study of physics itself." She smiled and acknowledged the welcoming applause with a slight nod, before she took a seat in one of the comfortable leather chairs provided for guests between opening remarks, rebuttals, guided discussion, and Q & A.

"Dr. Robert W. Smith is a research Professor of Philosophy at Houston Baptist University. He has written much on the reasonability of God." He, too, was welcomed with warm applause and turned to take his seat.

Although they were about to argue the fascinating facts that surrounded the relationship between *God* and *Science*, Dr. Csornock and Dr. Smith were friends who had long debated each other. Earlier that evening, they enjoyed a leisurely dinner and friendly conversation with the hosting members of Metanoia. One would have never known that they were about to spar.

Dr. Smith over-prepared for the debate, like a boxer who trained for a heavyweight title fight. As always, he thoroughly did his homework. He read Csornock's latest works and listened to her most recent lectures. It was obvious from her published work that she denied the existence of anything like a God—and as such, was an avowed atheist. She did, however, have Platonic leanings. This is the belief that physical objects were impermanent representations of unchanging ideas and that the ideas alone gave true knowledge, as they were known by the mind. To Dr. Smith, it was a flawed naturalistic way of thinking and a soft target.

Final introductions were dutifully made, and the rules completely read. You could feel a rarefied air of superiority that exuded from the atheist crowd. Although hard to place, it was as though they anxiously awaited the slaughter, as their atheist champion entered the ring.

Dr. Smith sensed it but had grown used to hearing misguided arrogance in the public arena. "These aren't the first garrulous debate supporters with an illusory superiority," he later related to his podcast fans. "They consistently and chaotically assail the compatibility of faith and reason."

No matter, he had done due diligence and knew his opponent's strengths and weaknesses. Throughout the evening, he smiled inwardly at her underlying pompousness, laziness, anxiety, and powerlessness to respond well to his calculated arguments and rebuttals. He knew that the rules for enhanced power in a debate were superior knowledge and focus. Dr. Robert Smith had both. He was cheerful and in control. For the moment of his opening statement, he was dialed-in, and ready to address the longueurs and lapses of her logic.

Dr. Csornock's followers positioned her, on-line, as having no equals and she certainly had the *ad hominem* swagger down. From the sound of the bell she was dismissively negative toward Dr. Smith and raised side issues or *red herrings* to detract from the worthy arguments at hand.

"Then who made God?" was her *coup de grace.* It was intended to be the final killing blow that would put him out of his misery and forever destroy the religious arguments.

"That's interesting Stephanie, because many naturalistic scientists and philosophers, like you, have historically believed that the universe was eternal. It either existed or somehow mustered the strength to create itself, right?" He looked toward Stephanie. "So, tell us…who created your universe? How did it get here? Much less, how did it in this limited few billion years, ever evolve a consciousness, much less the irreducible complexities of say, a flagellum?"

"Can I interject here?" Stephanie said looking toward the moderator.

"Yes, Stephanie, you may…" he held up the palm of his hand, "…when it's your turn." Then Smith pretended to answer a phone with his thumb and pinkie fingers extended across his cheek. "*Hello?*" He extended the imaginary phone toward his opponent. "The 19th Century called, and they'd like to have their scientific ideas back."

The audience roared.

You see, Stephanie, modern science happened. We now know that the universe isn't eternal."

"So, you say."

"No, so the evidence says. The beginning of the universe, the Second Law of Thermodynamics, fine-tuning, and the impossibility of an infinite regress have shown us otherwise."

"Your god of the gaps won't fly here, Bobby."

"No, you're still not listening. What won't fly are the half-baked ideas of anti-religious ideologues." He turned to speak more personally to the audience.

"You see, I have never believed in a god of the gaps, but in a God who created the whole show. I'm open to the science. Because, you see, I don't believe in a God who was made, but a God who is necessary, self-existing, and powerful enough to make everything else."

"That's not science and you're not a scientist," she asserted in protest as though nothing he said was admissible.

"No, I'm not."

"So, then let me tell you a story," Dr. Csornock said, "from *The Grapes of Wrath*. It was an economically depressed time in the late 1930's—with a lot of farmers searching for relief. To their dismay, there were representatives from the bank who came to repossess the land on which the tenant farmers had been living for years:

'Sure, cried the tenant men, but it's our land…We were born on it, and we got killed on it, died on it. Even if it's no good, it's still ours…. That's what makes ownership, not a paper with numbers on it.'

'We're sorry. It's not us. It's the monster. The bank isn't like a man.'

'Yes, but the bank is only made of men.'

'No, you're wrong there—quite wrong there. The bank is something else than men. It happens that every man in a bank hates what the bank does, and yet the bank does it. The bank is something more than men, I tell you. It's the monster. Men made it, but they can't control it.' That's what we have in religion—man made it, but they can't control it."

On her part, it was an intentional strategy because narrative was often more compelling than the facts, and negative emotions more salient than positive ones. It's the way we're built. Our brain, notably, gives them higher priority.

Nonetheless, Dr. Smith was calm, cool, and collected as he responded.

"I can see that you're neither a scientist nor a good storyteller," Dr. Smith said. "You see the bank in your story *needs, wants, insists*, and *must have* things as though it had *thoughts* and *feelings* independent of men—and determined, even dictated, the fate of men. There is no question about the meaning of purpose of the bank and how it came about. There is no choice in your story. They are preyed upon and consigned to their mindless, unguided fate. Your story lacks love, justice, or a happy ending that my God provides. In my story God is a maximal being, and nothing less than holy, just, eternal, infinite, true, beautiful, and loving.

Dr. Smith enthusiastically spoke with a lot of common sense. So much so, that Dr. Csornock was on her heels throughout most of the night. That invariably made her nervous and reckless and very thin on substantive responses. Though unnoticeable to the crowd, she was psychologically postured to flee. In her mind, she wanted to flee, but couldn't. That was when unaccounted things started to happen: acceleration of her heart and lungs, constriction and dilation of the blood vessels and pupils, auditory exclusion, and shaking. Dr. Smith saw the signs and used them against her with graceful precision.

He didn't have a vindictive or punishing style, but relished the worthy academic battles and intellectual jousting. In an *after the debate* comment, Kevin Wolf put it this way, "He has a calm pastoral spirit, but his opponents dare not hesitate, blink or be caught off guard. I recommend that you come well-armed, because his swift and sure mental prowess will be unleashed."

In Dr. Smith's mind, it was a spiritual war for the things that *mattered most* in the universe. The existential issues of meaning, purpose, and the existence of God. *If God exists, then what could be more important to talk about?* he thought. His spiritual foundation and hopes were grounded in the maxim that *the truth will set you free.* And, when necessary, he could be very pastoral about it.

The initial comments were pugnacious, if not hostile, and that was merely in the early stage as they warmed up. There was a palpable warrior spirit in the air as Kevin Wolf continued to set the stage and facilitate the debate with flash and flare. Earlier he had referenced the *Roman Gladiator* posters used to market and hype the debate and then loudly announced: "*Let the games begin!*"

CHAPTER ONE HUNDRED EIGHTEEN

"In the end there doesn't have to be anyone who understands you. There just has to be someone who wants to." ~ *Robert Brault*

RELATIONSHIPS

SENATOR CROXON TOOK the scenic route and flew Steven and the rest of the gang back to Annapolis from the Tazewell County Airport, two miles from Richlands. Missy and Chelsea were excited to tag along.

"This beauty is breathtaking," Steven said.

John nodded. "I'll circle around the town, so you get a bird's eye views."

"Oh, fly over our house, Daddy." He did, and dipped the wing, so they could the house and the Grist Mill and the Clinch River. He once again reminisced about life, growing up in a small town and the hope that it gave him.

"The sights and smells are magnificent, but it was the relationships that *mattered* most in these parts," John said. "They are the glue that holds everything else together." It was the relationships that brought his people here and the relationships that made them stay, work hard, overcome adversities, raise families, and worship their God.

"Daddy, are you thinking about something again," Chelsea asked. "Your forehead is all wrinkly.

"Why, yes, it is John," Steven said, amused.

John smiled. "Yeah, I was just thinking about when I told you that this is where *God started making Heaven.*"

"Yeah, I can see why," Steven said.

Chelsea nodded. "I like Richlands, Daddy, but Heaven is a *whole lot* prettier."

"Well, He's had your town to practice on," Mark added.

Missy and Peggy nodded, impressed with his impromptu answer.

Chelsea liked talking to the adults. And she was used to having meaningful conversations with her daddy. He gave her the gift of being present—even though it was impossible for him to grasp her having seen Heaven. However, her stories strengthened his faith.

"Well, sweetie," he squeezed her hand, "I love hearing your stories about Heaven, just as much you love my stories about Richlands."

John's vast knowledge of his family history and Christian education at *the Home* had provided him with a more robust Christian worldview, identity, integrity, and strong character. It was a place where people always looked you in the eyes whenever they spoke, and gave you a firm handshake. John was surrounded by people that he loved and supported, and people who loved and supported him as well. Through teaching, prayer, and incredible acts of kindness, his Church family was strongly connected and had indeed made their life here on Earth, a little bit more like Heaven.

"That's the old Cedar Bluff High School and Elementary School," he said pointing out the right window of the plane at an old building. "See that place? It's on College Hill. And it started out as a four room school in 1906."

"But now it looks more like a haunted house," Steven said.

"Yep, where they keep a watch on the *hollers*." He made a spooky face and grinned as he turned the plane and circled southeast.

"Why would they holler at us?" Chelsea asked. Her mom found that amusing and repeated the question: "Yes dear—why would they holler at nice people like us?"

"Okay—good question!" John said.

"I read that it evolved from Elizabethan English—and it's how people here say the word *hollow*," Steven said.

"That's right, it's what they call the depression or valley between two mountains—a holler!" John said slightly louder, as though he was hollering the word.

"Or maybe when they hollered, their voices echoed through the valley," Steven theorized, "And they could communicate with each other before there were phones."

John puckered his mouth and gave a noncommittal head nod.

Chelsea needed to find out more about *hollers*. So, when they returned home, later that evening, she insisted that they stop along the side of the road and put it to the test. John escorted her to the side of a hill, where they both strenuously yelled *Hellooo! Is anybody hooome?!* Missy waited in the car and laughed. Then, satisfied, they drove toward the house.

On the way through town, Chelsea noticed a big painting. "Oh, that's pretty!"

"That's a mural of Richlands," John said, as they slowly cruised down 2nd Street.

Chelsea tried to say the word mural, but asked, "What's a *moral*?"

"It's a mural, honey—a painting that they put on a wall. My second Cousin Ellen Elmes painted that on what used to be the W.B.F. White and Sons hardware store." The store was started in 1907 and changed hands a few times, but now sat empty.

"I'd like to paint a mural, too." Chelsea said.

"It's a history of the area—*and* I've got a history with that hardware store, as well," he said. His face screwed in a grimace. "I can thank them for the seven stitches I got rolling down their unguarded wooden stairs, to the basement."

"My goodness, Daddy—what happened?" Chelsea asked.

"Well, I was just about your age, I suppose—maybe a little younger. I was looking at the beautiful horse saddles hanging on the wall and didn't notice an unmarked hole in the middle of the store's wood floor."

"That must have really hurt!" Missy said.

"I don't remember—I woke up at the hospital with a bandage around my head. God spared me the pain and memory of it anyways. Pop-Paw told me the story many times: *I just grabbed you up and whisked you off in the car.* He was quick to point out that it was in his classic 1965 *Ford Galaxie* 500 that got me there lickity-split."

Chelsea loved the stories and listened intently to every word her daddy had to say. She liked that it was her hometown too.

"Growing up, I heard stories from my folks about the Pounding Mill, Chimney Cave, Indian Creek, and a two-headed Thunderbird symbol that still remains on the ledge at Paint Lick Mountain. And—I remember doing things, like helping Mom-Maw and Pop-Paw hoe potatoes and snap green beans. Afterwards, I watched Mom-Maw can homemade jams, apple butter, fruit, and vegetables." They were all stored and preserved in Mason Jars and stored in root-cellars, during a time of self-resilience."

"That was before we had a lot of grocery stores," Missy said.

"Yep, and it was open 24 hours a day," John smiled. "For as far back as I can remember, I enjoyed things we canned on our own. But sometimes, if I had an extra buck, I'd slip down to the *King Kone* for one of those strawberry milkshakes I told you about!

"Oh—there it is up ahead," Mrs. Croxon said. "Let's get a custard!"

"But—I want a *stwaw-berry* milkshake, Daddy! Like you used to drink."

"Ha, that's my girl," he said as he pulled into the parking lot and turned the car off. "It's still nice to see the familiar hangouts from my childhood."

CHAPTER ONE HUNDRED NINETEEN

"What we do in life echoes in eternity." ~ *Maximus (Gladiator)*

THE GAMES BEGIN

KEVIN WOLF WENT on to say, "You know—in the *1st* Century A.D., some Gladiators were lured to the arena by the thrill of battle and the roar of the crowds. Not unlike our gathering here tonight—where the fight is for hearts, minds, and I believe—souls. Fortunately, though—the only things that will die here tonight are ill-conceived arguments and ignorance," he said pausing for applause. "So—don't be alarmed if you change your mind—it's okay." He raised a finger and glanced at the Director of Metanoia. "No one will be hurt tonight—but we hope that you'll forever be changed." As everyone applauded again, he turned to shake hands with Dr. Smith and Dr. Csornock before he returned to the podium.

Kevin went on to explain that there would be a figurative *thumbs up* or *thumbs down* conducted for each presenter, via an on-line voting system that they had concocted. Everyone in the auditorium and those that listened via radio or social media could vote. "At the end of tonight's debate, we will announce a winner, but rest assured mercy is available to all!" he said. He extended both arms in the air, as though he was bestowing a reprieve. "Oh, and as per always—no animals will be harmed!" he said with a huge smile. Kevin was intentionally melodramatic and had a knack for making academic subjects much more palatable and memorable.

He pressed on with his colorful introductions. "Without further ado, let's welcome our adroit debaters for tonight." The audience responded with more enthusiastic and warm applause. "On my left..."

"Your far, far left," Stephanie inserted, with laughter erupting from the audience.

"Yes, in full disclosure—Professor Csornock is literally and figuratively to my far, far left. She is also a writer and research Professor of Philosophy at Brown University and a well-published, if not vocal, atheist—is that fair to say?" She nodded.

"To my right is Dr. Robert W. Smith. He is a writer and research Professor of Philosophy from Houston Baptist University in Texas—who is a theist with serious Christian leanings."

Dr. Smith nodded and said, "Yes, guilty as charged."

"Dr. Smith has presented a series of dialogues about the existence of God at Oxford, Tsinghua University, and will again here tonight in this grand Harvard University auditorium. In a moment, I'll have each of our debaters share with us some of their experiences and perhaps a glimpse of what we'll have to look forward to during tonight's event. But, first let me tell you a little about myself, Kevin Wolf. My spiritual path was a little different than most. My mother started out as a disillusioned hippie during the San Francisco Haight-Ashbury *Summer of Love* celebrations of personal expression, drug experimentation, and easy sexuality. By a miracle, she was reached and converted by one of those barefoot *Jesus Freak* evangelists that hungout with them in the Bay Area—and the rest, is as they say, His-story. She taught me about God, led me to Christ, and I've dedicated my life to serving him through a variety of radio and television ministries," he said. He then noticed the floor director drawing a few large circles in the air with her index finger. It was her signal to wrap up this portion of the intros. Since it was a live broadcast, each segment had an allotted amount of time and commercials to air. It was her duty to keep Kevin running on schedule—and get the bills paid.

"Well, I think it's time to get the show on the road here at Harvard Yard," he said in his thickest mock Harvard accent, looking all around the auditorium. "This is quite an extraordinary building—something between the Saturday Night Fever Disco and Notre Dame, of course minus Quasimodo begging for sanctuary." There were a few polite chuckles. Kevin read the audience perfectly and moved on. "Thank you—thank you so much for being here with me tonight! It should be a thought-provoking evening, and it is certainly a privilege to welcome you here to be in the presence of two revered and prestigious intellectuals, like our guests."

Dr. Csornock shook her head and rolled her eyes at the lofty accolades. Dr. Smith smiled and mouth the words *Thank You!*

"But I also think it's the topic that has brought us here tonight. There's something that we all find so compelling about the relationship between *God and Science*," he said looking around the auditorium, allowing the depth of the topic to penetrate their thoughts.

"The assumption, by some, is that *God and Science* or any religious belief, in general, have always been at extreme odds with one another, but in fact our history tells us a much different story. There have always been extraordinary collaborations between the two studies. A spirit and culture of learning shared from each other—and exchanging ideas with one another! So, you may ask—how have we gotten to the place, where we think that these two fields are bitter enemies?" He paused again to let the room noise settle to a thoughtful quiet.

"Could it be because of our insatiable appetite for fake news?" he said, to more silence. "Please, I left my Xanax at home—so, feel free to assuage my anxiety with your occasional affirmations of applause and laughter." He smiled and waited again. The erudite group indulged his dry sense of humor and filled the silence with the applause he sought. Kevin looked toward his old friend Dr. Smith with raised eyebrows and an—*I gave it my best shot* look on his face.

"Okay, perhaps it's not fake news, but I think you know what I mean. Many universities, books, and news programs leave you with the feeling that you've only heard part of the story, with social media, of course, hyping or skirting the truth for more clicks. Sometimes opposing opinions or alternate thoughts and ideas are cleverly omitted or couched in biased verbiage. Serious ideas are mocked without warrant and obscured by humor or personal, nasty, attacks" he said, in a more somber tone. "It even happens in debates like these—but not with fine people like you—I'm sure," he said, motioning with his hands, across the auditorium.

"As someone who works for a media organization, let me be perfectly frank: The media's number one mission isn't always to tell you the truth—Mine is, of course!" he stated emphatically. "But others are in this purely to make money. They make millions by framing stories with conflict, controversy, incivility, and self-righteous indignation. It can be like a Puccini opera with you as the aroused, gullible audience—thirsty for entertainment, gossip, sex, slander, rebellion, fights, and war.

No, not me—you say. *I'm smarter than that.* But let me ask you—how do you behave on social media? Are you friendly, tolerant, or hateful? Are you tolerant, if it's what you believe? What is it that you consume each day—watch, read, and talk about? Whatever it is—that is what's shaping you—that's who you are," Kevin Wolf announced. "My hope tonight is that we might actually be encouraged to think, share, and engage with each other—even if we disagree. And to do it with respect and dignity, even if you're on the polar opposite of an issue. Let's get to know our guests for tonight's event a little better."

"The Rope a Dope would not have existed without the Big Dope." ~ George Foreman

KO

"OUR DISCUSSIONS HERE at Harvard tonight have centered on the idea of a god or the lack thereof," Dr. Stephanie Csornock said with a pursed lip smile. "And I've learned quite a lot about where Dr. Smith is coming from—that I hadn't previously appreciated. He is earnest— earnestly misled, of course, and intends to provide arguments for the beliefs that he holds, despite an abundance of evidence to the contrary. His *Leibnizian* claim that if the universe has an explanation—it must be God—is the weakest argument I think I've ever heard. In fact, it's quite laughable when closely examined. In tonight's discussions I will point out where he is wrong and distorts the ideas of science with his so-called religious reasoning."

Dr. Smith was diminutive in size, but his deep resonant voice and intellectual mind were quite capable of fracturing dysfunctional syllogisms, which formed reasons and drew conclusions. So, he began. "First of all—let it be known that I embrace *good science*, not stilted, agenda driven assertions and narratives that you'll hear from Stephanie this evening. In fact, my cosmological arguments appeal directly to proper science in the areas of cosmology and fine-tuning. They are arguments in which the existence of a unique being, generally seen as God, is deduced or inferred from facts concerning causation, change, motion, contingency, and finitude in respect to the beginning of the universe or the processes within it."

Throughout the course of the debate, there was a calmness and surgical intricacy in Dr. Smith's delivery. His piercing blue eyes humorously deflected a barrage of contemptuous mockery, over substance. With reason, evidence, and warrant, he visibly wiped the testy, dyspeptic sneer from Dr. Csornock's face and disposed of her fallacy-filled propositions. Stephanie couldn't begin to shoulder the burden of proof necessary to carry a debate or argument in favor of atheism. In one desperate attempt, she appealed to pain and suffering in the world, but failed at every turn.

"You see, Dr. Smith, if your God is good, then there wouldn't be any evil. He could blow it out like a candle...so the fact is...we still see evil everywhere, so there is no god."

"Your response, Dr. Smith," Kevin said.

As, in every debate we've had, Stephanie has turned it upside down. My argument is that:

1. If God is all-good, he will defeat evil.

2. If God is all-powerful, he can defeat evil.

3. Evil is not yet defeated.

4. Therefore, God can and will one day defeat evil. Count on it."

Dr. Smith gave breviloquent, to the point definitions and answers, and at one point stopped to explain science. Dr. Csornock just threw her head back and rolled her eyes.

"Let me explain," Dr. Smith said. "The most basic goal of good science is to *develop a theory, paradigm, or model that provides a basis for research to understand the phenomena being studied.* We're always learning and changing theories—every day."

"It's not that fluid at all," Stephanie asserted.

"She's absolutely wrong there."

Stephanie shook her head.

"You see, even in Darwin's day, we thought the human cell was just a blob of jelly material, but we now know that it's as complex as the city of Detroit—but I digress." He knew he didn't have all day to finesse a complete answer, and complicated ones often confused people. He needed to zero-in. "Look, I categorically accept the Scientific Method, but realize that it, too, has its limitations."

Stephanie threw her arms up in the air, as if to say *see what I'm dealing with?*

"Those limitations are based on the fact that a hypothesis must be testable and falsifiable, and that experiments and observations be repeatable. That places certain topics beyond the reach of the scientific method. *Metaphysical things.* Science cannot prove or refute the existence of God or any other supernatural entity," Robert said, looking over at Stephanie. "That's not the job of science."

"Yeah, right—that's very tidy, isn't it!" She waved him off with a *whatever* tone in her voice. "Science has no limits—there are only those things that we haven't discovered yet."

"That's just a copout," Dr. Smith chided. "Moral judgments, aesthetic judgments, decisions about applications of science, and conclusions about the supernatural are outside the realm of science—and generally can't be resolved by science."

Stephanie rolled her eyes again but made no attempt at a rebuttal.

He added, "They are important realms of learning, actively studied by scholars. In fact, domains such as ethics, aesthetics, and religion fundamentally influence society and how we morally interact with science.

Stephanie smirked. It was all she had left.

"You see friends—most of Dr. Csornock's rebuttals were limited to ad hominem comments, dismissive smirks, and glib assertions. She may think that those tactics make good arguments.

They do not! In our debate tonight, she has yet to address any of my arguments head-on, with more than an eye roll. She has done nothing to support her case for scientific naturalism and she decided there is no God because evil exists. So, listen closely and think about her failing responses tonight."

Dr. Csornock began the debate overly confident and noticeably ill-prepared, but nonetheless aggressive in her popular approach to debating. That seemed to be the most effective weapon for atheists of her ilk, and the only one that she knew how to wield. She was riding a wave of popular thinking, and an arrogant, unfounded notion that Christians had left their brains at the narthex of the church. Boy had she miscalculated.

"Robert, I didn't come here tonight to kill off your ideas of God or gods. The fact is that throughout history there have been a lot of gods—and science has buried them all. In fact, my job has already been done for me." The atheists in the crowd erupted wildly with *oohs* and *aahs* and applause. "In a manner of speaking, we're all atheists, right? I don't believe in any of the gods, and you don't believe in them all either. You've chosen one to believe in, but you're an atheist about all the others. Don't get me wrong—I'm sure that religion can be emotionally helpful to some of you, but call it what it is—a crutch to help you through life," she said with mock empathy. Dr. Smith continued to focus and take notes from her half-cocked rebuttals.

In earlier months, they had settled on an adequate title for the debate: *God vs. Science.* It was direct and to the point and allowed them to discuss their philosophical foundations. It took a while to negotiate an agreed upon time, date, and subject matter, but it paid off. The debate was well attended. Dr. Csornock's status and brand, as a superstar among internet atheists, brought significant attention to the debate; some respectful, and some querulous. Her disrespectful manner had unfortunately been modeled to her fans—who sent out Twitter messages like this: *Where do these bigoted, anti-intellectual Neanderthals get off believing in a sky-god?*

As the evening progressed, she continued to rail against what she called Dr. Smith's *absurd belief in a god*, looking at him directly, at one point in the debate, and asking, "So, which god is it that you believe in? Those gods that pushed the moon, sun, and planets around and caused it to rain?" And then she turned to the audience. "You see my friends—science has buried those myths long ago, so why don't we spend our time on something more intelligible?" The atheists cheered loudly again. Their champion had struck a blow.

Dr. Csornock was great at riling her base and stirring the pot with unsubstantiated and emotional claims about the myths associated with the Judeo-Christian God. Most of these issues could have immediately been cleared up by reading the primary literature, but she had no interest in the truth. She repeated her unsupported mantras ad nauseam in all her public lectures, interviews, and books, which sold well. To her it didn't matter if it was true or not. It drew audiences and sold books—and since she didn't believe in God, *what more could one ask for in life?*

Throughout the debate Stephanie flitted from subject to subject, skipping unwarranted assertions across the pond of ideas, without causing any substantial ripples of evidence or addressing Dr. Smith's arguments. He had served a hitch in the Army Reserve, in Afghanistan, and compared her presentation to an ill-equipped band of Al Qaeda fighters who used ineffective old weapons, mismatched ammunition, and had widespread eye problems.

"Stephanie appears to have little to no organized training in modern warfighting," he said with amusement. "I would duck if I were you. She's been firing randomly tonight—missing all the main targets."

All though deliciously credentialed, Dr. Csornock's arrogance and academic blinders had been her undoing. Even when the gate had been opened, she continued to trot within her naturalistic coral. In her world there was no place to run, and she wasn't open to possibilities. This was where she had been broken and dare not jump the fence.

He not only confounded her with his thorough rebuttals, but also connected with the audience through his superior facts, narratives, and likeable sense of humor. Since the time he was a youth pastor in Walla Walla, he had learned how to persuasively and strategically engage uninformed or misinformed audiences. Teenagers had given him the best practice.

Dr. Robert Smith could turn a meme as well as the next guy, as demonstrated in his post-debate comments: "Stephanie is *more flair than finesse and more nonsense than nuance.* You'll notice that she caters more toward emotion."

It was notable to all that attended that she was bright, but condescending in her delivery, and raged against issues that he had never raised—rather than addressing the compatibility or incompatibility of *God and Science.* She repeatedly mocked the idea that some imaginary god would be engrossed by sin, virgin births, and sex. She consistently tried to shift the debate to fallacious claims about the impossibility of Jesus being buried and resurrected, and God commanding the extermination of all the Canaanites, including the children. Dr. Smith merely replied, "Those are *red-herring* theological issues that I've addressed in my other works—and not applicable to tonight's debate."

Kevin Wolf described it this way on a podcast: "If you were analyzing the debate as a boxing match, then you would say she exposed her chin during her jabs, dropped her right hand during the left hook, telegraphed the right hand, and exposed the body. She was wasting a lot of time and tiring fast. I'd characterize it as she *flailed with indignation, jolts of rudeness, and gimmicky fragments of insolence,* but soon succumbed to Dr. Smith's brilliant apologetics *rope-a-dope.* Dr. Smith easily won the debate in terms of the ideas and arguments he presented and ignored Stephanie's uninformed theology and useless jabs at his character. Naturally, most of the Harvard Yard curious onlookers came in with their own set of preconceptions and felt that they were being supported well by their own champion's arguments. Others had never heard such clever, intellectually rich repartee from a Christian debater and were more open-minded to religious ideas and discussions than ever before. It was a good night. Dr. Smith had undeniable *moxie.*"

Metanoia, the organization hosting the debate, posted this on their website with a link to the recording: "His words inspired believers, and caused the pseudo-intellectuals to tremble in their *Louis Vuitton* shoes. All Dr. Csornock could do was pop semantic smoke and retreat without detection."

Nothing was hidden from those seated in the Sander's Theatre or those listening around the world. Dr. Robert Smith concluded with "Tonight, I've presented five good reasons for God's existence. In a cumulative sense I think that you'll agree—they don't conflict with the practice of science:

1. God makes sense of the origin of the universe.

2. God makes sense of the fine-tuning of the universe for intelligent life.

3. God makes sense of objective moral values in the world.

4. God makes sense of the life, death, and resurrection of Jesus.

   And…

5. God can be immediately known and experienced.

"You, on the other hand," Dr. Smith said, "have not offered any good reasons to believe atheism is true. So, forgive me if I'm not persuaded." He looked out at the audience. "And you shouldn't be persuaded either. God isn't against science—quite the opposite—He created it."

CHAPTER ONE HUNDRED TWENTY-ONE

"More markets. Less hassle." ~ *FedEx*

FEDEX

DR. LUI WEI appeared in court Monday and was remanded into custody after he pled *not guilty*, according to court documents. His federal public defender said, "Charges have been made and he will be detained until a trial can take place."

Brad Manuszewski had first become suspicious of Dr. Lui in late February, after he observed him abruptly end phone calls, and hang up whenever someone entered the room. Later he had become lazy and incautious, openly communicated in Chinese. If he hadn't cleared his desk off and locked access to the computers, he wouldn't have raised suspicions as quickly as he did. He might have even escaped unnoticed.

"He is Chinese, and was usually speaking Chinese on the phone, so I didn't think too much about it," Brad Manuszewski testified. "But it seemed odd when he responded to what he said was a wrong number, in Chinese. After I bypassed the lockout, Sabrina and I noticed numerous unauthorized, encrypted, software downloads from the PSYCHONIX project."

Agents explained to them that an external source had been used to trick computer inspection capabilities and infiltrate PSYCHONIX computers. The infiltrators, Dr. Lui and Dr. Kahn, also had an intricate phone scheme, which used each other's cellphones as mailboxes, when necessary. "They also used a malicious program that remotely accessed computers—and tagged

557

files for download and delivery. Using their own phones, made it less obvious to the naked eye," an agent said.

The computer logs showed multiple other downloads from the PSYCHONIX server, just days prior to Dr. Lui Wei entering a Pennsylvania FedEx store to prepare and package classified materials for shipment. The footage from a surveillance camera caught him as he handed a clerk stacks of classified documents, to be scanned, and an SD card to ship with it. "It was the kind that could be inserted into cameras and mobile phones."

"Tradition: how the vitality of the past enriches the life of the present." ~ *T.S. Eliot*

CUSTOMS & TRADITIONS

THROUGH THE YEARS, the coming of railroads and coal camps brought significant changes to Christmas customs in Richlands. One that was driven by poorer times was the old tradition of *Calling for a Christmas Gift*. It was an opportunity for those less fortunate to call upon more prosperous homes for help without the appearance or stigma of begging. The event planners at Calvary Baptist Church, where the Croxons attended, opened their doors to everyone.

Coal mining communities like Richlands began having community Christmas trees and provided each child with a Christmas present early on in their history, usually collected from all the miners' paychecks. The first of those trees was memorialized on *Christmas Tree Hill*.

As they sat around the fireplace, drinking hot chocolate and admiring their Christmas tree, Pop-Paw shared a few of the old mountain traditions: "The way Appalachian families celebrated Christmas came in part from their Scotts-Irish heritage, but they also took on new customs as their Soldiers returned from World Wars I and II." He glanced toward John, who nodded at Chelsea. "Traditions that they had seen throughout the *Old Country*."

Some of the *old ways* were still the more cherished ways for the Croxon family: shooting matches, games, Christmas pageants, and friends and neighbors that dropped by without an invitation. "Folk in these parts will open their door at a moment's notice," Pop-Paw said.

"I like that," Missy said. She cherished the traditions being passed down and loved the mountain people.

"I heard a lot of mountain folklore growing up," John said, looking for the right file on his cellphone. "Ah—let me read some of them to you—it's just a short list." He scanned through his phone. "First, they say that children born on January 6th are special—and often develop powers for healing the sick." He glanced over his silver reading glasses at Chelsea and said, "You'll really like this part: animals kneel at midnight on Christmas Eve, as they did by the manger when Christ was born. They also talk during that time, but it's bad luck to catch them speaking."

"Did you ever catch an animal speaking, Chelsea?" Mom-Maw Croxon asked.

"Nooooo!" she squealed, drawing out the word to indicate how amazing it might be if one could speak.

"Me neither! Except maybe on Sesame Street," John said.

"That doesn't count," she said with a giggle. "That's pretend."

John continued reading from his list: "Here's another one—water apparently turns into wine at midnight on Christmas Eve, but it's bad luck to taste it," he said scanning down the list, skipping a few uninteresting ones. "Let's see—uh—okay, here are some more. If you sit under a pine tree on Christmas Day, then you can hear angels sing." He sipped his cocoa and smiled with his eyes.

"Really?" Chelsea beamed.

"But, beware! If you hear them, you'll be on your way to Heaven before next Christmas."

"That's okay—I've already been there."

Missy hugged an arm around Chelsea's shoulder as her daddy read more Mountain Folklore from his list: "Breads and cakes baked on Christmas Day have special healing virtues."

"That's great—cut me another slice of cake," Pop-Paw teased.

"Some folks even preserved them for use in curing illness during the coming year and—oh, this is a nice one—on Christmas Day, visits to neighbors' houses required eating a piece of stack cake or mince pie to ensure good luck."

It was quite a long list, and John felt like perhaps he was losing everyone's attention as they broke off in different conversations and enjoyed their cake. "I'll leave it at that and print a copy for anyone to read, if you want to." It was an amusing list that many of their visitors read. Interesting to see how people used to entertain themselves with imaginative Christmas stories before there were the distractions of all-night media. The rest of the list read like this:

8. Visits from twelve neighbors ensure good luck for the whole year—and make for bringing a whole lot of people closer together.

9. Coals and ashes from the Christmas fire should never be thrown out that day, and no coal of fire or light should be given away.

10. Angels are so busy celebrating the birth of Christ that, one hour before Christmas, the gates of heaven are left unattended. Anyone passing over at this hour has a good chance of sneaking into heaven without having to give account.

11. Christmas Day weather forecasts the kind of weather we'll have for the rest of the year: a warm Christmas foretells a cold Easter; a green Christmas, a white Easter; a windy Christmas means a good corn crop.

12. Single girls who visit the hog pen at midnight on Christmas Eve can find out the kind of man they'll marry. If an old hog grunts first, she will marry an old man. If a young hog grunts first, her husband will be young and handsome.

Everyone who read the list found the hog story hilariously funny and joked about it until it wasn't funny anymore. Although Pop-Paw got in the last word. "I guess when they got engaged you could say they were *be-troughed!*" The family roared with silly laughter.

CHAPTER ONE HUNDRED TWENTY-THREE

"My home is in Heaven. I'm just traveling through this world." ~ *Billy Graham*

ROOMS IN ROOMS

ON STEVEN'S NEXT trip he was led up a narrow path, through some magnificent tall trees. There was an unbelievable combination of rainbow eucalyptus, royal poinciana, and peacock flowers on one side. On the other side Japanese Wisteria, maple, and flamboyant trees. Some colors and combinations were beyond description and imagination. It was a delight to the eyes of Steven and Marlina as they strolled to her lovely cottage. Mama and Papa Millie were there, calmly rocking on the front porch. They erupted in joyous laughter when they saw Steven, in what could only be called *a first day in heaven celebration.*

Mama Millie greeted him with generous hugs and kisses. "It's-ah extra special to see you Steven!"

"I did not think Heaven could get any better." Papa Millie smiled and nodded, patting Steven's shoulder.

It was astonishing that everyone he loved looked and sounded the same as before, but were somehow younger and stronger and wiser. You could see it in their eyes. Neither in a haughty nor arrogant way, but a brilliant sparkle of contentment, joy, and love. They had a special connection that made them distinct, but one with all other souls. It was magnificent to see, but that's all he would see of them, this time, on this limited visit. He and Marlina entered the house together, as her parents sat back down and gently rocked in their chairs.

"It was worth the wait," she said looking at him and soaking in the beauty of her forever home. It was the best thing she could say about her forever-blessings.

It was worth the wait!

"Steven, you'll be surprised to learn that this is *so much more* than a modest country cottage." She pointed. "Look out that window and then peer across at that one, on the other side of the house," she said. Both of them were completely fascinated by what they saw...the colors and diversity of the landscapes. Steven did a double take. He blinked his eyes in bewilderment as he tried to comprehend the immensity of what he saw. When he looked out the kitchen window, there was a private sanctuary. It was a garden patio with an umbrella picnic table and a courtyard of textured gold and red fall leaves.

"You still get to enjoy the seasons—wow!" he said.

"Yes, and all the seasons and scenery evolve depending on where you are in the house and according to the desires of your heart!" She took his hand and pulled him through to the living room and from one room to another, looking out all the many windows. Steven quietly muttered to himself, "I love—," he exhaled, "Wow, I really—love this place!"

He was utterly speechless as they ambled through the cottage that had been designed according to the desires of Marlina's heart. They sat on a cushy rococo loveseat and sipped hot cocoa in front of a roaring log fire, and enjoyed their time together, as they watched the dancing snowflakes fall outside the lightly frosted windows. It was pleasantly warm and comfortably cozy and reminded them of their leisure times on Earth—in the Colorado Rockies and Swiss Alps—but with more lush scenery and endless sunshine.

Out one of the antique bedroom windows, there was the gentle patter of rainfall and a mild wind that whistled through the trees. It was one of a few rooms where you could enjoy sunsets, sunrises, and starlit nights. In another room, open vistas spanned a penthouse view of *The Eternal City*. Since every day was a clear day, when you wanted it to be, you could see beyond the city's Central Park and out to the windswept waves of the ocean. They could, but no one at ITL saw any farther than the window.

"How is this even—?" he asked in awe.

"Possible? I never asked," she said, before he could finish his thought. They walked on and continued the tour. "Remember, with God all things are possible."

"This is my literary retreat," she said, leading Steven into an intimate, wood-shelved library with a couple big cozy ottomans and berry-red-leather chairs. "It's filled with my favorite books and recommendations."

"Recommendations?"

She smiled. "Sure, why not—if *Amazon* can do it?"

He nodded. "Sure! God can do it better."

"And even here, there's nothing that compares to the feeling of holding a good old-fashioned book in your hands." She grabbed an old version of Shelley's Poetical Works off the shelf and leafed through it and read one:

See the mountains kiss high heaven
And the waves clasp one another
No sister flower would be forgiven
If it disdained its brother
And sunlight clasps the earth,

And the moonbeams kiss the sea;

What are all these kissings worth?

If thou kiss not me?

...and he did. They embraced and he kissed her warmly, softly, tenderly. It would have to last.

The arched windows of the library gave them a stunning view of a color-filled flower garden, as they enjoyed the perfectly snug sitting area and pillows. Outside another window was a showcase of exotic woodland plants that were in full bloom and a meandering stream that disappeared into the horizon. She could see it as it directed the melting snow from nearby mountain peaks toward the distant ocean.

"I love it here," she took another hot sip of her cocoa.

"I can certainly see why." They stood and held hands, not feeling a need to speak. All that *mattered* was that for a short time, they were together again.

"I just learned that I could travel from here," she said without blinking. "To anywhere I want to go."

"You can what?"

"I can travel—to most any point in the universe or within any of the dimensions.

"Like one of the ten?"

"Yeah, except there are a lot more. Things like prayer and your ability—or I should say our empathic ability—happens in the 5th dimension."

"The group?"

"No, silly."

He smiled. "I don't understand all that stuff.

"You don't have to," she said. "There are things that we could have never imagined through our natural limitations."

"Well, I'm certainly a witness to that."

"See that *pergola* with flowering vines growing down," she pointed, "at the back of the garden?"

He nodded. "I see it."

"Under it is a cast iron Victorian garden bench that I use as a portal to wherever we want to travel. I can sit on *Apolytrosis*, *25* billion light years from Earth, and watch the sunset."

"Okay, I'll take your word for it."

"You just sit there and imagine where you want to go—and you're transported."

Back at ITL Sabrina checked the PSYCHONIX monitors and annotated the time. Steven was still frozen in the *Amaranth*, but **5-hrs** flashed up in his vision, or nearly seven months given the dimensional shift. He noticed but didn't discuss it with Marlina.

Marlina continued, "Let's go downstairs."

They both took off like two little kids on Christmas morning, excited to see all their new toys. But to their surprise, they never got out of breath, not once, as they sped around the house and down the stairs. In the basement, there was an outdoor exit into another jaw-dropping world of discovery. It was an entirely different sphere. They stepped outside and found themselves in the heart of an expansive property, roughly the size of Disney World resort and parks; *30,000* acres. And like the cottage, it changed in size and shape, as imagined by those who enjoyed it. There was a tranquil pond and places to relax, eat, and to be entertained along the way. There were also paths that led them from glacier-carved ridges, into steep-sided valleys, and a spectacular waterfall.

"This is *Angel Falls*," Marlina said. "It was called that because it's where *Lucifer* first admired his reflection in the water. From then on, it became a reflection of God's providence. And look," she said, pointing. "It allows us to retrieve special moments from the past—and to see things now, and as they may unfold."

Just then, a reflection of their meeting at *DiBuono's Steak & Submarine Shop* in College Place appeared in the waterfall. That had been the exact wonderful day things started to really click between the two of them. Steven saw himself as he walked home, and ducked into their family restaurant to avoid a random Washington downpour.

"That was a special day," Steven gently squeezed her hand.

"Yes, and I can sit by the waterfall and enjoy it whenever I choose. This was a pretty special day too—Watch," she said. They sat on a stone bench by the plunge basin of the waterfall and when he looked up, he saw their wedding vows reflect from the cascading water.

"It's like a HD video," Steven said.

"Yes—Heaven Definition. But even more than that, it allows us to see if our loved ones are okay or in need. It also provides us an opportunity to pray for them and assist with future events." She didn't elaborate. The fact was that those in Heaven couldn't interfere with God's plans—ever. However, with signed approval of the Archangels, they could cooperate with other guardian angels—and sometimes that meant intercession on the part of a wayward soul.

The trip downstairs ate up another *seven hours* of Steven's visit. "We're over the halfway mark," Sabrina communicated to Steven through her PSYCHONIX headset.

He nodded.

"We'll need to initiate recovery," Dr. Starr abruptly announced. So, they began the slow procedure of defrosting and extracting him. Steven Scott's PSYCHONIX eye pulsated digital red lights, at the exact moment that the recovery protocols commenced.

Meanwhile, Marlina and Steven headed back upstairs, but this time by way of a *360 degree* Crystal-gilded elevator that slowly rotated and allowed them to survey every aspect of the cottage inside and out. They saw the entire landscape and all the glorious seasons unfold outside in a single, simultaneous moment.

"Willy Wonka, eat your heart out," Steven said, as the elevator accelerated upward. "What's upstairs?"

"You'll see," she said, as they stepped off the elevator. "It's the banquet room." Steven walked forward, and immediately grabbed the long, thin baroque handles. He tried to tug the double doors open, even though it wasn't possible for him to open the doors. Marlina gently stopped him, by placing her hand on top of his. "We can't go in there yet, Steven!" she said. He stubbornly pulled once again at the giant door handles. "Not yet."

Even though they were locked out, at this moment, they could easily see through the thin, transparent doors, and the beautifully decorated inner-walls, to the banquet hall and beyond. Everything was made from a type of luxurious gold leaf glass, decoratively fused between multiple layers of gems; diamonds, rubies, emeralds and many other types of construction materials one might only find lying around Heaven.

He yanked on the door handle once more. "Not even—for a peek?"

"No, they're not ready for us." She pointed elsewhere to swiftly distract Steven. "Look over there—that's where the heavenly banquet takes place after Jesus returns to Earth and brings all the believers back to the Father's house. It's also where people will see Jesus Christ for their first time in Heaven. I can't wait to attend and see it joyously unfold." She spoke of it as the grandest, happiest party that one could imagine. And that all the grieving, tears, trials, and tribulations would end forever—after God wiped away all sorrow and replaced pain and suffering with perfect joy.

"It's all we've ever hoped for, Marlina!"

She smiled and said, "It is our *hope,* Steven."

Behind the royal banquet door, there were rows upon rows of elegant tables, elaborately decorated, and nimble angels made their vital last minute arrangements. They decided on the placement of tables, and the just right ambiance. Some scurried about to decorate, and others prepared menus, seating, and entertainment.

"The theme finalization is the most important." Just then a group of angels, closest to the doors walk by with a banner that read:

𝔐arriage 𝔖upper of t𝔥e 𝔏amb!

They beamed with smiles and gestured with friendly waves, as they ascended into the air, soaring to-and-fro, to position the two-sided sign high in the center of the magnificent hall. One angel, with a pencil over his left ear, appeared to be the project supervisor. He motioned for them to lower the left side a skosh and then gave them a snappy thumbs up. He then looked down at his non-existent watch, before he turned toward the door and mouthed —*it's not time yet*—and waved a friendly goodbye, before getting back to his important work.

"Hah! Did you see that? I just waved at an angel?" Steven exclaimed.

"Yes, they are the kindest people."

"People?"

"Yeah, angels are pure spirits and personal beings, so each angel is, in essence, a person—and they do a lot of work around her," she said. To her it made perfectly good sense, if you thought about it for a second. "Isn't it a lovely, spacious hall?" she asked rhetorically. They both shook their heads in silent wonderment and in awe of the divine work being done. "Jesus will welcome us all here, compassionately and in absolute love—and we will worship Him forever."

"And, to think, some people believe Heaven to be a boring time of endlessly attending church and playing a harp."

"Right, Steven, and it's nothing like that. Just like on Earth we're richly given all things for our enjoyment—and it is here that relationships *matter* the most. Our relationship to God and our relationship to each other are completed here. We gather together in community, care for each other, learn new things, and worship God every day, in spirit and truth—and if you want to play a harp I can mention it to Jesus for you," she said with a sly wink.

"That's quite alright," he said.

"You will know more and do more in Heaven than you've ever thought possible. Why, even our thoughts are orchestrated and delivered to God as a worshipful harmony."

"Music to His ears! I sensed it since I arrived. That's nice."

"Yes, it is."

As Marlina spoke, her last words began to sound muted and mumbled to Steven. He asked her to slow down and repeat it, as he rubbed his eyes and ears. He hoped it would help him understand better, but there was a problem. ITL was initiating the egress protocol.

Nearly

24 hours had passed at ITL, and Steven was being recalled, rewarmed, and revived in the giant glass vacuum flask called the *Amaranth*. It would take many hours to reanimate him. The cryoprotectants warm up protocol began its laborious liquefaction process. It would be a while before vital signs were reestablished. Although highly technical, it was a boring procedure, so most of the crew left for home. Sabrina drew the short straw and stayed overnight in an adjacent office with a large observation window and a strong cup of coffee. She occasionally checked the monitors and began to read a *Jordon K. Stephens* thriller called H-311, as Steven's body continued to thaw. All you could see from the unlit room, and *Amaranth,* was the red glow of Steven Scott's PSYCHONIX eye.

CHAPTER ONE HUNDRED TWENTY-FOUR

"Integrity is doing the right thing, even when no one is watching." ~ *C.S. Lewis*

THE RIGHT THING

THE FEDEX CLERK, retired Army Sergeant Major Aubrey, noticed something fishy going on and when an old Army Sergeant Major noticed a shady deal, he didn't ignore it—retired or not. He couldn't let well-marked CLASSIFIED files go unchallenged.

"So, I discreetly walked to a back office to find a desk phone. But, by the time I got back, he skedaddled."

"He ran?" the investigating officer asked.

"Yep, he *cut-n-run* like a jack rabbit. I just knew something was up. Nobody brings classified papers into a FedEx—and that guy was sweat'n pretty bad too. I wouldn't have thought twice about it, except it was *32* degrees outside and he wasn't even wearing a coat. Oh, and I nearly forgot—the papers looked like they were on some type of government letterhead with words marked out, but it still had all of the classification designations."

"What do you mean?"

"Well, if it's still the same as when I was in the Army, you put those classification designations in a parentheses before each sentence: (U) for Unclassified, (C) for Confidential, (S) for Secret, and so forth."

"Yes sir, it's still the same."

"That rascal—he was hand'n me secret information. It coulda got me in a bunch of trouble, too."

"You did the right thing contacting us."

"I knew I had to do something, sir."

"Well, getting your report and the video footage will be a lot of help, sir." The Sergeant Major stood tall and smiled a proud smile under his Vietnam Veteran hat, when the Department of Justice agents said, "You're a great American."

The agents from DOJ thanked SGM Aubrey, and then they were on their way. They not only got the information, but the actual surveillance camera footage. They had him dead to rights. Back at the agency they watch the tape. Dr. Lui prepared to mail the classified material to the Chinese Foreign Intelligence Service and then quickly fled after being engaged by the FedEx clerk.

"Always let your conscience be your guide." ~ *Pinocchio*

PINOCCHIO

DR. STARR WORE many hats, and continued to teach his series of classes, as the *Mind-Body Problem* research projects continued. Today, the class he taught concerned the sentient implications regarding Pinocchio.

"Even if you tracked evolution back to some primordial ancestor, then you've still got the *BIG* scientific and philosophical questions of how consciousness emerged. Not to mention—where did the primordial soup come from in the first place, with its solution rich with organic compounds? I've often wondered how that could be the originating cause for life, meaning, purpose, and consciousness. How could the mind be responsible for everything that really *matters*, if it was a biological accident?" he asked. "If it is responsible, then truly nothing ultimately *matters* at all. Morality is what we decide it is." The students listened intently as he taught.

"The trouble is that if nature is all that exists, then everything would be determined through the laws of nature and the things it causes. All our thoughts and beliefs would be caused and determined by biophysical forces, not something else, like a soul." That peaked everyone's interest.

"If that's the case you're not *really* thinking at all. You're just a puppet being manipulated by your genes and natural selection with no hope of ever becoming a *real boy* like Pinocchio, who was rumored to utter self-determined phrases like, 'How ridiculous I was when I was a puppet! And how glad I am that I have become a well-behaved little boy!'"

He looked around the room. "Who put such personal and self-aware thoughts in Pinocchio's mind? Was there a conscious pine *Jiminy Cricket* residue seeping through his head that died when he was thrown into the fire or was Geppetto's design animated by a higher power? Was it a *matter* of workshop wishful thinking that manifested the *real boy* attributes in Pinocchio— which made him brave, truthful, and conscious?"

Dr. Starr didn't tell them what to think, but the class listened and understood the cause and effect analogies.

CHAPTER ONE HUNDRED TWENTY-SIX

Dorothy: How can you talk if you haven't got a brain?
Scarecrow: I don't know…but some people without brains do an awful lot of talking…don't they? ~ *Wizard of Oz*

FOLLOW THE YELLOW BRICK ROAD

DOCTOR FEINBURG PUT in her time teaching as well. She played a Wizard of Oz video clip to begin the lesson. *"I could while away the hours, conferrin' with the flowers. Consultin' with the rain. And my head I'd be scratchin' while my thoughts were busy hatchin', if I only had a brain."* All of her lessons were related to the brain, so what better person to highlight it than the scarecrow, who needed one?

Dr. Peggy Feinberg worked as a counselor in private practice and now as a subcontractor with ITL. Previously, she held important jobs like Director of the Neuromodulation and Advance Therapies Clinic at Johns Hopkins. You might imagine that she would be a nerdy, scientific stuffed shirt, but *au contraire.* She was quite adept at entertaining her studious audience. All of her lectures started with the unexpected and kept you engaged with funny videos or interesting photos or unusual quotes or intriguing questions. She was very interactive and theatrical in her presentations, hence the *Wizard of Oz* video clip.

"Oh yes! He could sing, dance, laugh, and had fears like all of us. Yet he still *desired*— above all else, to have a brain. Since he didn't have a brain, but could already talk and was quite animated, we have got to ask the obvious question—where did his thoughts, desires, and emotion come from?" she asked.

"Maybe his thoughts were merely a residual effect of Dorothy's head injury? Let's just suppose, for a moment, that Dorothy suffered a fractured skull, and tore a blood vessel in her brain when the tornado struck. It slowly formed a clot, large enough to increase the pressure inside her skull. Dorothy became confused and saw—what do you know—*Munchkins*. Those were little people that no one else in Kansas could apparently see, but her. In her state of consciousness, she walked and talked and started feeling drowsy. Sleep overcame her while she was running through fields of poppies and couldn't fight it any longer. So, she laid down and went to sleep. But back here in the real world, they discovered that she had died." The students all expressed frowns of sadness at the thought of Dorothy dying.

"Not Dorothy," said one young student who feigned sadness. "She's gonna find the *Great and Mighty Oz*, get the ruby slippers, and go home." The class applauded—approving of the classic scenario.

"Now, don't look so sad, people. Before class is done, I shall reunite Dorothy with Auntie Em and Uncle Henry in Kansas or the Emerald City. For the time being, let's just say that she was somewhere over the rainbow. And perhaps, momentarily, the pressure inside Dorothy's skull compressed the brain, to the point that it eventually stopped working, nerves began to die, and she had a near death experience. What if she transitioned through a dream to a new level of consciousness?" she said. Clearly, Dr. Feinberg was thinking about the *Mind-Body Problem* with Steven.

"Now, is Dorothy having an NDE, Near Death Experience? She's having an experience that's for sure, but is it a veridical, *true* experience or is she still dreaming? Many in our scientific community have asserted that NDE's are merely hallucinations, caused by the misfiring of neurons in the brain. Perhaps the little chemical messengers, which we call neurotransmitters, are screwing with her thoughts too. That's one theory, but what if her experiences were real?" she asked rhetorically.

"There are many verified events and testimonies concerning NDEs, as well. So, let's say that Dorothy is brain-dead after an overdose of opium that she got from a dealer in Kansas or from sleeping in the poppy field too long. She's out of it. In her mind, she's lying in a beautiful field with Tin Man, Scarecrow, and the Cowardly Lion. Then, she's off on an adventure.

Suppose that she's brain-dead for nine minutes and is then miraculously resuscitated. When she regained consciousness, she remembered seeing Uncle Henry take cash out of his wallet and hide it. He hid it in a chest of drawers, behind a secret panel, that operated as their family safe. She apparently saw it while she was brain-dead, but after being resuscitated she told them exactly where the money was located. Now, mind you, nobody knew it, except Uncle Henry.

You see—Dorothy remembered something that happened in reality, whereas dreams or hallucinations refer to experiences that don't correspond with objective reality. Interestingly enough, there are many other recollections like this outside the *Land of Oz*. In our world." She was clearly thinking of Steven Scott. "There have been numerous NDEs that correspond with actual verified events. Things that really happened—so let's follow the road where it leads us."

"It is a capital mistake to theorize before you have all the evidence. It biases the judgment."
~ *Sherlock Holmes*

FORENSIC INVESTIGATION

IN COURT, DR. Lui initially denied taking part in the scheme to steal PSYCHONIX specs

from the ITL computers. But he later begrudgingly admitted to removing two pairs of

PSYCHONIX goggles, circuit board units, a microserver, and a massive amount of data. These

were all critical elements of the project. He also admitted to accessing the inner-office servers,

to transfer data from Dr. Kahn's smart phone to his and other personal systems. That didn't bode

well for Kahn's case. Agents pulled up slides, and demonstrated under oath how he had

airdropped files, and accessed other files remotely from his home computer—downloaded and

transferred to a portable hard drive that they found in his carry-on bag.

Dr. Lui changed his stories and defended his actions. He admitted that he had taken the ITL

hardware and files because he thought it would be useful to him on another *psychokinetic*

project, which he was testing at home. As for the files, he said, "I wanted to telework and study

the data in my own time."

After examining Dr. Lui's hard drive, the FBI and CIA digital forensic investigations team

uncovered Sensitive Compartmented Information (SCI) or special access programs (SAP) that

were a *Top Secret* add-on for security. The sensitivity was based upon a calculation of the damage to national security that the release of the PSYCHONIX information could cause. "It's highly problematic," one of the agents stated. "The information he had on him could only be transferred via secure electronic communication circuits, approved for secret or higher information. Also, *Top Secret* Receipts and Access Records were required to be filled out—and he had none."

The policies were clear: *Computers approved for processing classified information will not be connected to any unclassified network, USB, wireless, or Bluetooth enabled equipment— unless authorized.*

Investigations unveiled some interesting details. Many of the files were already being translated into Mandarin Chinese and categorized as *Lumni: QIGONG* specific projects. That, along with the fact that Dr. Lui purchased a one-way ticket to Beijing, was enough to solidly condemn him. When Federal agents intercepted Dr. Lui, at Dulles International Airport, they found two pairs of PSYCHONIX goggles in his possession. They also found a small box, with the words *Confidential* and *Proprietary* written on all sides. In it was a cellphone, USB, and the tiny proprietary PSYCHONIX MDSL-1 processor.

He claimed the smartphone was a gift for his ailing father, but it was actually a cleverly designed spy phone, given to him by Chinese Intelligence. Its surveillance software included a mobile tracker application, which recorded incoming and outgoing phone calls, SMS to send and receive short messages, and surrounding signals. It tracked GPS locations and the browser activity and messages from applications like *Whatsapp, Facebook, Viber, Skype* and *Line*.

The *Top Secret* contents in Dr. Lui's bags were essential to the *Mind-Body Problem* projects. Something that the press would never be privy to. After agents secured the equipment, DOJ lawyers redacted FOUO documents that described any aspect of the PSYCHONIX developments.

Dr. Lui was scheduled to be arraigned July 27, according to court documents. If found guilty, he could face 10 years in a U.S. Federal Prison, along with a $500,000 fine. Dr. Kahn, his accomplice had also been detained, and was under house-arrest, pending further investigation and charges.

Dr. Kahn really slipped up. Through his arrogance, and in his greed, he became careless about providing secret information to a Chinese spy. He willingly gave Dr. Lui the necessary info, and access to everything he needed at ITL, but negligently left an unsecured trail of phone and text messages. It was in writing. He whined endlessly to the Chinese about the amount of money that he was being paid, and the huge risk he was taking. The forensic team uncovered their entire deleted chat history.

"Your objective is easy. Upload the files to your phone—I'll get them from you wirelessly on the conference table," read one email from Dr. Lui,

"My object is to get well paid," Dr. Khan said.

"You deliver and I'll deliver."

They became much too bold with their conversations, phone calls, and emails.

"At this point all the risk is on me. Make it worth it for me. Deposit my money today," Dr. Kahn demanded.

In another email, "This system sucks. It's too confusing," Kahn wrote.

"Look, that is your concern. I've put in a transposition code encryption in order for you to read them," Dr. Lui texted.

"I don't understand."

"You're paid to deliver," Dr. Lui texted.

Court documents revealed page after page of email and text communication. On one of the pages, it specifically spelled out that Dr. Kahn had agreed to provide research and equipment in exchange for $1.5 million in cash and a two-story penthouse in one of Baltimore's waterfront high-rise condominium towers.

CHAPTER ONE HUNDRED TWENTY-EIGHT

"The question isn't how to get cured, but how to live."
~ *Joseph Conrad*

RECOVERY

STEVEN SCOTT FELT clearheaded and calm when he returned from his death or Near Death Experience (NDE). He couldn't explain it but he was freed up from bad dreams and frightening thoughts from the past. His anxiety had settled down—and there was no desire to run.

"Can PTSD be cured?" he asked his brother Mark.

"No, like most mental illnesses, it's not strictly curable."

"No—."

"No, it's a chronic biological illness…that usually requires a lifetime of therapy and medication, but it's not a cure…"

"But?"

"But many people lead healthy and fulfilling lives, and can recover significantly, if they pursue treatment and manage it with medication, self-help strategies, and supportive therapies. The meds that you're taking now should be relieving your symptoms, so that may be the best you can hope for."

"I think I'm better."

"Why?"

"I don't know. I guess I knew it—the moment Jesus touched me, I felt different. I think He healed me. You saw it too Mark. You said that my body radiated beams of light when He touched me."

"Yeah, that was spectacular!"

"I believe that was the moment it happened."

"Okay—it's possible Steven, but we still have to be cautious—and avoid any relapses. You're doing well now, but that doesn't mean you're completely healed."

"But I am."

"You've been through a lot, big brother—so let's take it one step at a time."

"I know, but there's something else."

"Okay—."

"I knew exactly *what* you were going to say, prior to you saying it."

"Yeah, so what am I thinking now?"

"Well, you're first thought was *that's nuts*—and secondly, you're gonna ask me to move in with you while we figure this out."

"That's—astonishing! That's exactly what I was thinking."

"I know. So, when do you want to run the test?"

"I didn't say anything about tests."

"But you were thinking about it, right?"

"Steven, don't mention this to anyone!

"—and you want me to move in with you as soon as possible.

"Copy!"

"I'm open to that, but we've got to get packed up and drive to Richlands for Christmas. And first, I'd like to stop off in Bluefield to do some Christmas shopping with Vito before spending time with our Southern friends. I was thinking we could all drive together."

"I knew that," Mark said, and they both smiled.

CHAPTER ONE HUNDRED TWENTY-NINE

"It's easy to fool the eye, but it's hard to fool the heart."
~*Al Pacino*

SCARED

AT THIS POINT, prosecutors said that Dr. Gus Kahn was desperate, and ultimately just panicked. Toward the tail end of his transactions with Dr. Lui Wei, he feared that the CIA and FBI were onto him. It was an appropriate fear. Prosecutors also said that Kahn had formulated a thorough cover story and reached out to the CIA on his own. He told them that he thought he was being *recruited by Chinese spies*. And he sold it well.

"I believe they were looking for some high level of U.S. government secrets. They even mailed me a special phone for transferring documents. I can bring it in to be examined if you like."

Dr. Kahn was a smart man trying to cover his trail, but apparently, he didn't understand the intricacies of digital forensics. He thought that the damning personal communication data on his phone and computers had been wiped clean, but he wasn't quite thorough enough. FBI and CIA statements later revealed that Dr. Kahn had indeed covered up and lied multiple times. The digital forensic examiner detailed exactly how the phone worked, and that it had been used often to airdrop classified documents to Dr. Lui. It time-stamped each and every delivery, which was used as evidence in court. The signatures precisely matched Dr. Kahn's phone and computer downloads.

Late the next evening, the FBI entered Dr. Kahn's home with an arrest warrant and turned the place inside-out. Upon entry, they immediately found more damning evidence. Taped to the underside of his junk drawer, agents discovered and secured an SD card wrapped in a small piece of tinfoil. On it, he had stored seven classified documents, secret, and top secret, and instructions directly related to the *Mind-Body Problem* and PSYCHONIX projects. It was identical to the files that Dr. Lui had stored on his personal hard drive, and the SD card that he had attempted to mail at FedEx last March.

The agents tore through Dr. Kahn's home, from top-to-bottom, looking for any other duplicate files, malware, or surveillance equipment. It looked like a hurricane had blown through his house. The only other thing that they found in their thorough search was a kicked over ladder lying on the floor of his garage…and Dr. Kahn swinging by his neck above it—dead.

There are so many more great reasons for why I believe in God now. Especially since I've witnessed the miracle of my own brother's journey to Heaven, and his miraculous healing. To me, the mere fact that we can do mathematics is evidence of God, and that there is a universe of structure and discovery. That was the renaissance impetus for science in the first place, right? C.S. Lewis said it best, "Men became scientific because they expected law in nature, and they expected law in nature because they believed in a Legislator."

It seems so basic to say it takes intelligence to create information—our life and world is nothing but a vast amount of coded information *dancing to our DNA*. The brain itself is a machine, and machines, as we know them, don't create abstract intelligence. They record. Compile. Search. Compare. Pass on. Machines don't enjoy the art of cooking, making culinary decisions based on sight, taste, or smell. I knew it as a child. Machines can't give you authentic experiences, bonds, adventures. Machines don't function on the idea of something being true or not—it's purely input and output. Machines have no personal temperament that aspires to artistry or creativity. Machines don't have empathy. They don't have the capacity to express genuine human interest and care. Feelings. That requires a personal soul.

I like to think of myself, as a learned man of science, in the order of a James Tour or Francis Collins, with an innovative mind that continues to test the boundaries of science. Catch a glimpse of eternity and see what it does for you.

CHAPTER ONE HUNDRED THIRTY

"Sometimes you will never know the value of a moment
until it becomes a memory." ~ *Dr. Seuss*

BLUEFIELD VISIT

THE TOWN OF Bluefield had a festive atmosphere and Christmas music filled the air, as shoppers scurried about in the middle of downtown. There was something for everyone: ice skating, live music, elves, food, Santa, and more. As the holiday season moved into full swing, all the Bluefieldians were in high spirits, including Steven Scott, Mark, and Peggy, who were visiting Steven's son, Vito. They would make it a day of last minute shopping before they headed down to Richlands.

When they met at Vito's apartment, there was nothing to say that hadn't already been said. They all embraced and held each other tight.

"I miss her," Vito cried. "It's our first Christmas without Mom."

"Yeah, I do too, but she's okay—better than okay," he said, patting his son gently on the back. "She's in the arms of Jesus."

He nodded. "I know."

But he didn't know that his dad had seen her recently. Steven couldn't talk about that part of the project yet, and Mark wasn't going to mention it. It had to remain classified.

590

Despite the cold weather conditions, they smiled and hummed old Christmas songs, as they completed their shopping and caught up with each other. Once done with their shopping list, they looked for a place to eat.

"What's good to eat around here?" Steven asked.

"Well, in this neck of the woods, as they say, *Savory Flavors* has great barbecue."

"You've eaten there?" Mark asked.

"Yep—I know the owner, Kathy Kestner. She calls it *smokin' hot, smokin' good* barbecue—and it is."

Vito drove them to Virginia Avenue, and they had a real treat. Each of them looked oh-so satisfied coming out of the restaurant.

"Man, I'm not gonna eat for another week," Vito said, patting his belly.

"I'm not sure where I put that banana pudding," Steven said, also rubbing his stomach.

"*Oh my*, we better save room for all the home cooking we'll get in Richlands," Peggy said.

"No worries—that's just a warmup," Vito smiled. Aside from working on his feet as a nurse all day, he was a strong Italian American boy, who worked out in the gym, a lot, and had a huge appetite. "Speaking of our visit—I mostly got a bunch of Christmas cards and gift cards to give them. You think that's okay?"

"Sure, they'll love it—but don't worry about it," Steven said. "They're a special family and want us to relax. Like us, they've been through a lot this year."

"Right," Peggy said.

"I had a special Christmas ornament made for Chelsea."

"The little seven year old?" Mark asked.

"Yeah."

He pulled out a small box and showed them the delicate contents. On the white crystal ball was an engraved angel, with a *red feather* in her hair. "The feather represents strength, vitality, good fortune, and good health—something we all need this year."

CHAPTER ONE HUNDRED THIRTY-ONE

"The best of all gifts around any Christmas tree is the presence of family all wrapped in each other." ~ *Burton Hills*

314 GROVE STREET

IT WAS CHRISTMAS EVE, and the Annapolis clan celebrated the joyous occasion with the Croxon and Keene families—cousins and all. They were gathered at *314 Grove Street,* in the Dalton Edition. Everyone busily prepared for the big feast. There was a glorious scent of southern food wafting from the kitchen, just a few feet away. Aromas that instantaneously caused one's mouth to salivate in anticipation, *old-fashioned Stack and apple butter cakes, cooked strawberries, fried eggs, sausage, and fried potatoes.*

Steven sat in an easy chair, in the living room. "Man, that smells good," as he sniffed the air. "Not our typical fare in Washington State, is it, guys?"

Mark and Vito nodded.

"What better way to celebrate the birth of Christ, than with a celebratory country breakfast?" Maggie Croxon asked. She noticed Peggy's coffee cup was empty and quickly gave her a refill. It was country hospitality at its finest. She busily assembled the feast and enjoyed every minute of it—even as she chased away a few trespassers who were stealing morsels as they were being prepared or cooling on a pan.

"I can't argue with that," Steven said to Maggie.

The Christmas family reunion was all coming together with homemade butterscotch, chocolate, and pumpkin pies. "Mmm, this one's my favorite—buckeyes!" Chelsea said. Buckeyes were chocolate covered peanut butter balls, like a round *Reece's Cup*, but with coconut, and sometimes a few chopped-up walnuts added in. She looked around, as though she had made an amazing new discovery, then made her move. She gleefully smiled, and her little hand snatched a small handful from a large glass Christmas plate teetering on the edge of the kitchen bar.

"Now, let's save some for later," Mom-Maw Maggie said. She wasn't saying it in a scolding tone. This was the time of the year to let the goodies flow, and she was overjoyed that they were in such high demand.

"Well, I only want to test them," Chelsea repeated the clever words that she had heard her daddy say earlier.

Steven Scott reached his arm around Chelsea and sneakily popped one in his mouth. "That one's mine. You know testing was ALWAYS a tradition at my home too," he said with mock seriousness.

Just then, they all heard the squeaky shocks and revving of an old green, *Ford 100* truck engine that strained to pick up sufficient speed. It had climbed the curvy, pothole-riddled, gravel driveway of *314 Grove Street* so often that it had nearly developed its own cruise control. John's grandparents had just returned from a last minute Christmas errand, and didn't hesitate once as they bounced and creaked and maneuvered the rusty old truck into place. The loose play of the steering wheel made Pop-Paw look like he had one hand at the helm of an old battleship, preparing to dock.

You could hear it coming. It rocked and bounded up the access road, slinging gravel, as it elbowed to the right, puffed a final plume of exhaust, and gently coasted into a wide brick-paver-driveway, at the back of the house. That was where the main family entrance was located. One could easily squeeze eight vehicles in that driveway, if needed. Provided that no one needed to leave soon—and no one did.

It was Christmas Eve so, of course, everyone was staying. They would all sleep soundly, assigned to beds, couches, or whatever room there was to spread blankets, pillows, and sleeping bags. Being together was the primary consideration. So, you doubled-up, tripled-up, and made do. You slept where there was room to lay your head, until Santa Claus came.

Younger folks, who could walk up to the house without much effort, parked along *Grove Street*, at the bottom of the steep driveway. As they parked and got out, everyone who approached, peered up at the bay window, and saw the festive, retro silver Christmas tree sparkling through the colonial wood grilles. It was highlighted with multicolored strands of Christmas lights and frosted snow spray in the shape of snowmen, snowflakes, and Santa.

Chelsea stood gazing out the window, and watched for all the new arrivals, as she ate her buckeyes and cookies. Cousins, Aunts, and Uncles that were coming up the drive waved back at her and smiled. It was good to be home for Christmas.

CHAPTER ONE HUNDRED THIRTY-TWO

"When they saw the star they rejoiced exceedingly with great joy." ~ *Matthew 2:10*

PHONE HOME

HAVING APPLE CIDER, in the foyer of the Croxon's home church, had become a long-standing Christmas Day tradition. Prior to the evening service, everyone gathered and fellowshipped, as worshipful songs were played, and video loops of snow were displayed on two large side screens in the auditorium. They also showed various pictures and videos, from Christmas celebrations around the world; the U.S., Europe, Asia, Africa, or wherever saints gathered to celebrate the birth of Christ.

Centered above the auditorium stage, was the word HOPE, spelled out in large white cutout letters. The **O** in the word H**O**PE was in the shape of the *Star of Bethlehem,* with a long tail. Five minutes prior to the main service, *Three Wise Men* directed everyone to *follow the star*— pointing them toward the sanctuary and seats with their staffs. The house lights were dimmed, and soft music wafted from a six-piece orchestra, positioned on the balcony. On cue, the worship leader greeted and welcomed everyone to the Calvary Baptist Christmas Service. The house lights were turned off, and spotlights directed at three singers and two narrators who guided the service.

The congregation sang a large variety of their favorites, as the program began: *Hark The Herald Angels Sing, Joy To The World, O Holy Night, Mary Did You Know?, Angels We Have Heard On High, O Come All Ye Faithful, The First Noel, and Silent Night.*

There were also a variety of solos sprinkled throughout the program, with various narrators, who entered the spotlight, and read from the Scripture (Luke 2:1-7), as the children reenacted the story:

In those days, Caesar Augustus issued a decree that a census should be taken of the entire Roman world. And everyone went to his own town to register. So, Joseph also went up from the town of Nazareth in Galilee to Judea, to Bethlehem the town of David, because he belonged to the house and line of David. He went there to register with Mary, who was pledged to be married to him and was expecting a child. While they were there, the time came for the baby to be born, and she gave birth to her firstborn, a son. She wrapped Him in cloths and placed Him in a manger, because there was no room for them in the inn.

And there were shepherds living out in the fields nearby, keeping watch over their flocks at night. An angel of the Lord appeared to them, and the glory of the Lord shone around them, and they were terrified. But the angel said to them, "Do not be afraid. I bring you good news of great joy that will be for all the people. Today in the town of David a Savior has been born to you; He is Christ the Lord. This will be a sign to you: You will find a baby wrapped in cloths and lying in a manger. Suddenly a great company of the heavenly host appeared with the angel, praising God and saying, Glory to God in the highest, and on earth peace to men on whom his favor rests.

When the angels had left them and gone into heaven, the shepherds said to one another, "Let's go to Bethlehem and see this thing that has happened, which the Lord has told us about. So, they hurried off and found Mary and Joseph, and the baby, who was lying in the manger. When they had seen Him, they spread the word concerning what had been told them about this child, and all who heard it were amazed at what the shepherds said to them. But Mary treasured up all these things and pondered them in her heart. The shepherds returned, glorifying and praising God for all the things they had heard and seen, which were just as they had been told."

Toward the end of the narration, the *Three Wise Men* approached—each held a candle. They looked around, and slowly strolled down the aisles, in search of the baby Jesus. As they made their way toward the center-stage manger, each Wise Man lit someone's candle at the end of a row. That person, in turn, lit the candle of the person beside them. The narrator continued to read, as the auditorium lit up with a sea of lights.

"After Jesus was born in Bethlehem...Magi from the east came to Jerusalem and asked, where is the One who has been born king of the Jews? We saw His star in the east and have come to worship Him. When King Herod heard this, he was disturbed. Then Herod called the Magi secretly and found out from them the exact time the star had appeared. He sent them to Bethlehem and said, "Go and make a careful search for the Child. As soon as you find Him, report to me, so that I too may go and worship Him. After they had heard the king, they went on their way, and the star they had seen in the east went ahead of them until it stopped over the place where the child was. When they saw the star, they were overjoyed. On coming to the house, they saw the child with his mother Mary, and they bowed down and worshiped Him. Then they opened their treasures and presented Him with gifts of gold and of frankincense and of myrrh."

Steven, Mark, Peggy, and Vito hadn't enjoyed a Christmas program like this in many years. It wasn't a perfect Christmas, but they were with family and friends. Steven missed Marlina, and his daughter Donna was still deployed to Afghanistan, so how could it really be perfect? Donna couldn't make it home this year, but he got a nice Christmas card and pictures. That would have to do.

Soldiers, Sailors, Airmen, and Marines have always written letters home in their spare moments, sometimes outside the wire, on the front lines, or from the confines of their barracks. Letters received from family and friends were also vital to their morale and kept them connected to the home that they loved, and temporarily left behind. Nowadays, military service members use email, cellphones, or other video chat apps to chat or stream live. Operational Security or OPSEC was still paramount and obvious in their choice of words. It was important that they didn't disclose too much information that could be useful to the enemy. Even small details about family, friends, where they were, and what they were doing could be pieced together.

At the conclusion of tonight's wonderful Christmas service, the pastor got up and said, "Before we pray and head home to celebrate the birth of Christ and polish off our leftovers—we have one more delightful surprise. As you know, we're streaming our Christmas service on Facebook. It allows our *shut-ins* and deployed military members an opportunity to celebrate with us, wherever they are in the world. Tonight, one of them would like to speak to you. It's a special gift from *Lt. Donna Scott*, serving in Afghanistan. A special message for her father Steven Scott and family visiting with us tonight.

Steven looked up in surprise toward Vito. He shrugged his shoulders. They were dumbstruck, as the live video was projected and played out on two large video screens in the church auditorium.

Donna waved at the camera. "Hello and Merry Christmas, Daddy—and my brother Vito!" She didn't know that Mark was there, and didn't know Peggy at all. "First let me say that I'm okay…and I hope that you're not alarmed to see me speaking to you from a hospital bed."

Steven stressfully pursed his lips and narrowed his eyes.

"But I've had a rough week—to say the least," she smiled. "It seems that a poorly aimed Taliban rocket got a little too close to my hut. Happy Holidays, right?"

Steven stood up from the church pew—and gripped the seat in front of him. He couldn't get to her, but instinctively felt a need to protect his little girl, as she told her story.

"A few days ago, I was getting ready for bed, when I heard some pops—and a shrill noise—and suddenly something crashed through one of my walls, and out the other side. That's all I remembered—and then I woke up here in the Landstuhl Regional Medical Center, in Germany." The camera panned and zoomed out, to show others in the room. "These are the folks looking out for me now and they're doing a great job."

Steven slowly sat back down. Mark and Peggy patted him on the back.

"They said that there was a huge explosion of flames that roared through my quarters and caused casualties in a few buildings down from mine." Her lips quivered and she teared up. Steven did too. "I can't talk about them, since not all the families have been notified. But let's just say—I was the lucky one. Actually, more than lucky. I had an angel Soldier rush to my rescue, and she stayed by my side. Say hi, Nia."

Steven raised his hand to wave, even though she couldn't see him.

Nia leaned toward Donna and waved at the camera. "Hello, Colonel Scott. Your daughter is amazingly strong...so worry about anything." She gave Donna a little squeeze on the shoulder and a thumbs-up to the camera.

"She's the one who pulled me out, Dad."

Steven mouthed the words *thank you.*

"I'm calling to say *Merry Christmas* to everyone, but also because General Mary Hodge is here, and about to present me the Purple Heart.

Steven covered his mouth with the palm of his hand, as more tears streamed down his cheek.

"I wanted you to see it first, Daddy."

They paused and the camera operator positioned himself to get her and the General framed in the shot. "Attention to orders," an Airman shouted. It was how the military began an awards ceremony. Everyone in the clinic stood at attention, and every service member, in the church, whoever wore a uniform stood up. Everyone else followed.

The Airman then read off her *Purple Heart* citation, as others stood at attention, and the medal was pinned to her hospital gown. Donna couldn't stand up yet and her right arm was damaged from the explosion. That made rendering a left-handed salute acceptable. The General returned the salute and dropped military protocol by giving her a gentle hug.

Everyone, on the ground in Afghanistan and in the church applauded as Donna looked back at the camera and said, "As Nana used to say—*I love, love, love you,* and can't wait to get back home. You're my hero daddy!"

He stood up and mouthed back, *you're my hero sweetie.*

"I'll be home soon." She blew him a kiss at the camera. "Merry Christmas!"

He blew her a kiss back. He missed her and Marlina with every ounce of his aching heart. Indescribably, he sensed that Marlina had blown them both a *kiss from heaven.* And indeed, she had, as she watched from the base of Angel Falls. He looked up, smiled, and blew her a kiss too.

The video ended and the church Christmas images reappeared on the auditorium screens. Steven wiped his one good eye and looked over at the Croxon family. "Thanks John. I can't begin to tell you how incredibly special that was to me. How in the world—?"

"No thanks necessary. I got the message about Donna from my office in D.C. late last night—and I knew that we had to do this."

The pastor gave some final thoughts, prayed, and invited everyone to close the service in song. "Stand with me, as we sing, *We Wish You A Merry Christmas*."

CHAPTER ONE HUNDRED THIRTY-THREE

"One of the best ways to have a little Heaven in our home is to have someone you love in Heaven." *~ Unknown*

HOME

STEVEN SCOTT SELDOM spoke of his experiences in heaven, unless of course someone asked him about it. He knew how he would've reacted to that kind of incredible information. *You did what? You went to heaven, saw angels, and spoke to Jesus—oh, okay, I'm sure you did.* There were some strong cessationists that took issue, but most were open to God still having the power to do all things—and move in ways that seemed strange to us.

Most people would probably nod politely, in disbelief, while they looked for a man in a white coat with a giant butterfly net, and a syringe filled with tranquilizers, to chase the crazy person down. *Been there and bought the t-shirt,* Steven thought. Or they might sympathetically expect something so outlandish from a guy—who had cracked. Someone grieving over the death of his wife—not to mention his PTSD issues. *Poor guy!*

But none of that *mattered* to Steven any longer—because he knew his experiences were true. He had died and gone to Heaven. It wasn't an imaginative story he made up or read in a book. It had strengthened his faith, evangelism, and desire to read the Bible more. In the greatest sense, he had renewed his mind. He was healed from PTSD and his senses had opened up—or *loosed-up* as Marlina said. Life became more meaningful: art, music, history, relationships, and conversations with strangers—everything evoked a relationship with God and eternity. Throughout his life, he had heard people mock those *overly zealous, know-it-all, born again Christians*—and there were elements of truth to it. Christians could be annoying, but they certainly hadn't corned the market. Steven, however, remained respectful and courteous and patient and kind. If anything, he had evolved into a combination of C.S. Lewis, Billy Graham and the Pope in his enthusiasm and spirit. It was impossible for his experiences not to spill over into everything he did in life. Marlina would be proud.

Mark still asked Steven not to mention his increased ability to anyone for now. If it were discovered, who knew what might happen? They would move forward on their own terms.

"It could become a real circus show for you. The government would probably lock you up and classify you *Sensitive Compartmented Information,* just like the PSYCHONIX project and file you away somewhere in the District of Columbia…so for now, we've got to keep it close hold."

"So, what do you want to do?"

"Well, I've got some ideas—and so does Senator Croxon. I just got off the phone with him."

Steven Nodded. John had taken him aside while they were in Richlands and had a lengthy discussion about the PSYCHONIX project. He knew a great deal, but NSI hadn't shared everything—and NSI couldn't share what ITL hadn't revealed.

"As you know, he's Chairman of the Senate Intel Committee."

"Okay, so I can just about guess."

"He's a powerful and influential man and wants to meet with us in private about the project."

"Why?"

"He said that it would be in your best interest."

Steven nodded again. They had become close friends with Senator John Croxon and he understood the risk, dangers, and political games more than most. He would trust his advice.

"We'll talk it over, but I'm already sensing that we might have to dissolve the PSYCHONIX project and consider other options.".".

"Like?"

"I don't know," Mark said. "I'm going to talk it over in our next meeting and, but I'm open to suggestions. I heard your spiritual conversation, in the *Amaranth,* about being on assignment—what are your thoughts?"

"I'd like to serve—maybe whip up an organization that's a force for good."

"I'd like that."

"You think we're positioned well enough for it?" It was an unspoken question about finances and facilities. The *good idea fairy* could fly around all day making suggestions, but someone had to back the plans.

"No, but we could be. I'm interested in hearing what the Senator has to say. Maybe we'll protect the universe, like we did as kids," Mark said with a wink."

"Cool—it's kinda like I'm a *superhero* anyways, right?" he lifted his eyepatch and flashed his activated PSYCHONIX eye. It illuminated with a red digital swirl and then he re-covered it with the patch.

"Well that trumps being Emperor—I think." He jokingly referenced their childhood argument of figuring out who was in charge.

"Yeah, I can see it now," Steven proclaimed, "Faster than an apologist, more powerful than a concluding argument, and able to leap tall minds in a single bound—it's PSYCHONIX MAN!"

"Let's not get carried away."

CHAPTER ONE HUNDRED THIRTY-FOUR

"A spirit with a vision is a dream with a mission."
~ Neil Peart

NEW MISSION

STEVEN SCOTT LIVED with his brother Mark until he could find a place nearby and they could develop a solid plan forward for the use of PSYCHONIX. He looked for an apartment in downtown Annapolis, Maryland, so he could walk to the stores, restaurants, and water. Even though there had been a shooting involving his little friend Chelsea, it was still a reasonably safe place to live. It also gave him access to the Naval Academy, Andrews Air Force Base, and Ft. Meade. It was a great area for military retirees with an easy drive to Baltimore, DC, and Virginia.

For all intents and purposes, Steven had resumed a normal life with Mark's help. But he continued to monitor and exercise his profound abilities. For the next year he stayed under the watchful eye of his brother and developed ideas of how to best use it. He wondered if he could use his knowledge to protect others. In the interim, he also traveled, and supported Mark and Bobby as they spoke on college campuses and sold their new book: *Mind Over Matter*.

The ever-increasing ability that Steven Scott had was strangely comforting to himself and others. He not only felt an exceptionally strong connection to those he was near, but also to those that he thought about and interceded for. The one most surprising and miraculous aspect of all was his prescient connection to Marlina, whenever she gazed into *Angel Falls*.

Mark filed a lengthy report for the *NOUS* Secret Service Agents. He told them everything that the U.S Government needed to know: *The PSYCHONIX project hit a dead-end and stalled.* ITL would terminate the study, delete the files, and dissolve the team. He didn't have to lie with top cover coming from the Chairman of the Senate Intel Committee. What a great friend Senator Croxon had turned out to be. He spearheaded the effort and coded PSYCHONIX in such a canny way that it made *Cicada 3301* and *Liber Primus* look like child's play.

The report concluded: *There is nothing else to do or to report on the matter.*

The remainder of the paperwork would be reclassified, redacted, and buried deep within the political catacombs of Washington, D.C.

As far as the government was concerned, the *MDSL-1* processor had picked up stray audio signals from random local transmissions and it was really nothing more than an overpriced walkie-talkie. *It's a waste of government money*, Senator Croxon briefed to the committee. A few more inquiries and due-diligence interviews happened over subsequent months, but interest rapidly dwindled.

For all intents and purposes, the PSYCHONIX project was now a free agent for the rich and powerful. Except that very few knew—or would ever find out about it. As a U.S. Senator, John Croxon was neither rich nor exceptionally powerful, but he knew and understood the power of the research into *psychological bionics*. He could have never supported such an expensive undertaking on his meager six-figure, government salary alone. But as a successful philanthropist and a former corporate executive with multiple offshore accounts, he was independently worth a whole lot more. He also had a sizable portfolio with a financial stake in various manufacturing and biotechnology companies—some estimated upwards of $65 billion.

Although they didn't talk about money, specifically—that was the jist of the conversation between him and Mark Starr when they met. He would like to become a silent investor for the PSYCHONIX project. They talked it over in great detail and he was quite interested for three reasons: it was a sound investment, it would be a force for good in the world, and his good friend Steve Scott was currently the bearer of the technology.

"It could fail," Mark honestly admitted.

"Nothing's foolproof," Senator Croxon replied. "But at least I'll have the satisfaction of knowing we tried."

And there were some failures, Mark thought.

Ill-fated circumstances left Todd Lopez and Dr. Gus Kahn dead, but there was nothing that Mark could've done about those situations. It saddened him, but he now had other serious concerns. There were four other witnesses that had seen Steven Scott transition, including Peggy. He wasn't worried about her. The others might be a challenge, but he believed that he could recruit them. He was right and it proved to be a good risk. When Mark approached Brad, Sabrina, and Stanley with an offer, they overwhelmingly embraced the idea of continuing their work on the PSYCHONIX project. None of them were religious, but their beliefs changed the moment they witnessed Steven's NDE journey. It had even caused Dr. Kahn to question the reality that he kept bumping into.

The group was still transitioning but fully on-board and pumped about their innovative new mission. They believed that their game-changing projects could fuel cultural, educational, and spiritual changes like the world had never seen before.

"I like the name you came up for our new organization," Steven offered.

"I never told you the name."

"I still like it," he said. He smiled and walked over to one of Mark's dry-erase boards and wrote the words: **PSYCHONIX SOULUTIONS**.

CHAPTER ONE HUNDRED THIRTY-FIVE

"Somewhere, something incredible is waiting to be known." ~ *Carl Sagan*

JULY 11, 2025

FORTY-SEVEN YEAR OLD Steven Scott still pretended that he was living in the 24th century, whenever he watched the fictional Federation starship *USS Voyager* stranded in the Delta Quadrant, far from the rest of the Federation. He and his stepbrother Mark watched a couple short YouTube clips of their favorite episodes on an Apple iPad Pro 12.9-inch screens, as they barbecued on the back deck of Mark and Peggy's new riparian waterfront home. It was located in Whitehall Creek—close to Steven and a short boat ride to downtown Annapolis.

I died, and there was nothing. There was no one there. No Forest, Neelix said in an episode that dealt with his death, resurrection, and crisis of faith.

Even with the exceptional water views, Steven was still glued to the tiny screen, as Mark fired up the grill and tossed him a Coke. "Hey, it's like you read my mind."

In the distance were two young boys assembling a camouflage dome tent with their dad. It was good to see the father involved in their life. The mom lounged on their boat pier and nursed her baby. He would be brought up well too. *That was what a real family looked like,* Mark thought, as he flipped burgers.

Steven had his good, or rather natural, eye peeled on the computer screen, watching a rerun. In this episode, the viewer learned Neelix had been taught that *The Great Forest* was the afterlife, and that his ancestors would be there waiting for him by the Guiding Tree. *I took great comfort in knowing that we'd all be together again one day—but, it's not true!* Distressed that he hadn't perceived the afterlife while he was dead, Neelix began to question all of his religious beliefs.

Don't throw away a lifetime of faith because of one anomalous incident, First Officer Chakotay said, *Death is still the greatest mystery there is.*

I was there. I experienced it. There was nothing.

This had become one of Mark's favorite episodes, because it dealt with the apparent conflict between religion and science. In this scene, Neelix was killed while participating in an away mission—however, he was revived by the crew after having been dead for 18 hours, 49 minutes, and 13 seconds. Chakotay served as a counterpoint to his perspective and helped him embark on a spiritual vision quest. He encouraged Neelix not to abandon all faith.

You're being called back to your life again, Neelix. Don't turn your back on it. We're your family now.

It's not enough!

A family member in Neelix's vision quest seemed to communicate directly to him, and then crumbled to dust: *Life is irrelevant—you know what you have to do.* The entire experience had seriously challenged his religious faith. It convinced him that his existence was meaningless, and that life had no purpose—so, he decided to commit suicide.

"Isn't it crazy that he was going to kill himself over a vision?" Mark asked.

"Yeah, it could have just been some bad lasagna," Steven replied. "Why would he put so much stock in something like that?"

"How did he experience nothing?" Mark shook his head.

"I know. If it wasn't real, then it didn't matter, and if it was real, then there was someone communicating with him, right?"

"Right. So, how did that person communicate, if they didn't exist and why would you think their words mattered?"

Steven nodded.

In the end, Neelix found his life's purpose in being a cherished member of the crew and with the love and affection of a little girl who needed him to tuck her in and chase away an imagined monster. When she asked him whether or not the monster was in the replicator and under her bed, he said, *yes, but I chased him away.*

"The monster seems like it symbolized being frozen by our fears," Mark said. He peeked at the screen, but mostly kept an eye on the grill. "You know—the idea of choosing to enjoy your life, instead of running from your problems."

"Wow, you're deep."

"Shut up," Mark gave him a brotherly punch on the shoulder.

"It appears that Neelix's beliefs were seriously challenged, because he hadn't perceived an afterlife while he was dead," Steven said.

"But he perceived there was nothing," they bounced the conversation back and forth like an apologetics volleyball.

Steven fingered his goatee. "Hmm, who could that be?

"They left it out."

"That's Hollywood for you," Steven said. "It's a fun script but Gene Roddenberry was a humanist."

"Right. But how could you discover the universe, and not believe in God?"

Steven nodded. "Oh, hey—remember this one?" He hit play. It was the conclusion to the Measure of a Man episode.

"There are still many human emotions I do not fully comprehend: anger, revenge, jealousy. But I am not mystified by the desire to be loved, or the need for friendship. These are things I do understand," Data wrote in a message to Commander Maddox.

Steven and Mark still enjoyed debating the potential of an android robot gaining consciousness and self-determination.

"How does a machine gain wisdom, appreciate art, or understand the desire to be loved?" Mark asked.

"Simple—a writer puts it in the script."

Mark grinned and nodded again. "Yep, well they wrote in a lot of things that came true too—including android robots, designed to resemble humans."

"Yeah and my favorite, the tablet computer and AI bionics," Steven said as he held up his iPad and activated the red-light in his prosthetic eye, "like this."

The PSYCHONIX eye and processor remained a permanent part of Steven. He rightly believed that anything fused to your brain became personal property. He had already discussed it with Mark and Senator Croxon. *I'm not giving it back.* They agreed and knew that trying to surgically remove the processor would be dangerous.

Agents didn't bother with it, because Senator Croxon had already convinced them that it was an obsolete project and that removal could potentially kill him. They concurred. Also, the fact that Steven held a top secret clearance and had an Army Special Forces background didn't hurt. They relinquished any and all government control of his prosthetic eye.

They were actually happy to have it off their hands and off their records. Their only real interest had been in the apparent PSYCHON radiation discovered, but Dr. Starr deflated their understanding of that, too.

However, he knew it was still an exceptionally powerful computer—which gave Steven rather unique capabilities, beyond his own. He still picked up communication, but that was their secret.

Mark, curious about Star Trek's imaginative gadgetry—did a Google search. He tried to find out something about spin-offs from the popular show. The creators had anticipated and influenced a load of real-life innovations. He found a list and read it off:

"They came up with wearable badge communicators and translators, automatic doors, GPS, real-time universal translators, portable memory, hypo-sprays, teleconferencing, Bluetooth headsets, and bionic eyes—wow, you can't deny there were also some incredible Artificial Intelligence ideas."

"True, but all those machines had a common denominator," Steven said.

"They were thought of and created by—a person."

"Yep."

"And they don't have any immaterial parts nor do they know what it *feels like* to be a machine. They don't have self-determination."

"Copy, over."

"But we do, and I'm determined to get these burgers cooked."

"Pass me a bag of chips while I wait." He snatched it out of the air, as Mark tossed it— thinking: *a machine couldn't have made any of the adjustments that I just made to catch that can in mid-air.*

Just then, Peggy poked her head out the back door, "Would you hold the door, sweetie?" She turned, picked up a large pan of ribs and corn on the cob, and carried it out to the grill. She gave Mark a peck on the cheek, which he gladly accepted. Although there were times that he questioned their differences, he no longer felt that the female gender were aliens.

Donna Scott trailed behind Peggy on her crutches and took a seat at the picnic table. She was home for therapy at Walter Reed and would stay with her dad until she fully healed.

Steven, still glued to his iPad, played another clip. "Check this one out, Mark." He called up the court proceeding from *The Measure of a Man, Star Trek: The Next Generation* television series.

"Sir, there is a celebration on the Holodeck."

"I have no right to be there," Riker replied.

"Because you failed in your task?"

"No, god, no. I came close to winning, Data."

"Yes, sir."

"I almost cost you your life."

"Is it not true that had you refused to prosecute, Captain Louvois would have ruled summarily against me?

"Yes."

"That action injured you and saved me. I will not forget it."

"You're a wise man, my friend."

"Not yet, sir. But with your help, I am learning."

EPILOGUE

"HOPE ISN'T A plan" is a snarky cliché that tough guys sometimes like to throw around to win an argument or shut you down. They consider the term a lackadaisical abandonment of a solid game plan, but it's not. Biblical hope isn't that at all. It's the confident expectation of what God has promised and its strength in His faithfulness and the hope of a future with Him. It provides me with the hopeful attitude that I can bounce back from disappointments or major life events like sickness or the death of someone close to me and that there's objective meaning and purpose. It's the deep well from which our soul draws water. It's an acknowledgement that my knowledge and wisdom are limited—and that my steps are being guided by a higher power. God.

In that sense—Hope is definitely a plan!

Prayer of Saint Francis

Lord, make me an instrument of your peace.
Where there is hatred, let me bring love.
Where there is offence, let me bring pardon.
Where there is discord, let me bring union.
Where there is error, let me bring truth.
Where there is doubt, let me bring faith.
Where there is despair, let me bring hope.
Where there is darkness, let me bring your light.
Where there is sadness, let me bring joy.
O Master, let me not seek as much
to be consoled as to console,
to be understood as to understand,
to be loved as to love,
for it is in giving that one receives,
it is in self-forgetting that one finds,
it is in pardoning that one is pardoned,
it is in dying that one is raised to eternal life.

DISCLAIMER:

ACKNOWLEDGMENTS

Dr. J.P. Moreland is an American philosopher, theologian, and Christian apologist. He currently serves as a Distinguished Professor of Philosophy at Talbot School of Theology at Biola University in La Mirada, California. I never thought that one of the top 25 greatest philosophers alive would answer my email, but I'm glad you did. Your work on consciousness and the mind-body problem inspired much of this novel. Thank you for looking it over and for your encouraging words.

Dr. Gary Habermas is a distinguished research professor of apologetics and philosophy at Liberty's Rawlings School of Divinity. It's unbelievable to me that a world-renowned would pick up my novel, much less endorse it. Thank you for your generosity and kindness.

Pastor Holland David (P. HD) is the founder and senior pastor of Calvary Chapel in San Clemente, California. He is an author, bible teacher, and award-winning songwriter and the composer of the platinum-selling worship song "Let It Rise." I don't know how you do it all, but you're still never too busy for a Christian brother and fellow military brat.

Kevin Harris is the Co-Host and Producer of the Reasonable Faith Podcast with Dr. William Lane Craig; a program dealing with the most important apologetic questions of our day. In the face of great tragedy and adversity you have shined as an example of strong faith in Christ. You have been gracious to me with your time and talents. I know that if we had met earlier in life, there would be a radio show called *Kevin and MoonDog,* and that we'd already be broke from paying FCC fines. Maybe there still will be, but we'll be a lot nicer.

Dr. Terry Portis is the Director at Anne Arundel Community College. He is a psychology professional with 20 years of experience in educational leadership, association management, and the development of programs and services. I learn something new every time I sit in your Bible study, and your specialties in psychology and technology were invaluable to my understanding of mental health issues.

Dr. Brian Chilton is Senior Pastor, author, teacher, theologian, and apologist. As a fellow Liberty University Alumnus, you've been a supporter and cheerleader, from the beginning. Thanks for your mature insight and wisdom.

Jonathan Church is an attorney with the Prince George's County State's Attorney's Office and a retired police officer with the Anne Arundel County Police Department. Your legal attention to detail gave this novel the realism and depth it needed. I would say more, but I know that it could be held against me in a court of law. Thank you for taking the time to call me and talk things over.

Adrian Meshaw is an officer with the Annapolis Police Department/ S.W.A.T team. It's nice to have a humble, street-tough, man of God in our church, and on my beta-reader team. Your tactical insight was informative and renewed my respect for the men and women in blue. If I'm ever in trouble I'm going to pray and call you.

Brenda Shipman is author of *Embracing Hospitality: Help for the Hesitant Host.* I've known Brenda and her husband Greg since 1986, when we were stationed at an Army Post, in Bremerhaven, German. She had to hear me do the morning show for American Forces Radio, and yet we're still friends—amazingly. Thanks for your gentle feedback and insight in *the writing biz.*

Phyliss Orr is a dedicated bible teacher and pastor's wife, who somehow finds time to serve the church and edit novels from upstart authors, like myself. Thanks for the detailed notes and your honesty.

Suzanne Stratton is a retired high school Spanish teacher and an artist with no claim to fame, other than being the mother of Dr. Tim Stratton of FreeThinkingMinistries.com. Thanks for your wonderful book review and encouragement. I can see why Tim turned out so well.

Mike Stover is seeking to serve God through a media company called Valor, Inc. He is looking for ways to amplify your multimedia platforms and conferences. Thanks for reading the book and conducting my first video interview for PSYCHONIX. You have a beautiful family.

Cindy Rae is a mom, grandma, and close family friend. I have known Cindy since our times at AFN Aviano, Italy as broadcasters. Thank you for waking up to my early morning calls from Maryland to Washington State. All the readers will be forever grateful for you fixing my grammar and spelling errors.

Rick Morgan is the Webmaster at Christian Research Institute. Thank you for taking the time to give me feedback.

Cindee Martin Morgan is an author and founder of WalterMartinJude3.com. Her mature Christian insights have guided this novel to greater heights. Cindee loves the Lord, loves people, and was always available.

Sherri Burnette is my wife and is studying for her Master's Degree in Counseling. Sherri is the kindhearted and caring one in our family, who listens with her heart, pays attention, and provides wise counsel. Thanks for your faithful support and insightful feedback.

Michael Burnette, Jr. is my son. Last, but not least—no one has spent more time nor edited with such surgical precision, as my son Michael. His creative and corrective feedback put a blinding polish on this novel.

NAMI, the National Alliance on Mental Illness, provides advocacy, education, support and public awareness so that all individuals and families affected by mental illness can build better lives. Contact and support: nami.org. For help call: 703-236-6022

Made in the USA
Middletown, DE
16 September 2020